Robert Musil, born at Klagenfurt, Austria, in 1880, was a trained
scientist, philosopher and one-time army officer as well as a
novelist of genius. He was engaged on his unfinished masterpiece,
The Man Without Qualities, from the early 1920s until his death in
exile at Geneva in 1942. Among his other works are *Young Törless*
and *Tonka and Other Stories*.

ROBERT MUSIL

translated from the German and with a foreword
by Eithne Wilkins and Ernst Kaiser

The Man Without
Qualities One

A Sort of Introduction
The Like of It Now Happens (1)

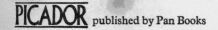**PICADOR** published by Pan Books

PUBLISHERS' NOTE Robert Musil's novel, *Der Mann ohne Eigenschaften*, was originally planned in two volumes, containing four parts, the titles of which were intended to be as follows:

First volume – First part: *Eine Art Einleitung.*
Second part: *Seinesgleichen Geschieht.*

Second volume – Third part: *Die Verbrecher.*
Fourth part: *Eine Art Ende.*

The first volume was published as intended (1930). The second volume, containing the third part, *Ins Tausendjährige Reich* (*Die Verbrecher*), was published in 1932. The third volume, which remained unfinished, was published posthumously and privately in Switzerland, and includes unrevised chapters from the manuscript.
The English edition is intended as follows:

The Man Without Qualities.
Volume I – Book 1: *A Sort of Introduction.*
Book 2: *The Like of It Now Happens* (I).
Volume II – Book 2 *continued*: *The Like of It Now Happens* (II).
Volume III – Book 3: *Into the Millennium* (*The Criminals*).
Volume IV – containing the unfinished conclusion of the work and some unfinished chapters.

First published in Great Britain 1954 by Martin Secker & Warburg Ltd
This Picador edition published 1979 by Pan Books Ltd,
Cavaye Place, London SW10 9PG
9 8 7 6
English translation © Secker & Warburg Ltd 1954
ISBN 0 330 25611 4
Printed and bound in Great Britain by
Richard Clay (The Chaucer Press) Ltd, Bungay, Suffolk

CONTENTS

FOREWORD

ROBERT MUSIL, born in Klagenfurt, Carinthia, on the 6th November 1880, an Austrian of partly Czech descent, who is almost unknown except to a small circle of readers, is one of the great figures in German literature and one of the most remarkable in the history of the modern novel. Robert Edler von Musil, to give him the full title that he himself never used, was the only child of Hofrat Alfred Edler von Musil and of Hermine, née Bergauer. Hofrat von Musil, who, like his son, was many-sided in his interests (he painted portraits and was a keen horseman), was professor of engineering, first at Klagenfurt, later at the Technical University at Brno, and was well known in his own field for improvements made in the construction of the steam turbine. Academic distinction was not unusual in the family : a cousin of his was Alois Musil, confessor to the last Austrian Empress and an archaeologist renowed for his *Arabian Itineraries*. Hermine Musil was a lady of lively personality who somewhat put her husband in the shade ; she too had artistic tastes, and was a gifted pianist. The relationship between son and parents was, it appears, not one of strong sympathy, but rather of a polite lack of understanding on each side for what the other side felt was important in life.

Robert Musil was destined for the army and was educated first at the military academy at Eisenstadt, in the Burgenland, and then at that at Weisskirchen (Hranice), in Moravia, the same grim school at which Rilke, only a very few years earlier, had been so desperately unhappy. Musil, about whom there was always something soldierly, both in spirit and in bearing, could stand up to such rigours. However, shortly before he was to be commissioned from the *k. & k.* Military Academy in Vienna, he suddenly changed his mind about his career and left, in 1897, in order to study civil engineering. He took his diploma as an engineer at the Technical University in Brno, in 1901. After

doing his military service he spent a year working in the engineering laboratories at the Royal Württembergian Technical College
in Stuttgart.   But mathematics and machines did not satisfy him
for long.   His interest in philosophy, especially in logic, and in
experimental psychology, took him to the University of Berlin.
For his degree in philosophy, which he took in 1908, he wrote a
thesis on Mach's epistemology.   He also invented a chromatometer that is known by his name.   He was always very proud of
this invention.   It seems symbolically significant, too, that it
should have been made by the philosopher with the scientific bent
who was to turn artist and become the creator of the Man Without Qualities.   The classical chromatometer, invented by Newton,
is that which, containing all the colours of the spectrum, when it
revolves fast enough turns white, so representing the unbroken
beam of light.   Musil, in writing his major work, went back, as
it were, to that ideal by creating a correspondence to it in Ulrich,
the man in whom all qualities merge spectrally into the whiteness
of none, the unbroken beam.

The period of studies in Berlin was one of the most important
in Musil's life and was the time when he, who was not by temperament intimate with anyone, made most friends, chiefly among
fellow-students of psychology.   One of his literary friends and
acquaintances whose name is most likely to be known to English
readers is Franz Blei, the critic, who was among the first to
recognise Musil's true vocation.   He was one of the very few
men on whom Musil relied and one whose stimulating society
he valued.

But this period was important for another reason too.   It was
now (1906) that Musil's first book, the novel *Die Verwirrungen
des Zöglings Törless*, appeared, bringing him some degree of
recognition, even of international notice.   This helped to make
him decide that he would decline all of several opportunities to
make a career as an academic philosopher (there was an opening
for him at Munich University as well as at Berlin) and would live
as an independent writer.

In *Törless* there is doubtless a good deal of his experiences at
the military academy at Weisskirchen.   No one can tell to what
extent the influence of that environment in his schooldays was
decisive in making him, not a professional philosopher or psycho-

logist any more than an army officer or an engineer, but an artist. We do not know to what extent the weird and terrifying experiences of the boy Törless correspond to those of the boy Robert. When Musil was asked whether the book was a portrait of that period of his life, he is said to have answered, laughing, that what he had written down was nothing compared to the reality. Yet although neither *Törless*—a seemingly heartless and yet passionate book that is an extraordinary study of torture and misery, a microcosmic prefiguration of the Nazi world—nor the much later and utterly different *Mann ohne Eigenschaften* is intended as autobiography in the strict sense, Törless, the schoolboy, and Ulrich, the Man Without Qualities, must both be regarded as aspects of Musil himself. We can draw conclusions as to Musil's own boyhood and development from the fact that no adult Törless ever came into existence : he would have been a monster. Perhaps the man Musil would have been a monster, and not the infinitely complicated and positive personality that he was, if he had not succeeded in evolving the boy Törless into the man Ulrich. So we need to superimpose on the image of Törless that of the boy that Ulrich remembers having been, if we are to get a picture of the writer in his early life, and see the origins of the psychological constitution that was the driving-force of that great engine of a mind. The ruthlessness, the sceptical curiosity, and the romanticism of Törless, and the intellectual integrity, even severity, of Ulrich who, among other things, ' should have become a pilgrim ', are obviously part of the one pattern. Both characters are austere and yet sensual ; in both the personal aloofness is counterbalanced by irony and searing humour, as well as by a capacity to come to terms with violence ; and both, however much they may seem to refrain from action of any kind, are actually on a quest—a quest for truth, for the first-hand thing, the immediate and ultimate experience. But the important difference is that in Ulrich's remembrance of his schooldays the sordid aspect is shed. Retrospectively that boyhood underwent a change : it was purified of its anguish and guilt, portrayed in a reconciled mood by the writer of the later and greater book.

It would be a mistake, however, to believe that because the element of ruthlessness in Musil's character did not develop in the way foreshadowed in *Törless* it was therefore no longer there.

It was always there, but it became constructive. There was an, as it were, ruthless impulse to go on from soldier to technician, mathematician, philosopher, in order to arrive finally at art, so turning it all to creative account. This impulse became organised into a single purpose. It became an uncompromising determination to say what he had to say, no matter where it would get him, and no matter what the obstacles were in his way. There is ruthlessness, although not only that, in these words from one of his note-books : " I state my case, even though I know it is only part of the truth, and I would state it just the same if I knew it was false, because certain errors are stations on the road to truth. I am doing all that is possible on a definite job in hand."

Just as all his studies were necessary to give him the equipment for his unique literary undertaking—the intellectual apparatus of a technician, scientist and philosopher, all of which the Man Without Qualities is also—so too, inevitably, his earlier writing, however significant in itself, was even more significantly the clearing of the way for *Der Mann ohne Eigenschaften*. It was a number of experiments with material that was to take final shape in his main work.

In 1911 a small volume containing two exquisitely written stories, *Vereinigungen*, was published. It is interesting to see how in the first story, *Vollendung der Liebe*, a pattern that is recurrent in Musil's work—the tensions between intellect and feeling, and above all erotic feeling, which sometimes becomes suffocatingly intense—is treated entirely in terms of sex: the intellectual man, representing the mind itself, who is later almost always to be the protagonist, here recedes into the background immediately, leaving the scene to the woman, and it is she who goes through the whole experience, the critical ordeal, triumph over which is necessary to make their relationship complete. Apart from *Törless*, however, the work that shows the shaping of the *Mann ohne Eigenschaften* most clearly is *Die Schwärmer*, a play that was published in 1921. Musil himself often declared that these two works were ' the direct way ' to the *Mann ohne Eigenschaften*.

It was, as such things go, not a long way ; but it was not easy. Musil had to write, and he had to live. After his marriage in 1910, he worked as a librarian at the Technical University of Vienna, but the hours, which were from ten till two, were fatally

disturbing to his writing. It was not only that he, who was an
early riser and always extremely regular in his habits, working
at his best in the first half of the day, was thrown out of his
rhythm; to have to give time and attention to some routine
earning of a living distracted and thwarted him, consuming
energy that should have been concentrated purely on his creative
work. In 1913 he returned to Berlin, to become one of the
editors of the *Neue Rundschau*. This was, in a different way,
even worse. The atmosphere of rush and the many social
obligations that were involved in working on a literary periodical
meant there was little chance of doing anything else, and it was
something of a relief to him when the outbreak of war brought
the whole thing to a standstill. Musil served as an officer with
the Austrian Army from 1914 to 1918, first at the front and later,
after a severe illness that left him unfit for active service, as a
staff-officer editing an army newspaper. In 1919 he was transferred to the Austrian Foreign Ministry, where, as a *Ministerialrat*,
he did liaison work with the press. This, and a period from 1921
as scientific adviser to the War Ministry, though it again kept him
from his writing, provided him with much material for satire in
Der Mann ohne Eigenschaften.

After 1922 he lived as a free-lance, which meant a return to his
own strict discipline. After spending the morning at work, he
would go for a walk with his wife, and in the afternoon either
continue working or, in the traditional Viennese style, go to his
usual café, where he would be sure of finding the usual circle,
consisting of Blei, Egon Erwin Kisch, the young Werfel, Alfred
Polgar, and others. In the evening he would write letters or read,
or sometimes go to the cinema (he was a particular admirer of
Chaplin and Fred Astaire). Apart from writing dramatic criticism
for various newspapers in Vienna and Prague, he contributed
essays and criticism to a number of literary journals, such as
Ganymed, *Der Neue Merkur*, and *Die Neue Rundschau*. In 1921
Die Schwärmer was published, and in 1924 a second play, *Vinzenz
und die Freundin bedeutender Männer*, to which he gave the description 'a farce'. He was not primarily a writer for the theatre,
but like other eminent novelists he was at least as enthusiastic
about his plays as about the rest of his work. He also had very
definite ideas about their casting and production. It was as a

result of disagreement on this head that the *Schwärmerskandal* arose : Musil made a public protest against a production of which he disapproved, and it was taken off after only one performance. He preferred to bide his time rather than have his work handled in a way he disliked.   After his death, it was all the same to him what was done with it, he remarked with reference to *Die Schwärmer.   Vinzenz,* in a production by Berthold Viertel, with the well-known actor Rudolf Forster in the title-role, ran for a month and was considered a moderate *succès d'estime.*   In 1923 the story *Grigia* appeared as a small volume, and the following year was republished with two other *novellen* under the title *Drei Frauen.*   These smaller writings, which have a fascination all their own, are incidentally valuable for revealing something one might not single out from the immense wealth of *Der Mann ohne Eigenschaften* : Musil's pin-point observation of natural detail and the way he uses it—the seated, lolling cows in the field, gazing towards the dawn, working their jaws as though in prayer ; the stream, where it runs over a stone, looking like an ornamental silver comb ; the little cat dying of mange and the sense of helpless guilt it arouses—to illuminate the relations of things, as though with a light at once from without and from within.

In 1927 was published the memorial address Musil delivered, in Berlin, in honour of Rilke, one of the rare literary contemporaries whom he ranked high and whose death the previous year had caused no more stir, as he said, ' than a film-première '.

Der Mann ohne Eigenschaften, which occupied Musil all the rest of his life, was begun early in the 'twenties, and the first volume was published in 1930.   The work remained unfinished. Even so, it is one of the longest novels in literature.   The first volume, of which the present volume is half, has over a thousand pages ; the second volume has over six hundred, and the third over four hundred, apart from about twenty unpublished chapters, some of them existing in as many as twenty versions.

Musil, whose favourite reading among the novelists was Dostoievsky, Tolstoy, and Balzac, in his writing kept to tradition. He was not an innovator.   That was not his function in literature. Perfunctory references to his work in surveys of modern German literature as, for instance, part of the ' aftermath of Expressionism ' are misleading and nonsensical.   He was the writer above all others who summed up and finished off the classical novel of tradition. *Der Mann ohne Eigenschaften* is indeed magnificently classical in its inclusiveness, its unhurried sweep—as though some vast bird, slowly wheeling at a great height, were taking its bird's-eye view of the revolving world. Not only does it comprehend infinitely many aspects of life, all bristling and rippling with ideas and glittering with wit, but it gives the reader the feeling that he is moving steadily through years, even decades, of experience. Yet the whole book's action takes place within the framework of less than one year. (On the face of it, this may seem a counterpart to Mr. Bloom's one day, as to the one night of H. C. Earwicker, and in the wider literary-historical sense it is ; this remains true in spite of the fact that the comparison annoyed Musil, who did not care for Joyce's work.) The book was to end with the outbreak of the first world war ; but it lingers on the brink in a way that is evidently due to something inherent in the situation and even stronger than the artistic plan. The story of the preparations for a nation-wide festival to celebrate the Austrian Emperor's jubilee and permeate the world with the spirit of ' our grand old Austrian culture ' (which many of the characters would certainly, if they had known our current expression, have called ' the Austrian way of life ') could not go on, of course, after the outbreak of the war that was to end the Austrian Empire. Yet even this end is never reached. It is as though it could not come about. It is as though the very material were rearing back from the abyss, piling up and growing, against the laws of matter, against the accomplished facts of historical time, into a space and time of its own. It is, in short, as though everything that was to happen, everything that in reality did happen—the 1914 of which the reader knows—could be changed retrospectively by some magical operation of the writer's will, and the monarchy that vanished under the weight of history, as Atlantis vanished overnight in the deluge, could, by force of the reality it has in the book, reappear in reality on the surface of the earth, with its ancient Hapsburg Court and the immense tracts of the proverbially ramshackle empire that, as Musil says, by means of huge expenditure on the army just managed to remain ' the second weakest great power in Europe '. Reading, we may not be quite conscious of the bitter ' if only ' principle involved ; rather, we are like the children watching a Punch-and-Judy show who, no matter how often they have seen it and how well they know the course events must take, still clamour their warnings to whoever is about to be hit on the head.

There is a link here with something said in 1915 by Henry James, with whom Musil has certain social-historical affinities. " To have to take it all now," James said, " for what the treacherous years were all the while really making for and *meaning* is too tragic for any words."   For Musil, the years were not ' treacherous ', since he was not deceived ; and for him nothing was—at least in the sense in which it so elaborately was for James—past words. Yet the resemblance is there. James in all his work revolves round a point he could never get to (" an elephant trying to pick up a pea ", H. G. Wells once said), and was taken unawares by the war ; Musil, in spite of looking back on it all afterwards and seeing it fall into shape all the more clearly for the clarity of his scientific mind, could never, in the chronology of what he was writing, and however much everything he wrote was always *to* the point, actually reach the point of fatality. Here, it must be, lies the inner reason why the book remained unfinished. It may even be that this unfinishedness is its real form. Another way of putting it would be to say that James's real 1914 is the manifestation of the very thing that is lacking in his work, whereas Musil has it all, but, for reasons that are profoundly personal as well as philosophic, will not let the long-accomplished doom manifest itself in his story except by implication—as indeed it does in every word, every glance, every gesture. The world of the beautiful and patriotic Diotima's Collateral Campaign cannot do otherwise than slide into 1914 ; the Collateral Campaign itself is one of those ideal projects that exist only to state their own unreality and failure. The blood and destruction of the years 1914–1918 were the manifestation, Musil recognised, of something that could not be fully said in terms only of blood and destruction. The war was in the last resort an anti-climax. And Musil was not a moralist. Showing the origins of the untold catastrophe says more, on the highest level of expression, about the evils and stupidities of the world than could be done by developing them in their historical chronology ; and in that sense this novel is also, as has been said more than once, a con-

tribution to the *Geistesgeschichte* of our era.   That is not to say
that the blood-curdling and hair-raising aspect is left out: it
is there, of course, as much in the petrol fumes and asphalt of
a spring day in town as in the peculiarly horrible murder of the
prostitute by the journeyman carpenter Moosbrugger.   But what
Musil was concerned with was a far larger problem than merely
that of depicting the new dark age, which he had known and
symbolically expressed long ago in *Törless*.

It would be useless to attempt a synopsis of *Der Mann ohne
Eigenschaften*, not only because of its length and complexity, but
also because the real action lies not on the surface, in what the
characters do (though that is often dramatic enough), but within,
in their states of mind, the fluctuations of their emotions, their
theories, and the counterpoint between the thoughts and behaviour
of them all, in themselves and in relation to each other, especially
to the Man Without Qualities himself, who is the nucleus, and
in relation to the demands of the indefinable pattern of this world
we live in.   There are two main themes bound up with each
other.   The first is the imposing Campaign, 'Collateral' because
it is in competition with a similar campaign in Germany—that
new-fangled empire snobbishly, jealously, and nervously disliked.
It involves the most diverse people—from Diotima, the wife of a
high-ranking civil servant and a distant connection of Ulrich's,
with her *salon* and her middle-class aspirations towards intellectual
aristocracy, and the Imperial Liege-Count Leinsdorf, whose
' bosom ' friend she is, to her little maid Rachel, for whom it is
all like a fairy-tale come true, or the banker Fischel, who puts
his philosophic finger on the essentially fantastic point in the
Campaign's inaugural proclamation by asking: " What is *true*
patriotism, *true* progress, the *true* Austria?"   Almost all of them
are in frantic and vain search for a guiding idea, for some formula-
tion of their vague yet fervent conviction that the Good, the
True, and the Beautiful must be realisable upon earth.   Ulrich, the
man who has given up his ' qualities ' as an ascetic might give up
the world, and who against his intentions drifts into becoming honorary secretary to the Campaign, is the one serious character among
them.   He is the only one who recognises that no such ideal can
be realised, and against the background of his irony it become apparent that the Campaign is a farce, a caricature quest for the Grail.

The second theme is the *cause célèbre* of Moosbrugger, the sexual maniac and murderer, whose fate—hanging or confinement in an asylum—is in the balance. The problem is that of the individual's responsibility before the law. What we are confronted with is the Good, the True, and the Beautiful in reverse. Only if those categories could be established could Moosbrugger's fate be settled in terms of true justice. The lack of the great idea, of any idea at all, not only indicates all the evil, the false, and the hideous, on a scale that dwarfs Moosbrugger, the monster ; it not only reveals that there are no standards by which his crime can be measured; it also reveals that there are no measurements for crime on any scale, and hence it implies that the *débâcle* is inevitable. So the Moosbrugger case drags on without getting anywhere, precisely like the Collateral Campaign, of which it is, indeed, the sombre reflection. Or, as it is expressed in Ulrich's thoughts : " If mankind could dream collectively, it would dream Moosbrugger."

A third, subsidiary theme, linking up with both these, is that of Walter and Clarisse, Ulrich's friends since his extreme youth, whose tragedy is that Walter is the intellectual and artistic Jack-of-all-trades and not the genius that Clarisse insists he ought to be. She is a harsh, inspired little creature (' like the month of March ', Ulrich says) with a streak of madness. Her growing frustration brings about a growing preoccupation with Moosbrugger, into whom she projects partly Ulrich—whom she suspects of being the man all of one piece that Walter is not—and partly herself, her vision taking on the dream-like outlines of the hero-genius, of all that she yearns for but hates when it is presented to her in Walter's impassioned playing of Wagner. And this oneness is in fact what Ulrich also yearns for but, floating in his ' interim scepticism ', does not care to do anything about. It is the reason why he also is deeply bound up with Moosbrugger, that embodiment of all sinister qualities, who is complementary to the utterly sane Man Without Qualities.

" Something beyond his understanding made Moosbrugger a closer concern of his than the leading of his own life ; Moosbrugger held him spellbound like an obscure and sombre poem in which everything was faintly distorted and displaced, revealing a mutilated significance drifting in the depths of the mind."

Just as this book ends without an end, at Musil's death, so too it has no plot that is important merely as a plot. Musil himself in a note-book, 1932, said : " What the story that makes up this novel amounts to is that the story that was supposed to be told in it is not told."

It is worth investigating what this means. We can get a glimpse of the writer's development and of his work in progress, and so of the story of the story, not only in the evolution of the boy Törless into Ulrich, but in particular from the plays, the characters of which irresistibly transform themselves into those of *The Man Without Qualities*, growing in both size and significance with the enlarging of the scope. A glance back over this development is extraordinarily illuminating, for what it shows is a steady re-shuffling and re-grouping of characters and their functions— as though according to some pre-established plan that the writer was compelled to follow—towards the achievement of the final constellation. What we then see is not the story of the Collateral Campaign or that of the murder case, both of which are told in detail, but that elusive thing, the story of Ulrich himself—the story that is ' not told '.

In *Die Schwärmer* the hero is the man of intellect, the professor who loses his wife to the good-for-nothing charmer, Anselm, and seems to gain his wife's sister as a partner for a possible new life, surmounting that betrayal and going on to something beyond the terms in which the betrayal could be committed. In the farce *Vinzenz* the hero is the man of intellect and the good-for-nothing charmer fused into one, the combination producing the ' brilliant failure ' who finally parts from Alpha, the *Freundin bedeutender Männer*, with the sardonically picaresque resolve to ' take service with a society lady or a financier '. In the novel this combination of intellect and feeling is carried a long stride further. Ulrich is the man above intellect. He refuses to go on, from being a ' promising young man ', to become a professor ; he refuses to take sides or commit himself or indeed ' be ' anything but a dilettante in feeling, quite unattached and independent. His neutrality is stressed by the fact that his surname is never mentioned. He does not earn a living. He is not married. The conflict between him and his main antagonist, Arnheim, the Prussian high-financier—who in

the end, incidentally, offers to take him into service as his confidant
and friend—is therefore not motivated by jealousy or ambition;
it is a matter of pure antagonism between two temperaments,
two conceptions of the world, two styles of living. Arnheim's
offer may be read as a higher mockery built on the mockery of
Vinzenz's conclusion, with the difference that what in *Vinzenz*
was an ironically coloured wish-dream born of despair now
becomes reality; but Ulrich, who stands out much bigger against
a much more gravely threatened world, is, because of all he is
and is not, constitutionally unable to accept what was never
offered to his more light-hearted and also more desperate fore-
runner. Similarly, what is the final chord of the farce becomes,
in the novel, an incident of less importance. To Ulrich, whose
sole occupation lies in reducing everything to its essentials, the
megalopolitan Arnheim's unspeakable wealth, culture, and reputation as a thinker are all the more preposterous because so much
' idealism' is involved in them. Arnheim in contrast sincerely
believes that one owes it to the world to get on in the world.
This is the secret of his success. It is this, too, that helps
to make him so solemnly fascinating to the high-minded
Diotima.

There is a curious parallelism in the male and female characters
of the plays. Just as the hero and his antagonist of the *Schwärmer*
fuse into one in *Vinzenz*, so the two women of the drama merge
into the one woman Alpha. It is equally significant that the
new combination of mind and feeling, Vinzenz, is confronted
with no single antagonist, but with a whole assembly of types:
The Man of Learning, The Politician, The Musician, The
Reformer, and so on. So too at the end of the farce there is no
Omega to Alpha. In the novel there is therefore necessarily a
new beginning, and it is made with a whole series of women:
Leona, the Junoesque night-club artiste who sings risqué songs
' with a housewifely air ', Bonadea, the maternal nymphomaniac,
Diotima, as chaste and beautiful as she is eager to be intellectual,
and Clarisse, the dementedly unmaternal, the vicarious artist.
With all of them, it is as though Musil were experimenting in
order to work up towards the final achievement, Agathe, which
means ' The Good '. This is not the place to go into the significance of names (*nomina sunt numina*), but it is interesting to notice

that two of these women are called by nicknames that are classical allusions, instead of by their real names, and also to see the parallelism between, on the one hand, Maria and Regine, one the professor's wife, the other his wife's sister—who, it is clear as the curtain falls, will either commit suicide or become his mistress —and, on the other, Agathe, Ulrich's sister, who, when the novel breaks off, seems to have become his lover. The mystical implications of ' Maria Regina ' and Agathe, the ultimate heroine, the perfected female principle, need not be stressed. That the brother-sister relationship was fascinating to Musil is known ; yet to take this development as either a piece of sensationalism or the result of a morbid compulsion would certainly be wrong. On the ritual incestuous love between brother and sister, with all its sacramental implications, a great deal has been written by those far better qualified to discuss it than the present writers, and there is no need to say more about it here. But there is no getting over the fact that from this point of view the splitting up of the female characters for the sake of achieving a higher unity precisely in the sister takes on a startlingly symbolic aspect, and that by following his feelings the Man Without Qualities steps out of life's ordinary conditions into a realm accessible only to divine heroes and kings.

Of the antagonist in the drama only straw-men, types or qualities, remain in the farce. And now these condense into two new characters, forming, together with the Man Without Qualities, a new pattern. Ulrich has absorbed the intellectual-erotic conflict into his own being, but to compensate for this he has his Moosbrugger like a shadow stalking after him. His one antagonist is Arnheim, the bachelor millionaire, who has his own little shadow in his Negro servant-boy, Soliman, whom—at least according to Soliman's own boastful, hate-ridden fantasies—he has robbed of his liberty. Arnheim is the big man, the public figure, allpowerful, universally admired. Ulrich is nothing of all that ; his existence is essentially private. At the same time, he is the only one who sees through Arnheim. And as Ulrich admits the importance to himself of Moosbrugger, it seems as if this must be applied by analogy to Arnheim's case, only that Arnheim cannot admit his bondage to Soliman. For although Ulrich and Arnheim cannot come together, in a peculiar way they do corre-

spond to each other. Walter, the other antagonist, is all the more
hostile to Ulrich since he knows of Clarisse's feelings and is jealous,
even frightened, of what may happen.

> "Ulrich . . . ruthlessly tampered with the very thing in her that
> Walter dared not touch—the cavern of disaster, all that was poor,
> sick, all there was of ill-omened genius in Clarisse, the secret empty
> room where something tore at chains that might some day rend
> apart."

So there is, we see, the dark aspect to each of these three figures
linking them together : the huge murderer, the little black boy,
and the chained horror in the cavern. It is from Clarisse that a
hint, if not an answer, comes as to what this means. For there
is evidently some connection between her belief that Ulrich owes
Moosbrugger—the destroyer of women—a mysterious debt, his
liberty, and the mysterious persistence with which Moosbrugger
haunts Ulrich's thoughts. It can be found in her madly cryptical
outcry to Ulrich : "This murderer is musical . . . you must do
something for him . . . liberate him . . . you would be transformed."
If Ulrich does not understand this, it is surely not because he is
incapable of experiencing something beyond the limits of what
is rational. That he is not incapable of it is proved by, among
many other things, a flash-back into his youth, "The forgotten
and extremely important affair with the Major's wife", a chapter
in which, on a lonely island, he renounces his love and enters into
a state of mystical union with Nature.

> "He was submerging himself in the landscape, although one
> might equally well say it was an unutterable state of being buoyed
> up and borne along ; and when the world overbrimmed the thresh-
> old of his eyes, its meaning lapped against him from within, in
> soundless waves. He had drifted into the very heart of the world.
> From him to the distant beloved was as far as to the next tree.
> Inscape had linked the living beings where space was no more, as
> in dreams two living beings can pass through each other without
> intermingling ; and this altered all their relations . . . All life's
> problems and events took on an incomparable mildness, softness
> and serenity, and at the same time an utterly transformed meaning."

Is it therefore that he does not want to understand the supra-
rational if it is mixed up with madness ? (It is not irrelevant to

mention here Musil's often professed distaste for music.) What is it Clarisse wishes Ulrich to liberate? Moosbrugger the murderer? The chained monster in her of which Walter knows? Or something in himself that is ' musical '—that might, diffidently, be called his soul? Does she see such a liberation bringing about Ulrich's transformation into the man who would give her the child she later comes to him to conceive and that she refuses to have by Walter? Or does she want to be destroyed by him, by the Moosbrugger in him? If Ulrich does not understand, is it because, like Musil, he does not want to be ' musical '? Does he deny her the child because he knows, as he must, that this is not the way to transformation? Here Musil intervenes. For it is precisely at this point that the news arrives of the death of Ulrich's father and not only prevents what might after all have happened, but leads Ulrich straight on towards his sister, Agathe, whom he has not seen since they were children.

It is only after seeing something of the pattern throughout Musil's writing that one can approach the question as to what he was really getting at—not his conscious intellectual intentions alone, but his attitude as a whole, all he was in his life and work ' making for and *meaning*'. Nobody seems to know to what extent he was conscious of this pattern, which—apart from the preoccupation it indicates—takes on an increasingly mythological aspect, a pattern of submerged values that barely creates a ripple on the surface realism. The problem is difficult, because Musil was, after all, a realistic writer. And this brings us to the question of the reality he was ultimately dealing with. He gave us all that we have from him by way of answer in the chapter of the third volume, *Atemzüge eines Sommertages*, in which Ulrich and Agathe, in solitary communion all one summer afternoon, move their deck-chairs over the lawn, turning as the sun turns, almost like plants or stars. The last words of this chapter, on which he was working on the morning of his death, and perhaps the last words he wrote, are:

" Of course it was clear to him that the two kinds of human being . . . could mean nothing else than a man ' without qualities ' and, in contrast, the man with all the qualities that anyone could manage to display. And the one might be called a nihilist, dreaming of God's dreams—in contrast with the activist, who is, however, with his impatient way of acting, a kind of God's dreamer too, and anything but a realist, who goes about being worldly-clear and worldly-active. ' And why aren't we realists ? ' Ulrich wondered. Neither of them was, neither he nor she : their thoughts and actions had for long left no doubt of that. What they were was nihilists and activists, and now one, now the other, according as it came."

As regards some of the manifestations of this underlying pattern in *The Man Without Qualities*, Musil's widow, the late Frau Martha von Musil, wrote in a letter to the present writers : " The mythological aspect of the novel was, I am sure, not *intentional*, but arose unconsciously and may be taken as confirmation of its inner truth. A friend who knows *Der Mann ohne Eigenschaften* as thoroughly as anyone does said to me : ' Every manifested truth (*Gestaltwahrheit*) rounds itself out in the direction of myth, but the mythological element cannot be manufactured. It reveals itself *retrospectively*.' "

It does not matter, in the last resort, whether such things were or were not intended by Musil. Indeed, what becomes the more apparent, if there was no intention of that kind, is a vital force working its way out as though spontaneously, pointing to, even perhaps revealing, something real in a way that no intention could have done. What we can, at any rate, take as probable is that Musil, who was well versed in the writings of the mystics and the Church Fathers, as he was also in experimental psychology, cannot have overlooked this entirely. If he scorned the attempts at mythological symbolism to be found in modern prose, was it not because he knew the difference between the conscious attempt and the real thing growing of its own accord ? But because he was, consciously, above all a realistic writer, it is safest to say only that he was reluctant to enter into controversy about such things. For however he strove to overcome the limitation of the human mind by artistic means, he had to face and admit them intellectually. He himself personified the eternal antagonism between the scientist and the artist, the one holding fast to facts, guarding the frontiers of the mind, the other charged with the mission of overstepping those frontiers, of breaking out of the confinement of matter and mind by the force of his vision and so enlarging the world of experience. Musil may have been a resolute positivist for the sake of intellectual truth, but that does not mean that he enjoyed the self-imposed restrictions. In the very last years of his life, in exile and solitude, he was, as he himself wrote, under the pressure of the outer crisis going through a crisis within, and he was making notes for what he called a ' layman's theology '.

This is not necessarily to suggest that he was trying to put a name to something that he always regarded warily. As Ulrich says to Diotima :

> " We infinitely overvalue the present moment, the sense of the present, the Here and Now. I mean, the way you and I are here together now in this valley, as though we had been put into a basket and the lid of the moment had fallen shut. We overvalue that. . . . But what really moves us, speaking at least for myself, is always —to put it carefully, for I'm not looking for an explanation and a name for it !—to a certain extent in antagonism to this way of experiencing things. It is displaced by so much Here and Now, so much Present. So it can't force its way through to becoming present ! "

All this is implicit too in the earlier novel, where Törless lies on the ground at midday, in late autumn, gazing up into the sky :

> " And suddenly he noticed—and it was as though it had happened for the first time—how high the sky really was.
>
> " It was almost a shock. Straight over him there was a small, blue, unspeakably deep hole between the clouds. He felt as though it must be possible to climb up and through there, up a long, long ladder. But the further he penetrated in, raising himself on his eyes, the more deeply the blue, shining depths drew back. . . . ' Infinity ! ' Törless knew the word from mathematics lessons. It had never meant anything special for him. . . . And now he was suddenly startled to realise that there was something terribly disturbing about this word. . . . Something going beyond reason, something wild. . . . There it was, in the sky, over him, alive and threatening and sneering."

If one looks back, in *Der Mann ohne Eigenschaften*, to the first volume from the last it seems superfluous any longer to raise the question whether Ulrich—whose way of thinking was ' not so much godless as God-free '—became a ' daylight mystic ' against Musil's will, so detaching himself from his creator. Does not all the evidence force us to assume that his experience is also Musil's ? And that brings us right back to the question whether Törless's experiences at school were Musil's own. Remembering the answer Musil gave to that question, we almost expect the answer here too to be : What is written down is nothing compared to the reality.

To whatever extent Ulrich is Musil's mouthpiece, he is certainly his eyepiece. And Musil was so many-sided that his view of the world should perhaps be described not as a bird's but as a fly's-eye view. It is into some vastly magnified, many-faceted fly's eye, with countless images mirrored in it, that the reader finds himself gazing.

Among Musil's pet philosophical notions was that of the fly-paper : man is irresistibly attracted by the sweet smell of life, as the fly is by that of the fly-paper, and each is doomed, with every movement of attempted escape, to sink a little deeper, so perishing in the sweet stickiness. With this allegory in mind one may wonder whether he felt himself indeed to be the super-fly with the gigantic facet-eye. Yet to take the fable of the fly-paper as the core of his ideas would be as wrong as to take the farce of the Collateral Campaign, or even the tragedy of Moos-brugger, for the central idea of *The Man Without Qualities*, as it would be equally wrong to take the book as a whole for the teachings of a modern mystic. Musil is no more a mystic merely because he knows and says a great deal about mysticism than he is a philosopher who merely uses the form of the novel for the propagation of his ideas ; moreover he is extremely entertaining on a high comic level, as neither a teacher of esoteric wisdom nor a professional philosopher commonly is. But neither is he a satirist or a humorist only. All these qualities combine in him, each transparently illumined by the others, each making the others a little sharper and more real. The sum of all the components making up this highly unusual man remains less than the whole, the *Gestalt*, which is reflected in this highly unusual book.

It may seem odd that this book, the first volume of which was published over twenty years ago by a leading German publisher, remained untranslated and is still practically unknown even to those who read the German language. But is this really so odd a phenomenon ? Cannot similar fates be found over and over again in the history of art and literature ? It is all not so much something that needs to be explained as—being part of the origins of modern man's predicament—something that cries out for a change of heart, a changed attitude to life and its values. Only, it is striking that a man and a work that would in any era deserve to be acclaimed great, now, in this desert, this vacuum, in which any greatness should stand out the higher, resound the more loudly, nevertheless have produced no resonance at all.   Is it just that in a vacuum there can be no echo ?   Does the explanation lie in the acoustics of the desert ?   Or is it that there is no one there to hear ?

In spite of his elaborate and complex subject-matter Musil's work is in the last resort simple, with what another great artist of our time called ' the higher, second simplicity '.   It is not really, as might be supposed, some great difficulty in the nature of Musil's communication that has barred his way.   Those who try can find out very quickly that this big book—which many of Musil's admirers, in the circumstances quite naturally, have treated as something rarefied, esoteric, a kind of secret hoard that could never be appreciated by a wider public—is far less difficult than is often suggested, and is not only deeply rewarding but also far more amusing than many much more widely read works that set out primarily to amuse.   Unfortunately, once a book has, by mischance, been classified as ' high-brow ' and difficult, the prejudice so generated may be a serious drag on the potential reader's imagination and receptiveness, and what many people, if left to themselves, might quite easily have taken in their stride, they then feel is too formidable a task for them ;   now when we all know so much about psychology there should be no need to emphasise what real trouble can be caused by imagined difficulties. And so Musil has remained remote from a larger readership not so much because he is entirely disinclined ever to play down to anyone as because the general public, following the path of least resistance, tends to be content with those entertainers who are not likely to be claimed as anybody's secret and most precious property.   One of Musil's own comments on public opinion (from *Aus einem Rapial*, a little collection of aphorisms) has some bearing not only on this but on the general way in which the important and the unimportant can be confused and become as it were interchangeable :

" One would think it would be more difficult to recognise what is important than, when it has once been recognised, to distinguish between it and the unimportant. Our experience of art, and indeed in general, always, however, teaches the very opposite : namely that it is easier by far to get a number of people to agree about what is important than to keep them from confusing it, at the very first opportunity, with what is unimportant."

Musil very well knew what a man had to be like if success was what he was after, that he had to be one of those who

" were not wicked. No, far from it. It was only that the good was adulterated with a little too much of the bad, the truth with error, and the meaning with a little too much of the spirit of accommodation. There positively seemed to be certain proportions in which these elements had to be blended for maximum success in the world. A little admixture of *ersatz* was all that was wanted, just enough to bring out the genius in a genius and the promise in a man of talent, precisely as, in some people's opinion, a certain addition of fig-coffee or chicory is needed to give coffee its proper full-bodied coffeeness. . . ."

Or worse :

" one of those unobtrusive talents that consist of forty-nine per cent. ability and fifty-one per cent. lack of it, and that are as a result so very good at everything that requires an energetic man but might be damaged by a strong man . . ."

It goes without saying that he could not adjust himself to suit such descriptions. He did not take part in any of the literary movements at the end of the first world war. He was not a man to belong to ' movements ', and the magnitude of the task he had set himself—colossal even if measured in terms of pages—forced him to concentrate on the job in hand instead of diffusing his energy in the more or less extraneous activities of a man of letters.

Still, although it is by no means an explanation that can excuse past neglect, it is not irrelevant—particularly with regard to such practical matters as publication and critical evaluation—that Musil's life and work was disturbed by two wars and fundamental political upheavals. He lost four years in the first world war (there were not even any essays in literary journals during that period), and it is impossible to say how gravely he was hampered by losing time after the war in his various—however respectable—

official positions. The first volume of *Der Mann ohne Eigen-schaften* appeared at a time of economic misery and unrest (in spite of which it was not only a ' literary ' success, but sold about 8,000 copies), and the second volume in the year the Nazis came to power. Only when we consider Musil as *par excellence* the writer of *Der Mann ohne Eigenschaften* (a way in which he did not wish to be considered) is it really so astounding that the standard German critical surveys mention him merely in lists and appendices. For, brilliant and mature though his earlier works are, their significance becomes fully apparent only retrospectively, in the light of the major novel, for the wide recognition of which there were no more than three years left in pre-Hitler Germany —three years, moreover, of rapidly sinking standards. This, and the period of barbarism that followed, partly explain, too, why his work was not accorded its proper place immediately after the Third Reich came to its end. By then standards in Germany were so degraded that it took long to remember Musil at all, and it must take even longer to arrive at a proper appreciation of his work.

Like some other great writers, Musil was slow to arrive at the point where he could stand forth in his full stature. This is a disadvantage that is often associated with artistic enterprises of monumental dimensions, and one that may, when the time factor plays such a large and unfavourable part as in his case, prove more than even genius can cope with.

Paradoxically, success with the public is especially important to a writer who is not out to gain it ; for without large sales from books quickly written only rich men can really afford to spend a lifetime writing those books that cannot count on immediate success but which do, after all, in the end make up a considerable part of the world's great literature. Musil could not produce pot-boilers. His satirical dicta on this whole problem are never quite without an undertone of resignation. Although he, like Stendhal, did not doubt that his work would have its place among the great works of world literature a hundred years after his death, he was disappointed that he did not receive wider recognition. Of his sixtieth birthday—traditionally an occasion when a literary man is fêted—he remarked that the silence was ' positively oppressive '.

This brings us to the simple question asked by the man (a distinguished Viennese art historian) who founded the small private society that for a time, during Musil's last years in Austria, enabled him to work in relative material security. It was : What does a man who writes such books live on ?

When Hitler came to power in 1933, Musil's situation became very grave. Only a few weeks before the seizure of power in Germany he returned to Vienna from Berlin, where he had been correcting the proofs of the second volume (which in his case meant re-writing it once more) in an atmosphere he found more suitable for this work than that of his home town. He had for some time been able to get advances from his German publisher, in spite of the slow pace at which he worked, which would doubtless have been maddening to any publisher. These supplies now stopped. Believing as he did that he would live to as great an age as his father (who was over eighty when he died), and being infinitely scrupulous in revising and polishing, Musil never let himself be hurried with his writing. Now, however, there was no longer any hurry in Germany where his book was concerned. Now he was dependent on the Austrian book-market, which was very much smaller, offering correspondingly less chance of reward. What enabled him to survive and carry on with his work was the foundation, after 1933, of what is known as the Musil-Gesellschaft. This was a small number of people—professional and business men—who banded together to give Musil financial support. He accepted this arrangement as his due, for he was a believer in patronage as an obligation owed to the artist, either by the State or by anyone else.

Accounts of this period give us some of the domestic background, as well as some of the lighter aspects of Musil's last years in Austria and of a situation that without the good will and admiration of these friends would have been desperate, even hopeless. The apartment in the Rasoumovskygasse that had been found after long search was very pleasantly situated overlooking the famous old Rasoumovsky Palace and its gardens, in quiet surroundings favourable to work. Inside, the apartment— still vividly remembered by those who frequented it then—was remarkable in that it consisted of a string of rooms each opening only into the next, the last of them—as if it were a citadel, or rather, the head of a living organism—being where Musil worked, surrounded by bookshelves reaching up to the ceiling. Characteristically, he worked not at an ordinary writing-desk, because no desk was large enough, but at a dining-room table, with another table beside him for all his papers. The necessity of this arrangement becomes clear from the fact that when the Musils travelled there were, among the luggage, always at least three suit-cases containing manuscripts, note-books, and so forth.

Here is the place to speak of his wife, Martha von Musil, who not only had faith in his work but was untiring in the management of his welfare. This encyclopaedic man, with his strict training in engineering, mathematics, and logic, paid slight attention, for the most part, to practical matters. (There is an example of this among the stage directions to Act III of *Die Schwärmer*, which indicates only a faint notion of how tea is made.) His unworldliness extended to many little everyday things, and it was his wife on whom he relied to buy his ticket for him on the tram, to stop him from getting over-excited in discussion, or, if he had over-excited himself, or smoked too much, or drunk more coffee than was agreed to be good for him, to administer a bromide. This child-like side of his character is also reflected in the naïvety with which he would on occasion assert himself in practical affairs, once he had come to the intellectual conclusion as to what was due to him. It is recounted that he liked to keep check on the contributors to the Musil-Gesellschaft and would, if it seemed necessary, ask why So-and-So had not yet paid up for the quarter. Although those who knew him well speak of his wit and brilliance, and of how wonderfully amusing he could be in conversation, he was fundamentally a quiet, reserved man and in society often retiring, even, it seemed, aloof. It was characteristic of him that he would not throw off random opinions on the spur of the moment and, where a real problem was concerned, preferred to say that he must go home and think about it. This precise habit of mind was reflected in his manner, which inclined towards the old-world style of etiquette, and in his personal appearance. He was extremely careful in matters of dress, even to the point of being slightly dandified, and as he was never comfortably off (in spite of the legend that he could extort uniquely large advances from publishers), he would at home go about in old track-suits in order to save his clothes. He was slightly under middle height, compactly built, very strong, and always in good trim. His ideal was not only the master-mind but also the master-body. He made something of a fetish of physical fitness (and indeed, in *The Man Without Qualities* he went near to developing the subject into a metaphysical system). This was why as an elderly man he would not give up his strenuous morning gymnastics, even when—especially combined with heavy smoking —they became a danger to his life. It was a threat he would not take seriously.

It must have been hard for him to feel at ease in the atmosphere of the petty fascism that soon prevailed in his native Austria, that small and in many ways backward country, the remnant of a great empire and once the heart of Europe. Although he could live and write there unmolested (even gaining some unofficial reputation) because his writing was not ' political ' in any sense that could menace the *Ständestaat*, yet, because it was equally of no use to that short-lived regime, he had to stand by and see literary nonentities attain fame practically overnight as patriotic men of letters and poets of the homeland. The irony of it is that probably no other Austrian has written about Austria—the old pre-1914 Austria of the Dual Monarchy—with such rare, mellow sympathy, blended with critical humour, a quality of reconciliation that comes from contemplation of a vista receding into the past, of a state of things and a way of living beyond recall, where

> " one was negatively free, constantly aware of the inadequate grounds for one's own existence and lapped by the great fantasy of all that had not happened, or at least had not yet irrevocably happened, as by the foam of the oceans from which mankind arose."

There is an element of anticipation of his own return to Vienna in the early 'thirties in Ulrich's return many years before—a return home in a spirit of scepticism and yet with a sort of trust that home-coming in itself could make all things well.

> " And one day one suddenly has a wild craving : Get out ! Jump clear ! It is a nostalgic yearning to be brought to a standstill, to cease evolving, to get stuck, to turn back to a point that lies before the wrong fork. And in the good old days when there was still such a place as Imperial Austria, one could leave the train of events,

get into an ordinary train on an ordinary railway-line, and travel back home."

But what Musil returned to was no longer Kakania, of which he had written :

> "There, in Kakania, that misunderstood State that has since vanished, which was in so many things a model, though all unacknowledged, there was speed too, of course ; but not too much speed. . . . The conquest of the air had begun here too ; but not too intensively. Now and then a ship was sent off to South America or the Far East ; but not too often. There was no ambition to have world markets and world power. Here one was in the centre of Europe, at the focal point of the world's old axes ; the words 'colony' and 'overseas' had the ring of something as yet utterly untried and remote."

That was the Austria of which his Count Leinsdorf is an embodiment—'merely a patriot' but also a 'progressive' Austrian who believes that everything will somehow turn out all right in the end, and who by virtue of this mixture arrives, for instance, at the view that a social-democratic republic with a strong sovereign at its head would be a far from impossible form of government. He and General Stumm von Bordwehr, perhaps the most lovable general in literature, in all they do and say wear something like a halo of absurdity, which one gradually comes to realise is essentially related to a mild realism of common sense, a distrust of overdoing it, that once, it seems, was not only the secret of Austria's charm but also the secret of a way of life that worked —a system of beautifully balanced compromises in every sphere that the Austrians call '*fortwursteln*' and the English, the only other people who have it, call 'muddling through'.

How difficult things were in the utterly different Austria of the nineteen-thirties can be seen from the fact that Musil's last small book of fables and aphorisms, with the melancholy title *Nachlass zu Lebzeiten*, was published (in 1936) in Switzerland. Nevertheless, thanks to the Musil-Gesellschaft, these few years, during which the third volume of *Der Mann ohne Eigenschaften* was begun, were probably the period of greatest independence as a writer that Musil ever knew. He continued to take his time. What was valuable in his work would be valuable later, no matter what might happen in the interval. Still, there is a perceptible difference in the tone of the three volumes, as though each were written in a different key. After the fresh morning quality of the first volume, where things are seen variegated, multitudinous, and as though through a reversed opera-glass, the focus shifts, becoming directed more towards the personal, the inner life, not only of Ulrich but of all the characters, who draw steadily nearer to us, closing in around us. Perhaps it is Musil's peculiar position—in his writing still approaching 1914, and at the same time feeling the new and even more appalling catastrophe overtaking him in reality—that changes the colour, as though the light were changing. The second volume has the brightness of midday, the third that of an afternoon already growing late, the light not yet fading, but the shadows already lengthening, the threat of nightfall in the air. And his awareness of new danger and darkness made him work if anything more slowly, more carefully, as he penetrated further into the depths.

In 1937, the year before the *Anschluss*, his lecture *Über die Dummheit*, delivered in Vienna in March, was published in pamphlet form there by a publisher who had emigrated from Germany and was soon to be forced to emigrate further. The last sentence of this lecture On Stupidity has a strangely double meaning:

> "And with one foot on the frontier I declare myself incapable of going further. For one step beyond the point where we have halted—and we should move out of the realm of stupidity, which is even theoretically still full of variety, and into the realm of wisdom, territory that is bleak and in general shunned."

In 1938 he himself emigrated to Switzerland. He must have been quite clear about it then that this meant giving up Austria and Germany, and with that his position as a German writer, for good. There were those who thought he need not have taken this step. It seems that a kind of recognition was now on its way. But it was not the kind he could accept; it did not come from those from whom he would accept it. Consequently his work was banned in Germany and Austria, and up to the time of writing (January 1952) it remains unobtainable there. His German publisher disposed of the rights of *Der Mann ohne Eigenschaften* to that emigrant publisher, now in Stockholm, who had published *Über die Dummheit*. It was incidentally the same publisher from whom Musil later withdrew the third volume when it was already in the press, choosing to re-write the book, which did not yet satisfy him, rather than benefit from its immediate publication. He and his wife spent almost a year in Zurich, and then moved to Geneva, the surroundings of which appealed to him more. There they led a very quiet, withdrawn existence. And it was there that he died, very suddenly, on the 15th April 1942.

He had spent the morning as usual at his writing-table and in the garden, and had gone upstairs to take a bath before luncheon. His widow wrote : " When he was satisfied with the way work was going—which was not often the case—he was cheerful. And I have rarely seen him so cheerful as he was five minutes before his death. He had written some sentences that were to stand." He was probably doing his gymnastics when he collapsed. The expression on his face when he was found a short while later was one of mockery and mild astonishment.

The third volume was posthumously and privately published in Switzerland, and it was only after the recognition of Robert Musil in England that in 1951 his old German publisher undertook to prepare an edition of the complete works. From 1945 until a short time ago, in spite of intensive book-production in Germany, no publisher could be found to take any interest in the matter. An anticipatory comment on these facts is contained in the following passage from a letter Robert Musil wrote in 1940 :

" In spite of the reputation as an artist that I undoubtedly have in Germany and abroad, I have always kept some slight distance from the main road of success. I am not the kind of author who tells his readers what they want to hear because they know it anyway. My attitude and my work tend rather more towards the severe, and my readers have gradually come to me, not I to them. By that I do not mean to suggest I have no feeling for what remains stronger and wiser than the individual, but only that it is on the whole difficult to find the right social measure for one as for the other. Granted the ability, granted also the possibility of making mistakes now and then, it seems to me that what is decisive is the passionate seriousness with which one sets about one's job and subordinates material advantage to it. This is something that I think I can safely say I possess to a more than adequate degree."

These words might serve as his epitaph.

E.W., E.K., *London*, 1952.

FIRST BOOK

A SORT OF INTRODUCTION

1

*Which, remarkably enough, does not get any-
one anywhere.*

THERE was a depression over the Atlantic. It was travelling
eastwards, towards an area of high pressure over Russia, and still
showed no tendency to move northwards around it. The
isotherms and isotheres were fulfilling their functions. The
atmospheric temperature was in proper relation to the average
annual temperature, the temperature of the coldest as well as of
the hottest month, and the a-periodic monthly variation in
temperature. The rising and setting of the sun and of the moon,
the phases of the moon, Venus and Saturn's rings, and many
other important phenomena, were in accordance with the fore-
casts in the astronomical yearbooks. The vapour in the air was
at its highest tension, and the moisture in the air was at its lowest.
In short, to use an expression that describes the facts pretty
satisfactorily, even though it is somewhat old-fashioned : it was
a fine August day in the year 1913.

Motor-cars came shooting out of deep, narrow streets into the
shallows of bright squares. Dark patches of pedestrian bustle
formed into cloudy streams. Where stronger lines of speed
transected their loose-woven hurrying, they clotted up—only to
trickle on all the faster then and after a few ripples regain their
regular pulse-beat. Hundreds of sounds were intertwined into
a coil of wiry noise, with single barbs projecting, sharp edges
running along it and submerging again, and clear notes splintering
off—flying and scattering. Even though the peculiar nature of
this noise could not be defined, a man returning after years of
absence would have known, with his eyes shut, that he was in
that ancient capital and imperial city, Vienna. Cities can be
recognised by their pace just as people can by their walk. Opening his eyes, he would recognise it all again by the way the

3

general movement pulsed through the streets, far sooner than he would discover it from any characteristic detail. And even if he only imagined he could do so—what does it matter ? The excessive weight attached to the question of where one is goes back to nomadic times, when people had to be observant about feeding-grounds. It would be interesting to know why, in the matter of a red nose, for instance, one is content with the vague statement that it is red, never asking what particular shade of red it is, although this could be precisely expressed in micro-millimetres, in terms of wave-lengths ; whereas, in the case of something so infinitely more complicated, such as a town in which one happens to be, one always wants to know quite exactly what particular town it is. This distracts attention from more important things.

So no special significance should be attached to the name of the city. Like all big cities, it consisted of irregularity, change, sliding forward, not keeping in step, collisions of things and affairs, and fathomless points of silence in between, of paved ways and wilderness, of one great rhythmic throb and the per-petual discord and dislocation of all opposing rhythms, and as a whole resembled a seething, bubbling fluid in a vessel consisting of the solid material of buildings, laws, regulations, and historical traditions.

The two people who were walking up a wide, busy thorough-fare in the midst of it all were, of course, far from having such an impression. They obviously belonged to a privileged section of society, their good breeding being apparent in their clothes, their bearing and their manner of conversing. They had their initials significantly embroidered on their underclothing. And likewise —that is to say, not outwardly displayed, but, as it were, in the exquisite underlinen of their minds—they knew who they were and that they were in their proper place in a capital city that was also an imperial residence.

Let us assume that their names were Arnheim and Ermelinde Tuzzi—but no, that would be a mistake, for Frau Tuzzi was spending this August in Bad Aussee, accompanied by her hus-band, and Herr Dr. Arnheim was still in Constantinople. So we are confronted with the enigma of who they were. If one has a lively imagination one is very often conscious of such enigmas in the street, but they become resolved in a remarkably easy manner by being forgotten, unless in the next thirty yards one can remember where one has seen these two people before. These two now suddenly stopped, having become aware of a crowd gathering in front of them. A moment earlier the regularity had been broken by a sudden oblique movement : something had spun round, skidding sideways—the abrupt braking, as it appeared, of a heavy lorry, which was now stranded with one wheel on the edge of the pavement. In an instant, like bees round the entrance to their hive, people had collected round a little island of space in their midst. The driver, who had climbed down from his seat, stood there, grey as packing-paper, gesticulating crudely, explaining how the accident had happened. The eyes of those joining the crowd rested first on him and then were cautiously lowered into the depths of the enclosed space, where a man had been laid on the edge of the pavement, apparently dead. It was owing to his own carelessness that he had been run over, as was generally admitted. In turns people knelt down beside him, trying to do something about him. They opened his jacket and buttoned it up again, tried to prop him up, and then again to lay him flat ; all that it really amounted to was that they were marking time until the ambulance arrived bringing expert, authorised aid.

The lady and her companion had also approached and, peering over heads and bent backs, contemplated the man lying on the ground. Then they stepped back and stood hesitating. The lady had a disagreeable sensation in the pit of her stomach, which she felt entitled to take for compassion ; it was an irresolute, paralysing sensation. The gentleman, after some silence, said to her :

" These heavy lorries they use here have too long a braking-distance."

Somehow the lady felt relieved at hearing this, and she thanked him with an attentive glance. Though she had doubtless heard the expression many times before, she did not know what a braking-distance was, nor had she any wish to know ; it was sufficient for her that by this means the horrible happening could be fitted into some kind of pattern, so becoming a technical problem that no longer directly concerned her. And now the shrill

whistle of an ambulance could be heard, and the promptness of
its arrival was a source of satisfaction to the waiting crowd.   How
admirable these social institutions are!   The casualty was lifted
on to a stretcher and then slid into the ambulance.   Men in a
kind of uniform attended to him.   The inside of the vehicle,
glimpsed for a moment, looked as clean and tidy as a hospital
ward.   People walked on with the almost justifiable impression
that what had occurred was an event within the proper framework of law and order.

" According to American statistics," the gentleman observed,
" there are over a hundred and ninety thousand people killed on
the roads annually over there, and four hundred and fifty thousand
injured."

" Do you think he is dead ? " his companion asked, still with
the unjustified feeling that she had experienced something
exceptional.

" I should think he's alive," the gentleman replied.   " It
looked as though he were when they lifted him into the ambulance."

2   *Abode of the Man Without Qualities.*

THE street in which this minor accident had occurred was one
of those long winding rivers of traffic that radiate from their
source in the centre of the city and flow through the surrounding
districts out into the suburbs.   Had the elegant couple followed
its course for a while longer they would have seen something that
would certainly have appealed to them.   It was an eighteenth-
or even perhaps seventeenth-century garden, still in parts unspoilt ; and passing along its wrought-iron railings one caught
a glimpse through the trees of a well-kept lawn and beyond it
something like a miniature château, hunting-lodge, or *pavillon
d'amour* from times past and gone.   More precisely, its original

structure was seventeenth-century, the garden and the upper storey had an eighteen-century look, and the façade had been restored and somewhat spoilt in the nineteenth century, so that the whole thing had a faintly bizarre character, like that of a super-imposed photograph. But the general effect was such that people invariably stopped and said: " Oh, look ! " And when this pretty little white building had its windows open, one could see into the gentlemanly calm of a scholar's house where the walls were lined with books.

This house belonged to the Man Without Qualities.

He was standing at one of the windows, looking through the delicate filter of the garden's green air into the brownish street, and for the last ten minutes, watch in hand, he had been counting the cars, carriages, and trams, and the pedestrians' faces, blurred by distance, all of which filled the network of his gaze with a whirl of hurrying forms. He was estimating the speed, the angle, the dynamic force of masses being propelled past, which drew the eye after them swift as lightning, holding it, letting it go, forcing the attention—for an infinitesimal instant of time—to resist them, to snap off, and then to jump to the next and rush after that.

And then, after doing sums in his head for a while, he laughed and put his watch back in his pocket, having come to the con-clusion that what he had been doing was nonsense. If one could measure the leaps that the attention took, the exertion of the eye-muscles, the pendulum-movements of the psyche, and all the efforts that a human being must make in order to keep him-self vertical in the flux of the street, then presumably—so he had thought, and had toyed with trying to calculate the incalculable— the result would be a quantity compared with which the force that Atlas needed to hold the world up was trivial, and one could imagine the enormous output of energy, nowadays, of even a man who was doing nothing at all.

At this moment the Man Without Qualities was such a man. And how about a man who was doing something ?

" There are two conclusions one can draw from this," he said to himself. The expenditure of muscular energy made by a citizen quietly going about his business all day long is considerably greater than that of an athlete who lifts a huge weight once a day.

Physiologically this has been established ; and so doubtless the social sum-total of little everyday exertions, as a result of their suitability for such summation, does bring far more energy into the world than do the deeds of heroes ; indeed, the heroic exertion appears positively minute, like a grain of sand laid, in some act of illusory immensity, upon a mountain-top.

The idea appealed to him. But, it must be added, it was not really because he liked a life of urban respectability that he liked this idea ; on the contrary, he was merely choosing to create difficulties for his own inclinations, which had once been different.

Perhaps it is precisely the common man who has an intuitive prophetic glimpse of the beginning of an immense new, collective, ant-like heroism ? It will be called rationalised heroism and will be regarded as very beautiful. But what can we know of that today ? However, at that time there were hundreds of such unanswered questions, all of the greatest importance. They were in the air ; they were burning underfoot. The time was on the move. People who were not born then will find it difficult to believe, but the fact is that even then time was moving as fast as a cavalry-camel ; it is not only nowadays that it does so. But in those days no one knew what it was moving towards. Nor could anyone quite distinguish between what was above and what below, between what was moving forwards and what backwards.

" It doesn't matter what one does," the Man Without Qualities said to himself, shrugging his shoulders. " In a tangle of forces like this it doesn't make a scrap of difference." He turned away like a man who has learned renunciation, almost indeed like a sick man who shrinks from any intensity of contact. And then, striding through his adjacent dressing-room, he passed a punching-ball that hung there ; he gave it a blow far swifter and harder than is usual in moods of resignation or states of weakness.

3

Even a Man Without Qualities has a father with qualities.

WHEN the Man Without Qualities returned from abroad some time earlier, it was only out of whimsicality and a detestation of the usual kind of apartment that he rented this little château, which had once been a summer residence outside the city gates, losing its meaning when the city grew out and round it, amounting in the end to nothing more than a neglected piece of real estate waiting for a rise in the price of land, and in the mean time untenanted. The rent was correspondingly low, but all the rest— getting the place into a state of good repair and bringing it into line with modern ideas of comfort—had cost an unexpectedly large amount of money. It had become an adventure that finally forced him to turn to his father for help, which was by no means agreeable ; for his independence was precious to him. He was thirty-two years of age, and his father was sixty-nine.

The old gentleman was aghast—not, actually, at being descended on in this way (although it was partly on that account too, since he detested imprudence) and not at the contribution levied on him, for at bottom he approved of his son's manifesting a need for domesticity and a proper establishment of his own. What affronted his feelings was the taking over of a building that one had no choice but to call a château, even though it were only in the diminutive ; it was the ill-omened presumption of it that upset him.

He himself had begun as a tutor in houses of the high nobility when he was a student and had continued in that capacity when a junior lawyer—though not from necessity, for his father before him had been comfortably off. Later, when he became a university lecturer and then professor, he felt the benefit of it all, for the careful nursing of these connections brought it about that he gradually rose to be legal adviser to almost all the old aristocratic families in the country, although he was by then even less in need of a professional side-line than formerly. Indeed, long after the fortune thus accumulated could very well stand comparison with the dowry provided by a Rhineland industrialist family for his early deceased wife, the mother of his son, these connections, established in his youth and strengthened in his prime, still did not lapse.　Although the savant, who had attained to honours, now retired from legal practice proper, only on occasion giving counsel's opinion for an exalted fee, every event that concerned the circle of his former patrons was still meticulously entered up in special records, which were very precisely carried forward from the fathers to the sons and grandsons ; and no official honour, no marriage, birthday or fête-day passed without a letter in which the recipient was congratulated in a delicate blend of veneration and shared reminiscence.　Each time, with equal punctilio, short letters came in reply, expressing thanks to the old family friend, the esteemed scholar.　So his son was from boyhood well acquainted with the aristocracy's talent for condescension, which unconsciously yet so accurately weighed and measured out the exact quantity of affability required ; and he had always been irritated by this subservience —of one who did, after all, belong to the intellectual élite— towards the possessors of horses, lands and traditions.　It was, however, not calculated servility that made the father insensitive on this score.　It was quite instinctively that he had made a great career in this manner, not only becoming a professor and a member of academies, sitting on many learned and official committees, but also being made Knight, then Commander, and even Grand-Cross of high orders, finally being elevated by His Majesty into the ranks of the hereditary nobility, subsequent to having been appointed a member of the Upper House.　Once there, the man so distinguished attached himself to the liberal bourgeois wing, which was sometimes ín opposition to the high nobility.　But, characteristically enough, none of his noble patrons bore him any ill-will for it or felt even the slightest surprise ; they had never regarded him as anything but a personification of the rising third estate.　The old gentleman took an assiduous part in the expert work of legislation, and even when a controversial division found him on the bourgeois side, the opposite side bore him no grudge, conscious as they were that he had not been invited to act otherwise.　In politics he did nothing but what it had formerly always been his function to do, namely combine his superior and sometimes gently emend-atory knowledge with the suggestion that his personal loyalty could nevertheless be depended upon ; and so he had risen without essential change, as his son declared, from being a tutor to the upper classes to being a tutor to the Upper House.

When the matter of the château came to his notice, it struck him as a violation of a boundary-line that had to be respected all the more punctiliously because it was not legally defined ; and he took his son to task in terms even more bitter than the many reproaches he had heaped upon him in the course of time, making it all positively sound like a prophecy that this would turn out to be the beginning of the bad end to which he was bound to come. It was an affront to the old man's fundamental feelings about life. As with many men who have achieved something of note, these feelings, far from being selfish, sprang from a deep love of what might be called the generally and suprapersonally useful, in other words, from a sincere veneration for what advances one's own interests—and this not for the sake of advancing them, but in harmony with that advancement and simultaneously with it, and also on general grounds. This is of great importance : even a pedigree dog seeks its place under the dining-table, undisturbed by kicks, and not out of doggish abjection, but from affection and fidelity. And indeed the most coldly calculating people do not have half the success in life that comes to those rightly blended personalities who are capable of feeling a really deep attachment to such persons and conditions as will advance their own interests.

4

If there is such a thing as a sense of reality, there must also be a sense of possibility.

IF one wants to pass through open doors easily, one must bear in mind that they have a solid frame : this principle, according to which the old professor had always lived, is simply a requirement of the sense of reality. But if there is such a thing as a sense of reality—and no one will doubt that it has its *raison d'être*—then there must also be something that one can call a sense of possibility.

Anyone possessing it does not say, for instance : Here this or that has happened, will happen, must happen. He uses his imagination and says : Here such and such might, should or ought to happen. And if he is told that something *is* the way it is, then he thinks : Well, it could probably just as easily be some other way. So the sense of possibility might be defined outright as the capacity to think how everything could 'just as easily' be, and to attach no more importance to what is than to what is not. It will be seen that the consequences of such a creative disposition may be remarkable, and unfortunately they not infrequently make the things that other people admire appear wrong and the things that other people prohibit permissible, or even make both appear a matter of indifference. Such possibilitarians live, it is said, within a finer web, a web of haze, imaginings, fantasy and the subjunctive mood. If children show this tendency it is vigorously driven out of them, and in their presence such people are referred to as crackbrains, dreamers, weaklings, know-alls, and carpers and cavillers.

When one wants to praise these poor fools, one sometimes calls them idealists. But obviously all this only covers the weak variety, those who either cannot grasp reality or are so thin-skinned that they have to dodge it, in other words, people in whom the lack of the sense of reality is a real deficiency. The possible, however, covers not only the dreams of nervously sensitive persons, but also the not yet manifested intentions of God. A possible experience or a possible truth does not equate to real experience or real truth minus the value 'real'; but, at least in the opinion of its devotees, it has in it something out-and-out divine, a fiery, soaring quality, a constructive will, a conscious utopianism that does not shrink from reality but treats it, on the contrary, as a mission and an invention. After all, the earth is not so very old and its issue has never yet been anything that it has in any real sense been blessed with. If one wants a convenient way of distinguishing between people with the sense of reality and those with the sense of possibility, one merely needs to think of any given sum of money. Everything in the way of possibilities contained in, for instance, a hundred pounds is undoubtedly contained in that sum whether one possesses it or not ; the fact that Mr. I or Mr. You possesses it adds as little to it as to a rose or to a woman. But a fool tucks it away in a stocking, the realists say, and an efficient man makes it work for him. Something is undeniably added to or taken away from even the beauty of a woman by the man who possesses her. It is reality that awakens possibilities, and nothing could be more wrong than to deny this. Nevertheless, in the sum total or on the average they will always remain the same possibilities, going on repeating themselves until someone comes along to whom something real means no more than something imagined. It is he who first gives the new possibilities their meaning and their destiny ; he awakens them.

Such a man is, however, by no means an unambiguous matter. Since his ideas, in so far as they are not mere idle phantasmagoria, are nothing else than as yet unborn realities, he too of course has a sense of reality ; but it is a sense of possible reality and moves towards its goal much more slowly than most people's sense of their real possibilities. He wants, as it were, the wood, and the others the trees ; and the wood in itself is something that it is very difficult to express, whereas trees mean so and so many cubic feet of a definite quality. Or perhaps it can be put better by saying that the man with an ordinary sense of reality resembles a fish that nibbles at the hook and does not see the line, while the man with the kind of sense of reality that one can also call the sense of possibility pulls a line through the water without any notion whether there is a bait on it or not. In him an extra-ordinary indifference to the life nibbling at the bait is in contrast with the probability that he will do utterly eccentric things. An unpractical man—and he not only appears to be so, but actually is—will always be unreliable and incalculable in his intercourse with other people. He will perform actions that mean something different to him from what they mean to others, but is reassured about everything as soon as it can be summed up in an extraordinary idea. And in addition to this he is today still far from being logically consistent. It is quite possible, for instance, that to him a crime by which someone else is injured appears to be merely a slip for which it is not the criminal who is to blame, but the organisation of society. On the other hand, it is a question whether he would regard getting his own face slapped as a disgrace to society or at least as something as impersonal as being bitten by a dog; probably in such a case he will first return the slap and then come to the conclusion that he should not have done so. Moreover, if someone else goes off with his mistress, as things are today he will not be able to ignore the reality of the incident entirely and so compensate himself with a surprising new emotion. This development is at present still in flux, and in the individual human being it indicates a weakness as well as a strength.

And since the possession of qualities presupposes that one takes a certain pleasure in their reality, all this gives us a glimpse of how it may all of a sudden happen to someone who cannot summon up any sense of reality—even in relation to himself— that one day he appears to himself as a man without qualities.

5   *Ulrich.*

THE Man Without Qualities of whom we are speaking was called Ulrich. And Ulrich—it is not agreeable to keep on calling somebody whom one has only just met by his first name, but his surname is withheld out of consideration for his father—had passed the first test of his character when he was still on the borderline between childhood and adolescence: it was in a school essay on a patriotic theme. Patriotism was a very special subject in Austria. German children simply were taught to despise Austrian children's wars, and to believe that French children were the descendents of enervate debauchees, running away in their thousands whenever a German *Landwehrmann* with a big beard so much as walked up to them. And with the roles reversed, and all desirable alterations made, exactly the same is learnt by French, Russian, and English children, who for their part have also often been on the winning side. Now, children like showing off; they like playing Bobbies and Thieves; and they are always inclined to believe that the Y family in Great X Street, if it happens to be their own, is the greatest family in the world. And so they are very susceptible to patriotism. In Austria, however, this was a little more involved. Although, of course, the Austrians had also been victorious in all the wars in their history, after most of these wars they had had to surrender something. Such a state of things starts one thinking; and in his essay on Love of Country Ulrich wrote that anyone who really loved his country should never think his own country the best. And then, in a flash that struck him as particularly beautiful, although he was more dazzled by its brilliance than able to see what was going on in the light of it, he had added to this suspect sentence a second, to the effect that even God probably preferred to speak of His world in the subjunctive of potentiality (*hic dixerit quispiam* = here it might be objected . . .), for God makes the world and while doing so thinks that it could just as easily be some other way.—He had been very proud of this sentence, but perhaps he had not expressed himself quite intelligibly, for it created a great stir, and he was almost expelled from the school. No decision was reached, simply because the authorities could not make up their minds whether his audacious remark was to be regarded as defamation of the fatherland or as blasphemy. He was then receiving his education at the Theresianum, that very select school for the sons of the nobility and gentry, which produced the noblest pillars of the State. His father's wrath being aroused at the shame brought upon himself by this almost unrecognisable chip of the old block, he was packed off abroad, to a town in Belgium nobody had ever heard of, to a small school that was run on shrewd and efficient business lines and did a roaring trade in the black sheep of other schools, at low fees. There Ulrich learned to extend his contempt for the ideals of others to international dimensions.

Since that time sixteen or seventeen years had passed as the clouds drift across the sky. Ulrich did not regret them, nor was he proud of them; he simply looked back on them, in his thirty-second year, with astonishment. In the meantime he had been in various places, and sometimes also for short periods in his own country; and wherever he had been he had found all sorts of valuable and of futile things to do. It has already been indicated that he was a mathematician, and no more need be said about that for the time being. The fact is—in every profession that is followed not for the sake of money but for love, there comes a moment when the advancing years seem to be leading into the void. After this moment had lasted for some time, Ulrich remembered that there is ascribed to a man's native land the mysterious capacity of making his musings take root and thrive in their proper climate; and he settled down at home with the feelings of a traveller sitting down on a bench for eternity, although he has a premonition that he will get up again almost immediately.

When he was setting his house in order, as the Bible expresses it, he went through an experience for which he had, in fact, only been waiting. He had put himself in the pleasant position of having to renovate this neglected little property of his entirely to his own taste, and from scratch. He had all principles at his disposal, from that of a stylistically pure restoration to that of complete recklessness; and all styles, likewise, offered themselves to his mind, from the Assyrian to Cubism. What was he to choose?

Modern man is born in hospital and dies in hospital—hence he should also live in a place like a hospital.—This maxim had just been formulated by a leading architect, and another one, a reformer of interior decoration, demanded movable partition-walls in flats, on the grounds that in living together man must learn to trust man and not shut himself off in a spirit of separatism. A new time had then just begun (for that is, after all, something that time is doing all the time), and a new time needs a new style. Luckily for Ulrich the little château, as he found it, already possessed three styles superimposed on each other, so that one really could not do with it everything that was insisted on; nevertheless he felt himself mightily stirred by the responsibility of getting a house ready to live in, and over his head hung the menacing proverb: 'Tell me what your house is like and I'll tell you who you are', which he had often read in art journals. After intensive study of these journals he came to the conclusion that he preferred, after all, to take the architectural completion of his personality into his own hands, and he began designing his future furniture himself. But whenever he had just thought out a shape that was solid and impressive, it occurred to him that one could just as easily put a slim, strong, technically functional form in its place; and whenever he designed a reinforced concrete shape looking as though it were emaciated by its own strength, he would recall the thin, vernal lines of a thirteen-year-old girl and sink into reverie instead of making up his mind.

All this—in a matter that did not, in all seriousness, affect him very closely—was the well-known incoherency of ideas, with their way of spreading out without a central point, an incoherency that is characteristic of the present era and constitutes its peculiar arithmetic, rambling about in a multitude of things, from a hundred possibilities to yet a thousand others, and always without a basic unity. Finally he gave up inventing anything but impracticable rooms, revolving rooms, kaleidoscopic interiors, adjustable scenery for the soul, and his ideas grew steadily more and more insubstantial. Here at last he had reached the point to which he was drawn by inclination. His father would have expressed it approximately as follows: He who is allowed to do as he likes will soon run his head into a brick wall out of sheer confusion. Or perhaps like this: He who can fulfil all his own wishes will soon not know what to wish for. Ulrich repeated this to himself with great enjoyment. This ancestral wisdom struck him as an extraordinarily new idea. In his potentialities, plans, and emotions, man must first of all be hedged in by prejudices, traditions, difficulties and limitations of every kind, like a lunatic in his strait-jacket, and only then will whatever he is capable of bringing forth perhaps have some value, solidity and permanence. Indeed it is hard to see all the implications inherent in this idea! Now, the Man Without Qualities, who had returned home to his own country, also took the second step towards letting himself be shaped by the external circumstances of life itself; at this point in his reflections he simply abandoned the fitting up of his house to the genius of his tradespeople, confident that they would provide all that was wanted in the way of tradition, prejudices and limitations. He himself only touched up the old outlines that remained from earlier times, the dark antlers under the white vaultings of the little hall, or the formal ceiling in the drawing-room, and added, besides, everything else that seemed to him useful and convenient.

When it was all finished, he was entitled to shake his head and wonder : Is this, then, the life that is to be my own ?—It was an exquisite little château that he now possessed ; one could hardly help calling it that, for it was exactly as one imagines such places, a delightful retreat for an important personage as visualised by leading furnishers, carpet-dealers and interior-decorators. There was only one thing lacking : this charming clock-work was not wound up. For then carriages with high dignitaries and noble ladies in them would have come bowling up the drive and footmen would have jumped down to ask Ulrich dubiously : " Where is your master, my good man ? "

He had returned from Cloudland, and had at once installed himself again in a castle in the air.

6   *Leona, or a shift of perspective.*

WHEN a man has set his house in order, he should also take to himself a wife. Ulrich's mistress in those days was called Leontine and was a singer in a small cabaret. She was a tall, plump girl, provocatively lifeless, and he called her Leona.

She had first caught his attention by the liquid darkness of her eyes, the dolefully passionate expression of her symmetrically beautiful long face, and the sentimental songs that she sang instead of *risqué* ones. All these old-fashioned little songs were about love, sorrow, constancy, loneliness, woodland whispers and twinkling trout. A tall girl, lonely to the marrow of her bones, Leona stood on a tiny stage and patiently sang them at the public in a homely voice ; and if here and there some little daring passages did crop up, the effect was all the more spectral because she accompanied both the tragic and the roguish sentiments with the same laboriously studied gestures. Ulrich was at once reminded of old photographs or pictures of beautiful women in bygone volumes of German family magazines ; and while he was losing himself in contemplation of her face, he observed in it quite a number of little characteristics that simply could not be real and yet made the face what it was. There are of course in all ages all kinds of countenance ; but there is also one that is exalted by the taste of the time and acknowledged to be the image of happiness and beauty, while all other faces try to approximate to it, even ugly ones succeeding more or less by the aid of hairdressing and fashion ; and the only ones that never succeed are those faces born to strange triumphs, those in which the regal and exiled ideal beauty of an earlier age is expressed without compromise. Such faces drift like corpses of earlier desires in the great insubstantiality of love's whirlwind ; and the men who gaped into the vast ennui of Leontine's singing, without knowing what moved them, felt their nostrils twitch with feelings quite different from those caused by the pert little *chanteuses* with the tango hair-style. So Ulrich decided to call her Leona, and it seemed to him that possession of her was as desirable as that of a large lion-skin rug.

But after their acquaintance had begun Leona revealed yet another uncontemporary quality : she was monstrously greedy, and that is a vice that went out of fashion long ago. In its origins her greed was a poor child's yearning for expensive delicacies ; now that it was at last liberated, it had all the vigour of an ideal that has burst out of its cage and seized power. Her father, it appeared, had been a respectable man in a small way of life, who always beat her when she went out with admirers. But she did so for no other reason than that she liked nothing in the world so much as to sit at a table outside a small *pâtisserie* and spoon up her ice while gazing in a ladylike way at the passers-by. For although one could not actually have asserted that she was un-carnal, one might say, in so far as it is permissible to say such a thing at all, that in this as in everything else she was downright lazy and work-shy. In her extensive body it took every stimulus wonderfully long to reach the brain, and it sometimes happened that in the middle of the day her eyes would begin to melt for no reason at all, although in the night they had been rigidly fixed on a point on the ceiling as though watching a fly there.   Similarly, in the midst of complete silence, she would sometimes begin to laugh at a joke she had just seen, although some days earlier she had listened to it without understanding it.   And so too when she had no particular reason for being the opposite, she was entirely respectable.   It could never be got out of her how it was that she had ever come to her occupation.   Apparently she herself did not remember exactly. It was evident, however, that she considered the activities of a cabaret-singer a necessary part of life and associated with them all that she had ever heard about the greatness of art and artists, so that it seemed to her quite proper, edifying, and distinguished to come out every evening on to a little stage wrapped in clouds of cigar-smoke and sing songs whose heart-rending appeal was an established fact.   Naturally, whenever it was necessary to liven up a rather staid number, she did not in the least shrink from an impropriety strewn in here and there ; but she was firmly convinced that the *prima donna* at the Imperial Opera did precisely the same as herself.

To be sure, if one is bent on calling it prostitution when a woman does not, as is customary, give her entire person for money, but only her body, then Leona did occasionally go in for prostitution.   But if one has known nine years long, as she had since her sixteenth year, how small the wages are in the lowest singing-hells, and if one has one's head full of the price of evening-dresses and underclothes, the deductions, the avarice and wanton despotism of the owners of such places, the commission on the food and drink consumed by patrons growing ' merry ' and also on the price of the room in the hotel round the corner, and if one has to deal with these things daily, having all sorts of rows about them and trying to be businesslike about them, then what the outsider can happily regard as debauchery turns out to be a *métier* full of logic and matter-of-factness, and with its own professional code.   And precisely prostitution is a thing in which it makes a great difference whether one is looking at it from above or from below.

But although Leona had a perfectly matter-of-fact attitude to the problems of sex, she also had her romantic side.   Only, with her, everything high-flown, vain and extravagant, all feelings of pride, envy, lust, ambition, and self-abandonment, in short, the driving-forces of the personality and all that makes one climb the social ladder, were, by some trick of nature, bound up not with what is called the heart, but with the digestive tract, the edacious processes—with which, moreover, they were regularly associated in former ages and still are today among primitive people or the guzzling peasantry, who are capable of expressing social standing, and all sorts of other things that confer distinction on human beings, by means of a banquet at which one ceremonially over-eats, with all the inevitable consequences. At the tables in the *boîte* where she worked Leona did her duty; but what she dreamed of was a protector who would liberate her from that obligation, a liaison of the same duration as her contract, permitting her to sit in a genteel pose before a genteel menu in a genteel restaurant. Whenever she was taken out she wished she could have eaten some of all the available dishes at one go, and it was a source of distressingly contradictory satisfaction to her to be at the same time in a position to show that she knew how to choose an exquisite dinner. It was only when she came to the little dessert dishes that she could give her fancy free rein, and generally this turned into an extensive second supper in reversed order. Leona restored her capacity by means of black coffee and stimulating quantities of drink and egged herself on with surprises until her passion was quenched. Then her body was so stuffed with genteel things that it only just kept from bursting. She gazed round her in radiant lethargy, and although she was never very talkative, in this condition she liked to supply retrospective commentary on the dainties that she had consumed. When she said Polmone à la Torlogna or Pommes à la Melville she slipped it in as another will mention, in an affectedly casual way, that he has been talking to his highness or his lordship of that name.

Because it was not altogether to Ulrich's taste to appear in public with Leona, he generally arranged for her feedings to take place at his house, where she was free to dine and wine surrounded by the antlers and period furniture. But in this way she felt cheated of her social satisfaction, and when the Man Without Qualities tempted her to solitary excesses by means of the most amazing dishes that a chef could concoct, she felt herself precisely as ill-used as a woman who notices that she is not loved for the sake of her soul. She was beautiful and a singer, she had no cause to hide herself away, and every evening she was desired by several dozen men who would certainly have agreed that she was in the right. But this man, although he wanted to be alone with her, could not even manage to exclaim : " Holy show, Leona, your bottom makes me crazy ! " and lick his moustache with gusto when he so much as looked at her, as she was accustomed to her admirers doing. Leona despised him a little, although of course she clung to him faithfully ; and Ulrich knew that. What was more, he knew very well what was appropriate in Leona's company, but the time when he could have worked himself up to such exclamations, and when he still wore a moustache, lay too far back in the past. And when one is no longer capable of something that one used to be capable of, no matter how silly it is, the situation is, after all, just as if a stroke had paralysed one's arms and legs. His eyes popped as he looked at her when food and drink had gone to her head. One could with care lift her beauty off her. It was the beauty of the duchess whom Scheffel's Ekkehard carried over the threshold of the convent, the beauty of the noble lady with the falcon on her glove, the beauty of the Empress Elizabeth, famed in legend, with her heavy braids of hair—this beauty was a delight meant for people who were all dead now. In fact, she reminded him of divine Juno too—not, however, of the eternal and immortal goddess, but of something that a vanished or vanishing age had called Junonian. So the substance was only loosely cloaked in the dream of its own life.

But Leona knew that one should give something in return for refined entertainment even when one's host did not express any wishes, and one must not let it go at merely being stared at ; and so, as soon as she was once more capable of it, she would stand up and tranquilly but full-throatedly lift up her voice in song. For her protector such evenings were like pages torn out of an album, animated by all sorts of inspirations and ideas, but mummified, as everything becomes when it is torn out of its context, loaded with the tyrannical spell of all that will now remain eternally the way it is, the thing that is the uncanny fascination of *tableaux vivants*, when it is as though life had suddenly been given a sleeping-draught : and now there it stands, rigid, perfectly correlated within itself, clearly outlined in its immense futility against the background of the world.

7 *In a state of lowered resistance Ulrich acquires a new* chère amie.

ONE morning Ulrich came home in a pretty battered condition. His clothes were in tatters, he had to put cold compresses on his bruised head, and his watch and wallet were missing. He did not know whether he had been robbed of them by the three men with whom he had got involved in a fight or whether they had been stolen by some unobtrusive philanthropist during the short time that he had lain unconscious on the pavement. He went to bed, and while his weary limbs were again beginning to feel gently buoyed up and blanketed, he went over the adventure once more in his mind.

The three heads had suddenly loomed up in front of him. Possibly he had brushed against one of the men in the dark and deserted street, for his thoughts had been wandering and occupied with something else ; but these faces had been ready for anger and already distorted when they entered the circle of the lamp-light. Then he had made a mistake. He ought to have recoiled at once, as though afraid, and in so doing backed hard into the fellow who had stepped up behind him, or rammed his elbow into his stomach and in the same instant tried to get away ; for it is no use taking on three strong men single-handed. Instead he had hesitated for a moment. That was his age, his thirty-two years ; by that time both enmity and love are a little slower in getting started. He had not wanted to believe that the three faces suddenly staring out of the night at him in anger and con-tempt were only after his money, but gave himself up to a feeling that it was hatred that had here condensed and materialised against him. And even while the hooligans were cursing and abusing him, he was enjoying the thought that perhaps they were not hooligans at all but good citizens like himself, only somewhat drunk and freed from inhibitions, whose attention had been caught by his passing figure and who were now discharging on him a hatred always ready waiting for him or any other stranger, like the thunder in the air. For he occasionally felt something similar himself. A great many people today feel themselves regrettably at loggerheads with a great many other people. It is a fundamental characteristic of civilisation that man most profoundly mistrusts those living outside his own *milieu*, so that not only does the Teuton regard the Jew as an incomprehensible and inferior being, but the football-player likewise so regards the man who plays the piano. After all, each thing exists only by virtue of its limitations, in other words, by virtue of a more or less hostile act against its environment : without the Pope there would have been no Luther, and without the heathens, no Pope, and so it cannot be denied that man's most deeply felt association with his fellow-men consists in dissociation from them. Of course he did not think it out in such detail ; but he knew this state of vague atmospheric hostility, with which the air is laden in this epoch of ours, and when it suddenly concentrates in three unknown men who afterwards disappear again for ever, it comes like thunder and lightning and is almost a relief.

However, it did seem that he had done a bit too much thinking, faced with three ruffians. For although, when the first of them attacked, he went flying back, Ulrich having met him with a blow on the chin, the second, who ought to have been tackled instantly afterwards, was only grazed by Ulrich's fist, for in the mean time a blow from behind him with a heavy object had almost cracked his skull. Ulrich's knees gave way under him, he was gripped, then recovered for a moment in that almost unnatural lucidity of the body that usually follows the first collapse, hit out into the tangle of strange bodies and was hammered down by fists growing larger and larger.

Now that he had identified the mistake he had made and found that it lay only in the athletic sphere—just as it may happen that one jumps short once in a while—Ulrich, who still had excellent nerves, quietly went to sleep, with exactly the same delight in the disappearing spirals of fading consciousness that he had already experienced at the back of his mind during his defeat.

When he woke up again he assured himself that his injuries were not of any significance, and went on musing over his experience. A brawl always leaves a bad taste in the mouth, a taste, so to speak, of over-hasty intimacy; and quite apart from the fact that he had been the one attacked, Ulrich had the feeling of having behaved improperly. But improperly in relation to what? Close to the streets where there is a policeman every three hundred yards to avenge the slightest offence against law and order there lie others that demand the same strength of body and mind as the jungle. Mankind produces Bibles and guns, tuberculosis and tuberculin. It is democratic, with kings and nobility; it builds churches, and universities against the churches; it turns monasteries into barracks, but allots chaplains to the barracks. Of course it also provides hooligans with rubber tubing filled with lead to beat a fellow human being's body black-and-blue, and afterwards it has featherbeds waiting to receive the solitary, man-handled body, beds such as that enveloping Ulrich at this moment as though it were filled with sheerest respect and consideration. This is the well-known matter of the contradictions, the inconsistency and imperfection of life. One smiles or sighs over it. But that was not Ulrich's way of reacting. He hated this blend of renunciation and foolish fondness that makes up the general attitude to life, a blend that is as indulgent towards life's contradictions and half-measures as an elderly maiden aunt to a young nephew's loutishness. Only he did not jump straight out of bed when it appeared that remaining there meant he was profiting from the chaos prevailing in human affairs; for in many senses one is only making a premature compromise with conscience at the expense of the cause, producing a short-circuit, escaping into a private world, if one avoids the bad and does the good where oneself is concerned, instead of striving to achieve order in the totality of things. Indeed, after his involuntary experience it even seemed to Ulrich that there was desperately little use in doing away with the guns here and the kings there, and in diminishing stupidity and knavery by any greater or lesser piece of progress; for the measure of all that is disagreeable and bad is instantly made up again by new forms of the same thing, as though the world were always sliding back with the one foot while it takes a step forward with the other. If only one could discover the cause of this, the secret mechanism of it! That of course would be vastly more important than being a good man according to obsolescent principles. And so in the sphere of morality Ulrich was more drawn to service with the general staff than to the everyday heroism of right-doing.

Now he once more summoned up a mental picture of the continuation of his nocturnal adventure. When he had come to his senses again after the brawl's unfortunate conclusion, a cab was drawn up close to the pavement, the driver was grasping the injured stranger under the arms and trying to lift him up, and a lady was bending over him with an angelic expression on her face. At such moments, when consciousness is welling up again from the depths, one sees everything as in the world of children's picture-books. But this state of semi-consciousness soon made way for reality; the presence of a woman attending to him refreshed his senses like a whiff of eau-de-Cologne, skin-deep and quickening, so that he instantly realised that he had not suffered much damage, and tried to get on his legs in good style. He did not at once succeed quite as well as he wished, and the lady anxiously offered to drive him somewhere where he might find help. Ulrich asked if he might be taken home, and as he really seemed to be still dazed and helpless, the lady agreed. In the cab, then, he recovered quickly. He felt something maternally sensual beside him, a tender cloud of charitable idealism in the warmth of which the little ice-crystals of doubt, and of the fear of some impetuous act, were now beginning to form, while he himself was becoming a man again; and they filled the air with the softness of falling snow. He recounted his experience, and the lovely lady, who seemed to be just a little younger than himself, that is to say, perhaps thirty years of age, inveighed against the brutality of human beings and considered him awfully to be pitied.

Naturally he now began a lively defence of what had happened, explaining to the astonished maternal beauty at his side that such battle experiences ought not to be judged by their outcome. Their charm in fact was that one had, in the smallest possible space of time, at a speed not occurring anywhere else in civil

life, and guided by scarcely perceptible signs, to perform movements so many, various, vigorous and nevertheless so precisely
co-ordinated that it became quite impossible to supervise them
with the conscious mind. On the contrary, every sportsman
knew that training had to be stopped several days before the
contest, and this for no other reason than that the muscles and
nerves might be enabled to reach a final agreement among themselves, without the volition, intentions, and consciousness being
involved or having any say at all. Then, in the moment of the
act, what always happened, Ulrich went on, was that the muscles
and nerves fought and leapt together with the ego. This, however, the entity of the body, the soul, the will—this whole and
chief person as identified and defined by civil law—was only
swept along by them like something perched on top, like Europa
on the bull's back, and whenever it was not like that, whenever
anything went wrong and let even the smallest ray of conscious
thought fall into this darkness, then the whole operation was bound
to fail.—Ulrich had talked himself into a state of enthusiasm.
Fundamentally, he now declared, it—and he meant this experience of almost complete ecstasy or transcending of the conscious
personality—was related to a now lost kind of experience that had
been known to the mystics of all religions, and hence it was, in
a way, a contemporary substitute answering to eternal needs ;
even if a poor one, still, at least it was one. Boxing, or similar
forms of sport that put all this into a rational system, was therefore a kind of theology, although one could not insist that this
should be generally recognised at this stage.

Doubtless Ulrich had addressed himself to his companion in
this lively way partly in the vain wish to make her forget the
wretched situation in which she had found him. In these circumstances it was difficult for her to be sure whether he was
talking seriously or merely jesting. In any case it might well
seem quite natural to her that he should try to explain theology
in terms of sport, and it was perhaps even rather interesting, since
sport was in keeping with the spirit of the times and theology,
on the other hand, was something about which one knew nothing
at all, although it certainly could not be denied that there were still
a great many churches. However that might be, she realised that
a lucky accident had enabled her to rescue a very brilliant man,

although she did wonder on and off whether he might be suffering from concussion.

Ulrich, who now wanted to say something intelligible, took the opportunity to point out in passing that, after all, love too was one of the religious and dangerous experiences, since it lifted people out of the arms of reason and set them afloat with literally no ground under their feet.

Yes—the lady said—but sport was so brutal, wasn't it?

Yes, indeed—Ulrich hastened to admit—sport was brutal. One might say it was the sediment of a most finely distributed collective hatred that was precipitated in athletic contests. What was generally maintained, of course, was the opposite, namely that sport brought people together and encouraged the team-spirit and all that sort of thing. But fundamentally it only proved that brutality and love were no further away from each other than were the two wings of a big, bright, voiceless bird.

He had put the emphasis on the wings and the bright, voiceless bird—a notion that did not quite make sense, but yet was filled with a little of that vast sensuality with which life simultaneously satisfies all the rival contradictions in its boundless and exorbitant body. He now became aware that his companion did not in the least understand what he meant; and yet the soft snowfall that she was diffusing inside the cab had become still denser. So he turned right round to her, asking whether she happened to have a distaste for speaking of such physical problems. The physical to-do was really coming far too much into fashion nowadays, and it did of course bring a feeling of horror with it, for when the body was in perfect training it had the upper hand and, without waiting for orders, responded to every stimulus with the accurate, automatic movements of a precision-machine, so accurately, indeed, that its owner was stripped of everything but the uncanny feeling of being left high and dry, while his character was being bolted with, so to speak, by some part or other of his body.

It did indeed seem that this problem touched the young woman deeply. She showed signs of being stirred by these words, breathing faster and cautiously moving a little further away. A mechanism similar to that just described—accelerated respiration, a flushing of the skin, palpitations of the heart, and perhaps one

or two other symptoms—seemed to have begun working in her.
But at this very moment the cab stopped outside Ulrich's house,
and he only had time to ask, smiling, for his rescuer's address,
in order that he might call and thank her.   But to his surprise
this favour was not granted.

And so it was an astonished Ulrich on whom the black wrought-
iron gate had slammed.   And the lady, presumably, had seen the
trees in an old garden stand out tall and dark against the electric
light from illuminated windows, and the low-built wings of a
dainty little château looking on well-tended emerald-green lawns
had opened up, giving a glimpse of walls hung with pictures or
brightly lined with shelves of books : the man who had just taken
his leave had now been absorbed into an unexpectedly delightful
environment.

That was what had happened.

And while Ulrich was now reflecting how boring it would have
been if he had again had to give up his time to one of those amours
that he had long ago grown tired of, a lady was announced—a
lady who would not give her name and who entered the room
heavily veiled.   It was she herself, who had refused him her
name and address, but who now took it on herself to continue
the adventure in this romantico-eleemosynary style, on the pretext of enquiring after his health.

Two weeks later Bonadea had already been his mistress for a
fortnight.

8 *Kakania.*

AT the age when one still attaches great importance to everything connected with tailors and barbers and enjoys looking in
the mirror, one often imagines a place where one would like to
spend one's life, or at least a place where it would be smart to
stay, even though one may not feel any particular inclination to

be there. For some time now such a social *idée fixe* has been
a kind of super-American city where everyone rushes about,
or stands still, with a stop-watch in his hand. Air and earth
form an ant-hill, veined by channels of traffic, rising storey
upon storey. Overhead-trains, overground-trains, underground-
trains, pneumatic express-mails carrying consignments of human
beings, chains of motor-vehicles all racing along horizontally,
express lifts vertically pumping crowds from one traffic-level to
another. . . . At the junctions one leaps from one means of
transport to another, is instantly sucked in and snatched away by
the rhythm of it, which makes a syncope, a pause, a little gap of
twenty seconds between two roaring outbursts of speed, and in
these intervals in the general rhythm one hastily exchanges a few
words with others. Questions and answers click into each other
like cogs of a machine. Each person has nothing but quite definite
tasks. The various professions are concentrated at definite places.
One eats while in motion. Amusements are concentrated in other
parts of the city. And elsewhere again are the towers to which
one returns and finds wife, family, gramophone, and soul.
Tension and relaxation, activity and love are meticulously kept
separate in time and are weighed out according to formulae
arrived at in extensive laboratory work. If during any of these
activities one runs up against a difficulty, one simply drops the
whole thing; for one will find another thing or perhaps, later
on, a better way, or someone else will find the way that one has
missed. It does not matter in the least, but nothing wastes so
much communal energy as the presumption that one is called
upon not to let go of a definite personal aim. In a community
with energies constantly flowing through it, every road leads to
a good goal, if one does not spend too much time hesitating and
thinking it over. The targets are set up at a short distance, but
life is short too, and in this way one gets a maximum of achievement out of it. And man needs no more for his happiness; for
what one achieves is what moulds the spirit, whereas what one
wants, without fulfilment, only warps it. So far as happiness is
concerned it matters very little what one wants; the main thing
is that one should get it. Besides, zoology makes it clear that
a sum of reduced individuals may very well form a totality of
genius.

It is by no means certain that things must turn out this way, but such imaginings are among the travel-fantasies that mirror our awareness of the unresting motion in which we are borne along. These fantasies are superficial, uneasy and short. God only knows how things are really going to turn out. One might think that we have the beginning in our hands at every instant and therefore ought to be making a plan for us all. If we don't like the high-speed thing, all right, then let's have something else! Something, for instance, in slow-motion, in a gauzily billowing, sea-sluggishly mysterious happiness and with that deep cow-eyed gaze that long ago so enraptured the Greeks. But that is far from being the way of it : we are in the hands of the thing. We travel in it day and night, and do everything else in it too : shaving, eating, making love, reading books, carrying out our professional duties, as though the four walls were standing still; and the uncanny thing about it is merely that the walls are travelling without our noticing it, throwing their rails out ahead like long, gropingly curving antennae, without our knowing where it is all going. And for all that, we like if possible to think of ourselves as being part of the forces controlling the train of events. That is a very vague role to play, and it sometimes happens, when one looks out of the window after a longish interval, that one sees the scene has changed. What is flying past flies past because it can't be otherwise, but for all our resignation we become more and more aware of an unpleasant feeling that we may have overshot our destination or have got on to the wrong line. And one day one suddenly has a wild craving : Get out ! Jump clear ! It is a nostalgic yearning to be brought to a standstill, to cease evolving, to get stuck, to turn back to a point that lies before the wrong fork. And in the good old days when there was still such a place as Imperial Austria, one could leave the train of events, get into an ordinary train on an ordinary railway-line, and travel back home.

There, in Kakania, that misunderstood State that has since vanished, which was in so many things a model, though all unacknowledged, there was speed too, of course ; but not too much speed. Whenever one thought of that country from some place abroad, the memory that hovered before the eyes was of wide, white, prosperous roads dating from the age of foot-

travellers and mail-coaches, roads leading in all directions like
rivers of established order, streaking the countryside like ribbons
of bright military twill, the paper-white arm of government holding the provinces in firm embrace. And what provinces ! There
were glaciers and the sea, the Carso and the cornfields of Bohemia,
nights by the Adriatic restless with the chirping of cicadas, and
Slovakian villages where the smoke rose from the chimneys as
from upturned nostrils, the village curled up between two little
hills as though the earth had parted its lips to warm its child
between them. Of course cars also drove along those roads—
but not too many cars ! The conquest of the air had begun
here too ; but not too intensively. Now and then a ship was
sent off to South America or the Far East ; but not too often.
There was no ambition to have world markets and world power.
Here one was in the centre of Europe, at the focal point of the
world's old axes ; the words ‘ colony ’ and ‘ overseas ’ had the
ring of something as yet utterly untried and remote. There was
some display of luxury ; but it was not, of course, as over-
sophisticated as that of the French. One went in for sport ; but
not in madly Anglo-Saxon fashion. One spent tremendous sums
on the army ; but only just enough to assure one of remaining
the second weakest among the great powers. The capital, too,
was somewhat smaller than all the rest of the world's largest
cities, but nevertheless quite considerably larger than a mere
ordinary large city. And the administration of this country was
carried out in an enlightened, hardly perceptible manner, with a
cautious clipping of all sharp points, by the best bureaucracy in
Europe, which could be accused of only one defect : it could not
help regarding genius and enterprise of genius in private persons,
unless privileged by high birth or State appointment, as ostenta-
tion, indeed presumption. But who would want unqualified
persons putting their oar in, anyway ? And besides, in Kakania
it was only that a genius was always regarded as a lout, but never,
as sometimes happened elsewhere, that a mere lout was regarded
as a genius.

All in all, how many remarkable things might be said about
that vanished Kakania ! For instance, it was *kaiserlich-königlich*
(Imperial-Royal) and it was *kaiserlich und königlich* (Imperial and
Royal) ; one of the two abbreviations, *k.k.* or *k. & k.*, applied to

every thing and person, but esoteric lore was nevertheless required in order to be sure of distinguishing which institutions and persons were to be referred to as *k.k.* and which as *k. & k.* On paper it called itself the Austro-Hungarian Monarchy; in speaking, however, one referred to it as Austria, that is to say, it was known by a name that it had, as a State, solemnly renounced by oath, while preserving it in all matters of sentiment, as a sign that feelings are just as important as constitutional law and that regulations are not the really serious thing in life. By its constitution it was liberal, but its system of government was clerical. The system of government was clerical, but the general attitude to life was liberal. Before the law all citizens were equal, but not everyone, of course, was a citizen. There was a parliament, which made such vigorous use of its liberty that it was usually kept shut; but there was also an emergency powers act by means of which it was possible to manage without Parliament, and every time when everyone was just beginning to rejoice in absolutism, the Crown decreed that there must now again be a return to parliamentary government. Many such things happened in this State, and among them were those national struggles that justifiably aroused Europe's curiosity and are today completely misrepresented. They were so violent that they several times a year caused the machinery of State to jam and come to a dead stop. But between whiles, in the breathing-spaces between government and government, everyone got on excellently with everyone else and behaved as though nothing had ever been the matter. Nor had anything real ever been the matter. It was nothing more than the fact that every human being's dislike of every other human being's attempts to get on—a dislike in which today we are all agreed—in that country crystallised earlier, assuming the form of a sublimated ceremonial that might have become of great importance if its evolution had not been prematurely cut short by a catastrophe.

For it was not only dislike of one's fellow-citizens that was intensified into a strong sense of community; even mistrust of oneself and of one's own destiny here assumed the character of profound self-certainty. In this country one acted—sometimes indeed to the extreme limits of passion and its consequences—differently from the way one thought, or one thought differently from the way one acted. Uninformed observers have mistaken this for charm, or even for a weakness in what they thought was the Austrian character. But that was wrong. It is always wrong to explain the phenomena of a country simply by the character of its inhabitants. For the inhabitant of a country has at least nine characters : a professional one, a national one, a civic one, a class one, a geographical one, a sex one, a conscious, an unconscious and perhaps even too a private one ; he combines them all in himself, but they dissolve him, and he is really nothing but a little channel washed out by all these trickling streams, which flow into it and drain out of it again in order to join other little streams filling another channel. Hence every dweller on earth also has a tenth character, which is nothing more or less than the passive illusion of spaces unfilled ; it permits a man everything, with one exception : he may not take seriously what his at least nine other characters do and what happens to them, in other words, the very thing that ought to be the filling of him. This interior space—which is, it must be admitted, difficult to describe—is of a different shade and shape in Italy from what it is in England, because everything that stands out in relief against it is of a different shade and shape ; and yet both here and there it is the same, merely an empty, invisible space with reality standing in the middle of it like a little toy brick town, abandoned by the imagination.

In so far as this can at all become apparent to every eye, it had done so in Kakania, and in this Kakania was, without the world's knowing it, the most progressive State of all ; it was the State that was by now only just, as it were, acquiescing in its own existence. In it one was negatively free, constantly aware of the inadequate grounds for one's own existence and lapped by the great fantasy of all that had not happened, or at least had not yet irrevocably happened, as by the foam of the oceans from which mankind arose.

Es ist passiert, ' it just sort of happened ', people said there when other people in other places thought heaven knows what had occurred. It was a peculiar phrase, not known in this sense to the Germans and with no equivalent in other languages, the very breath of it transforming facts and the bludgeonings of fate into something light as eiderdown, as thought itself. Yes, in spite

of much that seems to point the other way, Kakania was perhaps
a home for genius after all ; and that, probably, was the ruin of it.

9 *First of three attempts at becoming a man of importance.*

THIS man who had returned home could not remember any
time in his life that had not been animated by his determination
to become a man of importance ; it was as though Ulrich had
been born with this wish. It is true that such an urge may be
a sign of vanity and stupidity ; it is no less true, however, that
it is a very fine and proper desire, without which there would
probably not be many men of importance.

The only snag was that he did not know either how one became
such a man or what a man of importance was. In his schooldays
he had taken Napoleon for one ; this was partly out of youth's
natural admiration for criminality, partly because his school-
masters emphatically represented this tyrant, who had tried to
turn Europe upside down, as the most tremendous evil-doer in
history. The result was that as soon as he escaped from school
Ulrich became an ensign in a cavalry regiment. Probably even
then, if he had been asked the reasons for this choice of profession,
he would no longer have answered : ' so as to become a tyrant '.
But such wishes are Jesuits. Napoleon's genius only began to
develop after he had become a general—and how could Ulrich,
as an ensign, have convinced his colonel how necessary it was for
that condition to be fulfilled ? Even at squadron drill it not
infrequently appeared that the colonel was of an opinion different
from his. Nevertheless, Ulrich would not have cursed the
barrack-square—in which peaceful setting a real vocation is
indistinguishable from the pretensions to it—had he not been so
ambitious. At that time he did not attach the slightest importance
to pacifist phrases like ' educating the nation to militarism ', but

gave himself up to a passionate memory of heroic conditions of lordliness, power and pride. He went in for steeple-chasing and duelling, and recognised only three sorts of people : officers, women, and civilians, the last a physically undeveloped and intellectually contemptible class whose wives and daughters were the proper prey of the officers. He indulged in magnificent pessimism : it seemed to him that since the soldier's profession was a sharp, white-hot instrument the world must for its own salvation be burnt and cut with it.

Admittedly he had the good fortune not to get hurt, but one day he made a discovery. At a social gathering he had a slight *contretemps* with a well-known financier, which he wanted to settle in his usual magnificent manner ; but it turned out that even in civilian life there are men who are capable of protecting their female relations. The financier had a word with the Minister for War, whom he knew personally, and the result was that Ulrich had a somewhat lengthy heart-to-heart talk with his colonel, in which the difference between an ordinary officer and, say, an archduke was made clear to him. From then on the warrior's profession ceased to give him any pleasure. He had expected to find himself on a stage of world-shaking adventures in which he would be the hero, and suddenly saw a drunken young man roistering about a wide empty square where only the stones answered him. When he realised that, he took leave of the thankless career in which he had just attained the rank of lieutenant, and quitted the service.

10

The second attempt. First developments in the moral philosophy of being a Man Without Qualities.

BUT in going over from the cavalry to civil engineering Ulrich merely changed horses. The new horse had limbs of steel and ran ten times as fast.

In Goethe's world the clattering of looms was still considered a disturbance. In Ulrich's time people were beginning to discover the song of the workshops, the riveting-hammers and factory-sirens. It would of course be wrong to think people were quick to notice that a skyscraper is bigger than a man on horseback; on the contrary, even today, if they want to make themselves out to be something special they mount, not a skyscraper, but the high horse, and they go fast as the wind, and if they have sharp eyes they are eagle-eyed, not giant-refractor-eyed. Their feelings have not yet learnt to make use of their intellect, and between these two faculties there lies a difference in development almost as great as that between the appendix and the meninx dura mater. So it is no slight stroke of luck to discover, as Ulrich happened to do when he was only just out of his hobbledehoy period, that in all things concerned with high ideals mankind behaves in a way that is considerably more old-fashioned than one would expect from looking at its machines.

From the first moment when he entered the engineering lecture-rooms Ulrich was feverishly biased. What does one still want with the Apollo Belvedere when one has the new lines of a turbo-dynamo or the smoothly gliding movements of a steam-engine's pistons before one's eyes? Who can be interested any longer in that age-old idle talk about good and evil when it has been established that good and evil are not ' constants ' at all, but ' functional values ', so that the goodness of works depends on the historical circumstances, and the goodness of human beings on the psycho-technical skill with which their qualities are exploited? The world is simply ridiculous if one looks at it from the technical point of view. It is unpractical in all that concerns the relations between human beings, and in the highest degree uneconomical and inexact in its methods. And anyone who is in the habit of dealing with his affairs by means of a slide-rule finds that a good half of all human assertions simply cannot be taken seriously. A slide-rule consists of two incredibly ingeniously combined systems of figures and divisions; a slide-rule consists of two little white-enamelled rods, the cross-section of which is a flat trapezium, which slide into each other, a device by the aid of which one can instantly solve the most complicated problems, without wasting any thought on the matter; a slide-rule is a little symbol that one carries in one's breast-pocket, feeling it as a hard white line over one's heart. If one owns a slide-rule, and someone comes along with large assertions or grand feelings, one says : ' Just a moment, please—first of all let's work out the margin of error and the approximate value of the thing ! '

That was, undoubtedly, a mighty conception of engineering. It formed the frame for an entrancing future self-portrait, showing a man with resolute features, a stubby pipe clenched between his teeth, a tweed cap on his head, journeying, in superb riding-boots, between Cape Town and Canada, carrying out tremendous plans for his firm. In the intervals there would always be some time to spare to draw on one's store of technical ideas for suggestions regarding the organisation and administration of the world or to formulate aphorisms like that of Emerson's, which ought to hang on the wall of every workshop : " Mankind walks the earth as a prophecy of the future, and all its deeds are tests and experiments, for every deed can be excelled by the next."—Strictly speaking, this pronouncement was by Ulrich himself, and compounded of several pronouncements of Emerson's.

It is hard to say why engineers do not altogether live up to this. Why, for instance, do they so often wear a watch-chain that forms a lop-sided, sudden curve from the waistcoat-pocket to a button much higher up, or cause it to form one arsis and two theses over their stomach as though it were part of a poem ? Why do they like to stick tie-pins adorned with stags' teeth or small horseshoes in their ties ? Why are their suits constructed like the motor-car in its early stages ? And why do they seldom talk of anything but their profession ? Or if they ever do, why do they do it in a special, stiff, out-of-touch, extraneous manner of speaking that does not go any deeper down, inside, than the epiglottis ? This is far from being true of all of them, of course, but it is true of a great many ; and those whom Ulrich met when he took up his duties for the first time, in a factory office, were like this, and those he met the second time were also like this. They revealed themselves to be men who were firmly attached to their drawing-boards, who loved their profession and were admirably efficient in it ; but to the suggestion that they should apply the audacity of their ideas not to their machines but to themselves they would have reacted much as though they had been asked to use a hammer for the unnatural purpose of murder.

So there was an early end to the second and more mature attempt that Ulrich made, this time in the field of technical engineering, to become an extraordinary man.

11 *The most important attempt of all.*

TODAY Ulrich could shake his head over the time up to then, as though he were being told about his own soul's transmigration. Not so over the third attempt. It is understandable that an engineer should be completely absorbed in his speciality, instead of pouring himself out into the freedom and vastness of the world of thought, even though his machines are being sent off to the ends of the earth; for he no more needs to be capable of applying to his own personal soul what is daring and new in the soul of his subject than a machine is in fact capable of applying to itself the differential calculus on which it is based. The same thing cannot, however, be said about mathematics; for here we have the new method of thought, pure intellect, the very well-spring of the times, the *fons et origo* of an unfathomable transformation.

If the realisation of primordial dreams is flying, travelling with the fishes, boring one's way under the bodies of mountain-giants, sending messages with godlike swiftness, seeing what is invisible and what is in the distance and hearing its voice, hearing the dead speak, having oneself put into a wonder-working healing sleep, being able to behold with living eyes what one will look like twenty years after one's death, in glimmering nights to know a thousand things that are above and below this world, things that no one ever knew before, if light, warmth, power, enjoyment, and comfort are mankind's primordial dreams, then modern research is not only science but magic, a ritual involving the highest powers of heart and brain, before which God opens one fold of His mantle after another, a religion whose dogma is permeated and sustained by the hard, courageous, mobile, knife-cold, knife-sharp mode of thought that is mathematics.

Admittedly, it cannot be denied that in the non-mathematician's opinion all these primordial dreams were suddenly realised in quite a different way from what people had once imagined. Baron Münchhausen's post-horn was more beautiful than mass-produced canned music, the Seven-League Boots were more beautiful than a motor-car, Dwarf-King Laurin's realm more beautiful than a railway-tunnel, the magic mandrake-root more beautiful than a telegraphed picture, to have eaten of one's mother's heart and so to understand the language of birds more beautiful than an animal psychologist's study of the expressive values in bird-song. We have gained in terms of reality and lost in terms of the dream. We no longer lie under a tree, gazing up at the sky between our big toe and second toe ; we are too busy getting on with our jobs. And it is no good being lost in dreams and going hungry, if one wants to be efficient ; one must eat steak and get a move on. It is exactly as if that old-time, inefficient mankind had gone to sleep on an ant-hill, and when the new one woke up the ants had crept into its blood ; and ever since then it has had to fling itself about with the greatest of violence, without ever being able to shake off this beastly sensation of ant-like industry. There is really no need to say much about it. It is in any case quite obvious to most people nowadays that mathematics has entered like a daemon into all aspects of our life. Perhaps not all of these people believe in that stuff about the Devil to whom one can sell one's soul ; but all those who have to know something about the soul, because they draw a good income out of it as clergy, historians or artists, bear witness to the fact that it has been ruined by mathematics and that in mathematics is the source of a wicked intellect that, while making man the lord of the earth, also makes him the slave of the machine. The inner drought, the monstrous mixture of acuity in matters of detail and indifference as regards the whole, man's immense loneliness in a desert of detail, his restlessness, malice, incomparable callousness, his greed for money, his coldness and violence, which are characteristic of our time, are, according to such surveys, simply and solely the result of the losses that logical and accurate thinking has inflicted on the soul! And so it was that even at that time, when Ulrich became a mathematician, there were people who were prophesying the collapse of European civilisation on the grounds that there was no longer any faith, any love, any simplicity or any goodness left in mankind; and it is significant that these people were all bad at mathematics at school. This only went to convince them, later on, that mathematics, the mother of the exact natural sciences, the grandmother of engineering, was also the arch-mother of that spirit from which, in the end, poison-gases and fighter aircraft have been born.

Actually the only people living in ignorance of these dangers were the mathematicians themselves and their disciples, the natural scientists, who felt no more of all this in their souls than racing-cyclists who are pedalling away hard with no eyes for anything in the world but the back wheel of the man in front. As far as Ulrich was concerned, however, it could at least definitely be said that he loved mathematics because of the people who could not endure it. He was not so much scientifically as humanly in love with science. He could see that in all the problems that came into its orbit science thought differently from the way ordinary people thought. If for 'scientific attitude' one were to read 'attitude to life', for 'hypothesis' 'attempt' and for 'truth' 'action', then there would be no considerable natural scientist or mathematician whose life's work did not in courage and revolutionary power far outmatch the greatest deeds in history. The man was not yet born who could have said to his disciples: 'Rob, murder, fornicate—our teaching is so strong that it will transform the cesspool of your sins into clear, sparkling mountain-rills.' But in science it happens every few years that something that up to then was held to be error suddenly revolutionises all views or that an unobtrusive, despised idea becomes the ruler over a new realm of ideas; and such occurrences are not mere upheavals but lead up into the heights like Jacob's ladder. In science the way things happen is as vigorous and matter-of-fact and glorious as in a fairy-tale. 'People simply don't know this,' Ulrich felt. 'They have no glimmer of what can be done with thinking. If one could teach them to think in a new way, they would also live differently.'

Now someone is sure to ask, of course, whether the world is so topsy-turvy that it is always having to be turned up the other way again. But the world itself long ago gave two answers to this question. For ever since it has existed most people have in their youth been in favour of turning things upside-down. They have always felt that their elders were ridiculous in being so attached to the established order of things and in thinking with their heart—a mere lump of flesh—instead of with their brains. These younger people have always noticed that the moral stupidity of their elders is just as much a lack of any capacity to form new combinations as is ordinary intellectual stupidity, and the morality that they themselves have felt natural has always been one of achievement, heroism and change. Nevertheless, by the time they reach years of fulfilment they have forgotten all about it and are far from wishing to be reminded of it. That is why many people for whom mathematics or natural science is a job feel it is almost an outrage if someone goes in for science for reasons like Ulrich's.

However, since taking up this third profession some years earlier, in the opinion of experts he had done not at all badly.

12

The lady whose love Ulrich won after some talk about sport and mysticism.

IT turned out that Bonadea was also in quest of great ideas.

Bonadea was that lady who had rescued Ulrich on the night of his unfortunate fisticuffs and the next morning came, heavily veiled, to visit him. He had nicknamed her Bonadea, the Good Goddess, because of the way she had come into his life and also after a goddess of chastity who had a temple in ancient Rome, which by a queer reversal later became a centre of all debaucheries. She did not know that. She liked the sonorous name that Ulrich had given her, and on her visits she wore it like a sumptuously embroidered négligé. " And am I really your good goddess ? " she would ask, " your Bona Dea ? "—and the proper enunciation of these two words required that while uttering them she should put both arms round his neck and gaze at him feelingly, her head thrown slightly back.

She was the wife of a well-respected man and the fond mother of two fine little boys. Her favourite idea was that of the ' paragon ' ; she applied this expression to people, servants, shops and feelings, whenever she wanted to speak well of them. She was capable of uttering the words ' the true, the good and the beautiful ' as often and as naturally as someone else might say ' Thursday '. What was most deeply satisfying to her craving for ideas was the concept of a tranquil, ideal mode of life in a circle formed by husband and children, while far below that there floated the dark realm of ' Lead me not into temptation ', the awe of it toning the radiant happiness down into soft lamp-light. She had only one fault, and this was that she was liable to be stimulated to a quite uncommon degree by the mere sight of men. She was by no means lustful ; she was sensual in the way that other people have other troubles, such as sweating of the hands or blushing easily ; it was apparently congenital, and she could never do anything about it. When she got to know Ulrich in circumstances so romantic, so extraordinarily stimulating to the imagination, she had from the first instant been the destined prey of a passion that began as sympathy, after a brief but severe tussle went over into forbidden intimacies, and then continued as an alternation between the pangs of sin and the pangs of remorse.

But Ulrich was only one of heaven alone knows how many cases in her life. Men—as soon as they have grasped the situation—are generally in the habit of treating such nymphomaniac women little better than imbeciles, who can by the most trivial means be tricked into stumbling over the same thing time and time again ; for the tender aspects of masculine self-abandonment somewhat resemble the growling of a jaguar over a hunk of meat, and any interruption is taken gravely amiss. The consequence was that Bonadea often led a double life, like that of any citizen who, entirely respectable in the everyday world, in the dark interspaces of his consciousness leads the life of a railway thief ; and the moment she held no one in her arms, this quiet, majestic woman began to suffer from self-contempt, which was caused by the lies and degradations to which she had exposed herself in order to be held in someone's arms. When her sensuality was aroused, she was melancholy and kind ; indeed, in her mingling of rapture and tears, of crude naturalness and inevitably approaching remorse, in the way that her mania would bolt in panic before the threatening depression that was already lying in wait for her, she had a heightened charm that was exciting in much the same way as a ceaseless tattoo on a darkly muffled drum. But in the lucid intervals, in the state of remorse between two states of weakness during which she felt her helplessness, she was full of the claims of respectability, which did not make it any too easy to get on with her. One had to be truthful and good, to be sympathetic towards all misfortune, to be devoted to the Imperial House, to respect everything respected and in matters of morality to be as sensitive and gentle as at a sick-bed.

But even if one failed in this, it did not alter the course of events. By way of excuse she had invented the fairy-story that she had been reduced to her deplorable condition by her husband in the innocent first years of her marriage. This husband, who was considerably older and physically larger than herself, appeared in the light of a callous monster, and in the very first hours of her new love she had spoken of this to Ulrich in a sad and significant manner. Only some time later did he discover that this man was a well-known and very able lawyer, highly respected in his profession, with a harmless love, into the bargain, of a day's slaughter with the guns, a welcome figure at pub and club and in all places where sportsmen and legal men sat and talked about masculine affairs instead of art and love. The only shortcoming that this on the whole unaffected, good-hearted and jovial man had lay in the fact that he was married to his wife and hence found himself more frequently than other men in that relation to her which in the terminology of the law-courts is known as ' intimacy '. The psychological effect of years of gratifying the desires of a man whose wife she had become more from calculation than from real affection had been to develop in Bonadea the illusion that she was physically over-excitable, and had made this fantasy almost independent of her consciousness. An inner compulsion that was incomprehensible to herself chained her to this man so favoured by circumstances ; she despised him for her own weakness of will and was overcome by her weakness in order to be able to despise him ; she was unfaithful to him in order to escape from him, but while being so she talked about him, or the children that she had had by him, and at the most unsuitable moments ; she was never capable of becoming completely free of him. Her attitude, like that of many unhappy women, was moulded, in an otherwise pretty unstable personal environment, by her aversion from her solidly established husband, and she transferred her conflict with him into each new experience that was meant to liberate her from him.

There was hardly anything else to be done, in order to silence her lamentations, but to transport her as rapidly as possible out of the state of depression into that of frenzy. Then she would charge the man who did so, and who took advantage of her weakness, with having not a trace of proper feeling ; but her complaint laid a veil of moist tenderness over her eyes when she—as she was accustomed to express herself with scientific detachment— ' inclined ' to this man.

13 *A race-horse of genius contributes to the awareness of being a Man Without Qualities.*

IT is by no means irrelevant that Ulrich could congratulate himself on having done not at all badly in his subject. Indeed, his work had brought him recognition. Admiration would have been too much to expect, for even in the realm of truth admiration is reserved for elderly scholars and scientists on whom it depends whether one does or does not get one's fellowship or professorial chair. Strictly speaking he had remained what is called ' a young man of promise ', and this is the name that in the republic of the mind is bestowed on the republicans, that is, on those people who delude themselves with the belief that one ought to devote one's entire energy to the thing itself instead of applying a large part of it to the job of getting on in the world. These people forget that the individual's achievement is small, whereas to get on in the world is the wish of one and all. They neglect the social duty of pushing; but one must begin by being a pusher so that in the years of success one can be a pillar and a tower of strength to other climbers on their way up.

And then one day Ulrich stopped wanting to be a young man of promise. The time had already begun when it became a habit to speak of geniuses of the football-field or the boxing-ring, although to every ten or even more explorers, tenors and writers of genius that cropped up in the columns of the newspapers there was not, as yet, more than at the most one genius of a centre-half or one great tactician of the tennis-court. The new spirit of the times had not yet quite found its feet. But just then it happened that Ulrich read somewhere—and it came like a breath of too early summer ripeness blown down the wind—the phrase 'the race-horse of genius'. It occurred in a report of a spectacular success in a race, and it was quite possible that the writer was far from aware of the magnitude of the inspiration wafted into his pen by the spirit of contemporaneity. Ulrich, however, suddenly grasped the inevitable connection between his whole career and this genius among race-horses. For to the cavalry, of course, the horse has always been a sacred animal, and during his youthful days of life in barracks Ulrich had hardly ever heard anything talked about except horses and women. That was what he had fled from in order to become a man of importance. And now when, after varied exertions, he might almost have felt entitled to think himself near the summit of his ambitions, he was hailed from on high by the horse, which had got there first.

This doubtless has its historical justification, for it is by no means long ago that people still thought of an admirable, manly spirit as one in which the courage was moral courage, the strength the strength of conviction, and the firmness that of the heart and of virtue, and considered speed something boyish, feinting something not permissible, agility and *élan* something contrary to dignity. In the end, however, this spirit had no vigour left in it, and turned up only in the masters' common-rooms at boys' schools and in all sorts of literary pronouncements ; it had become an ideological spectre, and life had to look for some other image of manliness. While looking round for this, however, it made the discovery that the tricks and dodges used by an inventive mind in going through the logical operations of a mathematical problem are really not very different from the ring-craft displayed by a well-trained body ; there is a general psychological fighting-strength that is made cold and shrewd by difficulties and improbabilities, whether what it is trained to search out is the vulnerable spot in a problem or that in a physical opponent. If one were to analyse a powerful mind and a champion boxer from the psycho-technical point of view, it would in fact turn out that their cunning, their courage, their precision and their combinatory ability, as well as the quickness of their reactions on the territory that they have made their own, are approximately equal ; moreover, one can safely assume that in the virtues and abilities that make for their particular success they would not differ from a famous steeple-chasing horse—for one must not underestimate the number of important qualities brought into play in jumping over a hedge. But apart from all this there is one other advantage that a horse and a boxer have over a great mind, and that is that their achievement and importance can be indisputably assessed and that the best among them is really acknowledged as the best. In this way sport and functionalism have deservedly come into their own, displacing the out-of-date conceptions of genius and human greatness.

Where Ulrich is concerned, it must be emphasised that in this matter he was some years in advance of his time. For he had pursued science in exactly the same way that an athlete improves on his record by one victory, one inch or one pound. He wanted his mind to prove itself acute and strong, and it had performed labours that only the strong can perform. This delight in the power of the mind was made up of expectation, was a war-like game, a kind of undefined, masterful claim on the future. He was by no means sure what he would ultimately achieve with this power. One could do everything or nothing with it, one could become a saviour of the world or a criminal. And that is probably more or less what the general psychological situation is like, the existence of which provides the world of machines and discoveries with a ceaseless flow of reinforcements. Ulrich had regarded

science as a form of preparation, a process of toughening, a kind
of training.   If it turned out that this way of thinking was too
dry, sharp, narrow and without vision, then the fact simply had to
be accepted, like the expression of hardship and tension on a face
during great exertions of body and will.   For years he had loved
intellectual hardship.   He hated people who could not live up
to Nietzsche's words about ' suffering hunger in the spirit for the
sake of the truth '—all those who give up half-way, the faint-
hearted, the soft, those who comfort their souls with flummery
about the soul and who feed it, because the intellect allegedly
gives it stones instead of bread, on religious, philosophic and
fictitious emotions, which are like buns soaked in milk.   His
view was that in this century we and all humanity are on an
expedition, that pride requires that all useless questionings should
be met with a ' not yet ', and that life should be conducted on
interim principles, though in the consciousness of a destination
that will be reached by those who come after us.   The truth is
that science has developed a conception of hard, sober intellectual
strength that makes mankind's old metaphysical and moral
notions simply unendurable, although all it can put in their place
is the hope that a day, still distant, will come when a race of
intellectual conquerors will descend into the valleys of spiritual
fruitfulness.

But that only works well so long as one is not forced to switch
one's gaze away from a visionary distance on to the nearness of
the present, so long as one is not forced to read that, in the mean
time, a race-horse has attained to genius.   The next morning
Ulrich got out of bed on the wrong side, and groped about
hesitantly after his slippers.   That had been in a different town
and street from that in which he now lived, but only a few weeks
ago.   Cars were already darting past on the brown gleaming
asphalt under his windows ; the pure morning air was beginning
to fill up with the sourness of day.   And to him, now in the milky
light filtering through the curtains, it seemed unspeakably senseless to start bending his naked body backwards and forwards as
usual, lifting it from the floor with the abdominal muscles and
letting it sink again, and finally showering blows on a punching-
ball, as so many people do at the same hour, before going to
the office.   One hour daily is a twelfth of conscious life, and it

suffices to keep a trained body in a panther-like condition, ready for any adventure ; but this hour is spent thus for the sake of a senseless expectation, for the adventures that would be worthy of such preparation never happen. Exactly the same is the case with love, for which man undergoes preparation on the most tremendous scale. And in the end Ulrich realised that in science, too, he was like a man who has crossed one mountain-range after the other, never getting within sight of a goal. He possessed fragments of a new way of thinking, and of feeling, too, but the glimpse of something utterly new, which had at first been so intense, had blurred with the increasing number of details ; and after believing that he was drinking from the fountain of life, he discovered that he had drained almost all his expectations to the dregs. It was then that he stopped, right in the middle of a very important and promising piece of work. His colleagues appeared to him partly as inexorably maniacal public prosecutors and chief detective-inspectors of logic, partly as opium-addicts and eaters of a strange pallid drug that populated their world with a vision of figures and abstract relations. 'Good heavens !' he thought to himself, ' surely I can never have meant to spend the whole of my life as a mathematician ? '

Yet what had he really meant to do ? At this moment there was only philosophy left for him to turn to. But philosophy, in the state in which it was then, reminded him of the ox-hide being cut into strips in the story of Dido, while it remained very uncertain whether what was measured out with it was really a kingdom ; and what new elements were coming into it were similar in nature to the things that he himself had been doing, and failed to allure him. He could only say that he felt further away from what he had really wanted to be than he had felt in his youth, if indeed it had not remained wholly beyond his ken. He saw wonderfully clearly that—with the exception of that necessary for earning a living, which he did not need—he had in himself all the abilities and qualities favoured by the time in which he lived ; but he had somehow lost the capacity to apply them. And since, after all, when even footballers and horses have genius, it is only the use one makes of it that can still save one's individuality, he decided to take a year's leave from his life in order to seek an appropriate way of using his abilities.

14   *Friends of his youth.*

SINCE his return Ulrich had several times gone to visit his
friends Walter and Clarisse, whom he had not seen for some
years, for in spite of the fact that it was summer these two had
not gone away.   Every time when he arrived they were playing
the piano.   They took it as a matter of course not to notice him
until they had got to the end.   This time it was Beethoven's
Hymn to Joy; the millions sank, as Nietzsche describes it, into
the dust in awe, the hostile frontiers dissolved, the gospel of
universal harmony reconciled and united those who had been
separated.   The two of them had forgotten how to walk and talk
and were about to soar up, dancing, into the ether.   Their faces
were flushed, their bodies hunched, and their heads bobbed and
jerked up and down, while splayed claws battered at the rearing
bulk of sound.   Something immeasurable was happening.   A
dimly outlined balloon filled with hot emotion was being blown
up to bursting-point, and from the excited fingertips, from the
nervous wrinkling of the foreheads and the twitchings of the
bodies, ever more and more feeling radiated into the monstrous
private upheaval.   How often, one wondered, had all this
happened before?
   Ulrich had never been able to stand the sight of this always
open piano with its bared teeth, this big-mouthed, short-legged
idol that was a cross between a dachshund and a bulldog, which
had subjugated his friends' lives to itself, down to the very
pictures on the wall and the spindly lines of the arty-crafty reproduction furniture;   even the fact that there was no maid, but only
a daily woman who came in to cook and clean, was part of the
same thing.   Beyond the windows of this house the vineyards
rose, with their clumps of old trees and their crooked little houses,
towards the sweeping outline of the forest.   But nearer at hand
everything was untidy, bare, scattered and as though burnt by
acid, as it always is where the edges of big cities go seeping out

into the countryside. It was the piano that threw out the arc spanning that foreground and the pleasant distance; black and gleaming, it sent pillars of fire, all tenderness and heroism, flaring out through the walls, though indeed they crumbled into an infinitely fine ash of sound and fell to the ground only a few hundred yards away, without ever reaching the hill-side with the fir-trees where the tavern stood, a half-way house, on the road leading into the forest. And yet the rooms could make the piano roar and resound; they were one of those megaphones through which the soul sends its cry out, into the universe—like a rutting stag answered by nothing but the self-same rival belling of thousands of other solitary souls roaring at the universe. Ulrich's strong position in this house rested on the fact that he declared music to be a failure of the will and a confusion of the mind, and spoke of it with more contempt than he really felt; for to Walter and Clarisse music was at that time the paramount hope and dread. They partly despised him for his attitude, and partly venerated him like an evil spirit.

When they had got to the end of the music, Walter remained sitting, soft, drained-out, and forlorn, on his half-turned stool at the piano. But Clarisse got up and welcomed the intruder eagerly. Her hands and face were still twitching with the electric charge of the music, and her smile squeezed out under the tension of ecstasy and disgust.

" Frog-prince ! " she said, nodding back at the music or Walter. Ulrich felt the springy strength of the tie between himself and her tightening again. On his last visit she had told him about a terrible dream she had had: a slippery creature had tried to overwhelm her in her sleep, a belly-soft, tender and atrocious great frog, and it was a symbol of Walter's music. The two of them had few secrets from Ulrich. Scarcely had Clarisse welcomed him now, when she turned away from him again, whirled swiftly back to Walter, once more uttering her war-cry " Frog-prince ! ", which Walter apparently did not understand, and, her hands still twitching with the music, grabbed him wildly by the hair, both painfully and as though in pain. Her husband made an amiably disconcerted face and came another step nearer on his return out of the slippery void of music.

Then Clarisse and Ulrich went for a walk without him under

the slanting arrows of the evening sun.   He remained behind at the piano.

Clarisse said : " One's ability to forbid oneself something harmful is the test of one's vitality.   The weary man is tempted by corruption !   What do you say to that ?   Nietzsche declares it's a sign of weakness for an artist to be too much concerned with the moral aspect of his art."   She had sat down on a little mound.

Ulrich shrugged his shoulders.   When Clarisse had married his boyhood friend three years earlier she had been twenty-two, and he himself had given her the works of Nietzsche as a wedding-present.   " If I were Walter, I should challenge Nietzsche to a duel," he answered, smiling.

Clarisse's slender back, floating in delicate outline under the dress, arched like a bow.   Her face too was tense with violent emotion, and she kept it anxiously averted from her friend.

" You still combine the girlish and the heroic," Ulrich added. It might have been a question, or it might not ; it was a little joke, and yet it held a little touch of affectionate admiration. Clarisse did not quite understand what he meant, but the two words, which he had used once before, pierced her as a burning arrow pierces a thatched roof.

Now and then a wave of chaotically churning sound reached them.   Ulrich knew that she refused herself to Walter for weeks when he played Wagner.   And yet he did play Wagner, and did so with a bad conscience, as though it were a schoolboy vice.

Clarisse would have liked to ask Ulrich how much he knew about it, for Walter could never keep anything to himself.   But she was ashamed to ask.   Now Ulrich had sat down too, on a little mound nearby.   And in the end she said something quite different.   " You don't love Walter," she said.   " You are not really his friend."   It sounded challenging, but she laughed as she said it.

Ulrich gave an unexpected answer.   " The thing is, we're boyhood friends.   You were still a child, Clarisse, when we were already in the unmistakable relationship of a youthful friendship drawing to its close.   We admired each other innumerable years ago, and now we mistrust each other with intimate understanding. Each of us would like to free himself from the painful feeling that he once mistook the other for himself, and so we serve each other as incorruptible distorting-mirrors."

" So," Clarisse said, " you don't believe that he will still achieve something after all ? "

" There is no example of inevitability that can compare with the sight of a gifted young man narrowing down into an ordinary old man—not through personal misfortune, merely through the process of dehydration to which he was predestined."

Clarisse closed her lips tightly. Their long-standing youthful agreement that conviction should come before consideration for the other's feelings made her heart beat high ; but it hurt. Music ! Unceasingly the sounds came churning over towards them. She listened. Now, when they sat silent, one could distinctly hear how the piano was seething and boiling. If one was not on one's guard, it seemed to be coming up out of the little grassy mounds like the ' flickering flames ' around Brünnhilde.

It would have been hard to say what Walter really was. He was a pleasant person with eloquent, meaningful eyes—that at any rate was definite—even today, although he was already past his thirty-fourth year. For some time now he had had a job in some government office dealing with the fine arts. His father had procured him this comfortable position and added the threat that he would stop his allowance if he did not accept it. For actually Walter was a painter. While he was reading art history at the university he had also worked in a painting-class at the academy, and later had lived for some time in a studio. And when he had married Clarisse and shortly afterwards moved into this house on the edge of the town with her, he had still been a painter. But now, it seemed, he was a musician again. In the course of the ten years of his love he had sometimes been the one, sometimes the other, and even a poet into the bargain. He had edited a literary periodical, then, in order to be able to marry, had taken a job with a theatrical publisher, had given up the idea after a few weeks, and then, after some time, still in order to be able to marry, had become the conductor of a theatre-orchestra, after six months had realised how utterly impossible this was, and had become an art master, a music critic, a hermit, and much else besides, until his father and his future father-in-law, in spite of all their broad-mindedness, would not put up with it any longer. Such elderly people were in the habit of saying that he simply had no will-power ; but it might just as well have been said that he had all his life long only been a many-sided dilettante, and the remarkable thing was in fact that there had always been experts in the sphere of music, painting or writing who had expressed enthusiastic opinions about his future. In Ulrich's life, by way of counter-example, although he had achieved one or two things of undeniable value, it had never happened that someone had come up to him and said : ' You are the very man I have always been looking for, the man my friends are in need of ! ' In Walter's life that had happened every three months. And even though these people had not been exactly those whose judgment was most authoritative, still they had all been people who had some influence, who could make a useful suggestion, who knew of enterprises already under way and of jobs to be had, who had friends and knew the ropes, all of which they put at the disposal of the Walter whom they had discovered and whose life for this reason ran such a splendidly zigzag course. Something hovered over him that seemed to mean more than any definite achievement. Perhaps this was a quite special talent for passing as a man of great talent. And if that must be considered dilettantism, then the intellectual life of the German nation is to a large extent based on dilettantism ; for this talent exists in all degrees up to the level of those who are really very talented— and only there does it generally seem to be missing.

And Walter even had the talent to see through all this. Although he was, of course, as ready as anyone else to believe that his successes were the result of personal merit, his faculty of being so effortlessly borne upwards by every lucky accident had always worried him as indicating an alarming lack of weight ; and every time he changed his activities and human relations, it was not simply the result of fickleness—it was accompanied by great spiritual tribulations, and he was haunted by a fear of having to move on again, for the sake of the purity of his spiritual being, before he had taken root just where the illusion was already becoming apparent. His path through life was a series of stirring experiences, which gave rise to the heroic struggle of a soul that would have nothing to do with divided loyalties, never suspecting that in this way it was only contributing to its own division against itself.

For while he was suffering and struggling for the sake of morality in his intellectual actions, as befits a genius, and was paying the full price for his talent, which did not quite suffice for greatness, his destiny had quietly led him round in an inner circle back to nothingness. He had at last reached the place where there was nothing more to obstruct him ; the quiet, withdrawn work in his semi-scholarly job, where he was sheltered from all the uncleanliness of the trafficking that goes on in art, gave him all the independence and time he needed in order to give himself up to listening whole-heartedly to his inner call ; possession of the woman he loved removed the thorns from his heart ; the house ' on the brink of solitude ', where they had moved after their marriage, was as though made for creativeness. But when there was nothing left to be overcome, the unexpected happened, and the works that the greatness of his convictions had so long promised did not materialise. Walter seemed no longer able to work. He hid things and destroyed things. He shut himself up for hours every morning or when he came home in the afternoon ; he went for long walks with his sketch-book shut ; but the little that came out of all this he kept to himself or destroyed. He had hundreds of different reasons for this. But his views as a whole were also changing very markedly at this period. He no longer talked about ' contemporary art ' and ' the art of the future ', ideas that had been associated with him in Clarisse's mind since she was fifteen ; but he would draw a line somewhere—in music stopping at, say, Bach, in literature at Stifter, in painting at Ingres—and explain that everything that came later was florid, degenerate, over-sophisticated and on the downward path. And he became increasingly violent in his assertion that in a time so poisoned at its spiritual roots as the present an artist of real integrity must abstain from creation altogether. But the treacherous thing was that although such austere opinions issued from his mouth, what issued from his room, as soon as he had locked himself in, was, more and more often, the sound of Wagner's music, that is to say, a kind of music that in earlier years he had taught Clarisse to despise as the perfect example of a philistine, florid, degenerate era, and to which he himself had now become addicted as to a thickly brewed, hot, intoxicating potion.

Clarisse put up a fight against it. She hated Wagner, if for nothing else, for his velvet jacket and his beret. She was the daughter of a painter whose stage-décors were famous throughout the world. She had spent her childhood in a realm of back-stage air and the smell of paint, where three different jargons were spoken, that of the theatre, that of opera, and that of the painter's studio, surrounded by velvet, carpets, genius, leopard-skins, knick-knacks, peacock-feathers, oak chests and lutes. She therefore loathed all sensuality in art from the bottom of her soul and felt herself drawn to everything lean and austere, whether it was the metageometry of the new atonal music or the clearly apparent will of classic forms, stripped of its skin like a specimen of dissected muscle. It was Walter who had brought the first word of it into her maidenly captivity. 'Prince of light,' she had called him, and while she was still a child Walter and she had sworn not to marry until he had become a king. The history of his transformations and undertakings was at the same time a story of immeasurable sufferings and raptures, of which she had been the trophy. Clarisse was not as talented as Walter ; she had always felt that. But she believed genius to be all a matter of will. She had with wild energy tried to make the art of music her own ; it was not impossible that she was simply not musical at all, but she had the ten sinewy fingers of a pianist and she had resolution. She practised for days on end, driving her fingers like ten lean oxen that were to wrench some overwhelming weight out of the ground. She went in for painting in the same way. She had considered Walter a genius since she was fifteen, because she had always had the intention of marrying no one but a genius. She would not permit him not to be one. And when she became aware of his failure, she fought frantically against this suffocating, slow change in the atmosphere of her life. It was precisely there and then that Walter was in need of human warmth, and when his helplessness tormented him he clutched at her like a baby wanting milk and sleep ; but Clarisse's small, nervous body was not maternal. She saw herself as misused by a parasite that was trying to gain a hold on her, and she denied herself to him. She scorned the billowing wash-house warmth in which he sought consolation. Perhaps it was cruel of her. But she wanted to be the mate of a great man, and she was wrestling with destiny.

Ulrich had offered Clarisse a cigarette. What more could he have said after he had so uncompromisingly said what he thought? The smoke of their cigarettes, floating up the beams of the evening sun, united at some distance from them.

'How much does Ulrich know about it?' Clarisse wondered, sitting on her little mound. 'Oh, how could he possibly understand anything about such battles?' She called to mind how Walter's face disintegrated, racked to the point of extinction, when the agonies of music and sensuality crowded upon him and her resistance left him with no way out. No, she assumed that Ulrich knew nothing of the monstrosity of a love-play that was as though on the peaks of the Himalayas, built of love, contempt, fear, and the obligations of the sublime. She had no very favourable opinion of mathematics, and she had never considered Ulrich as gifted as Walter. He was intelligent, he was logical, and he knew a lot—but was that any more than barbarism? Admittedly, in earlier days he had played tennis incomparably better than Walter, and she could remember sometimes when he drove the ball with inexorable force how intensely she had felt 'this man will achieve what he wants', as she never felt it face to face with Walter's painting, music or ideas. And she thought: 'Perhaps he does know all about us, and only says nothing!' After all, just a moment ago he had quite distinctly alluded to her heroism. This silence between them was now intensely exciting.

But Ulrich was thinking: 'How nice Clarisse was ten years ago—still half a child, with that raging, fiery belief in the future all three of us would have.' And actually he had only once found her disagreeable, and that was when she and Walter had got married. Then she had shown that tiresome egoism à deux that often makes young women ambitiously in love with their husbands so insufferable to other men. 'That has improved a good deal since then,' he thought.

15   *Intellectual revolution.*

WALTER and he had been young in that now vanished time, shortly after the turn of the century, when a great many people were imagining that the century too was young.

The century that had then just gone to its grave had not exactly distinguished itself in its second half. It had been clever in technical and commercial matters and in research, but outside these focal points of its energy it had been quiet and treacherous as a swamp. It had painted like the Old Masters, written like Goethe and Schiller, and built its houses in the Gothic or Renaissance style. Insistence on the Ideal dominated all manifestations of life, like the headquarters of a police-force. But by virtue of that secret law that will not permit man any kind of imitation without his getting an exaggeration along with it, everything was at that time done with a correctness of craftsmanship such as the admired prototypes could never have achieved and the traces of which can still be seen in the streets and museums even today. And—it may or may not be relevant—the women of that time, who were as chaste as they were shy, had to wear clothes covering them from their ears down to the ground, but at the same time had to display a swelling bosom and a voluptuous posterior. For the rest, there are all sorts of reasons why there is no past era one knows so little about as the three to five decades that lie between one's own twentieth year and one's father's twentieth year. It may therefore be useful to be reminded that in bad epochs the most frightful buildings and poems are made according to principles exactly as beautiful as in the best epochs; that all the people who take part in destroying the achievements of a previous good period do so with the feeling that they are improving on them; and that the bloodless young people of such a time think exactly as much of their young blood as the new people of all other times do.

And each time it is like a miracle when, after such an epoch of shallow sloping plains, suddenly there comes a slight rise in the spiritual ground, as happened then. Out of the oil-smooth spirit of the two last decades of the nineteenth century, suddenly, throughout Europe, there rose a kindling fever. Nobody knew exactly what was on the way ; nobody was able to say whether it was to be a new art, a New Man, a new morality or perhaps a re-shuffling of society. So everyone made of it what he liked. But people were standing up on all sides to fight against the old way of life. Suddenly the right man was on the spot every-where ; and, what is so important, men of practical enterprise joined forces with the men of intellectual enterprise. Talents developed that had previously been choked or had taken no part at all in public life. They were as different from each other as anything well could be, and the contradictions in their aims were unsurpassable. The Superman was adored, and the Subman was adored ; health and the sun were worshipped, and the delicacy of consumptive girls was worshipped ; people were enthusiastic hero-worshippers and enthusiastic adherents of the social creed of the Man in the Street ; one had faith and was sceptical, one was naturalistic and precious, robust and morbid ; one dreamed of ancient castles and shady avenues, autumnal gardens, glassy ponds, jewels, hashish, disease and demonism, but also of prairies, vast horizons, forges and rolling-mills, naked wrestlers, the uprisings of the slaves of toil, man and woman in the primeval Garden, and the destruction of society. Admittedly these were contradictions and very different battle-cries, but they all breathed the same breath of life. If that epoch had been analysed, some such nonsense would have come out as a square circle supposed to be made of wooden iron ; but in reality all this had blended into shimmering significance. This illusion, which found its embodiment in the magical date of the turn of the century, was so powerful that it made some hurl themselves enthusiastically upon the new, as yet untrodden century, while others were having a last fling in the old one, as in a house that one is moving out of anyway, without either one or the other party feeling that there was much difference between the two attitudes.

So one need not overrate that past ' activity ' if one does not wish. It only went on, in any case, in that thin, fluctuating layer of humanity, the intelligentsia, which is unanimously despised these days by the people with the wear-and-tear-proof views—who have come to the top again, thank heaven—in spite of all differences among those views. It had no effect on the masses. But all the same, even if it did not become an historical event, it was at least an eventlet. And the two friends, Walter and Ulrich, when they were young, had just been in time to catch a glimmer of it. Something at that time passed through the thicket of beliefs, as when many trees bend before one wind —a sectarian and reformist spirit, the blissful better self arising and setting forth, a little renascence and reformation such as only the best epochs know; and entering into the world in those days, even in coming round the very first corner one felt the breath of the spirit on one's cheeks.

16   *A mysterious disease of the times.*

AND so (Ulrich thought when he was alone again) there they had really been, by no means so long ago, two young men to whom curiously enough the greatest illuminations not only came first and before they came to the rest of humanity, but—what was more—simultaneously; for one of them needed only to open his mouth in order to say something new, and there was the other already making the same tremendous discovery. There is something queer about youthful friendship: it is like an egg that feels its glorious bird-future in its very yolk, although all it shows to the world is as yet only a somewhat expressionless egg-outline, which is indistinguishable from any other of its kind.

He saw before his mental eye the schoolboy's and the student's room where they used to meet whenever he returned for a few weeks from his first outings into the world—Walter's writing-desk, covered with drawings, notes and sheets of music, antici-patively radiating the future glory of a famous man, and the narrow bookshelves facing it, where Walter sometimes stood in his ardour like Sebastian at the stake, lamplight on his beautiful hair, which Ulrich had always secretly admired. Nietzsche, Peter Altenberg, Dostoievsky, or whoever it was they had just been reading, would have to make the best of it, left lying on the floor or on the bed when they were no longer needed and when the current of talk would not suffer the petty interruption of putting them back tidily in their places. The overweeningness of youth, which finds the greatest of minds only just good enough to be made use of ' as desired ', now appeared to him quaintly endearing. He tried to remember the talks they had had ; but they were like dreams, as when in wakening one just catches the last vanishing traces of one's sleeping thoughts. And he reflected in mild astonishment : ' When we made assertions in those days, it was with another purpose besides that of being right—and that other purpose was our own self-assertion ! ' How much stronger in youth the urge to shine was than the urge to see by the light one had ! That youthful feeling of floating as though on beams of light came back to him in memory now, a grievous loss.

It seemed to Ulrich that at the beginning of his adult life he had found himself in the midst of a general lull, which, in spite of occasional quickly disappearing eddies, settled down into an ever more listless, erratic pulse-beat. It was hard to say wherein the change lay. Was it that there were all of a sudden fewer men of importance in the world ? Far from it ! And anyway they are not what counts, at all ; the heights that an epoch reaches are not interdependent with them. (For example, the lack of intellect in the 'sixties and 'eighties could no more do anything to prevent Hebbel's and Nietzsche's development than either of those men could do anything to remedy this deficiency among his contemporaries.) Had life in general reached a standstill ? No, it was mightier than ever ! Were there more paralysing contradictions than previously ? There could hardly be more than there had been ! Had no absurdities been committed in the past ? Masses of them ! Between ourselves : the world went all out for weak men and ignored the strong. It would happen that blockheads played a leading role and men of great talent played the part of eccentrics. Regardless of all this birth-travail, which he disposed of as decadent and morbid exaggerations, the true-born German went on reading his family magazines, and visited the crystal palaces and academy exhibitions in incomparably greater throngs than the *avant-garde* galleries. Least of all did the political world pay any attention to the views expressed by the new men and their journals ; and public institutions remained as carefully cordoned off against the new spirit as though it were the plague.—Might one not in fact say that everything has improved since then ? Men who were then merely the leaders of small sects have since become aged celebrities ; publishers and art dealers have grown rich ; new things are continually being started up ; all and sundry visit both the crystal palaces and the galleries of the *avant-garde* movements and those too of the *avant-garde* of the *avant-garde* ; the family magazines have cut off their long tresses ; the statesmen like to appear knowledgeable in art and culture, and the newspapers make literary history. So what is it that has got lost ?

Something imponderable. A prognostic. An illusion. Like what happens when a magnet lets the iron filings go and they tumble together again . . . Or when a ball of string comes undone . . . Or when a tension has slackened . . . Or when an orchestra begins to play out of tune . . . No one could have established the existence of any details that might not just as well have existed in earlier times too ; but all the relations between things had shifted slightly. Ideas that had once been of lean account grew fat. Persons who had previously not been taken altogether seriously now acquired fame. What had been harsh mellowed down, what had been separated re-united, those who had been independent made concessions for the sake of public approval, and established taste fell a prey to new uncertainties. Sharp borderlines everywhere became blurred, and some new, indescribable capacity for entering into hitherto unheard-of relationships threw up new people and new ideas. These people and ideas were not wicked. No, far from it. It was only that the good was adulterated with a little too much of the bad, the truth with error, and the meaning with a little too much of the spirit of accommodation. There positively seemed to be certain proportions in which these elements had to be blended for maximum success in the world. A little admixture of *ersatz* was all that was wanted, just enough to bring out the genius in a genius and the promise in a man of talent, precisely as, in some people's opinion, a certain addition of fig-coffee or chicory is needed to give coffee its proper full-bodied coffeeness—and all at once all the sought-after and important positions in the world of the mind were filled by such people, and all the decisions that were made were made according to their way of thinking. There is nothing that one can hold responsible for this. Nor can one say how it all came about. It is no use attacking persons or ideas or definite phenomena. There is no lack of talent or of good will, nor even of personalities. The fact is simply that there is as much lack of everything as of nothing. It is as though the blood or the air had changed; a mysterious disease has consumed the earlier period's little seedling of what was going to be genius, but everything sparkles with novelty, and in the end one can no longer tell whether the world has really grown worse or whether it is merely that one has grown older oneself. When that point is reached, a new time has definitely arrived.

That was the way the time had changed, like a day that begins with a brilliant blue sky and quietly hazes over; and it had not had the kindness to wait for Ulrich. And he paid his time back by regarding the cause of the mysterious changes that constituted its disease, consuming the genius in it, as downright ordinary stupidity. He did not mean it at all offensively. And after all, if stupidity did not, when seen from within, look so exactly like talent as to be mistaken for it, and if it could not, when seen from outside, appear as progress, genius, hope, and improvement, doubtless no one would want to be stupid, and there would be no stupidity. Or at least it would be very easy to combat it. But unfortunately there is something very winning and natural about it. If one finds, for instance, that there is more artistic achievement in a printed reproduction than in an oil-painting done by hand, well, the fact is that there is a kind of truth in this too, and one that can be proved more satisfactorily than the truth that van Gogh was a great artist. Likewise, it is very easy and rewarding to be more powerful as a dramatist than Shakespeare or a more even story-teller than Goethe; and a thorough-going platitude always has more humanity in it than a new discovery. The long and the short of it is, there is no important idea that stupidity does not know how to make use of, for it can move in all directions and is able to wear all the garments of truth.

Truth, on the other hand, has only one garment and one road and is always at a disadvantage.

But after a while Ulrich had a curious fancy in this connection. He imagined that the great churchman and philosopher, Thomas Aquinas (*ob.* 1274), after having, by unspeakable exertions, got the ideas of his time arranged in the most orderly system possible, had gone still further down to the bottom of it all and had only just finished ; and now, having by special grace remained young, he stepped out of his round-arched doorway, a pile of folios under his arm, and an electric tram shot past right in front of him. The uncomprehending amazement of the *doctor universalis*, as the past had called the celebrated Thomas, amused him.

A motor-cyclist came shooting along the empty street, thundering up the perspective, bow-armed and bow-legged, on his face all the solemn, monstrous self-importance of a yelling baby. It reminded Ulrich of a photograph of a famous woman tennis-player that he had seen in a magazine some days earlier : she was poised on tip-toe, one leg exposed up to the garter and beyond, the other leg wildly flung up towards her head, as she reached high with her racquet to hit a ball ; and while doing so she made a face like the proverbial English governess. In the same magazine there was a photograph of a woman swimmer being massaged after a contest. Standing, one at her feet and one at her head, were two female persons in street-dress, gravely looking on, while she lay naked on a bed, on her back, one knee drawn up in an attitude of abandon, and the masseur stood alongside with his hands resting on it, wearing a doctor's white coat, and gazing out of the picture as though this female flesh were skinned and hanging on a hook. Such things were beginning to appear at that time, and in some way or other one had to recognise their existence just as one recognised the existence of skyscrapers and electricity. ' One can't be angry with one's own time without damage to oneself,' Ulrich felt. And indeed he was always ready to love all these manifestations of life. What he could never manage, however, was to love them unreservedly, as is required for a general sense of social well-being. For a long time there had been a faint air of aversion hovering over everything that he did and experienced, a shadow of helplessness and isolation, a universal disinclination to which he could not find the complementary inclination. At times he felt just as though he had been born with a gift for which at present there was no function.

17

The effect of a Man Without Qualities on a man with qualities.

THE music that Ulrich and Clarisse had heard while they were outside, talking, sometimes stopped without their noticing it. Walter then went to the window. He could not see the two of them, but he felt that they were only just beyond the limits of his field of vision. He was tormented by jealousy. The base intoxication of sluggishly sensual music lured him back. The piano behind his back lay open like a bed that had been rumpled by a sleeper who did not want to wake because he did not want to face reality. He was racked by the jealousy of one who is paralysed and feels how the able-bodied walk ; and he could not bring himself to join them, for his anguish left him no way of defending himself against them.

When Walter got up in the morning and had to hurry to the office, when he talked to people during the day and when he travelled home among them in the afternoon, he felt that he was a significant personality and called to great things. He believed then that he saw everything differently ; he would be moved by things that others passed by unheedingly, and where others reached out for something unheedingly, for him the very movement of his own arm was full of spiritual adventure or of the paralysis of self-love. He was sensitive, and his feelings were always moved by broodings, full of depressions, billowing dales and hills ; he was never indifferent, but saw fortune or misfortune in everything and so always had occasion for vivid thoughts. Such people exert an unusual attraction over others, because the moral motion in which they continuously find themselves is transmitted to those others. In their conversation everything assumes a personal significance; and because one can be continuously preoccupied with oneself in one's association with them, they provide a pleasure that one can otherwise obtain only from a psychoanalyst or an individual psychologist—and for a fee— with the further difference that in the latter case one feels ill, whereas Walter made it possible for people to appear very important to themselves for reasons that had previously escaped their attention. With this quality of spreading intellectual preoccupation with oneself, he had also conquered Clarisse and in time driven all rivals from the field. Because with him everything turned into ethical emotion, he could speak convincingly of the immorality of ornament, of the hygiene of simple shapes, and of the beery fumes of Wagnerian music, as was in keeping with the new artistic taste; and even his future father-in-law, who had a painter's brain like an out-spread peacock's tail, had been intimidated by it. So it was beyond all doubt that Walter could look back on successes.

Nevertheless, these days, as soon as he got home, his mind full of impressions and plans, which were perhaps as ripe and new as never before, a discouraging change would take place in him. He only needed to put a canvas on the easel or a sheet of paper on the table, and it was the signal for a terrible flight from his heart. His head remained clear and the plan in it floated as it were in a very transparent, clear atmosphere, indeed the plan split, dividing into two or more plans that might have fought for supremacy; but it was as though there had been a cutting of the communications leading from the mind to the first movements necessary for the execution of any of them. Walter could not bring himself to the point of lifting so much as a finger. He simply did not get up from wherever he happened to be sitting, and the task that he had set himself slipped between his thoughts like snow melting as it falls. He did not know where the time went, but before he was aware of it, it was evening; and since after several such experiences he brought the fear of them home with him, whole rows of weeks began to slide and pass away as in a confused half-sleep. Slowed down by a sense of hopelessness in all his decisions and movements, he suffered from bitter melancholy, and his incapacity became a pain that often had its seat behind his forehead, like a bleeding from the nose, from the moment when he wanted to make up his mind to do something. Walter was easily frightened, and the manifestations that he observed in himself not only hampered him in his work but also caused him very great anxiety, for they were apparently so independent of his will that they often impressed him as being the beginnings of intellectual deterioration.

But while his condition had become steadily worse in the course of the last year, he had also found wonderful help in a thought that he had never before valued highly enough. This thought was none other than that Europe, in which he was forced to live, was irreparably decadent. In ages that outwardly fare well, while inwardly they undergo the regression that is probably the lot of every thing and hence also of intellectual development (if one does not by constant exertions keep it supplied with new ideas), presumably the most immediate question ought to be what one can do against this state of things. But the tangle of clever, stupid, vulgar, and beautiful is precisely in such times so dense and involved that to many people it evidently seems easier to believe in a mystery, for which reason they proclaim the irresistible decline of something or other that defies exact definition and is of a solemn haziness. It is fundamentally all the same whether this is thought of as the race, or vegetarianism, or the soul, for all that matters, as in the case of every healthy pessimism, is that one should have something inevitable to hold on to. And although in luckier years Walter had been able to laugh at such doctrines, when he himself began to try them out he soon discovered their great advantages. Had it up to then been he who was unfit for work and felt out of sorts, now it was the time that was out of sorts, and he the healthy one. His life, which had come to nothing, was all at once given a tremendous explanation, a justification, in terms of centuries, that was worthy of him; and indeed, there was now positively something in the style of a great sacrifice about it when he took up his pencil or pen and laid it down again.

Yet Walter still had his inner struggles, and Clarisse tormented him. She would not have anything to do with critical discussions of the spirit of the time, for she had a headlong belief in the idea of 'genius'. What this was, she did not know; but her whole body began to tremble and grow tense whenever the subject came up. 'Either you feel it or you don't' was her one piece of evidence. For him she always remained the cruel little fifteen-year-old girl. She had never quite understood his sensibility, nor had he ever been able to dominate her. But cold and hard as she was, and then again so enthusiastic, with her insubstantial, flaming will, she possessed a mysterious capacity for influencing him, as though shocks came through her from some direction that could not be fitted into the three dimensions of space. It sometimes bordered on the uncanny. He felt this especially when they played the piano together. Clarisse's playing was hard and colourless, obeying a law of excitement that was alien to him, and when their bodies glowed until the soul began to shine through, he would feel it coming over with frightening intensity. Something indefinable then tore loose in her, threatening to fly off with her spirit. It came out of a secret recess in her being that had to be very carefully kept shut. He did not know what made him feel this or what it was, but it tortured him with an unutterable fear and the urge to do something decisive against it, which he could not do, for nobody but himself noticed anything of it.

While looking through the window watching Clarisse come back, he knew half-consciously that once again he would be unable to resist the need to speak badly of Ulrich. Ulrich had returned at a wrong time. He had a harmful effect on Clarisse. He ruthlessly tampered with the very thing in her that Walter dared not touch—the cavern of disaster, all that was poor, sick, all there was of ill-omened genius in Clarisse, the secret empty room where something tore at chains that might some day rend apart.

Now she stood bare-headed before him, as she had just come in, her sun-hat in her hand, and he looked at her. Her eyes were mocking, clear, fond—perhaps a little too clear. Sometimes he had the feeling that she simply possessed a strength that he lacked. Even when she was a child he had felt her to be a thorn that would not let him rest, and obviously he himself had never wanted her to be different. This was perhaps the secret of his life, which the two others did not understand.

'How deep our sufferings are!' he thought. 'I think it can't often happen that two people love each other as deeply as we must do.' And without transition he began to speak.

"I don't want to know what Ulo had been saying to you, but I can tell you that his strength, which you so much admire, is nothing but a vacuum!"

Clarisse looked at the piano and smiled. Involuntarily he had sat down again beside the open instrument.

"It must be easy to have heroic feelings," he went on, "if one is insensitive by nature, and to think in miles if one has no idea of the abundance that may be hidden in every millimetre!"

They sometimes spoke of him as Ulo—as they had called him in their younger days—and for this he was especially fond of them in rather the same way as one preserves a smiling deference for one's nanny.

"He has come to a standstill," Walter added. "You don't notice it. But you needn't think that I don't know him!"

Clarisse had her doubts.

Walter said violently: "Everything is crumbling nowadays! An intellectual pit without a bottom to it! He has an intellect, I grant you that. But he has no notion of the power of an unbroken soul! What Goethe calls personality, what Goethe calls mobile order—that's something he hasn't got an inkling of! 'This beautiful conception of power and restraint, of wantonness and law, of liberty and moderation, of mobile order—'"

The lines floated in waves from his lips.

Clarisse watched these lips in amiable astonishment, as though they had sent a pretty toy flying up into the air. Then, remembering her role of good little housewife, she interrupted:

"Do you want some beer?"

"Hm? Why not? I always have some, don't I?"

"But I haven't any in the house!"

"Pity you asked me," Walter said with a sigh. "I mightn't have thought of it."

So far as Clarisse was concerned, that settled the question. But Walter had now lost his equilibrium and did not quite know how to go on. "Do you remember our talk about the artist?" he asked uncertainly.

"Which one?"

"The one we had a few days ago. I explained to you what a

living creative principle means to a human being. Don't you remember how I came to the conclusion that in the old days, instead of death and logical mechanisation, it was blood and wisdom that prevailed ? "

" No."

Walter was frustrated. He searched, he wavered. Suddenly he burst out : " He is a man without qualities ! "

" What's that ? " Clarisse asked, with a little laugh.

" Nothing. That's just the point—it's nothing ! "

But the expression had aroused Clarisse's curiosity.

" There are millions of them nowadays," Walter declared. " It's the human type that our time has produced." He was pleased with the expression that had so unexpectedly come to him. As though he were beginning a poem, the words drove him forward before he had got the meaning. " Just look at him ! What would you take him for ? Does he look like a doctor, or like a business man, or a painter, or a diplomat ? "

" But he isn't any of those things," Clarisse pointed out matter-of-factly.

" Well, do you think he looks like a mathematician ? "

" I don't know ! How should I know what a mathematician is supposed to look like ? "

" Now you've said something very much to the point ! A mathematician doesn't look like anything ! Which means, he will always look so generally intelligent that there is no single definite thing behind it at all ! With the exception of the Roman Catholic clergy, there is no one these days, absolutely no one, who still looks like what he should look like, for we use our heads even more impersonally than our hands. But mathematics is the peak of it all, it has got to the point of knowing as little about itself as human beings—some day when they are living on energy-pills instead of meat and bread—are likely to know about meadows and little calves and chickens ! "

In the mean time Clarisse had put the simple supper on the table, and Walter had already disposed of a good deal of it ; perhaps this had suggested the comparison to him. Clarisse watched his lips. They reminded her of his mother, who was dead ; they were strongly marked, feminine lips that dealt with eating as though it were housework, and were topped off by a small clipped moustache. His eyes shone like chestnuts fresh from the husk, even when he was only looking for a piece of cheese on the dish. Although he was small and rather more flabby than delicate in build, he was impressive, and was one of those people who always seem to be standing in a good light. He went on talking.

"You can't guess at any profession from what he looks like, and yet he doesn't look like a man who has no profession, either. And now just run your mind over the sort of man he is. He always knows what to do. He can gaze into a woman's eyes. He can exercise his intelligence efficiently on any given problem at any given moment. He can box. He is talented, strong-willed, unprejudiced, he has courage and he has endurance, he can go at things with a dash and he can be cool and cautious—I have no intention of examining all this in detail, let him have all these qualities! For in the end he hasn't got them at all! They have made him what he is, they have set his course for him, and yet they don't belong to him. When he is angry, something in him laughs. When he is sad, he is up to something. When he is moved by something, he will reject it. Every bad action will seem good to him in some connection or other. And it will always be only a possible context that will decide what he thinks of a thing. Nothing is stable for him. Everything is fluctuating, a part of a whole, among innumerable wholes that presumably are part of a super-whole, which, however, he doesn't know the slightest thing about. So every one of his answers is a part-answer, every one of his feelings only a point of view, and whatever a thing is, it doesn't matter to him what it is, it's only some accompanying 'way in which it is', some addition or other, that matters to him. I don't know whether I make myself quite clear to you?"

"Oh yes," Clarisse said. "But I think it's very nice of him."

Involuntarily Walter had been speaking with signs of growing dislike; the old feeling of being the weaker boy—which goes with so many friendships—magnified his jealousy. For although he was convinced that, apart from a few proofs of plain intellect, Ulrich had never achieved anything, in secret he could not shake off the feeling of always having been physically inferior to him. The picture that he had been drawing relieved him, like the successful conclusion of a work of art; it was not he who had brought it forth, but outwardly, linked with a mysteriously successful beginning, word had followed word, while inwardly something dissolved without his becoming conscious of it. By the time he had finished, he realised that Ulrich was the expression of nothing but this dissolved condition that all phenomena are in nowadays.

" You like that? " he asked, painfully surprised. " You can't possibly mean that seriously! "

Clarisse was chewing bread and soft cheese. She could only smile with her eyes.

" Oh, I know," Walter said, " we may have had a similar way of thinking, ourselves, in the old days. But one mustn't regard it as anything more than a preliminary stage! A man like that isn't really human at all! "

Clarisse had finished chewing. " That's just what he says himself! " she declared.

" *What* does he say himself? "

" Oh, I don't know! He says everything is dissolved, nowadays. He says everything has come to a standstill—not only himself. But he doesn't bear a grudge the way you do. He gave me a long talk about it once—if you analyse the nature of a thousand human beings, all you're left with is two dozen qualities, feelings, forms of development, constructive principles and so on, which is what they all consist of. And if you analyse the human body, all you're left with is water and a few dozen little heaps of matter floating round in it. We draw up water just as trees do, and animal bodies are formed of it just as clouds are. I think that's pretty. Only it makes it rather hard to know what to think of oneself. And what to do." Clarisse giggled. " So then I told him that you go fishing for days on end, when you have time off, just lying by the water."

" Well, what of it? I should like to know if he could keep it up for ten minutes! But *human beings*," Walter said firmly, " have been doing that for tens of thousands of years, staring up into the sky, feeling the warmth of the earth, and no more analysing it than one analyses one's own mother! "

Clarisse could not help giggling again. " He says it's got much more complicated since then. Just as we float on water, we float in a sea of fire, a storm of electricity, a sky of magnetism, a swamp of warmth, and so on. Only we don't feel it. Finally all that's left is formulae. And what they mean in human terms is something one can't quite express—that's the whole thing. I've quite forgotten what I learnt at school but it seems to be right enough. And, he says, if somebody today wants to call the birds his little brothers, like Saint Francis, or you, then he mustn't go and make it quite so easy for himself, but must make up his mind to plunge into the furnace, and flash down into the earth through the trolley-pole of a tram, or go splish-splash down the drain of the sink, into the sewers."

" Yes, yes ! " Walter interrupted this account. " First the four elements become several dozen, and in the end we're merely left floating around on correlations, on processes, on the dirty dish-water of processes and formulae, on something of which one doesn't know whether it's a thing, a process, a phantom idea or a God-knows-what ! Then there's no difference left between a sun and a match, nor any between the mouth as the one end of the digestive tract and the other end of it ! One and the same thing has a hundred sides, each side has a hundred aspects, and every one of them has other feelings attached to it. The human brain has then successfully split things up. But things have split the human heart ! " He had jumped up, but he remained standing at the table. " Clarisse ! " he said. " He is a menace to you ! Look, Clarisse, there is nothing that everybody needs so urgently today as simplicity, nearness to the earth, health—and, yes, definitely, you can say whatever you like—a child too, because a child is what ties one firmly to the ground. All the things Ulo tells you are inhuman. I assure you, I *have* got the courage, when I come home, simply to have my cup of coffee with you, and listen to the birds, go for a bit of a walk, have a little chat with the neighbours, and let the day fade out quietly. That is human life ! "

The tenderness of this picture had slowly drawn him closer to her. But as soon as from afar father-feelings raised their gentle bass voice, Clarisse became stubborn. Her face shut down, while he came nearer to her, and drew up lines of defence.

By the time he had reached her, he was radiating warm gentleness like a good farm-house range. Clarisse swayed for a moment

in these rays. Then she said : " Nothing doing, my dear boy ! "
She grabbed a piece of bread-and-cheese from the table and
kissed him quickly on the forehead. " I'm going out to see if
there are any moths about."

" But, Clarisse," Walter implored, " there aren't any more
Lepidoptera at this time of the year ! "

" Oh, you never can tell."

Nothing of her remained in the room but her laughter. With
her piece of bread-and-cheese she roamed through the meadows.
The district was safe, and she needed no escort. Walter's tenderness collapsed like a *soufflé* taken out of the oven too soon. He
heaved a deep sigh. Then, hesitantly, he sat down again at the
piano and struck a few notes. With or without his will, it turned
into improvisations on themes from Wagner operas, and in the
splashings of this dissolutely swelling substance, which he had
denied himself in the days of his pride, his fingers waded and
wallowed, gurgling through the flood of sound. Let them hear
it far and wide ! His spinal cord was paralysed by the narcotic
influence of this music, and his lot grew lighter.

18   *Moosbrugger.*

AT this time the Moosbrugger case was attracting much public
attention.

Moosbrugger was a carpenter, a big, broad-shouldered man
without any superfluous fat, with hair like brown lamb's-skin and
harmless-looking great fists. His face also expressed good-
hearted strength and the wish to do right, and if one had not seen
these qualities, one would have smelt them, in the rough-and-
ready, straightforward, dry, workaday smell that went with this
thirty-four-year-old man, from his having to do with wood and
a kind of work that called for steadiness as much as for exertion.

One stopped as though rooted to the spot, when for the first time one encountered this face so blessed by God with all the signs of goodness, for Moosbrugger was usually accompanied by two armed gendarmes and had his hands shackled before him to a strong steel chain, the grip of which was held by one of his escorts.

When he noticed that one was looking at him, a smile passed over his broad, kindly face with the unkempt hair and the moustache and little imperial. He wore a short black jacket and light grey trousers. He carried himself in a straddling, military way. But it was chiefly this smile that had kept the law-court reporters busy. It might have been an embarrassed smile, or a cunning one, an ironical, treacherous, grieved, mad, blood-thirsty, or uncanny one : one could see them groping for contra-dictory expressions, and they seemed to be desperately searching for something in this smile, something that they obviously found nowhere else in the whole honest look of the man.

For Moosbrugger had killed a street-woman, a prostitute of the lowest type, in a horrifying manner. The reporters had described in detail a throat-wound extending from the larynx to the back of the neck, as well as the two stab-wounds in the breast, which had pierced the heart, the two others on the left side of the back, and the cutting off of the breasts, which could almost be detached from the body. They had expressed their abhorrence of it, but they did not leave off until they had counted thirty-five stabs in the abdomen and described the long slash from the navel to the sacrum, which continued up the back in a multitude of smaller slashes, while the throat showed the marks of throttling. From such horrors they could not find their way back to Moos-brugger's kind face, although they themselves were kind men and yet had described what had happened in a matter-of-fact, expert way and obviously breathless with excitement. They made little use even of the most obvious explanation : that here they were confronted with a madman—Moosbrugger had already been in lunatic asylums several times on account of similar crimes—although nowadays a good reporter is very well up in such matters. It looked as though they were still reluctant to give up the idea of the villain and to dismiss the incident from their own world into that of the insane, an attitude in keeping with that of the psychiatrists, who had declared him normal quite as often as they had declared him not responsible for his actions. And there was, furthermore, the remarkable circumstance that, even when the facts had scarcely become publicly known, Moosbrugger's insane excesses had been felt to be ' something interesting, for once ' by thousands of people who deplored the sensationalism of the newspapers, by busy officials as by fourteen-year-old schoolboys and housewives wrapped in the haze of their domestic cares. Although indeed one sighed over such a monstrosity, one was inwardly more preoccupied with it than with one's own affairs. Indeed, it was quite likely to happen that some staid assistant under-secretary or bank-manager would say to his sleepy wife as they were going to bed : " What would you do now if I were a Moosbrugger ? "

When Ulrich's gaze fell on this face that bore the marks of being in God's own keeping, and on the shackles, he turned swiftly on his heel and gave a sentry at the *Landesgericht* nearby some cigarettes, asking about the convoy that must only just have left the gates, so discovering . . . Well, anyway, something of the sort must have happened at some time, or else one would not so frequently find it described in this manner. Ulrich almost believed in it himself; but the historical truth of that particular situation was that he had merely read it all in the newspaper. It was to be a long time yet before he got to know Moosbrugger personally, and previous to that he only once succeeded in seeing him in the flesh during the trial. The probability of learning something unusual from a newspaper is far greater than that of experiencing it ; in other words, it is in the realm of the abstract that the more important things happen in these times, and it is the unimportant that happens in real life.

What Ulrich in this way learnt about Moosbrugger's history was approximately the following.

As a boy Moosbrugger had been a poverty-stricken wretch, a shepherd-lad in a hamlet so small that it did not even have a village street ; and he was so poor that he never spoke to a girl. Girls were something that he could always only look at, even later when he was an apprentice, and even on his wanderings as a journeyman. Now, one must just imagine what that means. Something that one craves for just as naturally as one craves for bread or water is only there to be looked at. After a time one's desire for it becomes unnatural. It walks past, the skirts swaying round its ankles. It climbs over a stile, becoming visible right up to the knees. One looks into its eyes, and they become opaque. One hears it laughing, turns round swiftly, and looks into a face that is round and unmoving as a hole in the ground where a mouse has just disappeared.

So it was understandable that even after the murder of the first girl Moosbrugger had vindicated himself by saying that he was continually haunted by spirits, which called him day and night. They would throw him out of bed when he was asleep, and disturbed him at his work. Then he would hear them talking to each other and quarrelling all day and all night long. That was not insanity, and Moosbrugger extremely disliked hearing it spoken of as such, although he himself did sometimes embroider it all with reminiscences of sermons or 'pile it on' according to the advice one gets in prison on how to simulate. The material, however, was always there, ready, waiting—only fading out a little whenever one did not happen to be paying attention to it.

That was the way it had been on his journeyings, too. It is difficult for a carpenter to find work in winter, and Moosbrugger was often without a roof over his head for weeks. Now supposing one has been walking all day, and arrives at a village and cannot get shelter. One has to go on and on walking, far into the night. One has no money for a meal, so one drinks schnapps until two candles light up behind one's eyes and the body walks on its own. One doesn't want to ask for a doss-down at 'the station', in spite of the hot soup, partly because of the bugs and partly because of the insulting fuss they make; and so one collects a few coppers by begging, instead, and crawls into some farmer's haystack. Without asking him, of course—for what's the sense of asking and asking and only getting insulted? Of course in the morning there's likely to be a row and a charge of assault, vagrancy and begging, and the outcome is that there's a thicker and thicker file of such previous convictions, opened up by each new judge with a great air of importance, as though Moosbrugger himself were explained in it.

And who thinks of what it means not to be able to have a proper wash for days and weeks on end? One's skin becomes so stiff that it stops one from making any but rough movements, even supposing one wanted to make gentle, loving ones—the living soul sets and hardens under such a crust. It may not affect the mind so much; one goes on doing what is necessary quite sensibly. The mind is quite likely to keep burning like a little lamp in a huge walking lighthouse that is full of crushed earthworms or grasshoppers—but everything personal in it is squashed, and what walks about is only the fermenting organic substance. Then Moosbrugger on his wanderings, passing through the villages, or even on the lonely road, met with whole processions of women. First there was one, and then it might be half an hour before there was another woman, but even if they came at such long intervals and had nothing to do with one another, still, as a whole they were processions. They would be going from one village to the other or would just have slipped out of the house for a moment, they wore thick shawls or jackets that stood out in a stiff snaky line round their hips, they came into warm rooms or drove their children along in front of them or they were so alone on the road that one could have dropped them with a stone, like a crow. Moosbrugger insisted that he could not have committed murder for the pleasure of it, because he had always been inspired with feelings of disgust for all these females. And that seems not improbable, considering that one thinks one understands even the cat sitting in front of a cage in which a fat, fair-feathered canary is hopping up and down, or striking a mouse, letting it go, and striking it again, just for the sake of seeing it run away once more—and what is going on in a dog that runs after a turning wheel, biting at it, he, the friend of man? This relation to the living, moving, silently bowling or flitting thing points to a secret aversion from a fellow-creature delighting in its own existence.

And after all what was one to do when she screamed? One could either come to one's senses or, if one was simply incapable of that, press her face to the ground and stuff earth into her mouth.

Moosbrugger was only a journeyman carpenter, an utterly solitary man, and although he was well liked by his mates in all the places where he worked, he had no friend. An irresistible urge from time to time cruelly turned his personality inside-out.

Perhaps he would really have needed, as he said himself, only the upbringing, and the opportunity, to make something quite different of it and become a destroying angel, slaughtering thousands, an incendiary, setting theatres on fire, or a great anarchist (those anarchists who leagued themselves together in secret societies he referred to with contempt as 'impostors'). He was clearly not normal; but although obviously it was his diseased nature that was the cause of his behaviour and set him apart from other human beings, to him it felt like a stronger and higher awareness of his own personality. His whole life was a struggle—laughably and horribly clumsy—to extort acknowledgment of this. As an apprentice, he had broken the fingers of a master who had tried to beat him. From another master he ran away with money—for the sake of necessary justice, as he himself put it. He never stood it long in any place. So long as he could keep the men in awe, as he always did at first, huge-shouldered as he was, with his kindly calm ways and his taciturn manner of going about his work, he stayed. As soon as they became matey and began to treat him without respect, as though now they had seen through him, he cleared out, for then he was seized by an uncanny feeling as though he were not quite firmly fixed inside his own skin. Once he had left it too late. Then four bricklayers on the site had plotted to make him feel their superiority and to throw him down the scaffolding from the top storey. He even heard them tittering as they came up behind his back, and then he hurled himself on them with all his extraordinary strength, threw one of them down two flights and cut right through the arm-sinews of two others. That he had been punished for this had been a shock to his feelings, as he said. He went abroad. He made his way to Turkey, and then back again, for everywhere the world was in league against him; no magic formula was a match for this conspiracy, and no benevolence either.

Such expressions he had picked up eagerly in mental hospitals and prisons, with scraps of French and Latin that he stuck in at the most unsuitable places in his speeches, since he had found out that it was the possession of these languages that gave those in power the right to 'arrive at findings' where his fate was concerned. For the same reason he did his utmost to use educated speech during the trial, saying, for instance, 'this must serve as the basis of my brutality', or 'I had imagined her even crueller than I habitually estimate women of that sort'. But when he saw that even this failed to make an impression, he not infrequently rose to the heights of an immense theatrical pose, scornfully declaring himself a 'theoretical anarchist' who could get himself rescued by the Social-Democrats at any moment if he were prepared to accept anything from the hands of those worst of Jewish exploiters of the ignorant working-class. In this he too had his 'science', a field on to which the learned presumption of his judges could not follow him.

This usually earned him the comment 'intelligence—remarkable' in the opinion of the courts, respectful attention during the proceedings, and severer sentences; but fundamentally his flattered vanity regarded these proceedings as the high-lights of his life. Hence too he hated no one as fervently as the psychiatrists who believed they could dispose of his entire difficult personality with a few long Latin or Greek words, as though for them it were an everyday matter. As always happens in such cases, medical opinion as to his mental state fluctuated under pressure from the juristic body of ideas, which superimposed itself upon it. And Moosbrugger missed none of these opportunities during the public proceedings to prove his superiority to the psychiatrists and unmask them as swelled-headed dunces and charlatans, who knew absolutely nothing and would have to take him into the asylum if he chose to simulate, instead of sending him to jail, where he really ought to be. For he did not deny these acts of his. He wanted them understood as mishaps arising out of a grand attitude to life. Above all, the giggling womenfolk were in a conspiracy against him; they all had their fancy-boys, and a steady man's straightforward way of talking was something they despised, if they did not take it for a downright insult. He kept out of their way as much as he could, so as not to be irritated; but this was not always possible. Days came when a man got quite stupid in his head and could not get a proper hold on anything, with his hands sweating from restlessness. And then, when one had to give in, one could be sure that at the very first step, far off, like an advance patrol sent out by the others, such walking poison would cross one's path, a cheat, secretly laughing at the man while she was weakening him

and playing her tricks on him, if indeed she didn't do something
far worse to him, being utterly unscrupulous as they all are.

And so it had come to the end of that night, a night spent in
listless drinking—with a lot of shouting to keep down one's inner
uneasiness. The world is sometimes quite unsteady even when
one is not drunk. The walls that are the street sway like stage-
scenery, with something waiting behind it to step out at its cue.
On the fringe of the town everything grows quieter, there where
one comes out into the open fields lit up by the moon. There
Moosbrugger had to turn back in order to get home by the long
way round, and there it was, at the iron bridge, that the girl
accosted him. She was the kind of girl that hires herself out to
men down there by the meadows, an out-of-work, runaway
servant-girl, a little thing of whom there was nothing to be seen
but two inveigling mouse-eyes gazing out from under her kerchief.
Moosbrugger waved her away and quickened his steps. But
she kept on begging him to take her home with him. Moosbrugger walked on, straight ahead, round the corner, and finally
round and round, not knowing what to do. He took long
strides, and she ran along beside him. He stopped, and there
she stood like a shadow. He was drawing her along after him,
that was it. Then he made one more attempt to scare her off:
he turned round and spat into her face, twice. But it did not
help ; nothing could affront her.

This happened in the vast park that they had to cross at its
narrowest part. Then Moosbrugger became certain that some
fancy-man of the girl's must be somewhere about—for else how
would she have had the courage to follow him in spite of his
annoyance ? He reached for the knife in his trouser-pocket, for
surely he was being got at, perhaps they were again about to
attack him. Behind the women there was always the other man,
sneering at one. And, come to think of it, didn't she look like
a man in disguise ? He saw shadows moving and heard a crackling
in the bushes. And always the sneaking female at his side, like
the pendulum of a huge clock, time and again repeating her request.
But there was nothing there on which he could have rushed with
all his giant's strength, and he began to be frightened of this
uncanny way in which nothing was happening.

When they began to go down the first, still very gloomy street, there was sweat on his forehead, and he was trembling. He kept his eyes fixed straight ahead. Then he went into the café that happened to be still open. He tossed off a black coffee and three brandies one after the other and was able to sit quietly for a while, perhaps as long as a quarter of an hour. But when he paid, there again the thought was : What was he to do if she was still waiting outside ? There are such thoughts that are like string winding itself in endless nooses round one's arms and legs. And he had taken only a few steps out into the dark street when he felt the girl at his side. Now she was no longer humble, but brazen and self-confident ; nor did she plead any more ; she was merely silent. There and then he realised that he would never get rid of her, because it was he himself who was drawing her along after him. His throat filled up with tearful disgust. He walked on, and, again, the thing half behind him was himself. It was just the same way that he always met processions. He had once cut a big splinter of wood out of his leg himself, because he was too impatient to wait for the doctor ; it was very much the same, the way he felt his knife now, lying long and hard in his pocket.

But with an almost more than earthly exertion of his conscience Moosbrugger hit upon yet another way out. Behind the hoarding along which the street now led there was a sports-ground ; there one could not be seen, and so he entered. In the small ticket-booth he rolled up, with his head pushed into the corner where it was darkest. And the soft, accursed second self lay down beside him. So he pretended to go to sleep at once, in order to be able to slip away later.

When he began quietly crawling out, feet first, there it was again, winding its arms round his neck. And then he felt something hard in her or his pocket. He tugged it out. He was not clear about whether it was a scissors or a knife ; he struck home with it. She had insisted that it was only a scissors, but it was his knife. She fell with her head inside the booth ; he hauled her some way out, on to the soft earth, and stabbed and stabbed at her until he had cut her completely away from himself. Then he stood beside her for perhaps another quarter of an hour, gazing at her, while the night again grew calmer and strangely, wonderfully smooth. Now she could never insult a man again, clutching at him. Finally he had carried the corpse over the street and laid it down by a bush so that it could be more easily found and buried, as he declared, for now one couldn't blame her any more.

During the proceedings Moosbrugger made quite unpredictable difficulties for his counsel. He sat there at huge ease on his bench, like an onlooker, calling out " Hear! Hear! " to the public prosecutor whenever he made a point of Moosbrugger's being a public menace and did it in a way that Moosbrugger considered worthy of himself. He gave good marks to witnesses who declared that they had never noticed anything about him that pointed to his being not responsible for his actions. " You're a queer customer," the presiding judge said from time to time, in a flattering way, and conscientiously pulled tighter the noose that the accused had laid round his own neck. Then Moosbrugger would stand astonished for an instant, like a harried bull in the arena, his eyes straying, and seeing from the faces of those sitting round him—what he could not understand—that yet once again he had worked himself one layer deeper down into his guilt.

What attracted Ulrich particularly was that Moosbrugger's own defence was obviously based on an obscurely perceptible plan. He had not gone out with the intention of killing, neither did his dignity permit him to be insane; there could not be any talk of sexual ' gratification ', but only of disgust and contempt: and therefore the act could only be manslaughter, into which he had been lured by the suspicious behaviour of the woman—" this caricature of a woman," as he expressed it. It even seemed that he was demanding to have his murder regarded as a political crime, and he sometimes conveyed the impression that he was fighting, not for himself at all, but for this interpretation of the legal situation. The tactics that the judge employed against this were the usual ones of seeing in everything a murderer's clumsily sly efforts to divest himself of his responsibility.

" Why did you wipe your bloodstained hands ?—Why did you throw the knife away ?—Why did you change into a clean suit and underclothes after the crime ?—Because it was Sunday ? Not because they were bloodstained ?—Why did you go to an entertainment ? Evidently the crime did not prevent you from doing so ? Did you feel no remorse whatsoever ? "

Ulrich well understood the deep resignation that Moosbrugger felt when in such moments he regretted his insufficient education, which made it impossible for him to untie the knots in this net of incomprehension. But from the judge this only drew the emphatic reproof: "You always manage to shift the blame on to other people!" This judge rolled everything up into one, starting with the police-reports and the vagrancy, and then presented it to Moosbrugger as his guilt. But for Moosbrugger it all consisted of separate incidents that had nothing to do with each other, each of them with a different cause, which lay outside Moosbrugger and somewhere in the world as a whole. In the judge's eyes his acts were something that issued from him; in his, they had come towards him the way birds come flying along. For the judge Moosbrugger was a special case; for himself he was a world, and it is very difficult to say something convincing about a world. There were two kinds of tactics fighting each other, two kinds of unity and of logical consistency; but Moosbrugger had the less favourable position, for even a cleverer man could not have expressed his strange shadowy arguments. They came directly out of the bewildered solitude of his life, and whereas all other lives exist a hundredfold, being seen in the same way by those who lead them as by all the others who confirm them, his true life existed only for himself. It was like a vapour that is always losing its shape and taking on other forms. He might, of course, have asked his judges whether their lives were essentially different. But such things never occurred to him. Before the law, all that had been so natural while it was one thing happening after the other now lay within him, one thing beside the other, without any sense at all; and he made the greatest efforts, struggling to get sense into it, a sense that would be in no way inferior to the dignity of the gentlemen opposing him. The judge made an almost kindly impression in his attempts to support him in this and to put expressions at his disposal, even though they were such as would deliver Moosbrugger up to the most terrible consequences.

It was like a shadow fighting with a wall, and in the end Moosbrugger's shadow was only just a ghastly flickering. On this last day of the trial Ulrich was present. When the president of the court read the finding that declared him responsible for his actions, Moosbrugger rose and addressed the court : " I am satisfied, I have attained my object." Scornful incredulity in the eyes round about answered him, and he added angrily : " As a result of having forced the court to try me, I am satisfied with the conduct of the case ! " The president of the court, who had now become all severity and condemnation, rebuked him, remarking that the court was not concerned with whether he was satisfied or not. Then he read out the death-sentence to him, exactly as though the nonsense that Moosbrugger had been talking all through the trial, to the delight of all present, had now for once to be accorded a serious answer. To that Moosbrugger said nothing, lest it might look as though he were frightened. Then the proceedings were concluded, and it was all over. At this moment, however, his mind staggered, reeling back, powerless, before the high-and-mightiness of those who did not understand. He turned round as the warders were already leading him out, he fought for words, stretched his hands above his head and shouted in a voice that shook itself free of his guards' grip : " I am satisfied, even though I must confess to you that you have condemned a madman ! "

This was an inconsistency. Ulrich sat breathless. This was clearly madness, and just as clearly it was merely the distorted pattern of our own elements of existence. It was disjointed and steeped in darkness. Yet somehow Ulrich could not help thinking : if mankind could dream collectively, it would dream Moosbrugger. He came back to the present only when the ' miserable clown of a lawyer ', as Moosbrugger had once ungratefully called his counsel in the course of the trial, announced, on account of some details or other, that he would submit a plea of nullity, while his—and Ulrich's—gigantic client was led away.

19   *An admonitory letter and an opportunity*
        to acquire qualities.
        Competition between two imperial jubilees.

SO the time passed, until one day Ulrich received a letter from
his father.

" My dear son, Once again several months have gone by without
its being possible to gather from your sparse communications
that you have either made the slightest progress in your career
or taken steps to do so.

" I am happy to be able to say that in the course of recent
years I have had the satisfaction of hearing your achievements
praised in various esteemed quarters and, on the strength of it,
a promising future predicted for you. But on the one hand the
tendency that you have inherited, though certainly not from me,
to be impetuous in taking the first steps whenever a task is alluring
to you, but then, as it were, quite to forget what you owe to
yourself and to those who have placed their hopes in you, and
on the other hand the circumstance that I am unable to find in
your letters even the slightest indication from which to deduce
the existence of a plan for your further actions, both fill me with
grave concern.

" Not only are you of an age at which other men have already
secured themselves a definite position in life, but I may die at
any time, and the property that I shall bequeath to you and your
sister, in equal shares, although not small, is, however, in present-
day conditions not so large that possession of it alone could
assure you of a social position, which you must therefore now, at
long last, establish for yourself. What fills me with grave concern
is the thought that since you took your degree you have only
vaguely talked of plans that are to be realised in various fields
and which you, in your usual manner, perhaps considerably over-
estimate, but that you never write of any satisfaction that a
university appointment would afford you, nor of any preliminary
approach to one or the other university in connection with such

plans, nor indeed of any contact with influential circles. I certainly cannot come under suspicion of belittling a scholar's independence, I who forty-seven years ago, in my work, with which you are acquainted, *Samuel Pufendorf's Theory of the Imputation of Moral Actions and its Relation to Modern Jurisprudence*, the twelfth edition of which is now about to appear, by putting the problem in its true context was the first to break with the prejudices of the older school of criminal jurisprudence in this connection ; yet I am equally unable, after all the experience of a life always usefully employed, to grant that a man can rely on himself alone and neglect the academic and social connections which are what fundamentally sustains the individual's work, and through which it becomes incorporated in a fruitful and beneficial whole.

" I therefore hope and trust to hear from you very soon and to find the expenditure that I have incurred for the sake of your advancement rewarded by your taking up such connections now on your return from abroad, instead of neglecting them any longer. With this in mind I have also written to my old and tried friend and patron, the former President of the Treasury and present Chairman of the All-Highest *Familiengerichtspartikularität* attached to the Supreme Chamberlain's Office, His Excellency Count Stallburg, begging of him that he will incline a favourable ear to the request that you will in due course lay before him. My exalted friend has already been so good as to answer, and by return post, and you have the good fortune that he will not only see you but takes a warm interest in your personal progress as described to him by me. As a result of this, so far as it is in my power and to the best of my belief, and assuming that you are capable of favourably impressing His Excellency and at the same time of confirming the views held by influential academic circles with regard to you, your future is assured.

" As regards the request that, I am sure, you will gladly lay before His Excellency as soon as you know what it is : the subject of it is the following.

" In Germany, in the year 1918, more precisely on approximately the 15th July, there is to take place a great and impressive festival celebrating the Emperor Wilhelm II's jubilee on the completion of thirty years of his reign and reminding the world of Germany's greatness and power ; although there are still some years to pass before that time is reached, it is known from a reliable source that preparations are already being made, even though of course for the time being quite unofficially. Now, you are doubtless aware that it is in the same year that our revered Emperor celebrates his jubilee, the seventieth anniversary of his accession to the throne, and that the date of it is the 2nd December. In view of the modesty that we Austrians are far too much given to in all matters pertaining to our own country, there is reason to fear that we may—to make no bones about it—experience yet another Sadowa, that is to say, that the Germans will outmatch us with their methodical training in creating effects, just as at that time they had introduced the needle-gun before we knew where we were.

" Fortunately this fear of mine, which I have expressed, had already been anticipated by other patriotic personages with good connections, and I am in a position to disclose to you that a campaign is under way in Vienna to forestall the realisation of that fear and to make the most of the full weight of a reign of seventy years rich in blessings and sorrows as against one of a mere thirty years. Since the 2nd December naturally cannot by any power be moved ahead of the 15th July, the happy idea has arisen of turning the whole of the year 1918 into a jubilee year for our Emperor of Peace. Admittedly, I am informed on these matters only in so far as the institutions of which I am a member have had the opportunity of expressing their opinions as to the proposal ; the details you will learn for yourself as soon as you have your interview with Count Stallburg, who intends you for a position on the committee of organisation, which will be all the greater an honour in view of your youth.

" Likewise I urge upon you no longer to neglect—in a way that is positively embarrassing to me—to take up relations with Tuzzi, Permanent Secretary to the Ministry of Foreign Affairs and of the Imperial House, a connection that I have so long recommended to you, but to call immediately on his wife, who, as you know, is the daughter of a cousin of my late brother's wife and hence your cousin. She occupies, as I am informed, an outstanding position in the enterprise of which I have just been writing, and my revered friend Count Stallburg has already had the great goodness to announce your intended visit to her, for which reason you must not delay for a moment in carrying it out.

"Concerning myself, there is nothing further to report. Apart from my lectures, the work on the new edition of my aforementioned book absorbs all my time and the residue of energy that one has at one's disposal in old age. One has to make good use of one's time, for it is short.

"From your sister I learn only that she is in good health. She has a capable and excellent husband, although she will never admit that she is content with her lot and feels happy in it.

"With God's blessing,

Your affectionate Father."

SECOND BOOK

THE LIKE OF IT NOW HAPPENS (I)

20

The touch of reality. Despite his lack of qualities Ulrich acts with ardour and resolution.

THAT Ulrich really decided to call upon Count Stallburg was explained, last but not least, by the fact that his curiosity had been aroused.

Count Stallburg had his office in that Imperial and Royal citadel, the Hofburg. The Emperor and King of Kakania was a legendary old gentleman. Since that time a great many books have been written about him and one knows exactly what he did, prevented or left undone ; but then, in the last decade of his and Kakania's life, younger people who were familiar with the current state of the arts and sciences were sometimes overtaken by doubt whether he existed at all. The number of the portraits one saw of him was almost as great as the number of inhabitants of his realms ; on his birthday there was as much eating and drinking as on that of the Saviour, on the mountains the bonfires blazed, and the voices of millions of people were heard vowing that they loved him like a father. Finally, an anthem resounding in his honour was the only work of poetry and music of which every Kakanian knew at least one line. But this popularity and publicity was so over-convincing that it might easily have been the case that believing in his existence was rather like still seeing certain stars although they ceased to exist thousands of years ago.

The fist thing that happened when Ulrich drove to the Imperial Hofburg was that the cab, which was supposed to take him there, stopped in the outer court, and the cabman demanded to be paid off, asserting that although he was permitted to drive through he was not permitted to stop in the inner court. Ulrich was annoyed with the man, whom he took to be either a cheat or a coward, and tried to make him go on ; but he was helpless against the man's awed refusal, and suddenly it conveyed to him the aura of a power that was mightier than he.   When he walked into the inner court, he was suddenly struck by the countless red, blue, white and yellow coats, breeches, and plumed helmets, standing there in the sunshine, rigid as birds on a sandbank.   Till then he had taken the term ' Majesty ' for a meaningless word that was kept in use from sheer habit, just as one can be an atheist and yet say ' Thank God '.   But now his gaze rose up along the high walls and he saw an island lying there, grey, secluded, and armed, with the city's swift life heedlessly rushing past.

After he had stated his business, he was led up stairs and along corridors and through rooms large and small.   Although he was very well dressed, he felt himself being quite exactly sized up by every glance that he encountered.   It evidently did not occur to anybody here to mistake aristocracy of the mind for the real thing ;   and there was no other satisfaction left to him but that of ironical protest and a commoner's criticism.   He observed that he was moving through a large outer shell with little inside it.   The vast rooms were almost unfurnished, but this empty taste lacked the bitterness of a grand style.   Ulrich passed a casual succession of single guardsmen and footmen who formed a protection more awkward than magnificent, which might have been provided more effectively by half a dozen well-paid, well-trained detectives ;   and most of all, a species of servant, dressed and capped in grey like bank-messengers, moving to and fro among the flunkeys and guardsmen, made him think of a solicitor or dentist who does not keep his consulting-room and his private apartment sufficiently separate.   ' The feeling comes through quite clearly,' he thought, ' how all this must once have awed people of the Biedermeier period with its splendour, but nowadays it can't even stand comparison with the grandeur and comfort of a hotel, and that's why it tries the dodge of being all distinguished restraint and stateliness.'

But when he entered Count Stallburg's presence, he was received by His Excellency in a large hollow prism of the best proportions, in the middle of which this unpretentious-looking, bald-headed man stood before him, slightly stooping, with an orang-outang-like sagging at the knees, in a manner that could not possibly be the natural way for a high Court functionary of noble blood to stand ; it could only be in imitation of something. His shoulders were bowed, and his under-lip drooped ; he resembled an aged beadle or a reliable cerilcal worker. And suddenly there was no more doubt whom he was a reminder of : Count Stallburg became transparent, and Ulrich realised that a man who had been the All-Highest focus of supreme power for seventy years must find a certain satisfaction in stepping back behind himself and looking like the humblest of his subjects, as a consequence of which it simply became good manners in the vicinity of this All-Highest personage, and a natural expression of tact, not to look any more personal than this personage. This seems to be the meaning of kings so often calling themselves the first servants of their country. With a rapid glance Ulrich confirmed his feeling that His Excellency really wore those ice-grey, short-clipped mutton-chop whiskers that were worn by all the ushers and railway-officials in Kakania. There was a general belief that they were emulating their Emperor and King in their appearance ; but in such cases the deeper need is a mutual one.

Ulrich had time to make these reflections because he had to wait for a while before His Excellency spoke. The fundamental theatrical instinct for masquerade and transformation, which is one of the pleasures of life, here offered itself to him without the faintest tang, probably without even any notion of the theatrical ; and it was so strong that the middle-class custom of building theatres and turning acting into an art to be hired by the hour, when compared with this unconscious, permanent art of acting one's self, struck him as something entirely unnatural, late, and divided against itself. And when at last His Excellency lifted one lip from the other and said to him : " Your dear father . . ." and got no further, while there was at the same time something in the voice that drew attention to the remarkably beautiful yellowish hands and something like an aura of tautened moral rectitude around his whole figure, Ulrich was charmed and subsequently made a mistake that intellectual people are given to making. For His Excellency now asked him what he was and, when Ulrich had answered that he was a mathematician, said : " Ah, very interesting—at what school ? " and when Ulrich explained that he had nothing to do with any school, His

Excellency added : " Ah, very interesting. I see. Pure scholar-ship. University "—which seemed to Ulrich so familiar and so precisely the way one imagines a well-bred conversation-piece that he all at once began to behave as though he were at home here, following the trend of his own thoughts instead of the social demands of the situation. He suddenly remembered Moos-brugger. Here, right beside him, was the power to reprieve, and nothing seemed simpler than trying to find out whether one could make use of it.

" Your Excellency," he said, " may I turn this fortunate opportunity to account on behalf of a man who has been unjustly condemned to death ? "

At this question Count Stallburg opened his eyes wide.

" A case of sadistic homicide, it must be admitted," Ulrich conceded, but at this moment he himself realised that his be-haviour was quite impossible. " A maniac, of course," he said, hastily trying to save the situation, and almost went on to say : ' You are aware, Your Excellency, that in this respect our penal code, dating from the middle of the last century, is out of date,' but he gulped and got stuck. It was a *faux pas* to expect this man to enter into a discussion such as people who are fond of intellectual jugglery often go in for, in the most futile manner. Just a few words, suitably strewn in, might there be as fecund as loose garden soil, but in this place they were like a little clod of earth that someone had accidentally brought into the room on his shoes.

But now that Count Stallburg noticed Ulrich's embarrassment, he displayed truly great benevolence towards him. " Yes, yes, I remember," he said, after Ulrich, with something of an effort, had uttered the name. " And so you say he is a maniac, and would like to help the man ? "

" He's not responsible for his actions."

" Yes, those are always particularly disagreeable cases." Count Stallburg seemed to be very distressed by the difficulties that they presented. He gazed at Ulrich with a hopeless expression and asked him, as though nothing else were to be expected, whether Moosbrugger's sentence had yet been finally confirmed. Ulrich had to admit that this was not so. " Ah well then," the Count went on in a tone of relief, " so there's still plenty of time." And he began to talk of Ulrich's ' dear father ', leaving the Moos-brugger case behind in amiable ambiguity.

Ulrich had lost his presence of mind for a moment as a result of his slip, but oddly enough this *gaffe* had not made a bad impression on His Excellency. True, at first Count Stallburg had been almost speechless, as though someone had taken off his jacket in his presence ; but then this directness in a man so well recommended began to seem like ardour and resolution, and he was glad to have found these two words, for he was determined to be given a good impression. He at once used them (" I think we may hope to have found a helper full of ardour and resolution ") in the letter of introduction that he was composing to the chief personage in the great patriotic campaign. When Ulrich received this letter a few moments later, he felt like a child that is dismissed by having a piece of chocolate pressed into its little hands. He now held something between his fingers and received instructions concerning a further visit, instructions that might just as well have been a command as a request, without any opportunity occurring for raising an objection. ' This is all a misunderstanding, you know, I really had no intention at all——' he would have liked to say, but there he was, already on his way back, back through the vast corridors and State apartments. He suddenly stopped, thinking : ' Heavens, it bore me upwards like a cork and washed me up somewhere where I never meant to go ! ' He scrutinised the cunning simplicity of the décor with curiosity. He felt quite safe in telling himself that it made no impression on him even now : it was merely a world that had not been cleared away. And yet what was the strong and peculiar quality that it had nevertheless made him feel ? Damn it all, one could hardly put it otherwise than that it simply was surprisingly real.

21

The true invention of the Collateral Campaign by Count Leinsdorf.

THE real driving-force in the great patriotic campaign—which from now on, for the sake of brevity and because it was to ' make the most of the full weight of a reign of seventy years rich in blessings and sorrows as against one of a mere thirty years ', shall be known as the Collateral Campaign—was, however, not Count Stallburg but his friend, His Highness the Imperial Liege-Count Leinsdorf.

In this great nobleman's beautiful study with its high windows, at the centre of many layers of tranquillity, devotion, gold braid and the solemnity of fame, his secretary was standing with a book in his hand, at the time when Ulrich was paying his visit in the Hofburg, and was reading aloud to the Count a passage that he had been given the task of finding. This time it was something by J. G. Fichte, something he had lit on in the *Addresses to the German Nation* and considered very appropriate.

" ' For liberation from the original sin of sloth,' " he read out, " ' and from cowardice and falseness, which follow in its train, men have need of models to construe the enigma of freedom for them, such models, indeed, as have arisen in the founders of religions. The necessary instruction as to moral conviction take place within the Church, whose symbols are to be regarded not as moral tenets but only as educational implements for the promulgation of the eternal verities.' " He laid special emphasis on the words ' sloth ', ' models ' and ' Church '.

His Highness had listened benignantly. He asked to be shown the book, but then shook his head.

" No," he said, " the book would be all right, but this Protestant bit about the Church won't do."

The secretary looked as sulky as a small official who gets the draft of a regulation back from his principal for the fifth time, and raised a cautious objection : " But wouldn't Fichte make an excellent impression in nationalist circles ? "

" I think," His Highness replied, " we must make do without it for the present."

With the shutting of the book, his face shut down too, and at the wordless command in that face the secretary shut up in a respectful bow and received Fichte back—to be cleared away like a rejected dish and replaced in the adjoining library, among all the other philosophic systems of the world, for one does not do the cooking oneself, but has it done by one's servants.

" So for the time being," Count Leinsdorf said, " what we have is the four points : Emperor of Peace, European Landmark, True Austria, and Culture and Capital.   Those are the lines on which to draw up the circular letter."

His Highness had at this moment had a political idea, which, if translated into words, would have been something to this effect : ' They'll come of their own accord ! '   What he had in mind was those sections of the population who felt that they belonged less to his and their country than to the German nation.   They were distasteful to him.   Had his secretary found a more fitting quotation to flatter their sentiments (for that had been the reason for selecting J. G. Fichte), the passage would have been copied out ;   but the moment an inconvenient detail prevented this, Count Leinsdorf gave a sigh of relief.

His Highness was the inventor of the great patriotic campaign. It was to him, when the rousing news came from Germany, that the words ' Emperor of Peace ' had first occurred.   It had immediately become associated with the image of an eighty-eight-year-old sovereign, a true father of his peoples, and of seventy years of uninterrupted reign.   Although of course these two images bore the to him familiar features of his Imperial lord and master, the glory emanating from them pertained not to His Majesty but to the proud fact that his country possessed the oldest sovereign in the world, whose reign was also the longest in the world.   The unappreciative might now be tempted to see this as merely delight in a rarity (rather as though Count Leinsdorf had rated possession of the much rarer horizontally streaked ' Sahara ', with water-mark and one perforation missing, higher than that of a Greco, which in fact he did, although he possessed both and did not quite overlook the celebrated collection of pictures that bore the name of his house), but this is simply because they do not understand what enriching power lies in an allegory, making it superior even to the greatest of riches. For Count Leinsdorf there lay in this allegory of the aged sovereign the thought both of his country, which he loved, and of the world, to which it was to be an example. Great and agonising hopes stirred in Count Leinsdorf. He could not have said whether what moved him was more pain at not seeing his country occupying the place of honour due to it ' in the family of the nations ', or whether it was jealousy of Prussia, which had thrust Austria down from that place (in 1866, by trickery and cunning !), or whether he was simply filled with pride in the nobility of an old State and the desire to show the world that it was exemplary ; for in his view the nations of Europe were all whirling along in the vortex of a materialistic democracy, and he envisaged a lofty symbol that would be to them at once an admonition and a signal for a change of heart. It was clear to him that something must be done that would put Austria at the head of all, so that this ' magnificent demonstration of the spirit of Austria ' should be a ' landmark ' for the whole world, so helping it to find the way back to its own true nature, and that all this was bound up with the possession of an eighty-eight-year-old Emperor of Peace. That was actually all that Count Leinsdorf was sure of as yet. But one thing was certain : a great idea had taken possession of him. Not only did it kindle his passion—something against which a strictly and responsibly brought-up Christian should, after all, have been on his guard—but it flowed out, all bright clarity, straight into such sublime and radiant images as ' Sovereign ', ' Country ' and ' the happiness of the world '. And what obscurity still clung to this idea could not cause His Highness any uneasiness. He very well knew the theological doctrine of the *contemplatio in caligine divina*, contemplation in the darkness of God, which is in itself infinitely clear, though for the human intellect it is a dazzling darkness ; and for the rest it was his lifelong conviction that a man who does great things usually does not know why. As Cromwell said : " A man never rises so high as when he does not know where he is going." So Count Leinsdorf abandoned himself contentedly to the enjoyment of his allegory, the vagueness of which stirred him, as he himself felt, more intensely than anything definite could have.

Apart from allegories, however, his political views were of extraordinary solidity and had all the freedom that goes with greatness of character and is only made possible by a complete absence of doubts. He was by primogeniture a member of the Upper House, but he was not politically active nor did he hold any appointment at Court or in the State ; he was ' merely a patriot '. But precisely as a result of this and of the independence afforded by wealth he had become the nucleus for all other patriots who followed the development of the Empire and of humanity with concern. The ethical obligation not to be an indifferent onlooker, but to hold out to this development a helping hand ' from above', permeated his life. He was convinced that ' the people ' was ' good '. It was not only his many officials, employees and servants that were dependent on him, but so too, economically, were countless other human beings, and he had never come to know ' the people ' from another side, except on Sundays and holidays, when as a bright, jolly, bustling crowd it came pouring out from behind the scenery like the chorus in the opera. Anything that did not fit in with this conception he therefore attributed to ' subversive elements ' ; to him it was the work of irresponsible, callow and sensation-seeking riff-raff. Having been brought up in a religious and feudal atmosphere, never exposed to contradiction in intercourse with middle-class persons, not without reading, but, as a result of having spent a sheltered youth being educated by priests, all his life long unable to see anything in a book but agreement with or erring divergence from his own principles, he knew the outlook of people who were at home in this epoch only from the controversies going on in Parliament and the newspapers ; and since he had sufficient knowledge to recognise the many superficialities in them, with every day he was confirmed in his prejudice that the true bourgeois world, when more profoundly understood, was nothing other than what he himself meant. In general the expression ' the true ', prefixed to political opinions, was one of his auxiliary means of finding his way about in a world that, though created by God, too often denied Him. He was firmly convinced that even true socialism was in harmony with his own conceptions ; indeed, from the very beginning it was his most personal idea, which he still kept partly concealed even from himself, to build a bridge over which the socialists should march into his camp. It is quite clear, after all, that helping the poor is a knightly task and that for the true aristocracy there can actually be no such great difference between a middle-class factory-owner and one of his workmen. ' After all, we are all socialists at heart,' was a pet saying of his, and meant about as much as, and no more than, that in the next world there are no social distinctions. In this world, however, he considered them necessary facts, and what he expected of the working class was that, if one merely made concessions to it in questions of material welfare, it should dissociate itself from unreasonable slogans brought into its midst from outside and recognise the natural order of things in the world, where everyone had his duties and could flourish in his allotted place. The true nobleman therefore seemed to him as important as the true artisan, and the solution of political and economic questions actually amounted, for him, to a harmonious vision to which he gave the name ' the Country '.

His Highness could not have said how much of this he had been thinking during the quarter of an hour since his secretary left the room. Perhaps all of it. The medium-tall, approximately sixty-year-old man sat motionless at his desk, his hands clasped on his lap, and did not know that he was smiling. He wore a low collar, because he had a tendency to goitre, and an imperial and mustachios—either for the same reason or because it made him look slightly reminiscent of portraits of Bohemian noblemen in the time of Wallenstein. He was framed in a high room, and this in its turn was set in between the big empty spaces of the ante-room and the library, round which again there were laid—shell upon shell—more rooms, quiet, deference, solemnity, and the garland of two sweeping stone staircases. Where these last debouched into the entrance-hall, there in his heavy, braided coat, staff in hand, the tall doorkeeper stood, gazing through the opening of the archway into the bright fluidity of the day, and the pedestrians floated by as though in a goldfish-bowl. On the dividing-line between these two worlds the playful tendrils of a rococo façade rose upward, a façade famed among art historians not only on account of its beauty but also because it was higher than it was broad. It is nowadays considered the first attempt at drawing the skin of a broad, comfortable country manor over

the skeleton of a town house growing tall out of the urban con-
striction of its ground-plan, and hence one of the most important
examples of transition from feudal landed magnificence to the
style of bourgeois democracy.   Here it was that the existence of
the Leinsdorfs passed over—art-historically certified—into the
spirit of the world.   But anyone who did not know this saw as
little of it as a drop of water, skimming by, sees of the sewer-walls.
Such a person noticed only the mellow dim grey of the great
doorway in the otherwise solid street, a surprising, almost exciting
cavity, in the depths of which glimmered the gold of the braid
and of the big knob on the doorkeeper's staff.   In fine weather
this doorkeeper stepped out in front of the entrance.   Then he
stood there like a bright, far-flashing jewel in a row of houses that
never came into anyone's conscious mind, although it was only
their fronts that imprinted upon the multitudinous, anonymous
drifting throngs the orderly pattern of a street.   It is a safe bet
that a large section of the ' people ', over whose ordered existence
Count Leinsdorf ceaselessly and anxiously watched, linked his
name, when it was mentioned, with nothing but the recollection
of this doorkeeper.

But His Highness would not have seen any depreciation in
this.   It was likelier that he would have considered the possession
of such doorkeepers the ' true selflessness ' that befits the bearer
of a noble old name.

22

*The Collateral Campaign, in the shape of
an influential lady of ineffable intellectual
charms, waits in readiness to devour Ulrich.*

IT was this Count Leinsdorf on whom Ulrich should have called
in accordance with Count Stallburg's wish.   But he had resolved
not to do so.   On the other hand, he made up his mind to pay
on his ' grand cousin ' the call that his father had urged upon

him, because he was interested in seeing her for once with his own eyes. Although he did not know her, he had for some time felt a quite special dislike of her, because it was constantly happening that people who knew of the relationship and meant well by him would say: " She's a woman whom you of all people ought to get to know ! " It was always said with that peculiar emphasis on ' you of all people ' that is an attempt to single out the person so addressed as exceptionally equipped for the appreciation of such a jewel, and which may equally well be sincere flattery or a cloak for the conviction that one is just the sort of fool for such an acquaintance. Hence he had already often enquired as to the lady's particular qualities, but he had never received a satisfactory answer. He was told either: " She has an ineffable intellectual charm ", or: " She is the most beautiful and intelligent woman we have ", and some simply said: " She's an ideal woman ! "

" And how old is this lady ? " Ulrich would ask. But nobody knew and the person asked was usually astonished to realise that he himself had never wondered about it.

" And who, anyway—come to think of it—is her lover ? " Ulrich at last asked impatiently.

" A liaison, you mean ? " The not unsophisticated young man, to whom Ulrich put this question, was amazed. " You're right, of course. Nobody would ever dream of supposing such a thing."

' I see—a high-minded beauty,' Ulrich said to himself. ' A second Diotima.' And from that day on he called her so in his thoughts, after that celebrated female philosopher of love.

In reality, however, her name was Ermelinda Tuzzi and in fact, actually, just Hermine. Now although Ermelinda is not even the translation of Hermine, she had one day earned the right to this beautiful name as a result of intuitive inspiration, when it suddenly rang in her mind's ear as a higher truth, even if her husband continued to be called Hans and not Giovanni and in spite of his surname had not learnt the Italian language until he went to the Consular Academy. Ulrich was no less prejudiced against Permanent Secretary Tuzzi than against his wife. In a ministry that, as the Ministry of Foreign Affairs and of the Imperial House, was far more feudal even than the other government departments, he was the only commoner in a position of authority ; he was the head of the most influential department, was considered to be the right hand and, as rumour had it, even the brains of his ministers, and was among the few men who had an influence on the fate of Europe. But when a member of the middle class rises to such a position in such proud surroundings, one is justified in concluding that he has qualities advantageously combining personal indispensability with a faculty of remaining inconspicuously in the background; and Ulrich was not far from imagining this influential Permanent Secretary as a kind of thoroughgoing regimental sergeant-major of cavalry who has to drill highly aristocratic officer-cadets. The fitting complement to this was a spouse whom he imagined, in spite of the lauding of her beauty, as no longer young, ambitious, and encased in a middle-class corset of culture.

But Ulrich's surprise was great. When he called on her, Diotima received him with the indulgent smile of a woman of consequence who knows that she is also beautiful and who must forgive men, superficial creatures that they are, for always thinking first of that.

" I have been expecting you," she said. And Ulrich did not quite know whether this was meant kindly or as a rebuke. The hand that she gave him was pudgy and weightless.

He held it a moment too long. His thoughts were unable to let go of this hand immediately. It lay in his like a fleshy petal; the pointed nails, like a beetle's wings, seemed capable of at any instant flying away with it into improbability. He was overwhelmed by the extravagance of the female hand, of what is a fundamentally pretty shameless human organ, touching everything as a dog's muzzle does, though publicly considered the seat of fidelity, nobility and tenderness. In these seconds he observed that there were several rolls of fat on Diotima's neck, covered with the most delicate of skin; her hair was wound into a Grecian knot, standing out stiffly and in its perfection resembling a wasps' nest. Ulrich felt himself pressed hard by something hostile, by an urge to anger this smiling woman. But he could not quite resist Diotima's beauty.

Diotima, for her part, too, gazed at him long and almost critically. She had heard things about this cousin's private life that to her ears had a slight tinge of the scandalous, and, besides, the man was related to her.

Ulrich perceived that she could not quite avoid being influenced by his appearance. He was used to this. He was clean-shaven, tall, in good training, athletic and supple ; his face was clear and impenetrable ; in short, he sometimes seemed to himself most women's preconceived idea of an impressive youngish man, and simply did not always have the strength to disillusion them in time. But Diotima was resisting it by bestowing on him a compassion that was of the mind. Ulrich noticed that she was studying his appearance, obviously with not unpleasing sensations, while she was perhaps saying to herself that the noble qualities he seemed so perceptibly to possess must be suffocating under a vicious life and ought to be saved. Although she was not much younger than Ulrich and physically in the full blossom of womanhood, something about her suggested a spiritual virginity still in the bud, which formed a strange contrast with her self-possession. So they went on surveying each other even after they had begun to talk.

Diotima opened the conversation by declaring the Collateral Campaign to be an opportunity such as would positively never occur again for giving practical reality to the things one believed greatest and most important. "We must and will give reality to a really great idea. We have the opportunity and we must not fail to rise to the occasion ! "

" Have you something definite in mind ? " Ulrich asked naïvely.

No, Diotima had nothing definite in mind. How could she have ? Nobody who talks about the greatest and most important things in the world means to say that they really exist. But to what strange quality of the world does this correspond ? What it all amounts to is that one thing is greater, more important or more beautiful or sadder than the other, which means a hierarchy of comparatives—and is there then to be no acme, no superlative to this ? If however one points this out to someone who has just begun to talk about what is most great and most important, he will get the suspicion that he is dealing with a callous person quite lacking in ideals. So it went with Diotima, and it was so that Ulrich had spoken.

Being a woman whose mind was generally admired, Diotima found Ulrich's demurring remarks irreverent. After a while she smiled and replied : " There is so much of the great and the good

that has not yet been given practical reality that the choice will
not be easy.   But we shall set up committees from all sections of
the community to assist us.   Or don't you think, Herr von ——,
that it is a tremendous privilege to be in the position to send forth
a call to a whole nation, indeed, even to the entire world, on such
an occasion, summoning it to awaken to spiritual things in the
midst of the hustle and bustle of materialism ?   You must not
assume that our endeavour is directed to anything patriotic in a
sense long obsolete."

Ulrich dodged the issue with a little joke.

Diotima did not laugh ; she merely smiled.   She was accustomed to men of wit ; but they were all something else besides
that.   Paradoxes for the sake of paradox struck her as juvenile,
and this aroused in her the urge to draw the attention of this
relative of hers to the seriousness of real life, which lent the great
patriotic enterprise both dignity and weight.   She now spoke in
a different tone, both closing down and yet again opening up.
Involuntarily Ulrich sought between her words for the black-and-
yellow tape that was used for fastening the files together in government departments.   Yet what fell from Diotima's lips was by no
means only phrases fit for governmental use, but also such expressions of cultural connoisseurship as ' a soulless age, dominated by
mere logic and psychology ' or ' the temporal and the eternal ',
and suddenly in the midst of it all Berlin turned up, together with
the ' treasure-house of feeling ' that was still inherent in the
Austrian spirit in contrast with the Prussian.

Ulrich several times made an attempt to interrupt this speech
from the throne of the mind.   But instantly the incense of
exalted bureaucracy clouded over the interruption, gently blurring
his failure in tact.   Ulrich found it an amazing experience.   He
rose, his first visit being evidently at an end.

In these minutes of withdrawal Diotima treated him with the
bland courtesy—carefully and pointedly a little overdone—that
she had copied from her husband, who made use of it in dealing
with young aristocrats who happened to be his subordinates but
who might some day be his ministers.   In the manner in which
she invited him to come again there was something of the mind's
overweening uncertainty when confronted with a more robust
vitality.   When he was once more holding her mild, weightless

hand in his, they looked into each other's eyes. Ulrich had the definite impression that they were destined to be a great nuisance to each other through love.

' Truly, a hydra of beauty ! ' he thought. He had had the intention of letting the great patriotic campaign wait for him in vain, but it seemed to have assumed form in Diotima, ready to devour him. It was a semi-comical feeling ; in spite of his years and experience he felt like some noxious little worm that was being attentively scrutinised by a large hen. ' For heaven's sake,' Ulrich thought, ' anything so long as I don't let myself be provoked to petty atrocities by this soulful ogress ! ' He had his hands full with his affair with Bonadea and imposed on himself the obligation to observe the utmost restraint.

As he left the flat he was cheered by an agreeable impression that he had already had on his arrival. This was the little maid with the dreamy eyes, who now showed him out. Then, in the darkness of the hall, the glance of her eyes, fluttering up to him for the first time, had been like a black butterfly. Now as he went away it floated down through the darkness like black snow-flakes. There was something Arabian or Algerian-Jewish about the little thing, a suggestion that he had not quite got hold of, something so unobtrusively exquisite that now again he forgot to take a good look at her. Only when he found himself in the street did he feel how uncommonly alive and refreshing the glimpse of that slight creature had been after Diotima's presence.

23   *First intervention on the part of a great man.*

ON Ulrich's departure Diotima and her maid were left behind in a state of faint stimulation. But while the little black lizard, every time she accompanied a distinguished visitor to the door, felt as though she had been allowed to flit up a high, shimmering wall, Diotima treated her recollected impression of Ulrich with the conscientiousness of a woman who does not dislike the awareness of being affected in a not quite appropriate manner, because she feels herself invested with the power of gentle rebuke. Ulrich did not know that on the same day another man had entered her life, one who, as it were, rose up under her like some gigantic mountain with vistas unfolding all around.

Herr Dr. Paul Arnheim had paid a call on her shortly after his arrival.

He was immeasurably rich. His father was the most powerful ruler of 'iron Germany', and even Permanent Secretary Tuzzi had condescended to use this play on words. Tuzzi's principle was that one must be economical in expression and that puns, though one could not quite get on without them in witty conversation, must never be too good, because that was middle-class. He himself had recommended his wife to treat the visitor with marked distinction. For although people of this sort were not yet quite on top in the German Empire and could not compare with the Krupps as regards influence at Court, yet it might, in his opinion, very well be the case tomorrow; and he passed on to her the gist of a confidential rumour according to which this son—who was, as it happened, well into his forties—was far from merely striving to attain his father's position but, backed up by the trend of the times and his international connections, was preparing to take on a position as a minister of the Reich. In Permanent Secretary Tuzzi's opinion this was of course utterly out of the question, unless preceded by a world cataclysm.

He had no notion of what a storm he thus raised in his wife's imagination. It was naturally one of the convictions of her circle that one should not think too highly of anything to do with ' commerce '; but like all people of bourgeois outlook she admired wealth in those depths of the heart that are quite independent of convictions, and the personal encounter with so overwhelmingly rich a man had much the same effect on her as angels' pinions all of gold descending from on high. Ermelinda Tuzzi was not quite unaccustomed to associating with fame and wealth since her husband's rise to his position ; but fame, such as is acquired by intellectual achievements, melts away with remarkable rapidity as soon as one associates with those to whom it attaches, and feudal

wealth either manifests itself as youthful attachés' foolish debts
or is bound up with a traditional style of life, without ever attain-
ing the overbrimmingness of loosely and liberally piled-up mountains of money and the sparkling, cascading, awe-inspiring shower
of the gold with which great banks or world-combines carry on
their business.   The only thing that Diotima knew about banking
was that even employees of only moderate importance travelled
first-class when on duty, while she always had to travel second
when not accompanied by her husband ; and it was accordingly
that she imagined the luxury surrounding the topmost despots of
such an oriental apparatus.

Her little maid Rachel—it goes without saying that Diotima,
when she called her, pronounced the name as though it were
French—had heard things that were ' a dream '.   The least she
had to recount was that the nabob had come in his own private
train, had taken a whole hotel and had a little Negro slave with
him.   The truth was considerably more modest, if only because
Paul Arnheim never behaved ostentatiously.   Only the little
blackamoor was real.   Arnheim had picked him up, while travelling, years earlier, in the extreme South of Italy, among a troop
of dancers, and taken him on partly out of a wish to adorn himself
and partly out of the impulse to raise a human creature out of the
depths and carry out God's work by opening up the life of the mind
to him.   Before long, however, he had lost interest and now used the
boy, who was sixteen years old, only as a servant, whereas before his
fourteenth year he had been giving him Stendhal and Dumas to read.

But although the rumours brought home by her maid were so
childlike in their extravagance that Diotima could not help smiling,
she nevertheless made her repeat it all word for word, for she
found it as unspoilt as things could only be in this one city of
the world, which was ' brimming with culture to the point even
of innocence '.   And remarkably enough, the little black boy
touched even her own imagination.

She was the eldest of the three daughters of a secondary school-
master without private means, so that Tuzzi had been considered
a ' good match ' for her even then, when he was still no more than
an unknown, perfectly middle-class vice-consul.   In her girlhood
she had had nothing but her pride, and as this, in its turn, had
had nothing to be proud of, it had actually been only a rolled-up

correctitude bristling with stiff prickles of sensibility. But even that sometimes conceals ambition and day-dreams and can be a force difficult to assess.

If Diotima had at first been allured by the prospect of far-away complications in far-away countries, disappointment came soon. For all it amounted to after a few years was a discreetly exploited advantage over women friends who envied her for the breath of the exotic that clung to her, and it could not ward off the realisation that in its main outlines life at such posts remains the life one has brought out from home with the rest of one's luggage. Diotima's ambition had for a long time been near to ending up in the genteel hopelessness of the fifth grade of the service, until by chance her husband's ascent suddenly began when a benevolent minister of ' progressive ' outlook took this man of no family into the upper reaches of the Ministry itself. In this position Tuzzi now had many people coming to him, wanting something of him, and from this moment on, almost to her own surprise, something happened to Diotima : there opened up in her a store-house of memories of ' spiritual beauty and grandeur ', which she had allegedly acquired in a cultured parental home and in the great cities of the world, but in fact doubtless as a model pupil at a girl's high school ; and this she began carefully turning to account. The sober but singularly reliable intelligence of her husband inevitably attracted attention to her too, and now, as soon as she became aware that her intellectual merits were appreciated, she began with great enjoyment weaving in little ' high-minded ' ideas at suitable places in her conversation, all with utter naïvety, like a moist little sponge oozing out again what it has soaked up to no particular purpose. And gradually, while her husband continued to ascend, more and more people came seeking association with him, and her home became a ' salon ', gaining the reputation of a meeting-place for ' society and intelligentsia '. And now, in intercourse with people who were of some consequence in various fields, Diotima also began seriously discovering herself. Her correctitude, which went on minding its P's and Q's and paying attention just as in school, accurately remembering what it learnt and blending it all into an amicable unity, practically of its own accord turned into a mind, simply by extension, and the Tuzzi at-homes acquired a recognised position.

24   *Culture and Capital. Diotima's friend-*
          ship with Count Leinsdorf, and the office
          of getting distinguished visitors into accord
          with the soul.

BUT they only became an established institution through
Diotima's friendship with His Highness the Count Leinsdorf.

Speaking in terms of the parts of the body after which friendships are called : Count Leinsdorf's feeling of friendship was so
situated between head and heart that one could not describe
Diotima as anything but his bosom friend, if that expression were
still in use. His Highness revered Diotima's mind and beauty,
without permitting himself any unseemly intentions. Through
his patronage Diotima's *salon* not only gained an unshakable
position but—as he was accustomed to put it himself—fulfilled
an office.

Where he himself was concerned, His Highness the Imperial
Liege-Count was 'merely a patriot'. But the State does not
consist only of the Crown and the people, with the government
machinery in between ; there is yet something else in it : thought,
morality, the idea . . . ! However religious His Highness might
be, he did not shut his eyes—being penetrated as he was with a
sense of responsibility and having, moreover, set up factories on
his estates—to the recognition that nowadays the mind had in
many respects freed itself from the tutelage of the Church. For
he could not imagine how for instance a factory, or a Stock
Exchange manoeuvre in grain or sugar, could be conducted according to religious principles, while on the other hand modernised
large-scale landowning was rationally unthinkable without the
Stock Exchange and industry. And when he listened to his
business manager's statement and it became clear to him that a
certain deal could be done better in association with a foreign
group of speculators than shoulder to shoulder with the landowning nobility of his own country, His Highness in most cases
felt himself compelled to decide for the former ; for the practical

relatedness of things has a mind of its own, which one can't run counter to simply for sentimental reasons, when, as the head of a great estate, one is responsible not only for oneself but also for innumerable other people's welfare. There is such a thing as the professional conscience, which in certain circumstances is antagonistic to the religious conscience; and Count Leinsdorf was convinced that even the Cardinal Archbishop in such a case could not act differently from the way he did himself. Admittedly, Count Leinsdorf was also always willing to deplore this in public sessions of the Upper House and to utter the hope that life would return to the simplicity, naturalness, supernaturalness, soundness and inevitability of Christian principles. Whenever he opened his mouth to make such pronouncements, it was as though a contact-pin had been pulled out, and he flowed in a different circuit. And for that matter the same thing happens to most people when they speak in public. If anyone had charged Count Leinsdorf with doing for his private benefit what he combated in public, His Highness would, with sacred conviction, have stigmatised it as the demagogic talk of subversive elements lacking any notion of the extent of life's responsibilities. Nevertheless, he himself recognised that a connection between the eternal verities and business, which is so involved in contrast with the beautiful simplicity of tradition, was a matter of the greatest importance; and he had also come to recognise that this connection was not likely to be found anywhere but in the essence of bourgeois culture, which, with its great ideas and ideals in the spheres of law, duty, morality and beauty, extended even into the struggles of the day and everyday antagonisms and seemed to him like a bridge consisting of entangled living plants. True, it did not offer as firm and solid a foothold as the dogmas of the Church, but it was no less necessary and laden with responsibility; and for this reason Count Leinsdorf was not only a religious idealist but also a passionate idealist in secular matters.

It was entirely in keeping with these convictions of His Highness's that Diotima's *salon* was constituted. Her at-homes were famous for the fact that on 'great days' one ran into people with whom one could not exchange a single word, because they were too well known in some special field to be talked to about the latest news, while on the other hand it often happened that one had never before heard the name of the domain of knowledge in which they had earned world fame. One was quite likely to meet Kenzinists and Canisians, a Bo philologist might come up against a man doing partigen research, or a tokontologist against a quantum physicist, to say nothing of the representatives of those new movements in art and literature that changed their labels every year, who were allowed to put in an appearance there in limited numbers alongside such of their fellow-artists as had already reached the top. In general these gatherings were organised in such a way that all these people were jumbled up together and allowed to blend harmoniously. It was only the younger intelligentsia that Diotima usually kept apart by means of separate invitations, and the rare or special guest was something she had an unobtrusive way of singling out and, as it were, framing. And then, too, what distinguished Diotima's at-homes from all similar affairs was precisely—if it may be put so—the lay element, the representatives of the world of practically applied ideas, in short, the element of 'action'. This element—to use Diotima's own words—had once crystallised round the nucleus of divine studies, a community of toiling believers, indeed an order composed solely of lay brothers and sisters. But today, when divine studies had been driven to the wall by economics and physics, and her invitation-list of the spirit's stewards upon earth gradually began to resemble the Royal Society's Catalogue of Scientific Papers, the lay brothers and sisters consisted, correspondingly, of bankers, architects and engineers, politicians, senior civil servants, and ladies and gentlemen of high society and such circles as mixed with it. It was particularly the women that Diotima made a point of, though giving preference to 'ladies' rather than to 'intellectual women'. "Life today is overburdened with knowledge," she used to say, "too much so for us to be able to do without the Integral Woman." She was convinced that only the Integral Woman still possessed the magical radiation that could envelop the intellect with the forces of life itself, which, to her way of thinking, the intellect was obviously in dire need of for its salvation. This theory of the enveloping woman and the forces of life redounded, furthermore, much to her credit among those young noblemen who frequented her at-homes because it was considered 'the thing' and also because

Permanent Secretary Tuzzi was quite well liked ; for the idea of Non-Fractional Life is of course the very thing for the nobility. And, coming down to particularities, Diotima's drawing-room, where one could become absorbed in conversations *à deux* without attracting attention, was, without Diotima's having the slightest notion of it, even more favoured as a place for tender meetings and long heart-to-heart talks than even a church.

His Highness Count Leinsdorf—when he did not happen to be calling them ' the true élite '—summed up these two elements, so various in themselves, that intermingled at Diotima's in the term ' culture and capital '.   But he liked even better to think of them in terms of ' office ', that conception occupying a privileged place in his mind.   He held the view that every form of productivity —not only that of a civil servant, but equally that of a factory-worker or a concert-singer—represented an ' office '.   " Every-one," he was accustomed to say, " holds an office in the State— the working-man, the prince, the artisan, all are officials ! "   This was an emanation of his perpetual and in all circumstances impersonal way of thinking, which knew no favouritism, and in his eyes the gentlemen and ladies of the highest society, by chatting with the learned specialists on Boghaz Keui inscriptions or lamellibranchiate *Mollusca* and smiling upon the wives of high-financiers, were also carrying out an important, even though not precisely definable office.   This idea of ' office ' was for him the substitute for what Diotima referred to as that unity of religious feeling in all human activities that has been lost since the Middle Ages.

And fundamentally, all such enforced sociability as that at her at-homes, if it is not utterly naïve and uncouth, does spring from a need to create the illusion of a human unity embracing humanity's extremely varied activities, a unity that in fact never exists.   This illusion Diotima called ' culture ', and usually, with a special amplification, ' our old Austrian culture '.   This was an expression that she had learnt to make more and more frequent use of since her ambition had become spiritualised by expansion. What she meant by it was : the beautiful paintings of Velasquez and Rubens that hung in the Imperial museums ; the fact that Beethoven had been to all intents and purposes an Austrian ; Mozart, Haydn, the Cathedral of St. Stephen, the Burgtheater ;

the Court ceremonial heavy with the weight of tradition; the Innere Stadt, the district where the smartest *couturiers* and dress-shops of an empire with fifty million inhabitants were crowded together; the tactful demeanour of high officials; Viennese cookery; the aristocracy, which considered itself second to none except the English, and its ancient palaces; the social tone, which was permeated with sometimes genuine, but usually sham aestheticism. Another thing she meant by it was the fact that in this country so great a nobleman as Count Leinsdorf gave her his attention and transferred his own endeavours in the cause of culture to her house. She did not know that His Highness did this also because it seemed to him unfitting to open the doors of his own ancestral mansion to an innovation that might easily get out of control. Count Leinsdorf was often secretly dismayed by the freedom and indulgence with which his beautiful friend spoke of human passions and the confusions that they caused, or of revolutionary ideas. But Diotima did not notice this. She drew a line between what might be called official unchastity and private chastity, like a woman doctor or a woman social-welfare worker; she was as sensitive as though a sore spot had been touched if a word bore too personal a meaning, but so long as discussion remained impersonal she would talk about anything and could not feel otherwise than that Count Leinsdorf appeared to be greatly attracted by this mixture.

However, life does not build anything up without tearing the stones out somewhere else. To Diotima's sad surprise, a very small, dream-sweet almond-kernel of fantasy, which had once been the core of her existence when there was as yet nothing else in it and which had still been there when she made up her mind to marry that Vice-Consul Tuzzi who looked like a leather cabin-trunk with two dark eyes, had vanished in the years of success. Admittedly, much of what she meant by ' old Austrian culture ', such as Haydn or the Hapsburgs, had once been only a tiresome school-task, whereas now the knowledge that she herself was living in the midst of all this seemed enchantingly delightful and every bit as heroic as the midsummer hum of bees; in time, however, it became not merely monotonous but also strenuous and even hopeless. Diotima fared not otherwise with her famous guests than Count Leinsdorf with his banking connections:

however much one wished to get them into harmony with the soul, it would not work.   Motor-cars and X-rays, of course, were something one could talk about and even have some feelings about. But what was one to do about all the countless other inventions and discoveries that every day now brought forth ? what, except in a very general way admire human inventiveness ?—which at length begins to be rather a drag !

His Highness would drop in occasionally and talk to a politician or have a new guest introduced to him, and it was all very well for him to be enthusiastic about the profounder aspects of culture. But when one was on such close terms with it as Diotima was, it became apparent that the insuperable difficulty lay not in the depth but in the extent of it.   Even problems affecting one's own humanity so closely as, for instance, the noble simplicity of Greece, or the meaning of the prophets, resolved themselves, in one's conversation with experts, into an immense variety of doubts and possibilities.   Diotima learned from experience that even her distinguished visitors always talked in twos on her ' evenings ', for already at that time no man could talk sensibly and to the point with more than at the most one other person ; and she could not really do it with one.   In realising this, however, Diotima discovered in herself the affliction from which modern man is well known to suffer and which is called civilisation.   It is a frustrating state of affairs, full of soap, wireless waves, the arrogant symbolic language of mathematical and chemical formulae, economics, experimental research and mankind's inability to live in simple but sublime community.   And, in addition, the relationship of her own indwelling nobility of mind to the social nobility, a relationship that obliged her to observe great caution and in spite of all her successes earned her many a disappointment, in the course of time seemed to her increasingly of a kind typifying an age not of culture but merely of civilisation.

Accordingly civilisation meant, for her, everything that her mind could not cope with.   And hence too it had for a long time meant, first and foremost, her husband.

25 *Sufferings of a soul in matrimony.*

IN her sufferings she read a great deal and discovered that she had lost something, the possession of which she had previously not been much aware of : a soul.

What is that ? It is easily defined negatively : it is simply what curls up and hides when there is any mention of algebraic series.

But positively ? It appears that this is where it successfully eludes all efforts to grasp it. It may be that there had once been something fresh and natural in Diotima, an intuitive sensibility, at that time rolled up in the dress of her correctitude, which was threadbare from much brushing, something that she now called ' soul ' and rediscovered in Maeterlinck's batik-adorned metaphysics, in Novalis, but above all in the indescribable wave of skim-romanticism and yearning for God that the machine-age had for a time squirted out as an expression of spiritual and artistic protest against itself. It is also possible that this fresh and natural element in Diotima could be more precisely defined as something made up of stillness, gentleness, devotion and kindness, which had never got on the right road and, in the oracular casting of the lead that fate performs with us, had happened to set in the comical shape of her idealism. Perhaps it was imagination, or perhaps it was an inexpressible awareness of those instinctive, vegetative workings that go on underground, day after day, inside the husk of the body, that shining envelope which radiates the soulful expression of a beautiful woman gazing out at us. Perhaps it was only at certain indefinable hours that she felt widened and warm in herself, when her sensations seemed more inspired than usual, when volition and ambition fell silent, and she was seized with a hushed rapture at being alive, at the fullness of life ; and then her thoughts veered far away from the surface and down into the depths, even if only concerned with the smallest of things, and world events were remote as noise beyond a garden wall. It seemed to Diotima then that she had an immediate vision of truth within herself, quite effortlessly ; delicate experiences, as yet without a name, raised their veils; and she felt herself—to quote only some of the many descriptions that she found to hand in literature—harmonious, humane, religious, near to primal depths that sanctify everything rising out of them and make everything that does not have its source in them seem sinful. But even though all this was quite beautiful to think about, such hints and glimpses of a peculiar state were something that not only Diotima never got beyond; neither did the prophetic books that she consulted, which spoke of the same state in the same vague and mysterious language. Diotima was left with no alternative but to lay the blame for this also on an age of civilisation in which—this was the long and the short of it—the portals of the soul had been buried under a landslide.

Probably what she called 'soul' was nothing but a small capital of capacity for love that she had possessed at the time of her marriage. Permanent Secretary Tuzzi was not the right stock to invest it in. His superiority over Diotima had at first and for a long time afterwards been that of an older man; later there was added to this the superiority of the successful man in a mysterious position, who gives his wife little insight into himself and looks on indulgently at the trivialities that keep her busy. And apart from the period of honeymoon caresses, Permanent Secretary Tuzzi had always been a utilitarian and a rationalist, who never lost his equilibrium. Nevertheless, the well-cut repose of his actions and of his suits, the—one might almost say—urbanely grave aroma of his body and beard, the circumspectly firm baritone of his speaking-voice, all surrounded him with an aura that excited the soul of the girl Diotima similarly as the proximity of his master excites the soul of a retriever laying his muzzle on that master's knee. And just as a dog, wrapt in his sentimental satisfaction, trots along at heel, so Diotima too, under serious-minded, matter-of-fact guidance, had entered into the boundless landscape of love.

Here Permanent Secretary Tuzzi preferred the straight paths. His habits were those of an ambitious worker. He rose early, in order either to ride or, preferably, to take an hour's walk, which not only served to preserve the elasticity of his muscles but also typified a pedantically simple custom, which, carried out with unvarying regularity, fitted perfectly into the picture of responsibility and achievement. And it goes without saying that in the evenings, when they were not going out and had no visitors, he soon withdrew to his study ; for he was obliged to keep his great store of expert information at the height that constituted his superiority over his nobly born colleagues and chiefs. Such a life sets definite bounds and fits love into its proper place among all other activities. Like all men whose imagination is not seared by eroticism, in his bachelor days—even though he had now and then for the sake of diplomatic appearances shown up in the company of his friends with little chorus-girls—Tuzzi had been a quiet *habitué* of bawdy-houses, and he transferred the regular rhythm of this custom into his marriage. So Diotima learned to know love as something violent, spasmodic and abrupt, which was set free by an even stronger force only once in every week. This transformation in two people's nature, which began to the minute and a few minutes later passed over into a short conversation about such of the day's events as had not yet been discussed and thence into sound sleep, something of which, in the intervals, one never spoke, or at least only in hints and allusions (such as, for instance, making a diplomatic joke about the ' *patrie honteuse* ' of the body), nevertheless had unexpected and contradictory consequences for her.

On the one hand, it was the cause of her excessively inflated idealism, of that semi-official, extraverted personality whose capacity for love and whose spiritual yearning extended to everything great and noble that loomed up in her environment, sharing itself out among such things and linking itself with them so intensely that Diotima made that impression, so bewildering to masculine preconceptions, of a mightily blazing but platonic sun of love, the description of which had aroused Ulrich's curiosity to make her acquaintance. On the other hand, however, the broad rhythm of conjugal intimacy had in her developed, purely physiologically, into a habit that travelled along its own orbit and asserted itself, without relation to the higher aspects of her being, like the hunger of a farm-hand whose meals are few but nourishing. In time, when little hairs were beginning to sprout on Diotima's upper lip and her girlish nature was gradually taking on the masculine independence of the mature woman, this came as a shock to her consciousness. She loved her husband, but with a growing admixture of abhorrence, indeed a terrible affrontedness of soul, which ultimately could only be compared to the sensations that Archimedes, absorbed in working out his great problems, might have had if the foreign soldier, instead of slaying him, had made an indecent suggestion to him. And since her husband neither noticed this nor would have thought the same way, and since her body in the end and against her own will betrayed her to him every time, she felt herself in thrall to a despotic regime ; doubtless it was one that counted as not unvirtuous, but the course of it was exactly as tormenting to her as she imagined the emergence of a tic would be, or the inexorability of a vice. Diotima might perhaps as a result have only become a shade melancholy and yet more idealistic ; but unfortunately all this began precisely at the time when her *salon* was also beginning to cause her spiritual difficulties.

Permanent Secretary Tuzzi quite naturally encouraged his wife's intellectual exertions, since he had soon realised the advantage bound up with them where his own position was concerned ; but he had never taken a share in them, and it can be safely said that he did not take them seriously. For the only things this experienced man took seriously were power, duty, high birth and, some way further down the scale, reason. He even warned Diotima repeatedly against putting too much ambition into her management of cultural relations ; for although culture was, in a manner of speaking, the salt in the dish of life, yet the best society did not care for an over-salted cuisine. He said this entirely without irony, for it was his conviction. But Diotima felt herself disparaged. She felt the constant hovering of a smile with which her husband followed her ideal exertions. And whether he was at home or not, and whether this smile—if indeed he did smile, which was by no means always sure—was directed especially at her or was only part of the facial expression of a man who for professional reasons always had to look superior, in time it became more and more unendurable to her, without her being able to escape from the preposterous appearance of justification that it assumed. From time to time she put the blame on a materialistic period of history, which had turned the world into a wicked, futile game, the atheism, socialism, and positivism of which made it impossible for a human being with a soul to find the freedom in which to rise to his or her true nature. But even that point of view was not often of any use.

That was the way things stood in the Tuzzi household when the great patriotic Campaign quickened the pace of events. Ever since Count Leinsdorf, not wishing to compromise the nobility, had set up the Campaign's headquarters in Diotima's house, an atmosphere of untold responsibility had prevailed there ; for Diotima had made up her mind to prove to her husband, now or never, that her *salon* was no mere plaything. The Count had confided in her that the great patriotic Campaign needed a crowning idea, and it was her burning ambition to find it. The thought of having to give reality to something that was meant to be culture at its greatest and best, or, limited to more modest dimensions, perhaps something that would reveal the inmost essence of Austrian culture—and this with the apparatus of a whole empire at her disposal and before the watchful eyes of the world—had much the same effect on Diotima as if the door of her drawing-room had sprung open and there, lapping against the threshold, a continuation of the floor, had been the boundless sea.

It could not be denied that the first thing she felt at this point was the sudden opening up of an immeasurable void.

There is so often something in first impressions ! Diotima was sure that something incomparable was going to happen, and summoned up her many ideals ; she mobilised the high drama of the history lessons she had had as a little girl, when she had learnt to reckon in terms of empires and centuries ; she did absolutely everything that must be done in such a situation. But after some weeks had passed in this way, she could not help noticing that she had not had any inspirations. What she felt towards her husband at that moment would have been hatred if she had been at all capable of such a low emotion as hatred. As things were, it turned into melancholy, and she developed a hitherto unknown ' grudge against everything '.

It was at this point that Herr Dr. Arnheim arrived, accompanied by his little blackamoor, and shortly afterwards paid his momentous call on Diotima.

26

The union of soul and economics. The man who can accomplish this wants to enjoy the baroque enchantment of old Austrian culture.
Hence an idea is born to the Collateral Campaign.

DIOTIMA did not know what wrong thoughts were. But on this day there was probably a great deal hidden behind the thought of the innocent little black boy that had preoccupied her ever since she had sent her maid ' Rachelle ' out of the room. This mature and beautiful woman had kindly listened to the maid's story once again after Ulrich's departure, and she felt quite young and as though she were playing with a tinkling toy. Once upon a time the nobility, high society, had kept blackamoors. She called to mind charming pictures of sleigh-drives with gaily caparisoned horses, plumed lackeys and frost-white, glittering trees ; but this romantic side of high life had long vanished. ' Society life has become soulless nowadays,' she thought. There was something in her heart that took the part of the dashing outsider who was bold enough to keep a blackamoor, this urbane intruder who overstepped the limits of bourgeois decorum and put to shame the mighty lords with their inherited tradition, as once the learned Greek slave had put his Roman masters to shame. Her self-confidence, cramped and paralysed as it was by all sorts of scruples, went over to him with flying colours as a sister-spirit. And this emotion, very natural in comparison with all her other emotions, even made her overlook the fact that Herr Dr. Arnheim was said—although rumour was still contradictory and there was as yet no reliable information—to be of Jewish descent ; so much was indeed definitely asserted of his father, only his mother was so long dead that it would be some time before the facts could be established. For the rest, it was not impossible that a certain cruelly elegiac feeling in Diotima's heart did not even desire a *démenti*.

In a gingerly fashion Diotima allowed her thoughts to leave the blackamoor and approach his master.   Herr Dr. Paul Arnheim was not only a rich man ; he was also a man of notable intellect. His fame extended beyond the fact that he was the heir to world-wide business undertakings ; in his leisure hours he had written books that in advanced circles were regarded as outstanding.   The people who form such purely intellectual circles are above con-siderations of money and social distinction ; but it must not be forgotten that for this very reason there is a special fascination in it for them when a rich man decides to become one of them ; and what was more, in his pamphlets and books Arnheim preached nothiṇg less than precisely the union of soul and economics, or of ideas and power.   The sensitive minds of the time, endowed with the finest capacity for picking up the scent of things to come, spread the tidings that he in himself united these two poles, usually separate in the world, and they encouraged the rumour that here a modern force was on the way, ordained—when the time came—to guide the destinies of the Reich and, who knows, perhaps of the world too, towards better days.   For there had long been a widespread feeling that the principles and actions of old-style politics and diplomacy were driving Europe, post-haste, straight into the ditch ; and in fact the period of turning away from the specialists had even then set in everywhere.

Diotima's state of mind too could be expressed in terms of ervolt against the mode of thought of the older school of diplomacy. That was why she instantly understood the marvellous similarity between her position and that of this extremely brilliant outsider. Moreover, the famous man had called on her at the earliest possible instant, her house being by a long way the first to be distinguished in this manner ; and the letter of introduction written to her by a woman friend they had in common spoke of the age-old culture of the Hapsburg capital and its people, which this hard-worked man hoped to enjoy in the time left over from unavoidable business.   Diotima felt as eminent as a writer who is for the first time translated into the language of a foreign country, when she gathered from this that this famous foreigner knew of her intellectual renown.   She observed that he did not look in the least Jewish ; he was a polished and deliberate man of an ancient-Phoenician cast of features.   And Arnheim too was delighted when in Diotima he met a woman who had not only read his books but, as a Grecian figure swathed in almost imperceptible plumpness, corresponded to his ideal of beauty, which was Hellenic, only with a bit more flesh on it so as to make the classical line a little less rigid. It was not long before Diotima realised what an impression she was capable of making on a man of really international connections, in a conversation of twenty minutes' duration, and this was sufficient to dispel utterly all the doubts that her husband, biased by somewhat old-fashioned diplomatic methods, had inspired in her mind by casting aspersions on her importance.

With quiet, comfortable pleasure she went over the conversation in her thoughts. Almost the first thing Arnheim had said was that he had only come to this ancient city in order somewhat to recuperate, in the baroque enchantment of old Austrian culture, from the calculations, the materialism, the bleak rationalism in which civilised man nowadays toiled.

Indeed, there was such a blithe soulfulness about this city, Diotima had replied. And she was well content with that.

"Yes," he had said, "there are no longer any inner voices in us. We know too much these days. Reason tyrannises over our lives."

Thereupon she had replied: "I like to be with women, because they know nothing, they are integral."

And Arnheim had said: "And yet a beautiful woman understands far more than a man, who for all his logic and psychology knows nothing about life."

And then she had begun to tell him that a problem similar to that of the soul's liberation from civilisation, only projected into monumental and national terms, was occupying influential circles here. "One ought—" she had said, and Arnheim had interrupted her, exclaiming that this was quite wonderful, "one ought to bring new ideas, or, if one may put it so," here he had sighed faintly, "simply, for the first time, bring ideas into the domains of power." And she had gone on to say that it was intended to form committees, drawn from all sections of the community, in order to ascertain what these ideas were.

It was at this point that Arnheim had said something exceedingly important, uttering a warning in such a tone of warm friendship and respect that it left a deep mark on Diotima's mind.

It would not be easy—he had exclaimed—to bring about something great in such a manner. It was not a democracy of committees, but only individual strong personalities, deeply versed both in reality and in the realm of ideas, that would be capable of conducting this Campaign !

So far Diotima had gone over the conversation to herself word for word. But at this stage it dissolved into sheer splendour ; she could not remember what she herself had answered. A vague, thrilling sensation of happiness and expectancy had been carrying her higher and higher all this time, until now her mind was like a bright little toy balloon that had broken loose and was floating, gloriously radiant, high up towards the sun. And in the next instant it burst.

This was how an idea was born to the great Collateral Campaign, one that had hitherto been lacking.

27   *The nature and substance of a great idea.*

IT would be easy to say what this idea was, but nobody could possibly describe the significance of it ! For what distinguishes an overwhelmingly great idea from an ordinary, perhaps even incomprehensibly ordinary and mistaken one, is the fact that it is in a kind of molten state, as a result of which the ego enters into infinite expanses and the expanses of the universe enter into the ego, whereby it ceases to be possible to recognise what belongs to oneself and what to the infinite. Hence overwhelmingly great ideas consist of a body, which, like the human body, is compact but perishable, and of an eternal soul, which is what lends them their significance, but which is not compact—on the contrary, at every attempt to get hold of it in cold words it evaporates into nothingness.

After this preamble it must be said that what Diotima's great idea amounted to was simply that Arnheim, the Prussian, must take over the spiritual leadership of the great Austrian Campaign, even although this Campaign had a jealous sting aimed at Prussia-Germany.   But that is only the dead verbal body of the idea, and anyone who thinks it incomprehensible or ridiculous is maltreating a corpse.   As for the soul of the idea, however, it must be said that it was a chaste and proper one; and for all eventualities Diotima attached to her resolve, as it were, a reservation in favour of Ulrich.   She did not know that her cousin had also made an impression on her—although at a far lower level than Arnheim and screened by the effect of the latter—and she would probably have despised herself if it had become clear to her.   Instinctively, however, she had taken counter-measures by declaring him ' immature ' in the court of her consciousness, although Ulrich was older than herself.   She had made up her mind to be sorry for him, and this made it easier to arrive at the conviction that it was a duty to elect Arnheim instead of him to the leadership of this Campaign, with all its responsibilities; but then again, after she had given birth to this resolve, the feminine notion asserted itself that the slighted party was now in need of and deserving of her help.   If there was anything he lacked, there was no better way for him to obtain it than by co-employment in the great Campaign, which would offer him an opportunity to spend a great deal of time in her and Arnheim's proximity.   So Diotima resolved on this too.   These, however, were merely supplementary considerations.

28

A chapter that can be skipped by anyone who has no very high opinion of thinking as an occupation.

MEANWHILE Ulrich was at home, sitting at his desk, working. He had got out the analysis that he had broken off short some weeks earlier when he had made his decision to return from abroad. He did not intend finishing it ; it merely pleased him that he was still capable of doing this sort of thing. The weather was fine, but in the last few days he had only left the house on brief errands and did not even go into the garden. He had drawn the curtains and was working by shaded light, like an acrobat in the semi-darkness of a circus, performing dangerous new leaps in front of a gathering of experts before the public are let in. The precision, vigour and sureness of this kind of thinking, which has not its equal anywhere in life, filled him with something like melancholy.

He now pushed away the paper, covered with formulae and symbols, on which the last thing he had written was an equation of state of water, as a physical example, in order to apply a new mathematical operation that he was describing. But his thoughts must have strayed some time before that.

' Wasn't I talking to Clarisse about something to do with water ? ' he wondered, but could not clearly recollect. Still, it did not matter. His thoughts wandered on, idly.

Unfortunately nothing is so difficult to represent by literary means as a man thinking. A great scientist, when he was once asked how he managed to hit upon so much that was new, replied : " By keeping on thinking about it." And indeed it may safely be said that unexpected inspirations are produced by no other means than by the expectation of them. To no small extent they are a success due to character, permanent inclinations, unflagging ambition and persistent work. How boring such persistence must be ! And then again, from another aspect, the solution of an intellectual problem comes about in a way not very different from what happens when a dog carrying a stick in its mouth tries to get through a narrow door : it will go on turning its head left and right until the stick slips through. We do pretty much the same, only with the difference that we do not go at it quite indiscriminately, but from experience know more or less how it should be done. And although of course a head with brains in it has far more skill and experience in these turnings and twistings than an empty one, yet even for it the slipping through comes as a surprise, is something that just suddenly happens ; and one can quite distinctly perceive in oneself a faintly nonplussed feeling that one's thoughts have created themselves instead of waiting for their originator. This nonplussed feeling refers to something that many people nowadays call intuition, whereas formerly it used also to be called inspiration, and they think they must see something suprapersonal in it; but it is only something non-personal, namely the affinity and kinship of the things themselves that meet inside one's head.

The better the head, the less perceptible it is in all this. Hence thinking, so long as it is not completed, is really a thoroughly wretched condition to be in, not unlike a colic affecting all the convolutions of the brain ; and when it is complete, it no longer has the shape of the thought, the shape in which it was experienced, but has already taken on the shape of the thing thought, and this unfortunately is a non-personal shape, for the thought is then extraverted and adjusted for communication to the world. One cannot, so to speak, catch hold, when a man is thinking, of the moment between the personal and the non-personal. And for this reason thinking is obviously such a source of embarrassment to writers that they prefer to avoid it.

However, the Man Without Qualities was now thinking. From this the conclusion may be drawn that it was at least partly not a personal matter. What then was it ? The world going in and out, aspects of the world falling into shape inside a head . . . Nothing in the least important had occurred to him. After he had been dealing with water by way of example, nothing else occurred to him but that water is something three times as great as land, even if one takes into account only what everyone recognises as water—rivers, seas, lakes, and springs. It was long believed to be akin to air. The great Newton believed this, and most of his ideas are nevertheless still quite up to date. In the Greek view the world and life originated from water. It was a god, Okeanos. Later water-sprites, elves, mermaids and nymphs were invented. Temples and oracles were founded on its banks and shores. But were not the cathedrals of Hildesheim, Paderborn and Bremen built over springs ?—and here these cathedrals were to this day. And was not water still used for baptism ? And were there not water-lovers and apostles of nature-cures whose souls had a touch of peculiarly sepulchral health ? So there was somewhere in the world something like a blurred spot, or grass trodden flat.   And of course the Man Without Qualities also had modern knowledge somewhere in his consciousness, whether he happened to be thinking about it or not.   And there now was water, a colourless liquid, blue only in dense layers, odourless and tasteless (as one had repeated in school so often that one could never forget it again), although physiologically it also included bacteria, vegetable matter, air, iron, calcium sulphate and calcium bicarbonate, and this archetype of all liquids was, physically speaking, fundamentally not a liquid at all but, according to circumstances, a solid body, a liquid or a gas.   Ultimately the whole thing dissolved into systems of formulae that were all some-how connected with each other, and in the whole wide world there were only a few dozen people who thought alike about even as simple a thing as water ; all the rest talked about it in languages that were at home somewhere between today and several thousands of years ago.   So it must be said that if a man just starts thinking a bit he gets into what one might call pretty disorderly company.

And now Ulrich remembered too that he had actually said all this to Clarisse.   She was as ignorant as a little animal, but in spite of all the superstition of which she was made up, one vaguely felt a sense of community with her.   It gave him a prick like a hot needle.

He felt annoyed.

The well-known capacity that thoughts have—as doctors have discovered—for dissolving and dispersing those hard lumps of deep, ingrowing, morbidly entangled conflict that arise out of gloomy regions of the self probably rests on nothing other than their social and worldly nature, which links the individual being with other people and things ; but unfortunately what gives them their power of healing seems to be the same as what diminishes the quality of personal experience in them.   The casual mention of a hair on a nose weighs more than the most significant thought ; and acts, feelings and sensations when repeated convey the impres-sion that one has been present at an occurrence, a more or less great personal event, however ordinary and non-personal they may have been.

' Silly,' Ulrich thought, ' but there it is.'   It reminded him of that stupidly profound, exciting sensation, touching immediately

on the self, that one has when sniffing at one's own skin.   He
stood up and pulled the curtains back from the window.

The bark of the trees was still moist with morning dew.   Outside in the street there lay a violet-blue haze of petrol-vapour.
The sun was shining into it, and people were moving briskly.   It
was like spring hovering over the tarmac, an out-of-season spring
day in autumn, a day such as only cities conjure forth.

29   *Explanation and interruptions of a normal state of consciousness.*

ULRICH had agreed with Bonadea on a signal to show that he
was alone at home.   He was always alone now, but he did not
give the signal.   So he must long have been expecting Bonadea
to walk in, in hat and veil, all uninvited.   For Bonadea was beyond
all measure jealous.   And when she went to see a man—and even
if it was only to tell him that she despised him—she always arrived
in a state of inner weakness, with the impressions received on the
way and the glances of the men she had passed still rocking in
her like faint sea-sickness.   But when the man, divining this,
made straight for her, although for a long time he had been
neglecting her quite callously, she would be hurt and squabble
with him and make reproachful remarks, so postponing what she
herself could hardly bear to wait for any longer, somewhat resembling a duck, shot through the wings, that had fallen into the sea
of love and was trying to save itself by swimming.

And all at once there Bonadea really sat, weeping and feeling
ill-used.

At such moments, when she was annoyed with her lover, she·
mentally craved her husband's forgiveness for her misdemeanours.
According to a good old rule that unfaithful wives follow in order
to avoid betraying themselves by some careless word, she had told
him about the interesting scientist whom she sometimes met at

the house of a woman friend, but whom she did not ask to call because he was too much spoilt by social success to come to their place of his own accord and she did not care for him sufficiently to invite him in spite of that. The half-truth contained in this made it easier for her to lie, and for the other half she bore a grudge against her lover. What was her husband to think, she wondered, if now all at once she was again to cut down her pretended visits to her friend ? How was she to make him understand such fluctuations in her likings ? She valued truth highly, because she valued all ideals highly, and Ulrich was dishonouring her by obliging her to diverge further from it than necessary.

She made a tremendous scene; and when it was over, reproaches, asseverations and kisses cascaded into the vacuum thus created. And when that also was over, everything was just as it had been before. Regurgitating gossip filled the void, and time developed little bubbles like a glass of stale water.

' How much more beautiful she is when she gets wild,' Ulrich reflected, ' and how mechanically everything has happened all over again.' The sight of her had stirred him and moved him to caresses. Now, when it was all over, he felt again how little it concerned him. The incredible swiftness of such transformations, which turn a sane man into a frothing lunatic, now became all too strikingly clear. But it seemed to him that this erotic metamorphosis of consciousness was only a special case of something far more general ; for nowadays all manifestations of our inner life, such as for instance an evening at the theatre, a concert, or a church service, are such swift appearing and disappearing islands of a second state of consciousness temporarily interpolated into the ordinary one.

' And yet a short time ago I was still at work,' he thought, ' and before that I was walking down the street to buy paper. I said good-morning to a man I know from the Society of Physicists. I had a serious discussion with him a little while ago. And now, if Bonadea would only hurry up a bit, I could look something up in the books I can see over there, through the half-open door. Yet in the mean time we have been flying through a cloud of madness, and it is no less uncanny how the solid experiences close up again over that vanishing gap and re-assert themselves in all their tenacity.'

But Bonadea did not hurry, and Ulrich had to think about something else. His boyhood friend Walter, little Clarisse's husband who had grown so odd, had once said of him : " Ulrich always puts tremendous energy into doing the very things he doesn't consider necessary." He remembered it at this very moment and thought : ' That could be said about all of us today.' He recalled the scene quite well. There was a wooden balcony all round the summer villa where he was the guest of Clarisse's parents. It was only a few days before the wedding and Walter was jealous of him. Walter had a way of being wonderfully jealous. Ulrich was standing outside in the sunshine, when Clarisse and Walter came into the room opening on to the balcony where he was. He overheard their conversation, without concealing himself. However, he only remembered that one sentence now and the picture it all made—the shadowy depths of the room hanging like a wrinkled, slightly opened bag, against the glaring sunniness of the outside wall. In the folds of this bag Walter and Clarisse appeared. Walter's face was elongated in anguish and looked as though it must have long, yellow teeth. One might even express it by saying that a pair of long, yellow teeth lay there in a little casket lined with black velvet, with these two people standing beside it, flickering like spirits. The jealousy was of course nonsense ; Ulrich did not go in for his friends' women. But Walter had always had a quite special capacity for experiencing things violently. He never arrived at what he wanted, because he went through so much emotion. He seemed to carry about inside himself a very melodious amplifier of minor happiness and unhappiness. He always put into circulation emotional small change in gold and silver, while Ulrich operated on a large scale, so to speak with intellectual cheques made out for enormous sums ; but ultimately it was only paper. Whenever Ulrich wanted to imagine Walter in a thoroughly characteristic attitude, he saw him lying at the edge of a wood. He would be wearing shorts and, oddly enough, black stockings. His legs were not a man's legs, neither the stalwart muscular ones nor the lean sinewy ones, but those of a girl—a not very good-looking girl with gentle, plain legs. With his hands clasped behind his head, he gazed out over the landscape, and the heavens above him knew that then one was disturbing him. Ulrich could not recall having seen Walter like this on any definite occasion that had stamped itself on his mind ; it was rather that this image stood out in relief, an impression like that of a final and conclusive seal, after a decade and a half. And his recollection of Walter's having been jealous of him at that time now gave rise to a very pleasant excitement. All this had happened precisely at a time when one had still revelled in being oneself. And Ulrich thought : ' I have been to see them several times now, and Walter hasn't been to see me. Still, I could go out there again this evening. Why should I worry about that ? '

He made up his mind that he would send them word—if only Bonadea would finish dressing and go ! In Bonadea's presence such a step was not advisable, because of the tedious cross-examination that would inevitably follow.

And since thoughts are swift and Bonadea was far from having finished, it happened that something else occurred to him. This time it was a little theory ; it was simple, illuminating, and passed the time away. ' If a young man is intellectually alive,' Ulrich said to himself, probably still thinking of his boyhood friend Walter, ' he is continually sending out ideas in all directions. But only what produces resonance in his environment will radiate back to him and condense, whereas all the other messages are scattered in space and lost.' Ulrich assumed as a matter of course that a man who has intellect possesses every kind of it, which would indicate that intellect is pre-existent to qualities ; he himself was a man of many contraries and took the view that all the qualities that had ever become manifest in humanity were latent, fairly close to each other, in every man's mind if he had any mind at all. This may not be quite correct, but what we know about the origin both of good and of evil makes it seem most likely that although everyone is of a certain inner size, he can of course wear the most various clothes in that size if fate lays them out for him. And so it seemed to Ulrich that what he had just been thinking was not quite without meaning either. For if in the course of time one's ordinary and non-personal ideas intensify quite of their own accord and the extraordinary ones fade, so that almost every one of them steadily becomes more mediocre, with all the certainty of a mechanical process, well, this explains why, in spite of the multiplicity of possibilities that we have confronting us, the average human being is in fact average !

And it also explains the fact that even among those privileged human beings who make their way and attain recognition there is a certain mixture, consisting of about 51 per cent. depth and 49 per cent. shallowness, that is the most successful one. This had for a long time struck Ulrich as complicatedly senseless and insufferably sad, and now he would have liked to go on thinking about it.

He was put off by the fact that Bonadea still gave no sign of being ready. Cautiously peering through the half-open door, he perceived that she had interrupted her dressing. She regarded absent-mindedness as indecorous when it was a matter of the last exquisite drops of a *tête-à-tête* ; affronted by his silence, she was waiting to see what he would do. She had taken up a book, and by good luck it was a history of art, with beautiful pictures in it.

When he returned to his meditations, Ulrich felt irritated by this lingering on her part and got into a state of vague impatience.

30   *Ulrich hears voices.*

AND suddenly his thoughts contracted, and as though he were looking through a chink between them, he saw Christian Moosbrugger, the carpenter, and his judges.

In a manner that was tormentingly ridiculous for anyone who did not think the same way, the judge was saying : " Why did you wipe your bloodstained hands ?—Why did you throw the knife away ?—Why did you change into a clean suit and under-clothes after the crime ?—Because it was Sunday ? Not because they were bloodstained ?—Why did you go to a dance that even-ing ? Evidently the crime did not prevent you from doing so ? Did you feel no remorse whatsoever ? "

In Moosbrugger something began to flicker . . . old prison experience . . . one had to sham remorse. The flicker twisted Moosbrugger's mouth and he said : " Oh yes, I did ! "

" Yet at the police-station you said : ' I feel no remorse, but only hate and fury to the point of paroxysm,' " the judge instantly took him up.

" Maybe," Moosbrugger said, once more becoming firm and refined, " maybe at that time I had no other sensations."

" You are a big, strong man," the public prosecutor cut in. " How could you be frightened of Hedwig ? "

" Your honour," Moosbrugger answered, smiling, " she had become caressive. I imagined her even more cruel than I habitually estimate women of that sort. I may look strong, and I am in fact——"

" Well then," the president of the court grunted, leafing through the file.

" But in certain situations," Moosbrugger said loudly, " I am timid and even cowardly."

The president's eyes darted up from the file. Like two birds flying off a branch, they flew up from the sentence on which they had just been perching. " That time when you got into a scrap with your work-mates on the site, you were far from being cowardly ! " the president said. " You threw one of them down two storeys and went for the others with your knife."

" Your honour," Moosbrugger called out in a dangerous tone of voice, " I hold the point of view to this day——"

The president waved that aside.

" Injustice," Moosbrugger said, " this must serve as the basis of my brutality. I stood before the court as a simple man and thought their honours the judges would know all about it. But I have been disappointed ! "

The judge's head had for some time been bent over the file again.

The public prosecutor smiled and said in a kindly way : " But poor Hedwig was a perfectly harmless girl, wasn't she ? "

" She didn't appear so to *me* ! " Moosbrugger retorted, still worked up.

" It appears to *me*," the president of the court concluded with emphasis, " that you always manage to put the blame on to others."

" Well then, why did you go for her with your knife ? " the public prosecutor asked pleasantly, beginning all over again.

31   *Whose side are you on?*

WAS that a fragment of the trial at which Ulrich had been present
—or only something out of the reports he had read? The
recollection was as vivid as if he were actually hearing the voices
speaking now.   Never before in his life had he 'heard voices'.
Good lord, he wasn't that sort of man!   But if such a thing does
happen, it comes floating down, rather like the quiet of snow
falling.   All of a sudden there are walls standing round one,
reaching from the earth up into the sky.   Where there was air
before, one is now moving through soft, thick walls, and all the
voices that were hopping to and fro in their cage of air now roam
at large inside those white walls that are grown together to the
very core.

He was probably over-wrought.   When one has been working
too hard and is bored, such things do sometimes happen.   But
it was not such a bad thing after all, hearing voices.   And suddenly he said under his breath : " There is another country where
one is at home, where everything one does is innocent. . . ."

Bonadea was fiddling with a lace.   She had in the mean time
come over into his room.   The conversation displeased her ;
she found it indelicate.   She had long ago forgotten the name
of the murderer about whom there had been so much in the
newspapers, and it only returned to her memory reluctantly when
Ulrich began talking about him.

" But," he said after a while, " if Moosbrugger can produce
this disturbing impression of innocence, how much more so,
then, that poor, desolate, shivering creature with her mouse-
eyes looking out from under the kerchief, that girl Hedwig who
begged for a night's shelter in his room and for that was killed
by him."

" Do stop ! " Bonadea urged, shrugging her white shoulders.
For Ulrich had given the conversation this turn precisely in the
maliciously chosen moment when the half-resumed clothes of
his injured *amie*, who had come into his room thirsting for
reconciliation, once more lay on the carpet forming that small,

charmingly mythological foam-crater out of which Aphrodite rises. Bonadea was therefore ready to abhor Moosbrugger and to pass over his victim with a fleeting shudder. But Ulrich would not let go at that. He painted a vivid picture of the fate awaiting Moosbrugger. "Two men will lay the noose round his neck, without in the least harbouring any hostile feelings against him, but merely because they are paid to do so. Perhaps a hundred people will be looking on, some because it is their duty, some because everyone likes to have seen an execution once in his life. A solemn gentleman in top-hat, frock-coat and black gloves pulls the noose tight, and at the same moment his two henchmen hang on to Moosbrugger's two legs, so as to break the neck. Then the gentleman in the black gloves lays his hand on Moosbrugger's heart, with the anxious air of a doctor, investigating whether it is still beating. For if it is, the whole thing will be gone through once again, somewhat more impatiently and less solemnly. By the way," he asked, " are you for Moosbrugger or against him ? "

Bonadea had slowly and painfully come to her senses, like someone waked at the wrong time. 'The mood'—as she was accustomed to call her fits of adultery—had gone. Now, after her hands had for a while undecidedly held the sinking clothes and the opened corset, she had to sit down. Like every woman in similar circumstances, she trusted firmly in an established public order so well regulated that one could pursue one's private affairs without having to give it a thought. And now, when she was reminded of the contrary, a feeling of pitying partisanship for Moosbrugger, the victim, quickly took hold of her, sweeping aside any thought of Moosbrugger, the murderer.

"What it comes to, then," Ulrich insisted, " is that you are for the victim and against the act, every time."

Bonadea expressed the obvious sentiment that a conversation like this, in a situation like this, was out of place.

"But if you so consistently condemn the act," Ulrich answered instead of at once apologising, " how then, Bonadea, are you going to justify your adulteries ? "

It was, above all, the plural that made the remark so indelicate. Bonadea said nothing. She settled down, with a contemptuous air, in one of the comfortable armchairs, and, visibly affronted, gazed up at the dividing-line between wall and ceiling.

32   *The forgotten, exceedingly important affair with the major's wife.*

IT is not advisable to feel oneself akin to a notorious lunatic ; nor did Ulrich do so.   But why did one medical authority declare that Moosbrugger was a lunatic, and the other that he was not ? Where had the reporters got their nimble expertness in describing the work of his knife ?   And by what qualities did Moosbrugger cause the excitement and gooseflesh that for half of the two million people living in this city amounted to practically as much as a family quarrel or a broken-off engagement ?   Here the case stirred up personal emotions to an extraordinary extent, invading areas of the soul that at other times lay dormant, while in pro-vincial towns it was less interesting news, and in Berlin or Breslau, for instance, where from time to time they had Moosbruggers of their own, Moosbruggers in, as it were, their own family, it meant nothing at all.   This horrible way that society had of toying with its victims preoccupied Ulrich.   He felt the same thing going on in himself too.   There was no impulse in him either to liberate Moosbrugger or to go to the aid of the law, and yet all his feelings stood up on end like the fur on a cat's back.   Something beyond his understanding made Moosbrugger a closer concern of his than the leading of his own life ; Moosbrugger held him spell-bound like an obscure and sombre poem in which everything was faintly distorted and displaced, revealing a mutilated significance drifting in the depths of the mind.

' Grand Guignol ! ' he held against himself.   To admire the gruesome or the taboo in the permissible form of dreams and neuroses seemed to him thoroughly appropriate to this age of middle-class mentality.   ' Either one thing or the other ! ' he thought.   ' Either I like you or I don't !   Either I defend you in all your monstrosity, or I ought to slap my own face for toying with you and what you are.'   And, after all, a cool but practical compassion would meet the case too ; a great deal might be done these days to make it impossible for such things to happen and such people to exist, if society itself would make even half the moral effort that it demands of such victims. But then it turned out that there was also a quite different side from which the matter could be considered, and strange memories rose up in Ulrich's mind.

Our judgment of an act is never a judgment of the particular aspect of the act that God rewards or punishes. That was said, oddly enough, by Luther—probably under the influence of one of the mystics with whom he was for a time on friendly terms. Certainly it might have been said by many another believer. They all were, in a bourgeois sense, immoralists. They distinguished between sins and the soul, which could remain immaculate in spite of the sins, in much the same way that Machiavelli distinguished between the end and the means. The ' human heart ' was ' taken ' from them. ' In Christ too there was an outer and an inner man, and everything that he did in relation to outer things he did in his aspect as the outer man, and the inner man stood by the while, motionless and aloof,' Eckhart says. And might not such saints and believers have been capable, after all, of acquitting even Moosbrugger ? Doubtless mankind had progressed since then ; but though it would kill Moosbrugger, it still had the weakness to venerate those men who might—who knows ?—have acquitted him.

And now a wave of discomfort went through Ulrich and he remembered a sentence, which went : ' The soul of the Sodomite might pass through the throng without foreboding, in its eyes the limpid smile of a child ; for everything depends on an invisible principle.' There was not much difference between this and those other sayings, but this, in its faint exaggeration, exhaled the sweet, sickly odour of corruption. And now it came to him that there was a room associated with this aphorism—a room with yellow French paper-backs on the tables and glass-bead curtains instead of doors—and a feeling rose up in his breast as when a hand slides into the opened carcase of a hen to pull the heart out. For this sentence was one that Diotima had uttered during his visit. What was more, it was by a contemporary writer whose work Ulrich had been fond of in his early youth, but whom he had since come to regard as a drawing-room philosopher ; such aphorisms taste as bad as bread on which scent has been spilt, so that for decades to come one does not want to have any more to do with anything of the sort.

But however strong the dislike was that this aroused in Ulrich, at this moment it seemed to him shameful that he had all his life long let himself be kept from returning to the other, the genuine utterances that had been made in that mysterious language. For he had a special and immediate appreciation of them, or rather, something that might be called a feeling of intimacy that skipped the stage of understanding, without his ever having been able, however, to make up his mind to confess whole-hearted faith in them. Sentences like these—speaking to him in tones of closest kinship, with a soft, dark inwardness that was the opposite of the hectoring tones of the mathematical and scientific language, though without its being possible to say in what the difference consisted—lay like islands scattered among his activities, unconnected and seldom visited ; yet if he surveyed them, in so far as he had come to know them, it appeared to him that there was a perceptible coherence in them, as though these islands, separated from each other only by short distances, lay at the approaches to some coast still out of sight beyond them or were the remains of a continent that had gone down into the sea in ages immemorial.

He felt the softness of sea and mist and a low, black ridge of hills asleep in yellow-grey light. He recalled a little sea-voyage, an escape along the lines of the travel-bureau slogans ' See the world ! ' and ' Give yourself a change ! ' and remembered clearly the strange, ridiculously enchanted experience that by its deterrent force had interposed itself once and for all between him and all similar experiences. For one moment the heart of a twenty-year-old beat in his breast, the hairy skin of which had thickened and coarsened in the intervening years. This beating of a twenty-year-old heart in his thirty-two-year-old breast seemed to him like the perverted kiss that a boy gives a man. Nevertheless, this time he did not shrink from the memory. It was the memory of a passion that had come to a queer end, a passion that he as a twenty-year-old had felt for a woman who was considerably older than he, not only in years but above all in the degree of her domestic and social consolidation.

Characteristically enough, he recalled her appearance only

vaguely. A stilted photograph, and the memory of the hours when he was alone and thinking about her, took the place of actual memories of this woman's face, clothes, movements and voice. Her world had in the mean time become so alien to him that the fact that she had been the wife of a major struck him as amusingly incredible. ' By this time, I dare say, she's the wife of a retired colonel,' he thought. It had been generally recounted in the regiment that she was an artist, a trained pianist, but at her family's wish had never made public use of her accomplishment, and later on, naturally, her marriage had made it altogether impossible. She did in fact play the piano beautifully at regimental festivities, with the glittering splendour of a well-gilded sun floating high over chasms of emotion, and from the very beginning Ulrich had fallen in love less with this woman's sensual presence than with the idea of her. The lieutenant he was in those days was not bashful; his eye had already practised on small female fry and even scouted out the faintly trodden poacher's track leading to this or that respectable woman. But the ' grand passion ' was for such twenty-year-old officers, if they had any desire for it at all, something quite different; it was, in fact, an idea; it lay outside the range of their enterprises and was as poor in practical experience, and for that very reason as dazzlingly empty, as only really great ideas can be. And when for the first time in his life Ulrich discovered in himself the possibility of putting this idea into practice, it was bound to happen as it did; the major's wife had no other part to play in it all than that of the last contributory cause that brings about the eruption of a disease. Ulrich became love-sick. And since true love-sickness is not desire for possession, but only a gentle unveiling of the world itself, for the sake of which one willingly renounces possession of the beloved, the lieutenant explained the world to the major's lady—and indeed in an unusual and persevering manner such as she had never met with before. Constellations, bacteria, Balzac, and Nietzsche whirled in a vortex of ideas, always narrowing down—as she felt with increasing clarity—towards certain differences (which prevailing notions of decorum set beyond the pale) separating her body from the body of the lieutenant. She was bewildered by this insistent association of love with questions that to the best of her knowledge had never yet had anything to do with love.

When out for a ride with Ulrich one day, as they were walking beside their horses she left her hand in his for a moment and noticed in terror that the hand remained lying in his as though in a swoon. At the next instant a conflagration flared from her wrists to her knees, and a stroke of lightning went through both of them, so that they almost collapsed by the wayside ; and there they then found themselves sitting on the moss, passionately kissing and in the end becoming embarrassed because this love was so great and out of the ordinary that to their surprise it left them with nothing to say and do except what is the ordinary thing in the course of such embraces. It was finally the horses, growing restive, that freed the two lovers from this situation.

The love between the major's wife and this very young lieu-tenant remained unreal throughout its brief course. They were both astonished ; they clung to each other a few more times, they both felt that something was not going right and would not let them come body to body in their embraces even if they shed all the obstacles set up by clothing and morality. The major's wife did not wish to deny herself to a passion that was, she felt, beyond her power of judgment, but there were secret reproaches throbbing in her on account of her husband and the difference in age ; and when Ulrich one day informed her, making use of very threadbare pretexts, that he must go on long furlough, in the midst of her tears she gave a sigh of relief. Ulrich, however, was by that time so far gone in love that he no longer had any wish except to get as quickly and as far away as possible from the proximity of the origin of that love. He travelled blindly on and on until a coast-line put an end to the railway-track, had himself taken over in a boat to the nearest island he saw, and there, in an unknown place chosen at random, he remained, poorly lodged and boarded, and in the very first night wrote the first of a series of long letters to the beloved, letters that he never posted.

These dead-of-night letters, which also filled his thoughts by day, he later lost ; and that had doubtless been their predestined fate. In the first ones he was still at the stage of writing a great deal about his love and about all sorts of thoughts inspired by it, but that soon began to be displaced by the scenery. The sun drew him out of sleep in the mornings, and when the fishermen were out on the water, the women and children keeping to the houses, then it seemed that he and a donkey grazing among the shrubs and on hillocks between the two little villages on the island were the only higher specimens of life that existed in this quaint outpost of the world.   He followed Brother Ass's example and climbed up on one of the hillocks or lay down on the shore in the surrounding company of sea, rock and sky.   There was no presumption in this feeling of companionship, for the difference in magnitude disappeared, as also did the difference between mind and nature, animate and inanimate ;   indeed, every kind of difference between things grew less in such communion.   To put it quite soberly, these differences doubtless neither disappeared nor grew less, but they shed their significance and one was ' no longer subject to any of the separations that are the mark of mankind ', one was in the very condition described by those believers in God who have entered the state of mystic love, those of whom the young cavalry lieutenant at that time knew nothing at all. Nor did he reflect on these phenomena—as another man, like a huntsman on the trail, might try to track an observation down by thinking along after it—indeed, he was probably not even aware of them.   But he was absorbing them.   He was submerging himself in the landscape, although one might equally well say that it was an unutterable state of being buoyed up and borne along ;   and when the world overbrimmed the threshold of his eyes, its meaning lapped against him from within, in soundless waves.   He had drifted into the very heart of the world.   From him to the distant beloved was as far as to the next tree.   Inscape had linked the living beings where space was no more, as in dreams two living beings can pass through each other without intermingling ;   and this altered all their relations.   Otherwise, however, this state of mind had nothing in common with dream. It was clear, and abounding in clear thoughts.   Only nothing in it moved according to cause, purpose and physical desire, but everything went rippling out in circle upon circle, as when a continuous jet plays upon a pool of water.   And precisely this was what he described in his letters ;   nothing else.

It was an utterly changed form of life.   Everything about it was shifted out of the focus of ordinary attention and had lost its sharp outlines.   Seen in this way, it was all a little scattered and blurred, and yet manifestly there were still other centres filling it again with delicate certainty and clarity. For all life's problems and events took on an incomparable mildness, softness and serenity, and at the same time an utterly transformed meaning. If, for instance, a beetle, there, ran past the hand of the man sunk in thought, it was not a coming nearer, a passing by and a disappearing, and it was not beetle and man ; it was a happening ineffably touching the heart, and yet not even a happening but, although it happened, a state. And, aided by such tranquil experiences, everything that generally goes to make up ordinary life was imbued with transforming significance, wherever Ulrich met with it.

And in this state his love for the major's wife also rapidly took on its predestined form. He sometimes tried to imagine the woman of whom he was continually thinking, and to form a picture of what she might be doing at that moment, an attempt for which he was well equipped by his exact knowledge of her way of life. But the instant this was successful and he saw the beloved in his mind's eye, his sensibility, which had become infinitely clairvoyant, grew blind again, and he had to make a hurried effort to modify her image once more to that blissful certainty of existing-for-him-somewhere proper to a beloved of the first magnitude. It was not long until she had become the impersonal centre of energy, the subterranean dynamo that supplied his illumination, and he wrote her a last letter in which he explained to her that the grand ideal of living for love's sake actually had nothing at all to do with possession and the desire for it, which originate in the sphere of thriftiness, appropriation and gluttony. This was the only letter that he posted and this was approximately the point when his love-sickness reached its culmination, which was soon followed by its abatement and sudden end.

33   *Breaking off with Bonadea.*

MEANWHILE, since she could not go on gazing at the ceiling all the time, Bonadea had lain down flat on the divan, her tender maternal belly breathing freely under white batiste, unhampered by whalebone and laces ; she called this position ' thinking '. It flashed through her mind that her husband was not only a judge but also a hunter and at times would talk with sparkling eyes of the beasts of prey that went after the game ; it seemed to her that it must be possible to draw from this some conclusion in favour of Moosbrugger and of his judges too. On the other hand, however, she did not wish to let her husband be put in the wrong by her lover, except where love itself was concerned ; her family feeling required that the paterfamilias should appear a dignified and respected figure. So she came to no decision. And while this conflict was drowsily darkening her horizon like two banks of cloud amorphously merging with each other, Ulrich enjoyed the liberty of following up his thoughts.

This had now lasted somewhat too long, and because nothing had occurred to Bonadea that could have given the situation a new turn, her resentment at Ulrich's having carelessly offended her revived, and the time that he let slip by, without making it up to her, began to weigh on her provocatively.

" So you feel I am doing wrong by visiting you ? " This question she at last put to him, slowly and emphatically, sadly, but with all her fighting-spirit gathered behind it.

Ulrich shrugged his shoulders and said nothing. He had long ago forgotten what she was talking about ; at any rate he found it impossible to endure her at this moment.

" So you are really capable of reproaching *me* for our passion ? "

" To every question of that kind there cling as many answers as there are bees in a hive," Ulrich replied. " All mankind's spiritual disorderliness, with its never settled questions, clings to every single one of them in a way that's quite disgusting." With this he was of course saying nothing but what he had already thought several times that day. But Bonadea related the spiritual disorderliness to herself and decided that this was too much. She would gladly have drawn the curtains again, in order to do away with the quarrel in that manner, but she could just as easily have wailed with grief. And all at once she thought she understood that Ulrich had grown tired of her. Thanks to her nature she had up to then never lost her lovers in any other way than as one mislays something, losing sight of it when one is attracted by something new ; or in that other way of being as quickly separated from them as united with them, which, for all the personal annoyance it involved, yet had something of the mysterious ways of a higher power. Her first feeling, therefore, when confronted with Ulrich's calm resistance, was that she must have grown old. Her helpless and indecent situation, lying as she did half-naked on a divan, exposed to all insults, shamed her. Without thinking what she was doing, she got up and snatched her clothes. But the rustling and whispering of the silken chalices into which she was sliding back did not move Ulrich to remorse. The stabbing pain of helplessness was there behind Bonadea's eyes. ' He's a brute, he has hurt me deliberately ! ' she kept repeating to herself. ' He doesn't budge ! ' she concluded. And with every ribbon that she tied, and every hook that she fastened, she sank deeper into the abysmally black well of that long-forgotten childish anguish of being left all alone. Gloom now gathered around her. Ulrich's face stood out as though in the last light, asserting itself, hard and brutal, against the darkness of sorrow. ' How could I ever have loved that face ? ' Bonadea asked herself. But at the same instant the thought ' For ever lost ! ' made her breast tighten convulsively.

Ulrich, who guessed at her resolve never to return, did not interfere with it. Bonadea was now energetically smoothing her hair before the looking-glass. Then she put her hat on and tied her veil. Now that the veil was there before her face, it was all over ; it was solemn as a death-sentence or as when the lock on a cabin-trunk closes with a final click. He should not kiss her any more and he should have no premonition that he was missing the last opportunity of doing so !

And because of this she almost threw her arms round him for pity and could have cried her heart out on his chest.

34   *A hot ray and walls grown cold.*

WHEN Ulrich had escorted Bonadea out and was again alone, he no longer felt like working.   He went out, with the intention of sending a courier to Walter and Clarisse with a few lines announcing his visit that evening.   When he was crossing the little hall, he noticed a pair of antlers on the wall that somehow resembled a movement of Bonadea's when tying her veil before the looking-glass ; only they did not smile to themselves with a resigned expression.   He looked about him, and considered his surroundings.   All these circular lines, intersecting lines, straight lines, curves and convolutions, of which an interior consists and which had accumulated around him, were a product neither of nature nor of inner necessity, but, down to the last detail, bulged with baroque superabundance.   The current and heart-beat ceaselessly flowing through all the things of our environment had for a moment stopped.

' I am merely accidental,' necessity leered at him.

' I don't look essentially different from a face marred by lupus, if I am regarded without prejudice,' beauty confessed.

Fundamentally it did not take much doing : a varnish had flaked off, an illusion had lost its hold, a chain of habit, expectation, and tension had snapped, a flowing secret equilibrium of world and feeling had for an instant been upset.   Everything one feels and does goes somehow ' in the direction of life ', and the slightest movement out of that direction is difficult or frightening.   It is exactly the same even in the mere act of walking : one lifts the centre of gravity, moves it forward and lets it drop again— but let the slightest detail be changed, let there be only a trace of shrinking from this letting-oneself-drop-forward-into-the-future, or even surprise at it, and one becomes incapable of standing upright any longer.   One must not think about it. And it occurred to Ulrich that all the moments that had meant something decisive in his life had left him with the same feeling as this.

In the street he beckoned to a courier and handed him the

note.   It was about four o'clock in the afternoon, and he decided to walk out there very slowly.   The spring-like autumn day delighted him.   The air was in a ferment.   There was something about people's faces that was like spindrift.   After the monotonous exertion of his thoughts in the last few days, he felt as though lifted out of a dungeon into a soothing bath.   He did his best to walk in a friendly and relaxed way.   All the readiness to run and jump and fight that there is in a well-trained body today affected him as disagreeably as an aging actor's face, full of often-acted artificial passions.   In the same manner the striving towards truth had filled his inner being with forms of mental mobility, divided it into groups of thoughts in well-balanced exercise against each other, and given it a—strictly speaking—untrue and theatrical expression, one that everything, even sincerity itself, takes on in the moment when it becomes habit.   This was what Ulrich was thinking.   He flowed on like a wave among his wave-brothers, if it may be put so.   And why shouldn't it be put so of a man who has been working very hard in solitude, returning now into the community and feeling the happiness of flowing in the same direction as it does ?

At such a moment nothing may be so remote as the thought that the life they lead—and are led by—does not concern men much, does not concern them inwardly.   And yet every man knows it so long as he is young.   Ulrich remembered what such a day had been like for him in the same streets ten or fifteen years · earlier.   Then everything had been twice as glorious, and yet there had quite distinctly been, in that seething desire, an aching premonition of captivity, a disquieting feeling of ' everything I think I am reaching is reaching me ', a gnawing surmise that in this world the untrue, careless, and personally unimportant utterances will echo more strongly than one's own inmost, most real ones.   ' This beauty ? '—one thought then—' it's all very well, but is it mine ?   And is the truth that I am getting to know *my* truth ?   The goals, the voices, the reality, the seduction of it all, luring and leading one on, all that one follows and plunges into—is it the real reality or does one still get no more than a breath of the real, a breath hovering intangibly on the surface of the reality one is offered ? '   What is so perceptible to one's mistrust is the cut-and-dried way that life is divided up and the ready-made forms it assumes, the ever-recurring sameness of it, the pre-formations passed down by generation after generation, the ready-made language not only of the tongue but also of the sensations and feelings.

Ulrich had stopped in front of a church. Dear heaven, if there in the shadow a gigantic matron had been sitting, with a big belly shelving down as a flight of steps, her back leaning against the sides of the houses, and up above, on thousands of wrinkles, on warts and pimples, the sunset in her face—might he not just as easily have thought that beautiful? Lord, yes, and how beautiful this was! One was, after all, far from wanting to dodge the consequences of having been set down in life under the obligation of admiring this; but, again, it would be just as possible to think the broad, reposefully drooping forms and the filigree of wrinkles on a venerable matron beautiful—it is only that it is simpler to say she is old. And this transition from finding the things of the world old to finding them beautiful is about the same as that from young people's outlook to the higher moral view-point of adults, which goes on being a ridiculous piece of didacticism until some day, suddenly, one has it oneself.

It was only for seconds that Ulrich stood outside this church, but these seconds grew down into the depths, pressing upon his heart, setting up all the resistance of a primal instinct against this world petrified into millions of tons of stone, against this rigid lunar landscape of feeling into which one had been set down with no will of one's own.

It may be that for most people it is a convenience and comfort to find the world ready-made except for a few small personal details; yet although there is no reason at all to doubt that what persists as a whole is not only conservative but also the basis of all progress and revolution, mention must be made too of a deep, shadowy uneasiness that it causes in people living on what one might call their own hook. While Ulrich was contemplating the consecrated building, full of understanding of its architectural subtleties, it forced itself on his consciousness with surprising vividness that one could just as easily devour human beings as build such monuments or let them stand where they were. The houses beside it, the vault of the sky over it, altogether an indescribable harmony in all the lines and blocks of space that absorbed and guided the gaze, the appearance and expression of the people going past below, their books and their morality, the trees in the street—all these things are, after all, sometimes as stiff as lacquered screens and as hard as a printer's die-stamp and—one can hardly put it otherwise—so complete, so complete and finished, that beside it one is a superfluous mist, a little puff of breath exhaled, which God no longer bothers about.

At this moment he wished to be a man without qualities. But this is probably not so very different from what other people sometimes feel too. After all, by the time they have reached the middle of their life's journey few people remember how they have managed to arrive at themselves, at their amusements, their point of view, their wife, character, occupation and successes, but they cannot help feeling that not much is likely to change any more. It might even be asserted that they have been cheated, for one can nowhere discover any sufficient reason for everything's having come about as it has. It might just as well have turned out differently. The events of people's lives have, after all, only to the least degree originated in them, having generally depended on all sorts of circumstances such as the moods, the life or death of quite different people, and have, as it were, only at the given point of time come hurrying towards them. For in youth life still lies before them as an inexhaustible morning, spread out all round them full of everything and nothing ; and yet when noon comes there is all at once something there that may justly claim to be their life now, which is, all in all, just as surprising as if one day suddenly there were a man sitting there before one, with whom one had been corresponding for twenty years without knowing him, and all the time imagining him quite different. But what is still much queerer is that most people do not notice this at all ; they adopt the man who has come to stay with them, whose life has merged with their own lives and whose experiences now seem to them the expression of their own qualities, his destiny their own merit or misfortune. Something has had its way with them like a fly-paper with a fly ; it has caught them fast, here catching a little hair, there hampering their movements, and has gradually enveloped them, until they lie buried under a thick coating that has only the remotest resemblance to their original shape. And then they only dimly remember their youth

when there was something like a force of resistance in them—
this other force that tugs and whirrs and does not want to linger
anywhere, releasing a storm of aimless attempts at flight.   Youth's
scorn and its revolt against the established order, youth's readiness
for everything that is heroic, whether it is self-sacrifice or crime,
its fiery seriousness and its unsteadiness—all this is nothing but its
fluttering attempts to fly.   Fundamentally it merely means that
nothing of all that a young man undertakes appears to be the result
of an unequivocal inner necessity, even if it expresses itself in
such a manner as to suggest that everything he happens to dash
at is exceedingly urgent and necessary.   Someone or other invents
a magnificent new gesture, either of the body or of the soul—how
is one to interpret it ?   A vital pose ?   A mould into which mind
and soul pour like gas into a glass balloon ?   An expression of
pressure within ?   A technique of living ?   It may be a new
moustache or a new idea.   It is play-acting, but like all play-
acting it has of course a meaning—and instantly, like the sparrows
from the roof-tops when crumbs are strewn, the young souls dart
at it.   It doesn't take much imagining : when outside there is a
heavy world weighing upon tongue, hands and eyes, the ice-cold
moon of earth, houses, rites and customs, pictures and books,
and inside nothing but a straggling, shifting mist—what happiness
it must be then, when someone produces an expression in which
one seems to recognise oneself!   Is anything more natural than
that every passionate man should take possession of this new
form even before ordinary people do ?   It bestows on him the
moment of being, of balanced tensions between the world within
and the world without, between being flattened out and flying
to pieces.

   This then is also the sole basis—Ulrich thought, and of course
all this touched him personally too (he had his hands in his
pockets, and his face looked as quietly and sleepily happy as
though in the rays of sunlight that came whirling down he were
dying a mild death in the snow)—this then is also the sole basis
of the everlasting phenomenon that is called new generations,
fathers and sons, intellectual revolution, changes of style, evolution, fashion and revivals.   What makes a *perpetuum mobile* of
this yearning for the renovation of life is nothing but the calamity
that between one's own misty ego and one predecessors' ego,

which has already petrified into an alien shell, there is again
interpolated a pseudo-ego, a group-soul that fits only approximately. And if one is just a little observant, one can probably
always recognise in the latest future, which has only this very
instant arrived, the 'old days' to come. The new ideas are then
merely older by thirty years, but contented and slightly cushioned
with fat or past their prime, producing a like effect of likeness to
what they were to that a woman's dim and faded features have to
the shining young face of her daughter beside her ; or they have
had no success and are emaciated and shrunken into nothing more
than a reformist slogan, campaigned for by some old fool whom
his fifty admirers refer to as the great So-and-So.

Now Ulrich stopped again, this time in a square where he
recognised several houses and recalled the public controversies
and intellectual excitement that had arisen at the time when they
were built. He thought of the friends of his youth. They had
all been the friends of his youth, whether he had known them
personally or merely by name, whether they were of his age or
older—these rebels who wanted to put new things and people
into the world—and whether they had been here or scattered over
all the places he had known. Now these houses stood there in
the late afternoon light, which was already beginning to pale,
looking like well-meaning aunts in old-fashioned hats, quite neat
and irrelevant and anything but exciting. One was tempted to
smile. But the people who had abandoned these now unassuming
remains had meanwhile become professors, celebrities and
'names', a well-known part of the well-known progress of
evolution ; over a more or less short route they had got out of
the misty state into that of petrifaction, and hence some day,
when an account is given of their century, history will report :
Among those present were . . .

35

*Director Leo Fischel and the Principle of
the Insufficient Cause.*

AT this moment Ulrich was unexpectedly interrupted by an
acquaintance who addressed him. This acquaintance had, that
same day, when opening his despatch-case before leaving home
in the morning, been disagreeably surprised to find, in one of the
less used compartments, a circular letter from Count Leinsdorf,
which he had some time ago forgotten to answer because his
sound business instinct made him averse to patriotic enterprises
originating in high circles. 'Doubtful proposition' was probably what he had said to himself at the time (and he hoped to
heaven he had not said it publicly)—but then his memory had
played him a trick, as memories will, by acting on the emotional
and unofficial first reaction and negligently dropping the matter
instead of waiting for a considered decision. And hence it was
only now, when he opened the letter again, that he discovered
something extremely painful to him, something he had paid no
attention to before. It was actually only a phrase, only two little
words, which turned up at various places in the circular; but
these two words had cost this portly man several minutes of
indecision, standing with his despatch-case in his hand, before
leaving the house. And they were : 'the true'.

Director Fischel—for that was what he was called, Director
Leo Fischel, of Lloyd's Bank, though in fact he was only manager
with the title of director—and Ulrich was justified in calling
himself his young friend of earlier days and had, on his last stay
in this city, been quite good friends with his daughter Gerda,
whom he had however visited only once since his return—
Director Fischel knew His Highness as a man who made his
money work for him and kept up with modern methods, and at
the moment when he ran over the account in his memory—for
Lloyd's Bank was one of those institutions through which Count
Leinsdorf conducted his deals on the Stock Exchange—he recognised him as 'undoubted' (such is the business term), indeed as
a man of great consequence. Thus Leo Fischel failed to under-

stand how he could have been so careless as to ignore an invitation as compelling as this, in which His Highness had appealed to a select circle of people to hold themselves in readiness for a great work in common. He, Fischel, had been included in this circle only as a result of very special circumstances (to be referred to later), and all this was the reason why he rushed up to Ulrich the moment he caught sight of him. He had heard that Ulrich had something to do with the affair, and ' in a position of note ', what was more—which was one of those incomprehensible but not infrequent rumours that get the facts right before they are facts at all—and he put a triple question to him, like a three-barrelled pistol aimed at his breast :

" Tell me, what do you understand by ' true patriotism ', ' true progress ' and ' true Austria ' ? "

Startled out of his mood and yet still in the spirit of it, Ulrich answered in the style in which he had always carried on conversation with Fischel : " The P.I.C."

" The P.I.C. ? " Director Fischel repeated the letters in all innocence, this time not thinking that it was a joke, for although such abbreviations were then not yet as numerous as today, they were familiar from cartels and trusts, and they were very confidence-inspiring. Then, however, he said : " Look, please don't make jokes. I'm in a hurry, I have a conference."

" The Principle of the Insufficient Cause ! " Ulrich explained. " Being a philosopher yourself, you know of course what the principle of the sufficient cause is. Only, people make an exception where they themselves are concerned. In real life, by which I mean our personal and also our public-historical life, what happens is always what has no good cause."

Leo Fischel wavered, undecided whether to contradict him or not. Director Leo Fischel of Lloyd's Bank enjoyed philosophising (there are still such people in practical occupations), but he was really in a hurry. So he replied : " Don't pretend you don't know what I mean. I know what progress is, I know what Austria is, and I dare say I know what patriotism is too. But I don't know that I can quite imagine what true patriotism, true Austria and true progress are. And that's what I'm asking you ! "

" All right. Do you know what an enzyme is ? Or a catalyst ? "

Leo Fischel lifted one hand in a defensive gesture.

" It's something," Ulrich went on, " that contributes nothing materially, but sets events going. You ought to know from history that there has never been such a thing as the true faith, true morality, and true philosophy. And yet the wars, and all the vileness and viciousness, that have been let loose in their name have fruitfully transformed the world."

" Another time ! " Fischel implored, and tried to adopt an air of frankness. " Look, it's like this, I've got to deal with all this on the Stock Exchange and would really like to know what Count Leinsdorf's actual intentions are. What is he getting at with this supplementary ' true ' of his ? "

" I give you my solemn word," Ulrich replied gravely, " that neither I nor anyone else knows what ' the true ' is. But I can assure you it is on the point of realisation."

" You're a cynic," Director Fischel declared and turned to hurry away, but after the first step swung back and corrected himself : " Only a short time ago I was saying to Gerda that you would have made a magnificent diplomat. I hope you'll come and see us again soon."

36

Thanks to the above-mentioned principle the Collateral Campaign has a tangible existence before anyone knows what it is.

DIRECTOR Leo Fischel of Lloyd's Bank believed, as all bank directors did before the war, in progress. Being a man who was good at his job, he naturally knew that it is only in things one really knows about that one can have a conviction on which one is prepared to stake anything. The enormous diffusion of all activities does not permit conviction to develop elsewhere. Efficient, hard-working people, therefore, have no convictions outside the limits of their own very narrow field, none that they would not immediately abandon if they felt any pressure on it from without; one could go as far as to say that sheer conscientiousness compels them to act differently from the way they think. Director Fischel, for instance, could picture nothing at all under ' true patriotism ' and ' true Austria ', whereas, on the other hand, on the score of ' true progress ' he had an opinion of his own, one that was certainly different from Count Leinsdorf's. Worn out by stocks and bonds, or whatever he was dealing with in his department, with no recreation other than an evening at the opera once a week, he believed there was such a thing as general progress, which must somehow resemble the picture of ever-increasing lucrativeness presented by his bank. But when Count Leinsdorf set up to understand *this* better too, and began to exert pressure on Leo Fischel's conscience, Fischel felt that ' after all, one never knew ' (except of course with stocks and bonds); and since, although of course one doesn't know, one doesn't want to miss anything either, he resolved to enquire quite casually of his managing-director what *he* thought of the matter.

When he did so, however, the managing-director had for quite similar reasons already had a talk with the Governor of the National Bank and knew all about it. For not only the managing-director of Lloyd's, but, it goes without saying, the Governor of the National Bank too, had received an invitation from Count Leinsdorf; and Leo Fischel, who was only the head of a department, owed his simply and solely to his wife's family connections, since she came from the upper reaches of the bureaucracy and never forgot this link, either in her social relations or in her domestic conflicts with Leo. He therefore confined himself, when talking to his superior about the Collateral Campaign, to wagging his head significantly, which now meant ' a great proposition ' but earlier would have meant ' doubtful proposition '. This could do no harm in any case, although with regard to his wife it might well have pleased Fischel better if the proposition had turned out to be doubtful.

So far, however, von Meier-Ballot, the Governor, whose advice had been sought by the managing-director, had personally got the best of impressions. When he received Count Leinsdorf's inaugural letter, he went to the looking-glass—naturally enough, though not for that reason—and saw looking out at him, surmounting the tail-coat and the order-ribbons, the well-organised face o a bourgeois minister, in which all that remained of money's hardness was, at the most, a trace of something far back in the eyes, and his fingers hung down from his hands like flags on a windless day, as though they had never in their life had to carry out the hasty movements with which a junior bank-clerk counts his cash. This bureaucratically over-bred high-financier, who had hardly anything any more in common with the hungry, free-roaming, wild dogs of the Stock Exchange racket, saw vague but agreeably tempered possibilities before him ; and that same evening he had an opportunity to confirm this view of his, in talk with the former ministers von Holtzkopf and Baron Wisnieczky at the Industrialists' Club.

These two gentlemen were well-informed, distinguished and reserved persons in high positions of some kind, into which they had been shifted aside when the brief caretaker government between two political crises—the government of which they had been members—had again become superfluous ; they were men who had spent their lives in the service of State and Crown, without any wish to step into the limelight except when their All-Highest master commanded it.   They knew of the rumour that the great Campaign was to be given a delicate pin-point barb directed at Germany.   It was their conviction, now as well as before the collapse of their ministry, that the deplorable manifestations even then making the political life of the Dual Monarchy a focus of infection for Europe were extraordinarily involved. But just as they had felt in duty bound to consider these difficulties soluble when they were under command to do so, so now too they would not declare it impossible that something might be achieved by the means suggested by Count Leinsdorf ; above all they felt that a ' landmark ', a ' glorious demonstration of vitality ', a ' mighty stride forward into the outside world, which would at the same time have a salutary influence on conditions at home ', as Count Leinsdorf had expressed it, were wishes so much to the point that one could no more refuse to identify oneself with them than if the call had gone forth for every man to come forward who was on the side of the Good.

It is of course possible that Holtzkopf and Wisnieczky, as men of knowledge and experience in public affairs, felt various qualms, especially since they were entitled to assume that they themselves were destined to play some part in the Campaign's subsequent development. But it is all very well for ground-level people to be critical, rejecting whatever does not suit them. If, however, the balloon of one's life happens to be nine thousand feet up in the air, one doesn't simply step out of it, even if one doesn't agree with all that is going on. And since in these circles one is really loyal and, in contrast with the scramble of bourgeois life, does not care to act otherwise than one thinks, in many cases one has to content oneself with not giving a subject too much careful thought. These two gentlemen's pronouncements therefore did much to intensify Governor von Meier-Ballot's favourable impression of the affair; and even though, both personally and professionally, he had a certain tendency towards caution, what he heard sufficed to convince him that here was a proposition at the further development of which one would in any case be present, though without committing oneself.

Meanwhile, however, the Collateral Campaign had not really begun to exist, and what form it would exist in was something even Count Leinsdorf did not yet know. At any rate, the only definite thing that had occurred to him up to this moment was a list of names.

Yet even that was a great deal. For it meant that at this stage, without anyone's needing to have a clear conception of anything, there already existed a network of preparedness, covering a grand complex. And it is probably safe to say that this was the right sequence. For knives and forks had to be invented first, and it was only afterwards that people learnt to eat decently; that was how Count Leinsdorf put it.

37

A journalist causes Count Leinsdorf great inconvenience through the invention of The Austrian Year. His Highness calls frantically for Ulrich.

ALTHOUGH, to be sure, Count Leinsdorf had sent out invitations in many directions, with the object of ' quickening the idea ', he might very well not have made such rapid progress if it had not been for an influential journalist who had discovered that there was something in the air and had been quick to publish two big articles in his paper, in which he came out with everything that he surmised was brewing, and as though it were all his own suggestion. He did not know much—where, after all, could he have learnt anything ?—but that was not noticeable, or rather it was the very thing that made it possible for his two articles to have an irresistible effect. He was actually the inventor of the concept ' The Austrian Year ', on which he wrote in his column without himself quite knowing what it meant and yet in ever new sentences, all through which, as in a dream, these words went on fusing with others and continually changing, and so aroused tremendous enthusiasm.

Count Leinsdorf was at first horrified. But he was wrong. From this slogan ' Austrian Year ' one can judge what journalistic genius is ; it was the right instinct that had invented it. It set emotions resounding, emotions that would have given out no ring in response to the idea of an Austrian Century, while a demand that such an era should actually be brought about would have struck rational people as the kind of thing that no one takes seriously. It would be hard to say why this is so. It was perhaps not only Count Leinsdorf's feelings that were given wings by a certain vague metaphorical quality that lessened the sense of reality. For there is an elevating and magnifying power in vagueness.

It seems that reality is something that the worthy, practical realist does not ever wholly love and take seriously. As a child he crawls under the table, when his parents are not at home, by this brilliantly simple trick making their living-room into a place of adventure; as a growing boy he hankers after a watch of his own; as the young man with the gold watch he longs for the woman to go with it; as a mature man with watch and wife he hankers after the prominent position; and when he has successfully attained the fulfilment of this little circle of wishes and is calmly swinging to and fro in it like a pendulum, it nevertheless seems that his store of unsatisfied dreams has not diminished by one jot, for when he wants to rise above the rut of every day he will resort to metaphor and simile. Obviously because snow is at times dis-agreeable to him, he compares it to women's glimmering breasts, and as soon as his wife's breasts begin to bore him, he compares them to glimmering snow; he would be horrified if one day he and his ' little turtle-dove ' suddenly had horny bills to coo with, or if her lips really turned into coral, but poetically he finds it stimulating. He is capable of turning everything into anything— snow into skin, skin into blossoms, blossoms into sugar, sugar into powder, and powder back into little drifts of snow—for all that matters to him, apparently, is to make things into what they are not, which is doubtless proof that he cannot stand being any-where for long, wherever he happens to be. Above all, however, inwardly no Kakanian born and bred could stand living in Kakania. If now an Austrian Century had been required of him, it would have appeared to him as something like one of the punishments of Hell, which he was to impose upon himself and the world by means of ludicrous voluntary exertion. An Austrian Year, on the other hand, was something quite different. What it amounted to was : ' For once we're going to show what we could be if we tried,' but so to speak only until further notice, and for no more than a year at the outside. It was something that one could imagine as whatever one liked, it wasn't going to last for ever, after all, and that touched the heart in some indescrib-able way. It awakened the deepest love of country.

So it came about that Count Leinsdorf had an unexpected success. He too of course had originally conceived his idea in the guise of such a metaphor, but along with it there had occurred to him a list of names, and his moral nature aspired to something beyond this state of fluidity; he had a distinct awareness of the fact that the imagination of the people, or as he now put it to an obsequious journalist, the imagination of the public, must be directed towards a goal that was clear, sound, rational and in harmony with the true aims of mankind and of their own country. Spurred on by his colleague's success, this journalist wrote it all down immediately, and since he had the advantage over the first one of having got it ' from the horse's mouth ', it went with the technique of his profession that he referred to it in large type as ' information from influential circles '. And this was precisely what Count Leinsdorf had expected of him, for His Highness attached great importance to being no ideologist, but an experienced practical politician, and was anxious to see a subtle line drawn between the Austrian Year emanating from the brain of a journalistic genius and the due deliberation of responsible circles. For this purpose he made use of the technique employed by one whom he did not generally care to take as a model, namely Bismarck, which was to make newspapermen the mouthpiece of one's real intentions, in order to be able to acknowledge them or disavow them according to the needs of the hour.

But while Count Leinsdorf acted with such shrewdness, he overlooked one thing. For it was not only a man like himself who saw what was true, the thing we are all in need of ; innumerable other people also think themselves in possession of it. One can practically define this as a form of induration of the condition, previously mentioned, in which one still goes in for metaphor. Sooner or later the taste even for that disappears ; and many of the people in whom there remains a residue of finally unsatisfied dreams at this stage provide themselves with a dot to stare at in secret, as though it were there they expected a world to begin that is still owing to them. Within a very short time after he had sent out his statement to the press, His Highness believed he noticed that all the people who have no money make up for it by having an unpleasant crank tucked away somewhere inside them. This obstinate man within the man goes along to the office with him every morning and, being quite unable to protest in any effective manner against the way of the world, makes up for it by keeping his eyes glued, his whole life long, on a secret dot that everyone else refuses to see, although it is so very obviously the very dot from which originate all the calamities of a world that will not recognise its saviour. Such fixed points or dots, where the person's centre of gravity coincides with the world's centre of gravity, may be for instance a spittoon that can be shut with a simple catch; or the abolition of the kind of salt-cellars in restaurants that people poke their knives into, which would instantly stop the spread of that scourge of humanity, tuberculosis; or the introduction of Ohl's shorthand system, which by bringing about an incomparable saving in time would simultaneously solve the social problem; or conversion to a natural mode of living that would call a halt to the way the world is running to waste, as well as offering a metapsychical theory of the movements of celestial bodies, a plan for simplifying public administration and a reform of sexual life. Supposing circumstances treat a man well, he relieves his feelings by one day writing a book, or a pamphlet, or at least a newspaper article about his dot, so to some extent filing his protest in the records of mankind, which is tremendously soothing, even though nobody may read it. Generally, however, it attracts a few people who assure the author that he is a new Copernicus, after which they introduce themselves to him as unappreciated Newtons. This habit of going through each other's fur, picking out the dots, is very widespread and very comforting; but its effect is not lasting, because those concerned begin squabbling after a while and are then left quite on their own again. Yet it does also happen that one or the other gathers round him a small circle of admirers who send up a chorus of accusation to heaven for not sufficiently aiding its anointed son. And should a ray of hope suddenly descend from a great height upon such little agglomerations of dottiness— as actually happened when Count Leinsdorf let it be publicly known that an Austrian Year, if there really was going to be such a thing, which was as yet far from being definite, would in any case have to be in harmony with life's true aims—then they hail it like the saints receiving a vision from God.

Count Leinsdorf's thought had been that his work should become a mighty demonstration spontaneously rising out of the people's very midst. He had been thinking of the universities, the Church, of several names that were never missing from reports of charitable affairs, and even of the press. He was counting on the patriotic parties, the 'sound common sense' of the middle class, who hung out flags on the Emperor's birthday, and on the support of high finance ; he was even reckoning with the political element, for in his heart he hoped that with his great work he would be able to make precisely this superfluous by reducing politics to the common denominator of ' our fatherland ', which he intended later to divide by ' land ' in order to be left with nothing over but the ruler, the father of his people. But there was, as it happened, just this one thing that His Highness had not thought of, and he was taken unawares by the very widespread enthusiasm that was hatched out in the warmth of a great occasion, as maggots are in a conflagration. This was something His Highness had not reckoned with ; he had expected a very great deal of patriotism but he was not prepared for inventions, theories, cosmological systems and people demanding that he should release them from intellectual oubliettes. They besieged his beautiful town house, lauding the Collateral Campaign as a chance to help truth to come into its own at last. And Count Leinsdorf did not know what to do about them. Conscious as he was of his social position, he could not, after all, sit down at one table with all these people ; on the other hand, as one whose spirit was filled with high-pitched morality he did not feel able to dodge them, and since his education, though strong on the political and philosophic side, was far from covering natural science and technology, he could not make head or tail of whether there was anything in these proposals or not.

In this situation he yearned more and more intensely for Ulrich, who had been recommended to him as just the man he would have needed now ; for his secretary, and for that matter any ordinary secretary, was naturally not up to coping with such demands. Once indeed, when he had been very annoyed with his secretary, he had even prayed to God—although he was ashamed of it the next day—for Ulrich to come at long last. And when nothing happened, His Highness himself embarked on a systematic search for him. He got them to look Ulrich up in the directory, but Ulrich was not yet in it. He then went to his friend Diotima, who generally had some helpful suggestion to make ; and there it was, the admirable woman had indeed already had a talk with Ulrich, but she had forgotten to ask him to leave his address—or at least that was what she said, for she wanted to turn the opportunity to account by putting forward another and much better suggestion where the secretaryship of the great Campaign was concerned.   But Count Leinsdorf was very worked up and declared most positively that he had already got used to Ulrich, couldn't do with a Prussian, not even with a reformed one, and was altogether set on not having any more complications.   He was aghast to see that his dear friend at this showed signs of being hurt, and as a result got an inspiration of his own : he told her that he was now going to drive straight to his friend the President of Police, who must, after all, be able to produce the address of any and every citizen of the country.

38 *Clarisse and her daemons.*

WHEN Ulrich's note arrived, Walter and Clarisse were again playing the piano so violently that the spindly arty-crafty reproduction furniture was jumping about and the Dante Gabriel Rossetti prints were trembling on the walls.   The aged courier, who had found all the doors open and had walked in without meeting anyone, got the full blast of thunder and lightning in his face when he penetrated right into the living-room, and the sacred uproar into which he had wandered pressed him, awe-struck, up against the wall.   It was Clarisse who finally discharged the onward-urging musical excitement in two mighty crashes and set him free.   While she was reading the letter, the interrupted outpour still writhed under Walter's hands ; a melody ran along jerkily as a stork and then spread its wings.   Clarisse observed this distrustfully, while deciphering Ulrich's writing.

When she announced that Ulrich was coming, Walter said : " What a pity ! "

She sat down again beside him on her little revolving pianostool, and a smile, which Walter for some reason felt to be cruel, parted her sensual-looking lips.   It was the moment when pianists rein their blood in, in order to give it its head in one shared rhythm, and the axes of their eyes stand out of their heads like four long parallel stalks, while with their hindquarters tensed they hang on to their little stools, which keep wobbling on the long neck of the wooden screw.

The next moment Clarisse and Walter shot away like two railway-engines racing side by side. The music that they were playing came flying towards their eyes like the glittering rails, then vanished under the thundering engine and spread out behind them as a chiming, resonant, miraculously permanent landscape. During this furious, rushing journey these two people's separate feelings compressed into a single feeling : hearing, blood, muscles, all were swept helplessly along by the same experience. Shimmering, inclining, curving walls of sound forced their bodies on to the one track, bent them as one, and widened and contracted their breasts with their united breathing. Precise to a fraction of a second, gaiety, sadness, anger and fear, love and hatred, longing and weariness went flying on through Walter and Clarisse. It was a union like that in a great panic, when hundreds of people, who just a moment earlier were in all respects distinct from each other, make the same lashing movements of flight, utter the same senseless cries, open wide their mouths and eyes all in the same way, as they are swept to and fro together by the same aimless force, swept to left and to right, yelling, twitching, trembling, all pell-mell. But it had not the same mindless, overwhelming force that life has, in which such occurrences do not come about so easily, though when they do everything personal is utterly blotted out. The anger, the love, the happiness, the gaiety and sadness that Clarisse and Walter lived through in this flight were not the full and live emotions, but scarcely more than the physical shell of them worked up to frenzy. They sat stiff and transfigured on their little stools, were angry, in love, and sad at nothing, with nothing and about nothing, or each of them at, with and about something different from the other, thinking different things and each with his or her own problems in mind. Music's command united them in sublime passion and at the same time left something in them that was remote as in the compulsive sleep of hypnosis.

Each of these two people felt this in his or her own way.

Walter was happy and excited. Like most musical people he held these billowing surges and emotional stirrings of the soul, that is, the cloudily churned-up somatic sediment of the psyche, to be the simple language of the eternal, uniting all human beings. It delighted him to hug Clarisse to him with the strong arm of primal emotion. Today he had come home from the office earlier than usual. He had been seeing to the cataloguing of works of art that still had the shape of great and integral times and radiated a mysterious power of the will. Clarisse had welcomed him in a friendly way, and now in the enormous world of music she was bound firmly to him. Today everything bore a mysterious mark of success, a soundless march within, as when gods are on their way. ' Perhaps today is the day ? ' Walter thought. For he did not want to bring Clarisse back to himself by force ; he wanted understanding to rise from her innermost being and incline her gently towards him.

The piano was hammering glittering note-nails into a wall of air. Although in its origin this process was completely real, the walls of the sitting-room vanished, and in their place arose the flowing golden walls of music, that mysterious room where ego and world, perception and feeling, inside and outside melt whirling into each other, quite intangibly, while the room itself consists entirely of sensation, certainty, precision, indeed of a whole hierarchy of the glory of ordered details. It was to these sensual details that the threads of feeling were tied, ceaselessly being spun out of the wavering haze of the souls ; and this haze was mirrored in the precision of the walls and so to itself seemed clear. Like cocoons, these two people's souls hung among the threads and rays, and the more thickly wrapped in silken radiance they were, the more Walter wallowed in it ; and his dreams turned more and more into the swaddled shape of a little child, until he began here and there to give the notes a wrong and sentimental emphasis.

But before it came to that and caused a spark of everyday feeling to shoot through the golden mist and unite them both again on the level of earthly relationships, Clarisse's thoughts had in their very nature become as different from his as can only happen when two people are storming along beside each other with twin gestures of desperation and rapture. In fluttering mists images leaped up, melted into each other, overcast each

other, and vanished : that was Clarisse's kind of thinking.   In
this she had a way of her own.   Often there were several thoughts
there simultaneously, often none at all ; but then the thoughts
could be felt like daemons behind the scenes, and the temporal
sequence of experience, which to other people is a definite support, in Clarisse turned into a veil, now drawing its fabric together
in dense folds, now dissolving into a scarcely visible breath of air.

This time there were three persons round Clarisse : Walter,
Ulrich, and Moosbrugger the murderer.

It was Ulrich who had told her about Moosbrugger.

Attraction and revulsion mingled, casting a weird spell.

Clarisse was gnawing at the root of love.   It was a forked root,
a thing of kissing and of biting, of glances clinging to each other
and of a tormented last-minute aversion of the gaze.   'Does
getting on well together drive people into hatred ? ' she wondered.
'Does civilised life yearn for brutality ?   Does peacefulness call
for cruelty ?   Does order demand to be torn to shreds ? '   It was
this, and yet it was not this, which Moosbrugger excited.   Under
the thunder of the music a world conflagration was hovering about
her, a conflagration that had not yet broken out but was secretly
smouldering in the rafters.   But it was also the way it is in a
metaphor, where the things are the same and yet, again, quite
different from each other ; and out of the dissimilarity of the
similar, and out of the similarity of the dissimilar, two columns of
smoke went up with the fairy-tale aroma of baked apples and pine-
twigs strewn on the fire.

'One ought never to stop playing,' Clarisse said to herself when
they got to the end and, hastily flicking the pages back, she began
the music again at the beginning.

Walter smiled awkwardly and joined in.

"What actually does Ulrich do with his mathematics ? " she
asked him.

Playing on, Walter shrugged his shoulders.   He was like a man
at the wheel of a racing-car.

'One ought to go on and on playing, to the very end,' Clarisse
thought.   'If one could play without ever stopping, right to the
end of one's life, what would Moosbrugger be then ?   Appalling ?
A madman ?   A black bird from heaven ? '   She knew no answer.

She knew nothing at all.   One day—she could have worked

out to the very day when it had happened—she had waked up out of the sleep of childhood, and there was the conviction, all ready and waiting for her, that she had a call to bring something about, to play a particular part, perhaps even was chosen for some great purpose. At that time she still knew nothing at all of the world. Nor did she believe anything of what people told her about it—for instance her parents or her elder brother. What they said was only tinkling words, all very well and quite nice in its way, but one couldn't make it one's own ; one simply couldn't, any more than a chemical substance will absorb another that has not got the right properties. Then Walter came. That was the day. From that day on everything had the right properties. Walter wore a little moustache, a toothbrush-moustache. He addressed her as ' Fräulein Clarisse '. And all at once the world was no longer a desolate, disorderly, jagged plane, but a glittering disk with Walter a point at the centre, herself a point at the centre, the two of them coincident in one central point. Earth, buildings, fallen leaves not yet swept away, aching lines in the air (she remembered the moment, one of the most tormenting in her childhood, when she had stood looking at a ' view ' with her father, and he, the painter, went into raptures over it for endless ages, whereas gazing into the world along these long lines of air only hurt her as though she had had to run her finger along the edge of a ruler), such were the things that life had consisted of before. And then it had become her own, flesh of her own flesh.

Then she knew that she would do something titanic. She could not yet say what it would be, but at that time she felt it most violently in music and hoped then that Walter would be an even greater genius than Nietzsche—to say nothing of Ulrich, who came on the scene later and had merely given her Nietzsche's works as a present.

From then on things had begun to move. How quickly, it was now quite impossible to say. How badly she used to play the piano, how little she had understood about music ! Now she played better than Walter. And how many books she had read ! Where had they all come from ? She saw all this before her like swarms of black birds fluttering round a little girl standing in the snow. But a while later she saw a black wall with white spots on it. Black stood for everything she did not know, and although the white ran together into small and sometimes larger islands, the black remained endless and unchanging. From this black there emanated fear and excitement. ‘ Is it the Devil ? ’ she wondered. ‘ Has the Devil become Moosbrugger ? ’ Among the white specks she now noticed thin grey paths : that was how she had got from one thing to another in her life, those were events, departures, arrivals, excited arguments, conflict with her parents, marriage, the house, indescribable struggles with Walter. . . . The thin grey paths meandered. ‘ Serpents ! ’ Clarisse thought. ‘ Snares ! ’ These events twisted round her, clinging, holding her fast, not letting her get where she wanted to, were slippery and made her suddenly dart at a point that she had not wished to get at.

Snakes, snares, slippery—that was how life ran. Her thoughts began running like life. The tips of her fingers dipped into the music’s torrent. In the stream-bed of the music snakes and snares came drifting down. Then, safe as a silent bay, the prison where Moosbrugger was hidden away now opened up. Clarisse’s thoughts entered his cell in awe. ‘ One must go on playing music right to the end ! ’ she repeated to herself encouragingly, but her heart trembled violently. When it had calmed down again, the whole cell was filled with her Self. It was a feeling as mild as balm on a wound, but when she tried to hold it fast for ever, it began to open out and shift apart like a fairy-tale or a dream. There Moosbrugger sat, resting his head on his hand, and she loosened his fetters. While her fingers were moving, strength, courage, virtue, kindness, beauty and riches came into the cell, like a wind, summoned by her fingers, coming from various meadows. ‘ It doesn’t matter at all why I may be doing this,’ Clarisse felt. ‘ The only thing that matters is that now I am doing it.’ She laid her hands, a part of her own body, on his eyes, and when she withdrew her fingers, Moosbrugger had become a handsome young man, and she herself stood beside him, a wonderfully beautiful woman whose body was sweet and mellow as southern wine and far from being inflexible, as little Clarisse’s body usually was. ‘ This is our body of innocence ! ’ she realised in some deep-down layer of her consciousness.

But why was Walter not like that ? Rising up out of the depths of this dream in music, she remembered how childish she still

was when she began to love Walter, then when she was only
fifteen, and how she wanted to save him, by courage, strength
and kindness, from all the dangers menacing his genius. And
how wonderful it was when Walter saw those deep spiritual
dangers everywhere ! And she asked herself whether all that had
only been childish. Their marriage had irradiated it with a
disturbing light. Out of this marriage there suddenly sprang a
great embarrassment for their love. Although this last period
had of course also been wonderful, perhaps more full of meaning
and substance than that preceding it, yet the gigantic conflagration,
the flaring flames all over the sky, had turned into something like
the trouble caused by a domestic fire that would not burn properly.
Clarisse was not quite sure whether her struggles with Walter
were still really great. And life ran like this music vanishing
under one's hands. In a wink it would be over. Clarisse was
slowly being overwhelmed by utter terror. And then she noticed
that Walter's playing was becoming unsure. His emotion splashed
on to the keys like big drops of rain. She guessed at once what
he was thinking of : the child. She knew that he wanted to tie
her to himself with a child. That was their quarrel day in, day
out. And the music never stopped for a moment, the music
knew no denial. Like a net, whose meshes she had not perceived,
it tightened round her with terrible swiftness.

Then Clarisse jumped up in the middle of playing and banged
the piano shut, so that Walter could barely save his fingers.

Oh, how it hurt ! Still quite startled, he understood it all.
It was Ulrich's coming, the mere announcement of it, that got
Clarisse into such an over-wrought state of mind ! He did her
harm by callously stimulating the very thing in her that Walter
himself scarcely dared to touch, the ill-starred streak of genius in
Clarisse, the secret cavern where some ominous thing tore at
chains that might some day snap.

He did not stir. He merely gazed at her in bewilderment.

And Clarisse gave no explanations, simply stood there, breathing
hard.

She was not in love with Ulrich, not at all, she assured Walter
when he raised the subject. If she ever fell in love with him,
she would say so at once. But she felt herself kindled by him,
like a taper. She felt herself giving out more light and amounting

to more, when he was near her—whereas Walter only wanted to close the shutters all the time. And what she felt was no one's business, neither Ulrich's nor Walter's either!

And yet Walter believed that somewhere in the anger and indignation breathing out of her words he could sense a narcotic deadly grain of something that was not anger.

Dusk had fallen. The room was black. The piano was black. The shadows of two people who loved each other were black. Clarisse's eyes shone in the darkness, lit like candles, and in Walter's grievously restless mouth the enamel of a tooth glimmered like ivory. It seemed—even though outside in the world the high drama of history might be going on—that this, for all its painful aspects, was one of the moments for the sake of which God had created the earth.

39 *A Man Without Qualities consists of qualities without a man.*

BUT Ulrich did not get there that evening. After Director Fischel had hurried away, leaving him alone, he again became preoccupied with the question of his youth, wondering why all figurative and (in the higher sense of the word) untrue utterances were so uncannily favoured by the world. 'One always gets one step further ahead precisely when one is lying,' he thought. 'I ought to have told him that as well.'

Ulrich was a passionate man; but 'passion' here should not be taken as meaning the collective of what are called 'the passions'. There must have been something that had time and again driven him into the latter, and this was perhaps passion, but in the actual state of excitement and of excited actions his attitude was at once passionate and detached. He had gone in for more or less everything there was and felt that even now he might at any time plunge into something that need not mean anything at all to him if only it happened to stimulate his urge for action. So he could with little exaggeration say of his life that everything in it had fulfilled itself as if it all belonged together more than it belonged to him. He had always been ' in for a penny, in for a pound ', whether in contest or in love. And so he more or less had to believe that the personal qualities he had gained in this way belonged more to each other than to him, indeed that every one of them, when he examined it closely, was no more intimately bound up with him than with other people who might also happen to possess it.

But undoubtedly one was nevertheless conditioned by them and consisted of them, even if one was not identical with them, and so sometimes when at rest one seemed to oneself precisely as much a stranger as when in motion. If Ulrich had been asked to say what he was really like, he would have been at a loss ; for like many people he had never tested himself otherwise than in the performance of a task and in his relation to it. His self-confidence had not been damaged, nor was it coddled and vain, and it felt no need for that kind of overhauling and greasing that is called examining one's conscience. Was he a strong personality ? He didn't know ; on this score he was perhaps fatefully mistaken. But he was certainly a man who had always had confidence in his strength. Even now he had no doubt that this difference between having one's own experiences and qualities and remaining a stranger to them was only a difference in attitude, in a certain sense an act of will or a matter of living on a chosen latitude between generality and individuality. To put it quite simply, one's attitude to the things that happen to one and that one does can be either more general or more personal. One can feel a blow not only as pain but as an affront, which will intensify it intolerably ; but one can also take it in a sporting spirit, as an obstacle that must not be allowed either to intimidate one or get one into a state of blind rage, and then it not infrequently happens that one does not notice it at all. In this second case, however, nothing has happened but that one has sorted it into its place in a larger complex, namely that of combat, as a result of which its nature proves to be dependent on the task that it has to fulfil. And precisely this phenomenon—that an experience gets its significance, even its content, only from its position in a chain of logically consistent actions—is apparent in everyone who regards experience not merely as something personal but as a challenge to his spiritual strength. He too will then experience his actions more faintly. But, oddly enough, what is considered superior intelligence in boxing is called cold and callous as soon as it occurs, from a liking for an intellectual attitude to life, in people who cannot box. There are in fact also all sorts of other distinctions in use by the aid of which it is possible to adopt or insist on a general or a personal attitude, according to the situation. If a murderer proceeds in a matter-of-fact and efficient manner, it will be interpreted as particular brutality. A professor who goes on working out a problem in his wife's arms will be reproached with being a dry-as-dust pedant. A politician who climbs high over the bodies of the slain is described as vile or great according to the degree of his success. Of soldiers, executioners and surgeons, on the other hand, precisely the same cold-bloodedness is demanded as is condemned in others. It is not necessary to go into the moral of these examples any further in order to be struck by the uncertainty leading, in every case, to a compromise between objectively correct and personally correct conduct.

This uncertainty formed a wide background to Ulrich's personal problem. In earlier times one could be an individual with a better conscience than one can today. People used to be like the stalks of corn in the field. They were probably more violently flung to and fro by God, hail, fire, pestilence and war than they are today, but it was collectively, in terms of towns, of countrysides, the field as a whole ; and whatever was left to the individual stalk in the way of personal movement was something that could be answered for and was clearly defined. Today, on the other hand, responsibility's point of gravity lies not in the individual but in the relations between things. Has one not noticed that experiences have made themselves independent of man? They have gone on to the stage, into books, into the reports of scientific institutions and expeditions, into communities based on religious or other conviction, which develop certain kinds of experience at the cost of all the others as in a social experiment ; and in so far as experiences are not merely to be found in work, they are simply in the air. Who today can still say that his anger is really his own anger, with so many people butting in and knowing so much more about it than he does ? There has arisen a world of qualities without a man to them, of experiences without anyone to experience them, and it almost looks as though under ideal conditions man would no longer experience anything at all privately and the comforting weight of personal responsibility would dissolve into a system of formulae for potential meanings. It is probable that the dissolution of the anthropocentric attitude (an attitude that, after so long seeing man as the centre of the universe, has been dissolving for some centuries now) has finally begun to affect the personality itself ; for the belief that the most important thing about experience is the experiencing of it, and about deeds the doing of them, is beginning to strike most people as naïve. Doubtless there are still people who experience things quite personally, saying ' we were at So-and-So's yesterday ' or ' we'll do this or that today ' and enjoying it without its needing to have any further content or significance. They like everything that their fingers touch, and are persons as purely private as is possible. The world becomes a private world as soon as it comes into contact with them, and shines like a rainbow. Perhaps they are very happy ; but this kind of people now usually appears absurd to the others, although it is as yet by no means established why.

And all at once, in the midst of these reflections, Ulrich had to confess to himself, smiling, that for all this he was, after all, a ' character ', even without having one.

40

A man with all the qualities, but they are a matter of indifference to him.
A master-mind is arrested, and the Collateral Campaign gets its honorary secretary.

IT is not difficult to give a description of this thirty-two-year-old man, Ulrich, in general outline, even though all he knew about himself was that he was as far from all the qualities as he was near to them, and that all of them, whether they had become his own or not, in some strange way were equally a matter of indifference to him. Associated with his intellectual suppleness, which was based simply on a great variety of gifts, there was, in him, a certain bellicosity too. He was of a masculine turn of mind. He was not sensitive where other people were concerned and rarely tried to get inside their minds, except when he wanted to understand them for his own ends. He had no respect for rights when he did not respect those whose rights they were, and that happened rarely. For with the passing of time he had developed a certain readiness to adopt negative attitudes, a flexible dialectic of feeling that was inclined to tempt him into discovering defects in what was generally approved of and defending what was considered beyond the pale, and into rejecting obligations with an irritation arising out of a determination to create obligations of his own. In spite of this determination, however, with certain exceptions that he considered his due he simply left his moral conduct to that chivalrous code that is the guide of more or less all men in bourgeois society so long as they are living in settled circumstances ; and in this manner, with all the arrogance, ruthlessness and nonchalance of a man who is conscious of his own vocation, he led the life of another person who made more or less ordinary, utilitarian and social use of his tastes and abilities. It was natural to him to regard himself—quite without vanity—as the instrument of a not unimportant purpose of which he felt certain he would, all in good time, discover more ; and even now, in this newly begun year of groping unrest, after he had realised how his life had been drifting, the feeling of being on the way somewhere soon returned and he made no particular effort with his plans. It is not altogether easy to recognise the driving passion in a temperament like this, which has been ambiguously shaped by natural talents and by circumstances, so long as its fate has not been laid bare by any really hard counter-pressure. But the main thing is that it still lacks some factor unknown such as would make a decision possible. Ulrich was a man whom something compelled to live against his own grain, although he seemed to let himself float along without any constraint.

The comparison of the world with a laboratory reminded him

of an old idea of his.   Formerly he had thought of the kind of life that would appeal to him as a large experimental station, where the best ways of living as a human being would be tried out and new ones discovered.   The fact that this whole complex of laboratories worked more or less haphazardly, without any directors or theoreticians, was another matter.   It might even be said that he himself had wanted to become something like a dominant spirit and master-mind.   And who, after all, would not ?   It is so natural for the mind to be considered the highest of all things, ruling over all things.   That is what we are taught.   All and sundry adorn themselves with mind, use it as trimming wherever possible.   Mind and spirit, when in combination with something else, are the most widespread thing there is.   There is a masculine mind, a cultured mind, the greatest living mind, the spirit of loyalty, the spirit of love, 'keeping up the spirit' of this cause or that, 'acting in the spirit of our movement' and so forth.   How solid and unimpeachable it sounds, right down to the lowest levels !   Everything else, the everyday crime or bustling greed for gain, appears by contrast as that which is never admitted, the dirt that God removes from under His toe-nails.

But when the spirit stands alone, a naked noun, bare as a ghost to whom one would like to lend a sheet—what then ?   One can read the poets, study the philosophers, buy pictures and have discussions all night long.   But is it spirit that one gains by doing so ?   Assuming one does gain it—does one then possess it ?   This something called spirit, so firmly bound up with the form in which it happens to manifest itself, passes through the person who wants to receive and harbour it, leaving nothing behind but a slight tremor.   What are we to do with all this spirit ?   It is continually being produced on masses of paper, stone and canvas, in downright astronomical quantities, and is being as ceaselessly ingested and consumed with a gigantic expenditure of nervous energy.   But what happens to it then ?   Does it vanish like a mirage ?   Does it dissolve into particles ?   Is it an exception to the natural law of conservation ?   The dust-particles sinking down into us, slowly settling, are in no relation to all the trouble involved.   Where has it gone ?   Where, what, is it ?   Perhaps, if one knew more about it, there would be an awkward silence round this noun 'spirit' . . .

Evening had come.   Buildings, as though broken out of their setting in space, asphalt, steel rails—all this formed the now cooling shell of the city.   In this maternal shell, filled with childlike, joyful, angry human movement, every drip begins as a droplet, frothing and splashing, begins with a tiny explosion and is caught up by the walls and cooled off, becoming milder, more quiescent, clinging tenderly to the inner wall of the mother shell and finally solidifying, setting fast there as a little grain of substance.

'Why,' Ulrich suddenly thought, 'why didn't I become a pilgrim?'   A pure, unconditional way of living, hectically fresh as very clear air, spread out before his mind's eye.   Anyone who did not want to accept life as it was should at least reject it as the saints did ; and yet it was simply impossible to consider that seriously.   Nor could he become a traveller and adventurer, although that life might well have a touch of perpetual honeymoon, and he felt the impulse to it in his limbs as in his temperament.   He had not been capable of becoming either a poet or one of those disappointed people who believed only in money and power, although he had had the makings of either, as of everything.   He forgot his age, imagining he was twenty.   Nevertheless, it had been just as finally decided within him even then that he could not become any of these things.   There was something attracting him to everything there was, and something stronger that would not let him get to it.   Why did he live so vaguely and undecidedly ?   Undoubtedly—he said to himself—what kept him, as under a spell, in this aloof and anonymous form of existence was nothing but the compulsion to that loosing and binding of the world that is known by a word one does not like to encounter alone :   spirit.

And though he himself did not know why, Ulrich suddenly felt sad and thought :   ' It's simply that I'm not fond of myself.' In the frozen, petrified body of the town, in its innermost depths, he felt his own heart beating.   There was something in him that had never wanted to stay anywhere, but had groped its way along the walls of the world, thinking :   There are still millions of other walls.   It was this ridiculous drop of Self, slowly growing cold, that did not want to give up its fire, the tiny red-hot core within it.

The mind has learned that beauty can make things good, bad, stupid or enchanting.   The mind dissects and analyses a sheep and a penitent sinner and finds humility and patience in both. It investigates a substance and observes that in large quantities it is a poison, in smaller quantities a stimulant. It knows that the mucous membrane of the lips is related to the mucous membrane of the intestine, but knows too that the humility of those lips is related to the humility of all that is saintly. It mixes things up, unravels them again and forms new combinations. Good and evil, above and below, are for it not relative ideas tinged with scepticism, but terms of a function, values dependent on the context in which they appear. It has learnt from the centuries that vices may turn into virtues and virtues into vices, and actually regards it as sheer clumsiness if one does not in one lifetime succeed in turning a criminal into a useful citizen. It does not recognise anything as in itself permissible or impermissible, for anything may have a quality by which it some day becomes part of a great new relationship. It secretly has a mortal hatred of everything that behaves as though it were established once and for all, the great ideals and laws and their little fossilised imprint, the hedged-in character. It regards nothing as firmly established, neither any personality nor any order of things or ideas. Because our knowledge may change with every day, it believes in no ties, and everything possesses the value that it has only until the next act of creation, as a face to which one is speaking changes even while the words are being spoken.

For the spirit of man is the great opportunist, but cannot itself be seized hold of anywhere ; and one might almost believe that nothing is brought about by its influence but decay. All progress means a gain in each particular case, but also a severance from the wholeness of things ; and this means an increase in power, which leads to a progressive increase in powerlessness, and there is no leaving off. Ulrich was reminded of the almost hourly growing body of facts and discoveries out of which the mind has to peer forth today if it wants to scrutinise any question closely. This body grows away from the inner being. Although there are countless views, opinions, and classificatory ideas from all latitudes and ages, from all sorts of sound and sick brains, waking and dreaming brains, lacing it like thousands of sensitive little nerveskeins, yet there is no central point where they all unite. Man feels he is dangerously near the stage where he will suffer the same fate as those gigantic primeval animals that perished because of their size. But he can't leave off.

And this brought Ulrich back to that rather dubious notion in which he had long believed and which he had even now not quite rooted out of himself : that the world would be best governed by a senate of highly evolved men possessing great knowledge. It is, after all, very natural to think that man, who lets himself be treated by professionally qualified doctors when he is ill, and not by shepherd-lads, has no reason when in good health to let himself by treated, as he actually does in his public affairs, by windbags whose qualifications are no better than those of shepherd-lads. And that is why young people who have the essentials of life at heart start out by thinking everything in the world that is neither true nor good nor beautiful—such as for instance the inland revenue department or, to keep to the point, a parliamentary debate—unimportant. At least, that is the way they used to think in those days. Nowadays, thanks to education in politics and economics, they are said to be different. But even then, when one grew older—and on longer acquaintance with the smoking-chamber of the mind, where the world cures the bacon of its business—one learnt to adapt oneself to reality ; and the final condition of the qualified intellectual was approximately this—that he restricted himself to his ' subject ' and spent the rest of his life in the conviction that although perhaps everything ought to be different, there was certainly no point in thinking about it. This is a pretty fair picture of the inner equilibrium of the people who follow intellectual pursuits. And all at once the whole thing presented itself to Ulrich comically, in the question whether in the end, since there was certainly plenty of mind and spirit knocking about, all that was wrong was that the spirit was mere spirit and the mind had no mind ?

He felt like laughing at that. After all, he himself was one of those specialists who renounced all else. But disappointed ambition, still alive, went through him like a sword. In this moment two Ulrichs walked side by side.

The one looked around, smiling, and thought : ' So that's where I once wanted to play a part, against such a stage-décor. One day I woke up, not snug as in mother's little basket, but with the firm conviction that I must accomplish something. I was

that reached out for the lemonade and held the glass abstractedly, without the nabob's drinking from it. After this climax was passed she did her duty like a bewildered little automaton and made her way as rapidly as possible out of this room of world history, where everything was full of legs and talk, out into the hall again.

44

Continuation and conclusion of the great conference. Ulrich takes a liking to Rachel, and Rachel to Soliman. The Collateral Campaign is given a definite organisation.

ULRICH had a weakness for girls of this kind, who were ambitious and well-behaved and in their well-trained timidity resembled little fruit-trees whose sweet ripe fruit one day falls into the mouth of some young knight of Cockaigne, when he deigns to open his lips. 'They must be brave and hardy as the Stone-Age women who shared their warrior's bed by night and carried his weapons and the domestic utensils on the march by day,' he thought, although he himself, except in the prehistorically distant age of his awakening manhood, had never gone forth on such war-paths. Sighing, he sat down, for the session had been resumed.

Thinking about it, he was struck by the fact that the black-and-white vestments into which these girls were put were of the same colours as the garments that nuns wore ; he noticed it for the first time, and he marvelled at it. But now the divine Diotima was speaking.

She was declaring that the Collateral Campaign must culminate in a great sign. That was to say, it could not have just any goal that happened to be visible far and wide, however patriotic such a goal might be. On the contrary, their goal must stir the heart

given my cues, and I felt they did not concern me. Everything was filled with my own intentions and expectations, as though with flickering stage-fright. But in the meantime the stage revolved without my noticing it, I got a bit further on my way, and now perhaps I am already standing at the exit. In next to no time it will have turned me right out, and all I shall have spoken of my great part will be : " The horses are saddled." The devil take the lot of you ! '

But while the one walked through the floating evening, smiling at these thoughts, the other had his fists clenched in pain and anger. He was the less visible of the two. And what he was thinking of was how to find a magic formula, a lever that one might be able to get a hold of, the real mind of the mind, the missing, perhaps very small, bit that would close the broken circle. This second Ulrich had no words at his disposal. Words leap like monkeys from tree to tree ; but in the dark realm where a man is rooted he lacks their friendly mediation. The ground streamed away under his feet. He could hardly open his eyes. Can a feeling blow like a storm and yet not be a stormy feeling at all ? If one speaks of a storm of emotion, one means the kind in which man's bark groans and man's branches fly as though they were about to break. But this was a storm with a quite calm surface. It was almost, but not quite, a state of conversion, of reversion. There was no shift in the expression of the face, but inwardly no atom seemed to remain in its place. Ulrich's senses were unclouded, and yet each person he went past was perceived differently from usual by his eye, each sound differently by his ear. It would be wrong to say : more sharply ; nor was it more deeply either, nor more softly, more naturally or more unnaturally. Ulrich could not say anything at all, but at this moment he thought of the strange experience that ' spirit ' is as of a beloved by whom one has been deceived all one's life long, without loving her any the less for that ; and this united him with everything that came his way. For when one loves, everything is love, even when it is pain and loathing. The little twig on the tree and the pale window-pane in the evening light became an experience sunk deep in his own essential nature, an experience that could scarcely be expressed in words. Things seemed not to be of wood and stone ; it was as if their fabric were a grand and infinitely delicate

immorality, which, in the moment when it came into contact with him, turned into a shock of deep moral emotion.

That lasted as long as a smile. And Ulrich was just thinking : ' Now for once I'll stay put where it has swept me ' when, as bad luck would have it, this tension crashed against an obstacle.

What happened now actually originated in an utterly different world from that in which Ulrich had just been experiencing trees and stones as a sensitive extension of his own body.

For a working-class paper had, as Count Leinsdorf would have put it, poured destructive venom on the Great Idea, asserting that it was merely a new sensation for the ruling class, following up the last sexual murder ; and this inflammatory talk had affected a worthy labourer who had drunk a little too much. He brushed against two respectable citizens who were feeling contented with their day's business and who, secure in the consciousness that right and proper opinions could be aired at any time, were somewhat loudly expressing their approval of the patriotic Campaign, of which they had read in their paper. There was an exchange of ' words '. And because the proximity of a policeman was as encouraging to the loyal citizens as it was provoking to the attacker, the scene became increasingly impassioned. The policeman at first watched it over his shoulder, and then turned round, and gradually drew closer ; he was present as an observer, like a protruding arm of the iron machinery of the State, complete with buttons and other metal parts. The fact is, living permanently in a well-ordered State has an out-and-out spectral aspect : one cannot step into the street or drink a glass of water or get into a tram without touching the perfectly balanced levers of a gigantic apparatus of laws and relations, setting them in motion or letting them maintain one in the peace and quiet of one's existence. One knows hardly any of these levers, which extend deep into the inner workings and on the other side are lost in a network the entire constitution of which has never been disentangled by any living being. Hence one denies their existence, just as the common man denies the existence of the air, insisting that it is mere emptiness ; but it seems that precisely this is what lends life a certain spectral quality—the fact that everything that is denied reality, everything that is colourless, odourless, tasteless, imponderable and non-moral, like water, air, space, money and

the passing of time, is in reality what is most important. Man is at times seized with panic as in the helplessness of dream, by a gale of movement, wildly lashing out like an animal that has got into the incomprehensible mechanism of a net. Such was the effect the policeman's buttons had on the labourer, and it was at this moment that the officer of the law, feeling that he was not being paid due respect, proceeded to make the arrest.

This did not take place without resistance and repeated manifestation of a seditious attitude. The sensation so caused was flattering to the drunk man, and a previously concealed total dislike of his fellow-creatures now broke out into the open. A passionate struggle for self-assertion began. A higher sense of his own ego came into conflict with an uncanny feeling of not being quite firmly fixed in his own skin. And the world too was not quite solid ; it was an unsteady mist, continually becoming distorted and changing its shape. Buildings stood crookedly broken out of space. Between them were ridiculous, swarming, yet all kindred silly fools, the people. ' I am called to put things straight here,' felt the man in this extraordinary state of drunkenness. The whole scene was filled with something flickering. Some piece of what was happening came clearly towards him like a few yards of road, but then the walls revolved again. His eyes felt as if they were standing out of his head on long stalks, while the soles of his feet clung to the ground. A strange and wonderful outpouring came from his mouth ; out of his innermost being came words of which there was no telling how they had first got in there, and possibly they were words of abuse. It wasn't so easy to be sure. The outside and inside of things collapsed upon each other. This anger was no inner anger, but only the bodily shell of anger worked up to fury, and a policeman's face came very slowly closer to a clenched fist, and then it was bleeding.

But the policeman had trebled meanwhile. As the policemen came hurrying up, a crowd gathered. The drunk man had thrown himself on the ground and was resisting arrest. Then Ulrich committed an imprudence. He had heard the words " insulting His Majesty " and now remarked that in his present condition the man was not capable of insulting anyone, and that he ought to be sent home to sleep it off. He did not think anything of it, but he had met with the wrong people. The man

shouted that for all he cared Ulrich and His Majesty could both go and be . . . And a policeman, who obviously attributed the blame for this relapse to the interference, barked at Ulrich to move on. Now, as it happened, Ulrich was not accustomed to regard the State as anything but a hotel in which one was entitled to civility and service, and he objected to the tone in which he had been addressed. This quite unexpectedly caused the police to see that one drunk was not sufficient reason for the presence of three officers of the law, whereupon they took Ulrich in charge as well.

The hand of a uniformed man clutched his arm. His arm was a good deal stronger than this offensive clutch, but he could not very well break out of it unless he wanted to let himself in for a hopeless boxing-match with the armed minions of the State. So there was nothing else for him to do but to utter a polite request that he might be allowed to come along voluntarily. The station was in the district headquarters building. When he came in, the floor and walls reminded Ulrich of barracks. They showed signs of the same sombre battle between the dirt that was being continually carried in and the crude detergents used against it. The next thing he noticed was the appointed symbol of civil authority : two writing-desks, each topped by a little ornamental balustrade from which several little columns were missing, hardly more than a crate for writing on, the cloth inlay torn and scorched, the whole thing resting on very low ball-feet and showing the last chipped traces of the yellow-brown varnish with which it had once been coated, away back in the days of the Emperor Ferdinand. The third thing was that the room was permeated by the dense feeling that this was a place where one had to wait without asking questions. Ulrich's own policeman, after reporting the grounds for arrest, stood beside him like a pillar. Ulrich tried to give some explanation at once. The sergeant in control of this fortress raised an eye from a form that he had been filling in when prisoners and escort came in, and surveyed Ulrich ; the eye then sank again, and he continued filling in the form. Ulrich got a whiff of infinity. Then the sergeant pushed the form aside, took a book from the shelf, made an entry, sprinkled sand on it, put the book back, took another, made an entry, sprinkled sand, pulled a file out of a bundle of similar files and continued his

activities with this. Ulrich got the feeling that now a second
infinity was unfolding, in the course of which the constellations
went on their predestined cycles, without his being in the world
at all.

From this office an open door led into a corridor with the cells
on each side. That was where Ulrich's protégé had been taken
immediately, and since there was no further sound from him, it
seemed likely that the blessing of sleep had descended upon him.
But there was also the feeling of uncanny other things going on.
The corridor with the cells along it must have a second entrance.
Ulrich repeatedly heard heavy-footed comings and goings, slam-
ming of doors, lowered voices. And all at once, when some other
person was brought in, one of these voices rose and Ulrich heard
it implore in despairing tones : " If you have a spark of human
feeling, don't arrest me ! " The voice broke, and there was
something oddly out-of-place, almost laughable, in this appeal to
a functionary to have feelings, since functions are after all only
carried out in a matter-of-fact way. The sergeant raised his head
for a moment, without quite withdrawing his attention from his
file. Ulrich heard the violent shuffling of many feet, the bodies
of which were evidently mutely pushing a resistant body. Then
came the sound of two feet alone, stumbling as though after a
push. A door slammed shut, a bolt clicked, the uniformed man
at the writing-desk bent his head again, and in the air lay the
silence of a full stop that has been set at the right place at the
end of a sentence.

But Ulrich seemed to have been mistaken in his assumption
that as far as the cosmos of the police was concerned he was not
yet created. For the next time the sergeant raised his head
he looked at him and the lines he had written last remained
moist and glimmering, without being sprinkled with sand, and
Ulrich—or rather, the case he was—all at once turned out to
have been in official existence for some time. Name ? Age ?
Occupation ? Address ? . . . Ulrich was being questioned.

He felt as though he had got caught up in a machine, which
was splitting him up into impersonal, general component parts
even before there was any mention of his guilt or innocence. His
name—those two words that are conceptually the poorest, but
emotionally the richest in the language—here counted for nothing.

His work, which had brought him honour in the scientific world (usually considered so solid), did not exist for this world here ; he was not asked about it even once. His face counted only from the point of view of ' description '. He had the feeling that he had never before thought about the fact that his eyes were grey eyes, belonging to one of the four officially recognised kinds of eyes in existence of which there were millions of specimens. His hair was fair, his build tall, his face oval, and his special peculiarities were none, although he himself was of a different opinion on this score. To his own way of feeling he was tall, his shoulders were broad, his chest expanded like a filled sail from the mast, and the joints of his body fastened his muscles off like small links of steel whenever he was angry or quarrelsome or, for instance, had Bonadea clinging to him. On the other hand, he was slim, lightly built, dark, and soft as a jelly-fish floating in water whenever he was reading a book that moved him or was touched by a breath of that great and homeless love whose presence in the world he had never been able to fathom. And so even at this moment he could also appreciate the statistical disenchantment of his person, and the methods of measurement and description applied to him by the police officer aroused his enthusiasm as much as might a love-poem invented by Satan. The most wonderful thing about it was that the police could not only dismantle a human being in this way, so that nothing remained of him, but that they would also put him together again out of these trifling components, unmistakably himself, and recognise him by them. All that is needed for this achievement is the addition of something imponderable, which they call ' suspicion '.

Ulrich all at once realised that it was only with the coolest of intelligence that he would be able to extricate himself from this situation into which his foolhardiness had got him. The questioning went on. He wondered what effect it would have if, when asked for his address, he were to answer : ' My address is that of a person I do not know.' Or if, in answer to the question why he had done what he had done, he were to answer that he always did something different from what he really cared about. But in outward reality he sedately named street and house-number and tried to invent an extenuatory account of his behaviour. The inner authority of the mind was meanwhile most distressingly

to meddle with the unsurpassable criticism of the suggestions made hitherto, which had all been magnificent. Nevertheless, now at the conclusion he would like to put forward the following ideas for their indulgent consideration. The intended demonstration was to have an influence abroad. But what had an influence abroad was a nation's might. Moreover, the situation in the European family of nations was, as His Highness had said, such that a demonstration of this kind would certainly not be without avail. Now, the idea of the State was, after all, that of might. Or, as Treitschke said : the State was the power of self-preservation in the struggle of the nations. He was only touching a well-known sore spot if he reminded them of the unsatisfactory condition in which the apathy of Parliament left the building up of our artillery—and of the navy too. He would therefore urge them to consider, in the event of noother aims being found, which was as yet by no means certain, that a broad popular interest in the questions of the army and its equipment would then be a very worthy aim. *Si vis pacem para bellum !* The strength that one displayed in peace warded off war, or at least made it much shorter. So he could certainly assure them that such a measure would also have the effect of reconciling the nations with each other and would in fact be an impressive demonstration of peaceful intentions.

At this moment there was something very odd indeed in the room. Most of those present had at first had the impression that this speech was not quite in keeping with the actual task for which they had gathered ; but as the General extended himself acoustically further and further, it began to sound like the reassuring march-step of well-ordered battalions. The Collateral Campaign's original meaning, 'Better than Prussia', rose shyly as though far off a regimental band were trumpeting the march of Prince Eugenius who rode forth against the Turks, or the *Gott erhalte* . . . Though of course if now His Highness had risen—which, however, he had not the slightest intention of doing—to suggest that they should put their Prussian brother Arnheim at the head of the regimental band, then, in the uncertain inner state of levitation in which they found themselves, they would have imagined they were hearing *Heil dir im Siegerkranz* and would scarcely have been able to object.

At the key-hole ' Rachelle ' signalled : " Now they're talking about war ! "

That she had hurried back into the hall at the end of the interval had to some extent also been occasioned by the fact that this time Arnheim had really brought his Soliman in his wake. The weather having changed for the worse, the little blackamoor had come after his master with an overcoat. He had made an impudent little face when Rachel opened the door to him, for he was a demoralised young Berliner whom women spoilt in a manner that he could not yet turn to the right account. But Rachel had thought that he must be talked to in the blackamoor language, and it had simply not occurred to her to try in German. As she had absolutely had to make herself understood, she had straightaway put her arm round the sixteen-year-old boy's shoulders, pointed to the kitchen, brought forward a chair for him and pushed in front of him what was close to hand in the way of cakes and drinks. She had never done such a thing before in all her life, and when she straightened up from the table, her heart was thudding like sugar being pounded in a mortar.

" What's your name ? " Soliman asked.

Goodness, he spoke German !

" Rachelle," Rachel had said and run away.

In the mean time Soliman had made the most of the cakes, wine and sandwiches in the kitchen, lit a cigarette and struck up a conversation with the cook. When Rachel came back from waiting on the guests, it gave her a stab. " In there," she said, " they're going to have another talk about something very import- ant any minute now ! " But that made no impression on Soliman ; and the cook, who was an elderly person, laughed.

" It may even turn into a war ! " Rachel added excitedly. And now the climax came in her announcement from the key- hole that it had almost got to that point.

Soliman pricked up his ears. " Are there any Austrian generals there ? " he asked.

" Look for yourself ! " Rachel said. " One has come already." And together they went to the key-hole.

Through the key-hole the glance fell now on a sheet of white paper, now on a nose ; now a big shadow went by, now a ring flashed. Life broke up into bright detail. Green baize stretched

away like a lawn. A white hand rested nowhere in particular, unrelated, pale as in a waxwork show. And if one looked through slantwise, one could see the General's gold sword-knot gleaming in a corner. Even the *blasé* Soliman showed signs of emotion. Life dilated uncannily, like a fairy-tale, when seen through a little opening in a door and through the imagination. The stooping position made the blood buzz in one's ears, and the voices beyond the door rumbled now like tumbling rocks, now slid as though on smoothly polished floorboards. Rachel straightened up slowly. The ground seemed to heave under her feet, and she was enveloped by the spirit of the occasion, as though she had put her head under one of those black cloths that conjurers and photographers use. Then Soliman straightened up too. The blood drained tremulously out of their heads. The little black boy smiled, and behind the blue lips the gums flashed scarlet.

While this instant in the hall, among the hung-up overcoats of influential personages, faded slowly, like a bugle-call, in the room there within a general resolution was being passed, after Count Leinsdorf had given utterance to the sentiment that they were all very grateful to the General for his most valuable suggestions, yet that for the present they would not go into detail but only deal with fundamental problems of organisation. In addition to this, however, apart from adapting the plan to the needs of the world according to its main aspects as represented by the ministries, all that was needed was a final resolution to the effect that those present unanimously agreed, as soon as the people's wish should have become apparent as a result of their mediation, to submit that wish to His Majesty with the most humble petition that it might be His Majesty's gracious pleasure to dispose freely of the means for its material fulfilment, which would have to be provided by then. This had the advantage that the people would thus be enabled to set itself the aim that it had recognised as the most worthy, and at the same time do so through the mediation of His Majesty's gracious will. And a resolution to this effect was passed at His Highness's particular wish, for although it was only a matter of form he found it important that the people should not attempt to do anything solely of its own accord and without the consent of the second constitutional factor—not even if it were in honour of this latter.

The other persons present would not have made quite such a point of this, but that was also precisely the reason why they had no objections to it. And it was quite in order, too, that the meeting concluded with the passing of a resolution. For whether one brings a brawl to an end with the knife, or at the end of a piece of music strikes the keys a few times with all ten fingers simultaneously, or the dancer bows to his lady, or one passes a resolution—it would be an uncanny world if events were simply to slink away without at the end once more giving proper assurance that they have taken place. And so that is why it is done.

45   *Silent encounter between two mountain peaks.*

WHEN the meeting was over, Herr Dr. Arnheim inconspicuously manoeuvred things so that he remained behind, the last. The impulse had come from Diotima. Permanent Secretary Tuzzi was observing a formal period of absence in order to be sure of not returning to his house before the end of the conference.

In these minutes between the guests' departure and the consolidation of the situation that then remained, passing from one room into the other, obstructed by little criss-cross arrangements, considerations and the unrest that a great event, fading into the distance, leaves in its wake, Arnheim smilingly followed Diotima with his gaze. Diotima felt that her flat was in a state of trembling motion. All the things that had had to leave their places on account of the event now returned, one after the other. It was like a big wave ebbing down the sand again out of countless little hollows and ditches. And while Arnheim waited in urbane silence until she and this movement around her should have settled down again, it struck Diotima that although many people had been entertained in her house, never before had a man

—apart from Permanent Secretary Tuzzi—been so domestically alone with her that the mute life of the empty apartment could be felt. And suddenly her chastity was baffled by a quite unaccustomed notion : her now empty flat, from which even her husband was missing, seemed to her like a pair of trousers into which Arnheim had slipped. There are such moments ; like the monstrous progeny of the night, they can visit the most chaste of people. The wonderful dream of a love in which soul and body are wholly one lit up in Diotima.

Arnheim was not in the slightest aware of this. His trousers stood, in impeccable perpendicular lines, on the gleaming parquet ; his morning-coat, his cravat, his calmly smiling patrician head, were devoid of utterance, so perfect were they. He had actually intended to reproach Diotima for the incident on his arrival and to take precautionary measures for the future. But, instead, at this moment something was there that made this man who hob-nobbed with American tycoons and had been received by emperors and kings, this nabob who could offer any woman her weight in platinum, stare spellbound at Diotima, whose name in reality was Ermelinda or even just Hermine Tuzzi and who was merely the wife of a high official. For this ' something ' here once again the word ' soul ' must be used.

This is a word that has already appeared frequently, though not precisely in the clearest of connections. For instance, as that which the present time has lost or that which cannot be combined with civilisation. As that which is in antagonism to physical urges and connubial habits. As that which is stirred, not only into repugnance, by a murderer. As that which was to be set free by the Collateral Campaign. As religious meditation and *contemplatio in caligine divina* with Count Leinsdorf. As a love of metaphor and simile with many people. And so on. Of all the peculiarities that this word ' soul ' has, however, the oddest is that young people cannot pronounce it without laughing. Even Diotima and Arnheim were shy of using it without qualification ; for that someone has a great, noble, cowardly, daring or base soul is something that can just about be asserted, but to say outright ' my soul ' is something one cannot bring oneself to do. It is distinctly a word for older people ; and this can only be under-stood by assuming that there is something that makes itself more

and more felt in the course of life, something for which one urgently needs a name, without finding it, until in the end one reluctantly makes use of that which was originally spurned.

And how then is one to describe it? One can stand still or move on as one will, the essential is not what lies straight before one, what one sees, hears, wants, takes hold of, and masters. It lies ahead, a horizon, a semicircle; but the ends of this semicircle are joined by a sinew, and the plane of this sinew goes right through the middle of the world. In front, face and hands look out of it; the sensations and strivings run along ahead of it; and no one doubts that what we do there is always reasonable or at least impassioned. That is, circumstances external to us demand our actions of us in a way that is comprehensible to everyone; or if, involved in passion, we do something incomprehensible, that, after all, is also something with a way and a nature of its own. But however completely understandable and self-contained it all seems, it is accompanied by an obscure feeling that it is merely half the story. There is something the matter with the equilibrium, and man advances in order not to sway, like a tightrope-walker. And as he advances through life, leaving behind him what he has lived through, a wall is formed by what is still to be lived and what has been lived, and in the end his path resembles that of a worm in the wood, which can twist any way it likes, even turning backwards, but always leaves an empty space behind it. And this dreadful feeling of a blind space, a space cut off behind all the fullness, this half that is always still lacking even although everything has become a whole, is what finally causes one to notice what one calls the soul.

One thinks it, feels it, has premonitions of it all the time, naturally, in the most various kinds of surrogates and according to one's temperament. In youth it is a distinct feeling of uncertainty, in everything one does, as to whether whatever it is is really the right thing. In old age it is amazement at how little one has done of all that one actually intended. In between it is the comfort of being a hell of a chap, efficient, and a good sort too, even though not everything one does can be justified in every detail; or that after all the world isn't what it ought to be, either, so that in the end all that one has done wrong still amounts to a fair enough compromise; and finally, some people even think, away out

beyond everything, of a God who has the missing piece of themselves in His pocket. Only love occupies a special position in all this ; for it is in this exceptional case that the second half grows on. The loved person seems to stand where otherwise there is always something missing. The souls unite, as it were *dos à dos*, so making themselves superfluous. This is why after the passing of their one great youthful love most people no longer feel the absence of the soul, so that this so-called foolishness fulfils a meritorious social function.

Neither Diotima nor Arnheim had ever loved. Of Diotima we know this already. But the great financier too possessed a—in a wider sense—chaste soul. He had always been afraid that the feelings he aroused in women might not be for himself, but for his money ; and for this reason he lived only with women to whom he, for his part, gave not feelings but money. He had never had a friend, because he was afraid of being used ; he only had business friends, even if sometimes the business deal was an intellectual one. So he was wily in the ways of life, yet untouched and in danger of being left on his own, when he encountered Diotima, whom destiny had ordained for him. The mysterious forces in them collided with each other. What happened can only be compared to the blowing of the trade winds, the Gulf Stream, the volcanic tremors in the earth's crust : forces vastly superior to man, related to the stars, were set in motion between the two of them, over and above the limits of the hour and the day—measureless, mighty currents.

At such moments it is quite immaterial what is said. Upward from the vertical crease of his trousers Arnheim's body seemed to stand there in the solitude of God in which the mountain giants stand. United with him by the wave of the valley, on the other side Diotima rose, luminous with solitude—her dress of the period forming little puffs on the upper arms, dissolving the bosom in an artfully draped looseness over the stomach and being caught in to the calf again just under the hollow of the knee. The strings of glass beads in the door-curtains cast reflections like ponds, the javelins and arrows on the walls were tremulous with their feathered and deadly passion, and the yellow Calman-Lévy volumes on the tables were silent as lemon-groves. Reverently we pass over their opening words.

46

Ideals and morality are the best means of filling the big hole that one calls the soul.

ARNHEIM was the first to shake off the magic spell. For to linger in such a state for any length of time was, to his way of thinking, impossible ; it meant either sinking into a muffled, vacant, blissfully reposeful brooding or propping up one's devotions with a solid scaffolding of thoughts and convictions, which would however no longer be of the same essential nature.

Such a means of, admittedly, killing the soul, but then as it were storing it in little tins for general use, has always been the linking of it with reason, convictions and practical action, as it has been successfully performed by all systems of morality, all philosophies and religions. God knows—as has already been said—what a soul is anyway ! There can be no doubt whatsoever that the burning wish to hearken to it alone leaves one with an immeasurable field open for action, a thorough state of anarchy, and we have examples of so to speak chemically pure souls committing downright crimes. On the other hand, as soon as a soul has morality or religion, philosophy, and intensive bourgeois education and ideals in the realms of duty and of the beautiful, it is endowed with a system of regulations, conditions and directives for operation, which it has to fill out before it is entitled to think of itself as a respectable soul, and its heat, like that of a blast-furnace, is conducted into beautiful squares of sand. What remains then is fundamentally only logical problems of interpretation, of the kind as to whether an action comes under this or that commandment ; and the soul presents the tranquil panorama of a battlefield after the battle, where the dead lie quiet and one can at once observe where a scrap of life yet stirs or groans. And so man makes this transition as fast as he can. If he is tormented by religious doubts, as occasionally happens in youth, he goes straight over to the persecution of unbelievers ; if love deranges him, he turns it into marriage ; and if any other enthusiasm overwhelms him, he disentangles himself from the impossibility of living perpetu-

ally in the fire of it by beginning to live for that fire. That is, instead of filling the many moments of his day, each of which needs a content and an impetus, with his ideal state, he fills them with the activity for the sake of his ideal state, in other words, with the many means to the end, the hindrances and incidents that are a sure guarantee that he never need reach it. For only fools, the mentally deranged, and people with *idées fixes*, can endure unceasingly in the fire of the soul's rapture. A sane man must content himself with declaring that life would not seem worth living without a flake of that mysterious fire.

Arnheim's life was filled out with activity. He was a man of reality and had listened, with a benevolent smile and not without an appreciation of the social good form of the representatives of Old Austria, to the discussion, at the meeting of which he had been a witness, which had included an Emperor-Francis-Joseph Soup-Kitchen and the connection between the sense of duty and military marches. He was far from making fun of it, as Ulrich had done, for he was convinced that following great ideas indicated far less courage and superiority than admitting the touching core of idealism in such everyday, somewhat ridiculous, well-bred minds.

But when in the midst of it all Diotima, this classical beauty with the Viennese *je ne sais quoi*, had uttered the expression 'Universal Austria', an expression that was as hot and humanly almost as incomprehensible as a flame, something had stirred his heart.

A story was told about him.

In his house in Berlin he had a large room full of Baroque and Gothic sculpture. Now, the thing is that the Catholic Church (and Arnheim had a great love for it) mostly depicts its saints and the standard-bearers of the Good in very blissful, even ecstatic poses. There were saints dying in all postures, and the soul wrung the bodies out as one squeezes water from a piece of washing. The attitudes of the arms, like crossed sabres, and of the wry necks, removed from their original surroundings and brought together in an irrelevant room, gave the impression of a gathering of catatonics in a lunatic asylum. This collection was highly esteemed and brought to Arnheim many art historians, with whom he had cultured conversations. But often

too he sat down in this room of his, all by himself, a solitary man, and then he felt quite different : then he was overcome by startled amazement, as though looking at a half-demented world. He could feel that once there had been an ineffable fire burning in morality, and looking at this now even a mind like his could not do much more than stare into the cold clinkers. This dark hint of something that all religions and myths express in the story that the commandments were primally given to men by the gods, in other words, the intuitive glimpse of a primary state of the soul, one that must have been somewhat uncanny and nevertheless pleasing to the gods, then formed a strange margin of unease round the otherwise so complacent lay-out of his thoughts. And Arnheim had an under-gardener, a plain man but profound, as Arnheim put it, with whom he often conversed about the life of the flowers, because one could learn more from such a man than from the learned. And then one day Arnheim discovered that this under-gardener was stealing from him. What it amounted to was that he carried off, almost desperately, everything he could lay hands on, saving up the proceeds in order to set up on his own, this being the one thought that obsessed him day and night. But once a small piece of sculpture also disappeared, and the police, who had been called in, discovered the connection. In the evening of the day when Arnheim was informed of this discovery he sent for the man and reproached him all night long for the paths of error on to which his passionate urge for gain had led him. It was said that he himself had been very upset and at times near to weeping in the darkness of an adjacent room. For he envied this man, for reasons that he could not explain to himself. And the next morning he had the police take him away.

This story was confirmed by close friends of Arnheim's.

Now he experienced similar sensations, standing alone in one room with Diotima and feeling something like the soundless flames of the world leaping all round about the four walls.

47

What all others are separately Arnheim is in one person.

IN the following weeks Diotima's *salon* got going in a tremendous way. People came in order to learn the latest news of the Collateral Campaign and to see the new man, whom it was said Diotima had prescribed for herself, a German nabob, a rich Jew, an eccentric who wrote poems, dictated the price of coal and was the personal friend of the German Emperor. It was not only ladies and gentlemen from Count Leinsdorf's and from diplomatic circles who made their appearance ; the bourgeois spheres of commerce and the intelligentsia also showed themselves increasingly attracted.   So specialists in the Ewe language and composers ran into each other, each never before having heard a syllable or a sound of the other's work ; shooting-box met confessional box ; people mingled in whom the word ' course ' evoked thoughts of the race-course, the course of exchange, or a course of studies.

But now something happened that had never happened before : there was a man who could talk to each of them in his own language, and this was Arnheim.

After his painful experience at the beginning of the first one, he held aloof from the official meetings ; besides that, however, he did not always attend the social gatherings either, for he was often out of town.   There was of course no further mention of the secretaryship ; he himself had explained to Diotima that this idea would not be acceptable to either side.   And although Diotima could not look at Ulrich without feeling he was a usurper, she yielded to Arnheim's judgment.   He came and went.   Three or five days would pass in a flash, and he would return from Paris, Rome or Berlin.   What was going on at Diotima's was only a small slice of his life.   But he had a preference for that slice and was there in it with his whole personality.

It was understandable that he could talk to big industrialists about industry and to bankers about finance ; but he was capable of chatting just as freely about molecular physics, mysticism or pigeon-shooting.   He was an extraordinary talker ; once he had

begun he did not stop, any more than a book can be finished before everything has been said that has to be said in it. But he had a quietly dignified, fluent manner of speaking, a manner that was almost melancholy about itself, like a stream overhung by dark bushes, and this gave his loquacity a touch of necessity. His reading and his memory were in fact of unusual extent. He could give experts the subtlest cues in their own field of knowledge, but he was just as well acquainted with every important personage of the English, French or Japanese nobility and was at home on race-courses and golf-links not only in Europe but also in Australia and America. So even the chamois-hunters, hard riders and those who kept their box at the Imperial theatres, who had come to see a crazy rich Jew (' something a bit out of the ordinary '—as was their way of putting it), left Diotima's house wagging their heads respectfully.

His Highness once took Ulrich aside and said to him : " You know, the high nobility have had bad luck with their tutors in the last hundred years. Once these tutors used to be the kind of people of whom a good many afterwards got into the encyclopaedia. And they brought along in their wake music masters and drawing-masters who showed their gratitude by doing things we now refer to as our ancient culture. But since there's this new universal education, and some people from my circles— forgive my saying so—go in for taking university degrees, somehow the tutors have fallen off. Our young men are quite right, you know, to go shooting pheasants and wild boar, riding, and picking out pretty women for themselves—there's little to be said against that when one is young. But in the old days the tutors used to divert part of that youthful energy to recognising that the mind and the arts have to be kept up just as, say, pheasants have to be preserved. And we haven't got that nowadays."

This had just struck His Highness. Such things did strike him at times. Suddenly he turned to face Ulrich and concluded : " You see, it was that fateful year, '48, which made the middle classes independent of the aristocracy, to their common loss."

He gazed round at the company in concern. It vexed him every time that opposition speakers in Parliament made great play with bourgeois culture, and he would have been glad if it had been possible to find true bourgeois culture only under the aegis of

the aristocracy. But the poor aristocracy could not find anything worth while in it ; for them it was an invisible weapon with which they were always being defeated. And as they had been steadily losing power in the course of this development, they finally came to Diotima and had a look at the thing for themselves. This was what Count Leinsdorf sometimes felt, grieved at heart, when he was watching what went on here. He would have wished to see the high office, to which the opportunity was given in this house, taken more seriously.

" You know, sir, the middle classes are today faring exactly the same with the intellectuals as the high aristocracy once did with their tutors," Ulrich said, trying to comfort him. " They are strangers to them. Just look at how they are all gaping at this Herr Doktor Arnheim."

But Count Leinsdorf had been looking only at Arnheim all the time, anyway.

" Incidentally," Ulrich said, referring to the object of this gaping, " that is something one can no longer call a mind. It is a phenomenon like a rainbow that one can seize hold of at each end and really feel under one's hands. He talks about love and economics, about chemistry and canoeing trips, he is a learned man, a landowner and a stock-jobber. In short, what we all are separately he is in one person. And this is what amazes us. You shake your head, sir ? But I am convinced the cloud of the so-called progress of the time, into which no one can see, is what has parked him down here in front of us."

" I wasn't shaking my head at what you were saying," His Highness said in rectification. " I was thinking about Herr Doktor Arnheim. All in all one must admit he is an interesting personality."

48

The three causes of Arnheim's fame and the Mystery of the Whole.

BUT all this was only the usual effect of Herr Dr. Arnheim's person.

He was a man on a grand scale.

His activities extended over continents of the earth and continents of knowledge. He knew everything : the philosophers, economics, music, the world, sport . . . He could express himself fluently in five languages. The world's most famous artists were his friends, and he bought the art of tomorrow when it was still green in the ear, before the prices had been pushed up. He went in and out at the Imperial Court ; he talked with workmen. He owned a villa built in the most modern style, photographs of which were reproduced in all the periodicals dealing with contemporary architecture, and a ramshackle old castle somewhere in the sandiest wastes of the aristocratic Mark Brandenburg, which looked positively like the half-crumbled cradle of the Prussian idea.

Such comprehensiveness and receptivity is seldom accompanied by original achievements ; but in this too Arnheim was an exception. Once or twice a year he retired to his country estate and there wrote down the experiences of his intellectual life. These books and dissertations, of which he had now composed quite an imposing number, were much sought after, went into big editions, and were translated into many languages. For nobody has any confidence in a sick physician, but everyone feels there must be a good deal that is true in what is said by someone who has known how to look after himself so well. This was the first source of his fame.

The second arose out of the nature of science and learning. They are in high repute among us, and rightly so. But although it may certainly fill a man's life entirely if he devotes himself to research into the physiology of the kidneys, yet even then there are moments, what one might call humanist moments, when he

Ulrich actually felt quite a liking for this naïve old aristocrat, who was now standing talking to Diotima and Arnheim, and almost some slight jealousy. For the conversation seemed to be very lively. Diotima was smiling, Count Leinsdorf had his eyes wide open, as though in alarm, in order to follow the better, and Arnheim was holding forth, with all the composure of distinction. Ulrich caught the expression : " bringing ideas into spheres of power ". He could not endure Arnheim, could not endure him in principle, simply as a form of existence, the Arnheim pattern. This combination of mind, business, good living and well-readness was something he found in the highest degree intolerable. He was convinced that Arnheim had already the previous evening arranged everything so that in the morning he would arrive at this meeting neither as the first nor as the last, that nevertheless he had certainly not looked at the clock on setting out, but had probably done so for the last time before sitting down to breakfast and listening to the report of his secretary, who handed him his mail ; so doing, he had transformed the time at his disposal into the mental activity that he wanted to complete before setting out, and if he then abandoned himself unhampered to that activity, he was sure that it would exactly fill the time, since the right thing and the time it takes are connected by a mysterious force, just like a piece of sculpture and the space it fills, or a javelin-thrower and the target that he hits without looking at it. Ulrich had heard a great deal about Arnheim and had read some of his writings. In one of his books there was the statement that a man who scrutinises his suit in the looking-glass is not capable of acting consistently. For the looking-glass, originally created for delight—so it was expounded—had become an instrument of anxiety like the clock, which is a compensation for the failure of our activities to follow each other any longer in a natural way.

Ulrich had to distract himself in order not to stare rudely at the neighbouring group, and his gaze came to rest on the little maid who was tripping about between the chatting groups and offering refreshments, reverentially casting up her eyes. But little Rachel did not notice him. She had forgotten him and even omitted to come to him with her tray. She had drawn near to Arnheim and offered her refreshments up to him as to a god ; she would have liked best to kiss the short-fingered, quiet hand

Papa," and chose her men friends from among a horde of Germanico-Christian contemporaries, who did not hold out the slightest prospect of being able to support a wife, but made up for it by despising capitalism and preaching that there had never yet been a Jew who had been capable of setting up a great symbol of humanity. Leo Fischel referred to them as anti-semitic louts and would have forbidden them the house. But Gerda said : " You don't understand these things, Papa, it's all just symbolic " —and Gerda was nervy and anaemic and always got so worked up if one didn't treat her carefully. So Fischel put up with this association, as Odysseus once had to put up with having Penelope's suitors in his own house, for Gerda was the ray of light in his life. But he did not put up with it in silence, for that was not his nature. He considered that he himself knew what morality and great ideas were, and he said so at every opportunity, in order to exert a good influence on Gerda. And Gerda always answered : " Yes, you would be absolutely right, Papa, if this whole thing didn't have to be looked at from a fundamentally different point of view from the way you go on looking at it."

And what did Klementine do when Gerda talked like that ? Nothing ! She remained silent, with a look of resignation on her face. But Leo could be sure that behind his back she would support Gerda in her attitude—as though *she* knew what symbols were ! Leo Fischel had always had every cause to assume that his good Jewish brain was superior to his wife's, and nothing made him so indignant as observing that she turned Gerda's craziness to her own advantage. Why should he, of all people, suddenly be no longer capable of thinking along modern lines ? It was a systematic campaign ! Then he would remember the night. This was no longer a matter of picking holes in one's honour, this was digging it up by the roots ! At night a man has only a nightshirt on, and what comes next under that is the character. No expert knowledge and expert cleverness can shield him. One has to stake one's whole personality. Nothing else will do. So what did it mean that, whenever Germanico-Christian views were under discussion, Klementine assumed an expression conveying that she thought him a savage ?

Now, man is a being that can no more stand up to suspicion than tissue-paper can stand up to rain. Since Klementine no longer thought Leo handsome, she found him unbearable ; and since Leo felt himself doubted by Klementine, he sensed a conspiracy in his house at every turn.   For all this Klementine and Leo, like everyone in the world who is talked into it by prevailing morality and literature, laboured under the delusion that they were dependent on each other through their passions, characters, destinies and actions.   In fact, of course, life is more than half made up not of actions but of harangues, the gist of which one absorbs, and of opinions and corresponding counter-opinions, and of the accumulated non-personality of all one has heard and knows.   The destiny of these two spouses to a great extent depended on a dreary, tough, unordered stratification of thoughts that were not even their own but were part of public opinion and had changed with it, without their being able to protect themselves against the process.   Compared with this dependence, their personal dependence on each other was only a tiny fraction, a madly over-estimated residue.   And while they were persuading themselves that they had a private life and were questioning each other's character and will, the desperate difficulty lay in this conflict's unreality, which they covered up with every thinkable kind of irritation.

It was Leo Fischel's misfortune that he neither played cards nor found it amusing to take pretty girls out, but, tired after his work, suffered from a marked yearning for family life, while his wife, who had nothing to do day and night but be the bosom of this family, was no longer led astray by any sort of romantic illusions.   Sometimes Leo Fischel was overcome by a feeling of suffocation, which, without being at all tangible, attacked him from all sides.   He was a good hard-working little cell in the social organism, one that did its duty sturdily and yet got poisoned humours from everywhere.   And although it went much further than what he needed in the way of philosophy, he began—now that he was left in the lurch by his life-partner, an aging man who saw no reason to give up the rational outlook of his youth—to glimpse the profound insubstantiality of spiritual life, its formlessness, which is an everlasting changing of forms, a slow but unquiet revolution always taking everything with it as it turns.

On one such morning, when his thoughts were taken up by family questions, Fischel had forgotten to reply to His Highness's invitation, and on many subsequent mornings he was given descriptions of what was going on in the circle of Permanent Secretary Tuzzi's wife, all of which made it appear very regrettable that such an opportunity for Gerda to enter into the best society should have been missed.   Fischel himself had a not quite clear conscience, since after all his own managing-director and the Governor of the National Bank went there ; but, as is well known, one refutes reproaches all the more violently the more tensely one feels oneself stretched between guilt and innocence. But every time that Fischel tried to make fun of this patriotic affair with the superiority of a serious man of business, it was explained to him that a financier abreast of the times, like Paul Arnheim, happened to think quite differently.   It was amazing how much Klementine and Gerda too—who normally of course went against her mother's wishes—had come to know about this man.   And since on the Stock Exchange, too, many odd stories were going round about him, Fischel felt himself forced on to the defensive, for he simply could not keep up with this, nor could he assert, of a man with such business connections, that he was not to be taken seriously.

But when Fischel felt himself forced on to the defensive, appropriately enough it took on the form of bearing the market ; that is to say, he kept up as impenetrable a silence as possible in the face of all allusions to the Tuzzi household, Arnheim, the Collateral Campaign and his own failure to do anything, made enquiries as to where and how long Arnheim was staying, and furtively waited for something to happen that would at one blow reveal the inner hollowness of it all and bring down the soaring family market with a crash.

52

Permanent Secretary Tuzzi notes the existence of a lacuna in his Ministry's apparatus.

SOON after his resolve to get himself a clear picture of Herr Dr. Arnheim, Permanent Secretary Tuzzi had the satisfaction of discovering a substantial lacuna in the structure of His Majesty's Ministry of Foreign Affairs and of the Imperial House, the ministry that was the object of his care : it had no equipment for dealing with persons like Arnheim.   Apart from memoirs, where *belles-lettres* were concerned he himself read no books except the Bible, Homer and Rosegger, and he somewhat prided himself on this because it saved him from dissipating his mental powers ; but the fact that in the whole of the Foreign Ministry there was not a man to be found who had read a book by Arnheim was something he recognised as a deficiency.

Permanent Secretary Tuzzi had the right to summon the heads of departments. But on the morning after that night made uneasy by tears he himself went along to the chief of the press department, guided by a feeling that one could not very well grant full official status to the matter that he felt the need of discussing. The chief of the press department admired the abundance of detailed personal information that Permanent Secretary Tuzzi possessed concerning Arnheim, admitted that he himself had also often heard the name, but instantly denied the possibility of this man's occurring in his department's files, since so far as he could remember Arnheim had never been the object of any official consideration and the handling of newspaper material, understandably enough, did not extend to covering the thoughts and actions of private persons. Tuzzi admitted that anything else was really not to be expected, but commented that the line of demarcation between the official and the private significance of persons and phenomena was not always clearly definable nowadays, which the chief of the press department thought a very acute observation, whereupon the two high officials were of one mind in concluding that they were confronted with a very interesting deficiency in the system.

It was manifestly a morning when Europe was having some slight repose, for the two chiefs sent for the head clerk and had a file opened, to be inscribed Arnheim, Dr. Paul, even though for the present it remained empty. After the head clerk, it was the turn of the registrar and the clerk in charge of the press-cutting files, both of whom were able to say instantly, out of their heads and beaming with efficiency, that there was no Arnheim in their records. Finally the press-relations officers were sent for, who had to go through the newspapers every day and lay the cuttings before their chiefs, and they all put on solemn expressions when asked about Arnheim and gave the assurance that he was very often and very favourably mentioned in the papers they read. They were however unable to give any information as to the contents of his writings, because his activities, as they were at once able to say, did not enter into the sphere covered by official news-sifting. The faultless functioning of the Foreign Ministry's machinery proved itself at the mere pressing of the button, and all these officials left the room with the feeling of having shown their reliability in the best light.

" It's just as I said," the chief of the press department said with satisfaction, turning to Tuzzi. " Nobody knows a thing."

The two high officials, who had listened to the reports with smiling dignity, sitting—their surroundings as it were embalming them for eternity, like flies in amber—in magnificent leather arm-chairs, on the soft red carpet, against the dark red curtains of the high windows, in the white and gold room dating from the times of Maria Theresa, acknowledged that the lacuna in the system, which at least they had now discovered, would be difficult to close.

" In this department," its chief said, mildly glorying, " every public pronouncement is dealt with. But one must draw a line somewhere in defining the term ' public '. I can vouch for the fact that every interjection that a deputy has made in any Diet in the course of the current year can be found in our records inside ten minutes, and every interjection made in the last ten years, if it has reference to foreign policy, in half an hour at the outside. The same applies to every political article in the newspapers. The work in my department is done very thoroughly. But those are tangible, so to speak responsible utterances, relating to tangible

conditions, forces, and ideas. And if I ask myself, purely as an
expert, under what heading the clerk who compiles the excerpts
or the catalogue is to enter an essay by somebody who—only as
a private person—well, whom shall I take as an example ? "

Tuzzi helpfully mentioned the name of one of the youngest
writers who frequented Diotima's drawing-room.

The chief of the press department glanced up at him with
the uneasy look of someone hard of hearing. " Well, let's say
him. But where is the line to be drawn between what one takes
notice of and what one passes over ? There have even been such
things as political poems before now. Is every writer of jingles
to be—— ? Or perhaps only authors of Burgtheater standing ? "

The two officials laughed.

" How is one ever to make an abstract of what such people
mean, even if it's Schiller and Goethe themselves ? There's
always a higher meaning in it, of course, but for all practical
purposes they contradict themselves at every second word."

In the mean time it had become apparent to the two that they
were running the risk of exercising themselves about something
' impossible ', even perhaps with that added nuance of the socially
ridiculous of which diplomats have such a subtle awareness.
" One can't very well attach to the Ministry a whole staff of
literary and dramatic critics," Tuzzi observed, smiling. " But
on the other hand, once one's attention has been drawn to it, it
cannot be denied that such people are not without their influence
in helping to form the views prevailing in the world, and hence
they also have their effect in politics."

" It isn't done in any Foreign Ministry in the world," the chief
of the press department came to his aid.

" Certainly. But constant dropping wears the stone." Tuzzi
felt that this proverb very well expressed a certain danger. " Perhaps one really ought to try something in the way of organisation ? "

" I don't know. I have qualms," his colleague ventured.

" So have I, naturally," Tuzzi added. Towards the end of
this conversation he had begun to have an uncomfortable feeling
like a coated tongue and could not be quite sure whether what he
had been saying was nonsense or whether it might after all turn
out to be an instance of the perspicacity for which he was celebrated. The chief of the press department was similarly unable

to distinguish. Hence the two gentlemen assured each other that they would have another talk on this subject another time.

The chief of the press department gave instructions that Arnheim's complete works should be ordered for the Ministry library, so that the matter might be brought to some sort of conclusion, and Permanent Secretary Tuzzi went along to one of the political departments, where he gave instructions that the Embassy in Berlin should be asked to provide a detailed report on the man Arnheim. This was the only thing left for him to do at the moment ; and until this report arrived, he had only his wife from whom to get information about Arnheim, a thing that had become entirely disagreeable to him. He recollected Voltaire's dictum that people use words only in order to conceal their thoughts and make use of thoughts only in order to justify their acts of injustice. Certainly, that was what diplomacy had always meant. But it disturbed him to realise that anybody could speak and write as much as Arnheim in order to conceal his real intentions behind words. It was something new to him and he would have to get to the bottom of it.

53 *Moosbrugger is removed to a new prison.*

CHRISTIAN MOOSBRUGGER, the murderer of a prostitute, was forgotten a few days after the reports of his trial ceased to appear in the newspapers, and public excitability was diverted to other matters. Only a circle of experts still continued to take an interest in him. His counsel had entered a plea of nullity, demanded a new examination of his mental state, and taken several other steps. The execution had been postponed for an indefinite period, and Moosbrugger was removed to another prison.

The precautions that were taken in doing so flattered him : loaded rifles, many people, irons on arms and legs. They were paying him attention, they were frightened of him, and Moosbrugger liked that. When he stepped into the prison van, he looked around for admiration, trying to catch the astonished gaze of the passers-by. A cold wind blowing down the street tossed his curly hair. The air drained his strength away. It lasted only two seconds. Then an armed guard gave him a push on the buttocks to make him get into the van.

Moosbrugger was vain. He did not like to be pushed like that. He was afraid the guards might knock him about, shout at him or laugh at him. The fettered giant did not dare to look at any of his escort and voluntarily slid down to the front of the van.

But he was not afraid of death. There is a great deal that one has to put up with in life that definitely hurts more than being hanged, and whether one lives a few years more or less doesn't really matter at all. The passive pride of a man who has been in prison a great deal forbade him to be afraid of his punishment ; but even apart from that he did not cling to life. What should he have loved it for ? Not, surely, for the spring wind or the open road or the sun ? That only makes a man tired, hot and dusty. Nobody who really knows it loves it. And Moosbrugger thought : ' It'd be different talking about I had a lovely bit of roast pork yesterday, at the inn on the corner ! ' That was more like it. But even that was something one could get on without. What would have pleased him was some satisfaction of his ambition, which had always met only with stupid affronts.

A confused rumbling from the wheels came through the bench and into his body. Beyond the iron bars on the door the cobblestones ran the other way, heavy waggons were left behind, sometimes men, women or children staggered across the barred field of vision. From far behind a cab was gaining on them, growing larger, coming close, beginning to spit forth fiery life like a smith's anvil when the sparks begin to fly. It seemed as though the horses' heads would push through the door. Then the clatter of the hooves and the soft sound of the rubber-tyred wheels ran on past, outside.

Moosbrugger slowly turned his head back and looked at the ceiling again, where it joined the side of the van, there in front of him. The noise outside roared and blared, was stretched like a screen over which now and then the shadow of some happening flickered. For Moosbrugger this journey was a change, although he did not take much notice of its details. Between two dark, inert prison periods there flashed a quarter of an hour of opaquely white frothing time. This was the way he had always experienced his freedom. Nothing so very wonderful. ' All that fuss,' he thought, ' with the last breakfast, and the prison chaplain, the hangmen and the quarter of an hour till it's all over, that won't be so very different, either. It'll skip along on wheels too, keeping a man busy all the time, just like this trying not to slide off the bench when it jolts. Won't see and hear much of it for all the people dancing around. It'll all be for the best, I dare say, to be shut of it all at last.'

The superiority of a man who has freed himself from the wish to live is enormous. Moosbrugger remembered the superintendent who had been the first to question him at the police-station. He'd been a real gentleman, talked quietly. " Look here, Herr Moosbrugger," he had said, " I'm simply asking you a favour. Don't grudge me this bit of success ! " And Moosbrugger had answered : " All right, if it's success you want, let's draw up the statement now." The judge, later on, could hardly believe it, but the superintendent had confirmed it in his evidence. " Even if you don't want to relieve your conscience on your own account, why don't you let me have the personal satisfaction of having you do it for my sake ? " This the superintendent had repeated in front of the whole court, and even the president had smirked understandingly. Moosbrugger had risen to his feet. " My best respects to this statement on the part of his honour the superintendent ! " he had proclaimed in a loud voice. And with an elegant bow he had added : " Although your honour's last words to me were ' I don't suppose we shall ever meet again ', I nevertheless have the privilege and pleasure of seeing your honour here again today."

Moosbrugger's face was lit up by a smile of self-approval, and he forgot the armed guards sitting opposite him, being flung to and fro by the jolting of the van, just like himself.

54

Ulrich shows himself a reactionary in con-
versation with Walter and Clarisse.

CLARISSE said to Ulrich: " Something must be done for
Moosbrugger ! This murderer is musical ! "

Ulrich had at last made use of a free afternoon to pay the visit
that he had been prevented from paying by his arrest, which had
been so fraught with consequences.

Clarisse was holding the lapel of his jacket, and Walter was
standing beside them with a not quite sincere expression on
his face.

" What do you mean—musical ? " Ulrich asked, smiling.

Clarisse looked merrily shamefaced. It was involuntary, as
though shame were oozing out all over her face and in order to
hold it in she had to tighten up her features into merriment.
She let go of his lapel. " Well, just like that," she said. " You're
an influential man now, aren't you ? " It was not always easy
to know what to make of her.

Winter had made a beginning and then stopped again. Here,
outside the city, there was still snow on the ground—white fields
and between them, like dark water, the black earth. The sun
spread a thin film of light over everything. Clarisse was wearing
an orange jacket and a blue woollen cap. The three of them were
out for a walk, and here in the midst of Nature's chaotic disarray
Ulrich had to explain Arnheim's writings to her. In them there
was talk of algebraic series and benzol rings, the materialist
philosophy of history and the universalist one as well, bridge-
piles, the evolution of music, the spirit of the motor-car, Hata 606,
the theory of relativity, Bohr's atomic theory, autogenous welding,
the flora of the Himalayas, psychoanalysis, individual psychology,
experimental psychology, physiological psychology, social psychology and all the other achievements that prevent a time that
has been enriched by them from producing good, whole, integral
human beings. But all this came up very soothingly in Arnheim's
writings, for he assured his readers that everything one did not
understand only amounted to some excess committed by sterile

intellectual forces, whereas the true was always the simple thing, the dignity of man and the instinct for suprahuman truths, an instinct that anyone could acquire by simply living and being in concord with the stars. " Many people make similar assertions these days," Ulrich explained, " but people believe Arnheim because they are at liberty to imagine him as a big, rich man who is sure to know all about what he is talking about, has been to the Himalayas himself, owns motor-cars and wears as many benzol rings as he likes ! "

Clarisse wanted to know what benzol rings looked like, vaguely associating them with cornelian rings.

" You're a dear girl all the same, Clarisse," Ulrich declared.

" Thank God she doesn't need to understand all this chemistry nonsense ! " Walter defended her. But then he began defending Arnheim's writings, which he had read. He would not go so far as to say that Arnheim was the best that one could imagine, but still, he was the best that the present age had produced. This was the modern mind ! Sound science, on the one hand, but at the same time, too, going beyond the limits of science !

In this way their walk came to an end. The final result for all of them was wet feet, an irritation in the brain—as though the thin, bare branches of the trees, sparkling in the wintry sun, had been left behind like splinters on the retina—a low yearning for hot coffee, and a sense of human forlornness.

Steam went up from the snow melting on their shoes. Clarisse was pleased with the mess it made on the floor. And Walter kept his sensuous, feminine lips pursed the whole time, because he was in search of a quarrel. Ulrich talked about the Collateral Campaign. When Arnheim cropped up again, the quarrel began again.

" Let me tell you what I have against him," Ulrich resumed. " Scientific man is something quite inevitable these days. One can't not want to know ! And at no time has the difference between the expert's experience and the layman's been as great as it is now. Everyone sees it in the skill of a masseur or a pianist. Nobody will even race a horse these days without special pre-paration. It's only where being a human being is concerned that everyone still believes he's entitled to judge. An old prejudice still insists that one is born and dies a human being. But once

I know that women five thousand years ago wrote word for word the same letters to their lovers as women do now, I can't read another such letter without asking myself whether there oughtn't to be a change for once!"

Clarisse showed herself inclined to agree. Walter on the other hand smiled like a fakir who is not going to flicker an eyelid when a hat-pin is run through his cheeks.

"All this means, then," he threw in, "is that until further notice you refuse to be a human being!"

"That's about it. It has such a disagreeable touch of the dilettante. But," Ulrich continued after some thought, "I am even prepared to admit something else, something quite different. The experts never get to the end of anything. It's not only that they haven't got to the end of anything today. But they can't even picture the idea of their activities ever being complete. Perhaps they can't even wish it. Can one imagine, for instance, that man will still have a soul once he has learnt to understand it completely and manage it biologically and psychologically? And yet that is the state of things we are trying to achieve! There it is. Knowledge is an attitude, a passion. Actually an illicit attitude. For the compulsion to *know* is just like dipsomania, erotomania, and homicidal mania, in producing a character that is out of balance. It is not at all true that the scientist goes out after truth. It is out after him. It is something he suffers from. The truth is true and the fact is real without taking any notice of him. All he has is the passion for it. He is a dipsomaniac whose tipple is facts, and that leaves its mark on his character. And he doesn't care a damn whether what comes of his discoveries is something whole, human, perfect—or indeed, *what* comes of them! It's all full of contradictions and passive suffering and at the same time enormously active and energetic."

"Well?" Walter asked.

"What do you mean—well?"

"You're surely not going to assert that one can simply leave it at that!"

"I should like to leave it at that," Ulrich said quietly. "Our view of our environment—and for that matter, of ourselves—changes every day. We are living in a period of transition. Perhaps, if we don't tackle our profoundest problems any better than we have so far, it'll go on as long as the world lasts. But still, if one is set down in the dark, one mustn't be like a child and whistle to keep one's courage up. And it's only whistling to keep one's courage up if one behaves as if one knew how to behave in this world here below. You can bellow for all you're worth, but it's still only from fear. Apart from that, one thing I'm convinced of is—we're galloping ! We're still a long way from our objectives, they don't get any nearer, we can't even see them, we shall often ride astray and often have to change horses. But some day—the day after tomorrow, or in two thousand years— the horizon will begin to flow and will come rushing and roaring towards us ! "

Dusk had fallen. 'No one can see my face now,' Ulrich thought. ' I don't even know myself whether I'm just making this up.' He had been talking the way one does when, in a moment of uncertainty, one sums up the result of decades of certainty. It came back to him how after all this youthful dream, which he was holding up to Walter, had long become hollow. He didn't want to go on talking.

" And so," Walter retorted sharply, " you think we ought to do without any meaning in life ? "

Ulrich asked him what he really needed a meaning for. One got along all right without it, he commented.

Clarisse giggled. She did not mean to be unkind, but the question had struck her as comical.

Walter turned on the light, for he did not think it necessary that Ulrich should in Clarisse's presence exploit the advantage of the man in darkness. An irritating glare poured over the three of them.

Ulrich went on doggedly explaining. " What one needs in life is merely the conviction that one's own business is going better than one's neighbour's. That means, your pictures, my mathematics, somebody else's children and wife—everything that assures a person that although he is in no way anything unusual, nevertheless in his own way of being in no way anything unusual he will not easily meet his match ! "

Walter had not yet sat down again. He was full of unrest, and now suddenly of triumph. " Do you know what you're saying ? " he exclaimed. " Muddling through ! You're simply an

Austrian.   You're preaching the Austrian national philosophy of muddling through ! "

" That may not be such a bad thing as you think," Ulrich replied.   " A passionate desire for sharpness and exactness or for beauty may very well bring one to the point of liking muddling through better than all exertions in the spirit of modern times. I congratulate you on having discovered Austria's world mission."

Walter wanted to retort.   But it became apparent that the feeling that had driven him to his feet was not only triumph but also—how does one put it ?—the wish to leave the room for a moment.   He wavered between the two wishes.   But both could not be combined, and his glance slid from Ulrich's eyes towards the door.

When they were alone, Clarisse said : " This murderer is musical.   That is to say——" she paused, and then continued mysteriously : " One can't say anything, but you must do something for him."

" But what can I do ? "

" Liberate him ! "

" You must be crazy ! "

" Surely you don't mean everything the way you say it to Walter ? " Clarisse asked, and her eyes seemed to be urging him to make some answer that he could not guess at.

" I don't know what you want," he said.

Clarisse gazed obstinately at his lips.   Then she came back to her point : " All the same, you ought to do what I said.   You would be transformed."

Ulrich considered her.   He did not quite understand.   He must have missed something she had said, some comparison, some sort of ' as if ' giving meaning to these words of hers.   It was very odd to listen to her speaking without that meaning and as naturally as though it were about some ordinary experience she had had.

But here Walter returned.   "Well, I am prepared to admit——" he began.   The interruption had taken the edge off the discussion.

He sat down again on his stool at the piano and gazed contentedly at his shoes, to which there was some earth clinging.

He thought : ' Why is there no earth on Ulrich's shoes ? It is the last hope of salvation for European man.'

But Ulrich looked at the legs above Walter's shoes ; they were clothed in black cotton stockings and had the unlovely shape of soft girlish legs.

" One must value it if there's a man still left nowadays who is striving to be something integral," Walter said.

" There's no longer any such thing," Ulrich countered. " You only have to look into a newspaper. You'll find it's filled with immeasurable opacity. So many things come under discussion that it would surpass the intellectual capacity of a Leibniz. But one doesn't even notice it. One has become different. There is no longer a whole man confronting a whole world, but a human something floating about in a universal culture-medium."

" Very true," Walter said at once. " There is in fact no longer any such thing as a universal education in Goethe's sense. But that is why today to every thought we also have a counter-thought and to every tendency an immediate counter-tendency. Today, every act and its opposite are accompanied by the subtlest intellectual arguments, with which one can both defend them and condemn them. I can't understand how you can bring yourself to speak up for such a state of things ! "

Ulrich shrugged his shoulders.

" One must withdraw entirely," Walter said in a low voice.

" One can manage as it is," his friend replied. " Perhaps we are on the way to the ant-State, or to some other unchristian distribution of labour."

Ulrich thought to himself that it was just as easy to agree as to argue. In politeness the contempt lay as transparently obvious as a tit-bit in aspic. He knew that his last words would also annoy Walter, yet he began to feel a longing to talk, for once, to somebody with whom he could wholly agree. There had once been a time when Walter and he had had such talks. Then the words are drawn out of the breast by some mysterious power, and none of them misses its mark. But if one talks with antipathy, they rise like mist from an icy plain. He gazed at Walter without resentment. He was sure that Walter too had the feeling that the further this conversation went, the more his inmost convictions were being deformed, and that he was blaming him, Ulrich, for that. ' All one thinks is either sympathy or antipathy,' Ulrich thought. And at this moment this so vividly struck him as being right that he felt it as a physical pressure, like the bodily contact of people swaying in unison when they are jammed up against each other. He looked round for Clarisse.

But Clarisse seemed to have stopped listening some time ago. She had at some point picked up the newspaper lying before her on the table and she had begun probing into her mind to find out why this caused her such profound pleasure. She felt before her eyes the immeasurable opacity of which Ulrich had spoken, and felt the newspaper in her hands. Her arms, themselves opening up, unfolded the darkness. Her arms formed two cross-beams with the trunk of her body, and between them hung the news-paper. That was the pleasure ; but the words to describe it had no existence in Clarisse. She merely knew that she was looking at the newspaper without reading and that it seemed to her there was something barbarically mysterious hidden in Ulrich, a force akin to herself, although she could not formulate it any more clearly. Her lips had opened as though she were about to smile, but it happened unconsciously, loosely and yet in rigid tension.

Walter went on in a low voice : " You're right in saying there's nothing serious, rational or even intelligible left nowadays. But why won't you realise that it's precisely increasing rationality that's to blame ? It's a disease rotting everything. Everyone's brain has been infected with the desire to become more and more cerebral, to rationalise life more than ever, to specialise, and at the same time with the inability to imagine what will become of us if we explain, analyse and normalise everything, transforming everything into machines, standardising everything. It can't go on like this."

" Good lord," Ulrich replied composedly, " in the monkish ages the Christian had to be a believer, although he could only imagine a heaven that was pretty boring, with those clouds and harps. And we're afraid of the heaven of rationality, which reminds us of the rulers, straight benches and ghastly chalk diagrams of our schooldays."

" I can't help feeling," Walter added thoughtfully, " that the consequences will be unbridled excesses of the sheer fantastic." There was some slight cowardice and cunning in this remark.

He was thinking of the mysterious anti-rational thing in Clarisse, and while he talked about reason, which was driving this thing to excesses, he was thinking of Ulrich.   The two others were not aware of this, and that filled him with the pain and triumph of the misunderstood.   He would really have liked to ask Ulrich not to enter the house again for as long as he remained in this city— if only it had been possible to do this without exciting Clarisse to mutiny.

So the two men observed Clarisse in silence.

She suddenly noticed that they had stopped arguing.   She rubbed her eyes and blinked amiably at Ulrich and Walter, who sat illumined by yellow light against the dusky blue of the window-panes, as though in a glass cabinet.

55   *Soliman and Arnheim.*

HOWEVER, the murderer Christian Moosbrugger had a second female well-wisher.   The question of his guilt or his affliction had some weeks earlier taken as vigorous a hold on her heart as on many others, and she had a conception of the case that somewhat diverged from that of the court.   The name Christian Moos-brugger rather appealed to her, and with it she associated a lonely, tall man sitting by a moss-grown mill, listening to the thundering of the water.   She was firmly convinced that the accusations made against him would be cleared up in a quite unexpected way.   When she was sitting in the kitchen or the dining-room, with her needlework, it would happen that Moos-brugger, having shaken off his chains, came up beside her, and then utterly wild fantasies began.   In them it was far from impossible that Christian, if he had got to know her, Rachel, in time, would have given up his career as a murderer of girls and would have developed into a robber-chieftain with an immense future.

This poor man in his prison had no notion of the heart that, bent over the mending of Diotima's underclothes, was beating for him. It was not at all far from Permanent Secretary Tuzzi's apartment to the *Landesgericht*. From one roof to the other, it would have taken an eagle only a few wing-beats. But for the modern soul, for which it is mere child's play to bridge oceans and continents, there is nothing so impossible as to find the contact with the souls dwelling just round the corner.

So the magnetic currents had dissolved again, and for some time now Rachel had loved the Collateral Campaign instead of Moosbrugger. Even if inside the rooms things did not get going quite as they should have, in the ante-chambers there was a good deal going on. Rachel, who had previously always found leisure to read the newspapers drifting from the master and mistress into the kitchen, no longer had time for it since from morning till late she stood as a little sentinel in front of the Collateral Campaign. She loved Diotima, Permanent Secretary Tuzzi, His Highness the Imperial Liege-Count Leinsdorf, the Nabob, and, since she had noticed that he was beginning to play a role in this house, Ulrich as well. So does a dog love the friends of his master's house—it is one emotion and yet various smells that provide exciting change. But Rachel was intelligent. Where Ulrich was concerned, for instance, she was quite well aware that he was always a little at variance with the others, and her imagination had begun ascribing to him a special and not yet quite clearly defined role in the Collateral Campaign. ›He always looked at her in a friendly way, and little Rachel observed that he regarded her at especial length when he thought she was not looking. She thought it certain that he wanted something of her. Well, let it come. Her soft white skin contracted in expectation, like that of a little animal, and out of her beautiful black eyes a tiny golden dart now and then shot across at him. Ulrich felt the sparking of this little person, without being able to account for it, as she flitted round the stately furniture and visitors, and it provided him with some distraction.

He owed his share of Rachel's attention not least to mysterious ante-chamber conversations, as a result of which Arnheim's dominant position was undermined; for, without knowing it, that shining example of a man had besides Ulrich and Tuzzi a third enemy in his little servant Soliman.

This little blackamoor was the sparkling clasp of the magic girdle that the Collateral Campaign had laid around Rachel. This funny little chap, who had come following his master from fairyland into the street where Rachel was in service, had simply been taken possession of by her as the part of the fairy-tale especially intended for her. This was the proper social arrangement : the Nabob was the sun and belonged to Diotima, Soliman belonged to Rachel and was a delightfully bright splinter, twinkling in the sun, which she had picked up for herself. But this was not quite the boy's view of it. Although he was quite small, he was nearly seventeen, a creature full of romanticism, malice and personal pretensions. Arnheim had once taken him away from a troupe of dancers in southern Italy and kept him. The weird, fidgety little boy, with his mournful monkey-gaze, had touched his heart, and the rich man resolved to open up a higher life to him. It was done out of a yearning for an affectionate, faithful companion, a feeling that not infrequently overcame the solitary man, a kind of weakness, but one that he generally hid behind increased activity ; and until Soliman's fourteenth year he treated him more or less on the same casual terms of equality on which rich families once brought up the foster-brothers and foster-sisters with their own children, letting them share in all games and amusements, until the moment in which it became evident that the same milk was of less value when it was a mother's than when it was a wet-nurse's. Soliman used to crouch day and night at his master's desk or at his feet, behind his back or on his knees, during long hours of conversation with famous visitors. He read Scott, Shakespeare and Dumas, when Scott, Shakespeare and Dumas happened to be lying about on the tables ; he had learnt to read out of handbooks of philosophy and the social sciences. He ate his master's sweets and early began to smoke his cigarettes too, when no one was looking. A private tutor came and— somewhat erratically because of the great amount of travelling they did—gave him an elementary education. All this bored Soliman dreadfully and he liked nothing so much as the duties of a valet, in which he was also allowed to have a share, for that was a real, grown-up activity, flattering to his urge for action. But one day—and it was not so long ago—his master had summoned him and told him, kindly, that he had not quite fulfilled the hopes set on him, that he was now no longer a child and that he, Arnheim, as his master, was responsible for seeing that Soliman, the little servant, turned out a decent citizen. For this reason he had resolved from now on to treat him exactly as that which he would one day have to be, so that he would have time to get used to it. Many successful men—Arnheim had added—had begun as boot-blacks and dish-washers, and precisely this had been the source of their strength, for the most important thing in life was to put one's whole heart into things right from the start.

That hour, when he had been promoted from the uncertain status of a pet kept in luxury to being a servant with free board and lodging and a small wage, had caused a devastation in Soliman's heart of which Arnheim had not the faintest notion. Soliman had not in the least understood the disclosures that Arnheim had made to him, but he had instinctively guessed what it all meant and he hated his master since the change that he had had to undergo. Not that he now refrained from taking books, sweets and cigarettes ; but whereas previously he had merely taken what he enjoyed, now he was deliberately stealing from Arnheim, and his sense of revenge was so difficult to satisfy that he sometimes simply smashed things, hid them or threw them away, so that they never turned up again and Arnheim, who obscurely recalled them, was left with a vague sense of puzzlement. While Soliman was thus taking his revenge, like a kobold, in the matter of carrying out his duties and presenting a pleasant appearance he pulled himself together to a surprising extent. Now, as ever, he was a sensational success with all cooks, housemaids, hotel staff, and women visitors, was exquisitely spoiled by their glances and their smiles, was gaped at, mockingly enough, by street-urchins, and continued to feel that he was a fascinating and important personage, even although he was being oppressed. Even his master still sometimes favoured him with a pleased and complacent glance or with some wise and friendly words ; he was praised by all as a handy, obliging boy ; and if it so happened that Soliman had a short time before laden his conscience with some particularly objectionable offence, then, obsequiously grinning, he would enjoy his superiority as though it were a ball of searingly cold ice that he had just swallowed.

Rachel had won this boy's trust in the moment when she confided in him that in this very house preparations might actually be under way for a war; and since then she had had to listen to the most disgraceful revelations concerning her idol, Arnheim. In spite of the fact that he was so *blasé*, Soliman's imagination was like a pin-cushion bristling with swords and daggers, and in all he told Rachel about Arnheim there was the thunder of horses' hooves and the swaying of torches and rope ladders. He confided in her that his name was not really Soliman at all and uttered a long, strange-sounding name, which he pronounced so quickly that she could never remember it. Later he added the secret that he was the son of an African prince and had when a baby been stolen from his father, who possessed thousands of warriors, heads of cattle, slaves and jewels. Arnheim, he said, had bought him in order some day to sell him back to the prince for a frightful lot of money, but he was going to run away and had only not been able to do it before this because it was so far to where his father lived.

Rachel was not so silly as to believe these stories, but she believed *in* them because in all that had to do with the Collateral Campaign there was no measure of the incredible great enough for her. She would also have liked to forbid Soliman to talk about Arnheim like this. But she had to content herself with a horrified mistrust of his presumption, for somehow, in spite of all her doubts, she felt the statement that his master was not to be trusted as a tremendous, imminent, thrilling complication in the Collateral Campaign.

These were thunder-clouds behind which the tall man by the moss-grown mill disappeared, and a lurid light gathered in the wrinkling grimaces of Soliman's little monkey-face.

56

Intense activity in the Collateral Campaign's committees. Clarisse writes to His Highness, suggesting a Nietzsche Year.

AT this time Ulrich had to go to His Highness's two or three times every week. The room he found prepared for him was high and elongated, delightful in its very proportions. At the window was a large Maria-Theresa writing-desk. There was a dark picture on the wall, with patches of red, blue and yellow glowing out of its depths, representing some horsemen driving their lances into the abdomens of other horsemen rolling on the ground ; and on the opposite wall was a solitary lady whose abdomen was carefully protected by a gold-embroidered bodice fitting closely to her wasp-like waist. It was not clear why she should have been exiled to solitude on that wall, for she obviously belonged to the Leinsdorf family, and her young powdered face resembled the Count's as closely as a footprint in dry snow resembles a footprint in wet clay. Ulrich had little opportunity, however, to study Count Leinsdorf's face. Outwardly the Collateral Campaign had received such impetus since the last meeting that His Highness never had time to give his mind to the great ideas, but was taken up with reading correspondence and seeing visitors, with discussions and driving about town. He had for instance already had a talk with the Prime Minister, a discussion with the Archbishop, a conference at the Chamberlain's office, and had several times sounded members of the high aristocracy and the ennobled bourgeoisie in the Upper House. Ulrich was not called in at these consultations, and all he learnt was that strong political resistance on the part of the opposition was generally expected, for which reason all quarters declared they would be able to support the Collateral Campaign all the more vigorously the less their names appeared in connection with it and for the present had themselves represented on the committees only by observers.

Gratifyingly enough, these committees made great progress

from week to week. As had been resolved at the inaugural meeting, they divided up the world according to those great aspects of it, religion, education, commerce, agriculture and so on, a representative of the corresponding ministry now being on each committee, and all committees already devoting themselves to their task, which consisted of each committee's waiting, in agreement with all the other committees, for the representatives of the respective organisations and sections of the population, in order to deal with their wishes, suggestions and petitions and pass them on to the executive committee. In this way it was hoped to supply this last body with a constant stream of the nation's 'number one priority' moral forces, all summarised and classified; and it was satisfactory to see the tide of correspondence rising. It was not long before the various committees' memoranda to the executive committee could refer to other memoranda that had already been sent to the executive committee, and began to begin with a sentence that became weightier each time, its first words being: "With reference to our ref. number such-and-such, alternatively number so-and-so, oblique . . ." followed by yet another number, this time in Roman figures; and with every communication these numbers became larger. Here already was something that looked like healthy growth. In addition, even the embassies began, through semi-official channels, to report on the impression this vigorous display of Austrian patriotism was making abroad. The foreign ambassadors were cautiously looking for ways of getting information. Parliamentary deputies, now on the alert, were asking questions. Private initiative began to manifest itself in enquiries from business houses, who took the liberty of putting forward suggestions or of respectfully seeking a clue that would be of help in establishing a relation between their firm and the cause of patriotism. The machine was there; and because it was there, it had to work, and once it was running, it began to accelerate. And when, for instance, a car begins to travel across a wide open space, it will always cover a definite, indeed very impressive and remarkable course even if there is no one sitting at the steering-wheel.

And so there was soon a tremendous driving-force; and it made itself apparent to Count Leinsdorf. Putting on his pince-nez, he read all the in-coming correspondence from beginning to end, with the greatest of seriousness. It no longer consisted of the suggestions and wishes of unknown, impassioned persons, such as had inundated him at the start, before the course of the affair had been regulated ; and even if these applications or enquiries originated from the ranks of the people, still, they were signed by the chairmen of Alpine associations, rationalist societies, girls' welfare guilds, working-men's associations, social and sports clubs, and others of those nondescript little groupings that are bowled along in the transition from individualism to collectivism as little heaps of street-sweepings are set whirling by a stiff breeze. And even if His Highness was not in agreement with everything that was asked of him, he did observe considerable all-round progress. He would take off his pince-nez, hand the communication back to the *Ministerialrat* who had passed it to him, and nod in a satisfied manner, without comment. He had the feeling that the Collateral Campaign was going ahead in a right and proper way and that the true way was sure to be found before long.

The *Ministerialrat*, taking the letter back again, generally laid it on a pile of other letters, and when the last one lay there, he read what was in His Highness's eyes. Then His Highness's mouth would open and speak. " All this is excellent, but one can't say either yes or no so long as we have nothing settled in principle as to the focal point of our aims." This, however, was what the *Ministerialrat* had already read in His Highness's eyes after every previous letter, and it was also precisely his own opinion. He held in his hand a gold-cased pocket-pencil with which he had already written at the bottom of each letter the magic formula : " *Ass.*" This magic formula, which was in use in the Kakanian civil service, stood for *Asserviert*, which means as much as *Awaiting further consideration*, and was an example of the circumspection that does not lose sight of anything and does not try to rush anything. For instance, a very minor civil servant's application for a grant of special assistance in view of his wife's confinement would be filed, *Awaiting further consideration*, until the child was grown up and earning its own living, and for no other reason than that by that time the matter might have been dealt with by legislation and that the senior official could not find it in his heart, meanwhile, to reject the application. But what was also filed with the remark *Ass.* was any application from an influential person or official department that must not be offended by a refusal, although one knew very well that some other influential quarter was opposed to the granting of the application. And on principle everything that came up before a department for the first time was kept on file, *Awaiting further consideration*, until a similar case occurred that could be used as a precedent.

But it would be quite wrong to make fun of this custom prevailing in government departments, for outside the civil service there is still far more that is perpetually *asserviert*. How little it means, for instance, that monarchs on their accession take an oath that still includes swearing to wage war against the Turks or the heathen becomes apparent if one bears in mind that never yet in the history of mankind has a sentence been completely cancelled out or completely finished, as a result of which progress at times hurtles along at a bewildering rate, suggesting a winged ox. And yet some things, at least, get lost in government departments ; in the world nothing does. Hence *Asservation* is one of the basic formulae in the structure of our life.

However, if something struck His Highness as particularly urgent, he had to choose another method. Then he would first send the suggestion to Court, to his friend Count Stallburg, with an enquiry whether it might be regarded as what he called ' provisionally definitive '. After some time then the answer would always come back that no expression of His Majesty's most gracious wishes on this point could be conveyed at present and that it seemed, indeed, desirable to begin by letting public opinion take on its own shape and to reconsider the suggestion at a later date in accordance with whatever its reception might have been and in relation to whatever other contingencies might arise. The file into which the suggestion had in this way been transformed was then passed to the appropriate ministerial department, whence it came back with the remark attached that ' this department ' did not consider itself authorised to arrive at any independent decision. And when this stage was reached, Count Leinsdorf made a note to propose, at one of the next meetings of the executive committee, that an inter-departmental sub-committee should be set up to study the matter.

There was only one case in which he was inexorably resolute, namely when a communication came in that did not bear the signature of the chairman of either a society or an officially recognised religious, scientific or artistic body. Such a letter had recently come from Clarisse. In it she had mentioned her acquaintance with Ulrich and suggested organising an Austrian Nietzsche Year, which should be combined with doing something for that maniacal murderer of women, Moosbrugger. As a woman herself, she felt called to suggest this—she wrote—and then too because of the significant coincidence that Nietzsche had been mentally deranged and Moosbrugger was too. Ulrich only just managed to conceal his annoyance behind a joke when Count Leinsdorf showed him this letter, which he recognised at first glance by the oddly immature writing scarred by thickly crossed T's and heavy underlinings. However, Count Leinsdorf, who seemed to perceive his embarrassment, said seriously and kindly : " It is not uninteresting. Indeed, one might say it is ardent and energetic. But I'm afraid we must shelve all such individual suggestions, or else we shall never get anywhere. Perhaps, since you seem to know the lady who wrote it, personally, you would pass this letter on to your cousin ? "

57 *Great exaltation. Diotima's strange discoveries about the nature of great ideas.*

ULRICH put the letter in his pocket, to get it out of sight. It would not have been easy to discuss it with Diotima anyway, for since the article on the Austrian Year had appeared, she felt herself in a chaotic state of exaltation. Not only did Ulrich hand over to her (if possible, unread) all the files that came to him from Count Leinsdorf, but apart from this the mail daily brought piles of letters and newspaper-cuttings, booksellers sent her huge masses of books on approval, the traffic in her house swelled as the sea swells when wind and moon tug at it in unison, the telephone too had not a minute's rest, and if little Rachel had not officiated at it with the fervour of an archangel, dealing with most of the enquiries herself because she saw that her mistress could not be bothered continually, Diotima would have collapsed under the weight of the demands made upon her.

This never quite materialising nervous breakdown, constantly quivering and pulsating in her body, did, however, give Diotima a happiness she had never known before. It was a shuddering as though under a state of awe, spray of significance, a crackling like that of the pressure in a stone set in the apex of the cosmic vault, a prickling like the awareness of the void one feels when standing on a mountain-peak high above everything far and wide. In short, it was the sense of her position that suddenly awoke in her, the daughter of a humble secondary-schoolmaster and the young wife of a middle-class vice-consul—for that, after all, was what she had hitherto remained in the most vernal aspects of her being, in spite of her rise in society. Such a sense of one's position is one of the unnoticed but fundamentally important conditions of life, like being unaware of the earth's revolutions or of the personal share that we contribute to our perceptions. Having been taught that he must not carry it in his heart, man carries the greatest part of his vanity under his feet, in that he walks about on the soil of a great motherland or fatherland, or on the ground of his religion or income-tax grade, and in default of such a position he even makes do with what anyone can have, which is poising on the momentarily highest point on the pillar of time that has risen out of nothingness, in other words, living precisely now, when all one's predecessors have turned to dust and one's successors are not yet there. Yet if this vanity, which is usually unconscious, should from any causes suddenly mount from the feet into the head, a mild form of madness may result, similar to that of those virgins who believe they are about to give birth to the round Earth itself.

Even Permanent Secretary Tuzzi now paid Diotima the tribute of enquiring how things were going, and of sometimes asking her to take over this or that little mission for him ; and at such moments the smile with which he generally spoke of her *salon* gave way to dignified gravity. It was still not known to what extent the plan, for instance, to appear at the head of an inter-national pacifist demonstration would be pleasing to Most

Gracious consideration; but in touching on this possibility he
repeatedly uttered the anxious request that Diotima should not
take the slightest step into the field of foreign affairs without
previously asking his advice. At this point he even gave her to'
understand that if at any time the suggestion for an international
peace-campaign should show signs of taking shape in earnest,
caution would at once have to be observed lest it created political
complications. There was of course no need to turn down such
a beautiful idea—he explained to his wife—not even in the event
of there being a possibility of its becoming reality; but it was
absolutely necessary to keep the terrain free all along for all
possible manoeuvres and withdrawals. He then expounded to
Diotima the distinctions between disarmament, a peace-confer-
ence, and a meeting of potentates, down to that foundation, already
referred to, for the adornment of the Hague Peace Palace with
murals by Austrian artists. Never before had he talked to his
wife in such a matter-of-fact way. Sometimes he would even
come back into the bedroom with his brief-case under his arm
in order to supplement his exposition, as, for instance, when he
had forgotten to add that he personally considered everything
linked with the idea of Universal Austria only possible, it went
without saying, in connection with a pacifist or humanitarian
enterprise, if one was not to create the impression of being
dangerously irresponsible—or the like.

Diotima would answer with a patient smile. " I shall do my
best to comply with your wishes, but you mustn't get any exaggerated ideas as to the importance foreign affairs have for us.   There
is at present a positively redeeming exaltation of inner life, arising
out of the anonymous depths of the nation. You can't imagine
the floods of petitions and suggestions that overwhelm me
every day."

She was admirable. For, without letting it become noticeable,
she had to contend with enormous difficulties. In the delibera-
tions of the great central committee, which was organised under
the headings of Religion, Justice, Agriculture, Education and so
on, all the more sublime suggestions met with the same icy and
timorous reserve that Diotima knew so well in her husband, from
days when he had not yet been so attentive; and she sometimes
felt quite discouraged, from sheer impatience, and could not con-

ceal it from herself that this resistance on the part of the inert world would be hard to break. However clearly the Austrian Year existed for her as the Universal-Austrian Year and was to present the Austrian nations as the model of universal nationhood, for which purpose actually nothing else was needed than to prove that the mind and spirit had their true home in Austria, it became equally clear that for those inclined to lethargy this scheme would need to be given a special content and to be supplemented by some idea that, by consisting more in obviousness than in generality, would meet understanding half-way. And so Diotima spent hours and hours in studying a great many books, looking for an idea that would do this, and naturally it was also to be in some special way a symbolically Austrian idea. But Diotima made some strange discoveries about the nature of great ideas.

It became apparent that she was living in a great time, for the time was full of great ideas. Yet it is extraordinary how difficult it is to put into reality what is greatest and most important among great ideas, as soon as all the pre-conditions are fulfilled except one —namely, knowing what *is* greatest and most important. Every time when Diotima had almost decided in favour of one such idea, she could not help noticing that it would also be a great thing to give reality to the opposite of it. Well, that's the way it is, and she wasn't to blame. Ideals have remarkable qualities, among them that of suddenly turning into their opposite the moment one tries really to live up to them. There were, for example, Tolstoy and Berta Suttner—two writers whose ideas were talked about to pretty much the same extent in those days. But how, Diotima wondered, can humanity provide itself even with roast chicken without violence? And what's to be done with the soldiers if, as these two writers demanded, one is not to kill? They'll be unemployed, the poor fellows, and there'll be golden days for criminals. But such proposals had actually been made, and one even heard of signatures being collected. Diotima could never have imagined a life without eternal verities, but to her amazement she discovered that each eternal verity exists twice over and even in a multiplicity of forms. That is why rational man—and in this case this was Permanent Secretary Tuzzi, whose honour was, as a result, to some extent vindicated—has a deeply rooted mistrust of eternal verities; although he will never deny that they are indispensable, he is convinced that people who take them literally are mad. According to Tuzzi's way of thinking—which he helpfully put at his wife's disposal—ideals make excessive demands on human nature, such as must lead to ruin if one does not from the very beginning avoid taking it all entirely seriously. The best proof of this that Tuzzi could bring forward was that in offices, where people were concerned with serious matters, such words as ' ideal ' and ' eternal verity ' simply did not arise ; an administrative officer going as far as to use such expressions in an official communication would instantly be advised to apply for leave of absence on grounds of ill-health. But though Diotima listened to her husband mournfully, from such hours of weakness she did in the end always draw new strength to plunge back into her studies.

Even Count Leinsdrof was surprised by her mental energy when at last he found time to turn up for a consultation. What His Highness wanted was a demonstration rising from the midst of the people. He sincerely wished to establish what the will of the people was and to refine it by means of a cautiously exerted influence from above, for he wanted, when the time came, not to present it to His Majesty as a gift bearing the stigma of Byzantinism, but to lay it at his feet as a sign of a change of heart on the part of the nations adrift in the vortex of democracy. Diotima knew that His Highness was still set on the ' Emperor of Peace ' idea and on a magnificent demonstration of True Austria, even though he did not in principle reject the Universal-Austria suggestion, so long as it could serve to convey effectively the feeling of a family of nations gathered around their patriarch. From this family His Highness did, it must be added, covertly and tacitly exclude Prussia, although he found nothing to object to in the person of Herr Dr. Arnheim and even expressly referred to him as ' an interesting person '.

" We certainly don't want to have anything patriotic in any worn-out sense of the word, do we ? " he reminded her. " We must shake up the nation, and indeed the world. The idea of having an Austrian Year is an admirable one, I think, and as a matter of fact I myself said to the journalists that the public imagination must be directed to such an aim. But have you ever considered, my dear, what—if we fix on this Austrian Year—we are to do in it ?   That's the point, you see !   We must know that too. It'll mean a little helping on from above, or else the irresponsible elements will gain the upper hand. And I simply don't find time to have any ideas myself ! "

Diotima thought His Highness seemed worried, and replied animatedly : " The Campaign must culminate in a great sign or not at all ! That is certain. It must move the heart of the world, but it does also require an influence coming from above. That cannot be denied. The Austrian Year is an excellent suggestion, but in my opinion a Universal Year would be still finer—a Universal-Austrian Year, for the European spirit to recognise Austria as its true home ! "

" Careful !   Careful ! " Count Leinsdorf said warningly. He had quite often been startled by his friend's intellectual audacity. " Your ideas are always, perhaps, just a little too grand, Diotima ! You did speak of this before, I know, but one can never be quite careful enough. Well now, what have you thought out for us to do in this Universal Year ? "

With this question, however, Count Leinsdorf, acting with the straightforwardness that made his way of thinking so sturdily characteristic, touched on precisely the sorest spot in Diotima's mind. " Count," she said after some hesitation, " you are asking me for an answer to the most difficult question in the world. What I intend to do as soon as possible is to invite here a circle of our most distinguished men, including writers and philosophers, and I want to wait and see what suggestions are put forward by that gathering before I say anything."

" That's the very thing ! " His Highness exclaimed, instantly won over to the idea of waiting and seeing. " The very thing ! One can't be too careful !   If you only knew what I have to listen to now, day in, day out ! "

58

The Collateral Campaign causes qualms. But in the history of mankind there is no such thing as turning back of one's own free will.

ONCE, too, His Highness had time to talk things over with Ulrich in more detail. " I don't altogether care for this Herr Dr. Arnheim," he confided in him. " Extremely brilliant man, of course, one can't wonder at your cousin—but a Prussian, after all. It's the way he looks on, you know. I remember, when I was a little chap, in '65 it was, my late lamented father had a shooting-party at Chrudim Castle, and one of the guests was a fellow who had that way of looking on, too, and a year afterwards it turned out that not a soul knew who had brought him along anyway, and that he was a major on the Prussian general staff ! Naturally, I don't want to suggest anything, but I don't altogether care for the idea that this fellow Arnheim knows all about us."

" Sir," Ulrich said, " I'm glad you have given me an opportunity to speak my mind. It's time something was done. I come across things that have started me thinking, and they are by no means suitable for a foreign observer. After all, the Collateral Campaign ought to stir up cheerful feelings in people, oughtn't it ? That is what you intend, I think ? "

" Well, yes, naturally ! "

" But the very opposite is happening ! " Ulrich exclaimed. " I have the impression it's putting educated people into a strikingly thoughtful and melancholy frame of mind."

His Highness shook his head and twiddled his thumbs, as he always did when his spirit was overcast by gloomy thought. He had indeed himself made observations similar to those of which Ulrich was now telling him.

" Since it has got around that I have something to do with the Collateral Campaign," Ulrich went on, " whenever anyone I see starts talking to me on general topics, hardly three minutes pass without his saying : ' What actually are you getting at with the Collateral Campaign? After all, there's no such thing as great achievements or great men left these days.' "

" Yes, only they never mean themselves," His Highness interjected. " I hear plenty of that too, I know it well. The big industrialists run down the politicians for not giving them sufficiently high protective tariffs, and the politicians run down industry for not stumping up enough for party funds."

" Quite so," Ulrich said, taking up the point. " Surgeons, for instance, undoubtedly do think surgery has made progress since Billroth's day, but they say that the rest of medicine and scientific research as a whole does too little to help surgery. I should even go so far as to say, if you would permit me to do so, sir, that the theologians, too, are convinced that theology is in some way further ahead nowadays than in the time of Christ . . ."

Count Leinsdorf raised one hand in indulgent protest.

" I'm sorry, sir, I didn't mean to say anything unseemly, and it wasn't really necessary at all. For what I am getting at seems to indicate something quite general. The surgeons, as I was saying, assert that scientific research doesn't quite come up to what might be expected of it. On the other hand, if one talks to a research scientist about the present time, he will complain that generally speaking he would like to broaden his mind a little, but he finds the theatre a bore and he can't discover any entertaining and stimulating novels. If one talks to a poet, he's bound to say nobody believes in anything nowadays. And—as we are now leaving the theologians aside—if one talks to a painter one can be pretty sure he will declare that painters can't give of their best in a time with such rotten literature and philosophy. The sequence in which each one puts the blame on the other is of course not always the same, but it always somehow reminds one of Eeney Meeney Miney Mo, if you know what I mean, sir, or Puss in the Corner. The principle on which it is based, or the law it obeys, is something I can't work out. I'm afraid it must be admitted that each individual man is just about satisfied with himself, but, collectively, for some universal reason or other, no one seems to feel quite at home in his own skin, and it seems that the Collateral Campaign is destined to bring that to light."

" Good gracious me," His Highness said in response to this

analysis, and added, without its being quite clear what he meant :
" Nothing but ingratitude ! "

" Apart from that," Ulrich went on, " I already have two files
full of written proposals of a general nature, which I have not
yet had an opportunity of returning to you.   One of them I have
headed : ' Back To ——'.   The fact is, there are a remarkably
large number of people informing us that in earlier times the
world was in a better way than it is now and all the Collateral
Campaign need do is to lead it back to that stage.   Putting aside
the quite natural demand ' Back to Belief ', we are still left with
' Back to the Baroque ', ' to the Gothic ', ' to Nature ', ' to
Goethe ', ' to old Germanic law ', ' to moral purity ', and quite
a number of other things."

" H'm, yes.   But perhaps, don't you think, there may be a
true idea in it somewhere, and one shouldn't discourage it ? "
Count Leinsdorf said diffidently.

" That's quite possible.   But how is one to reply ?   ' After
careful consideration of your esteemed communication of the
such-and-such, we regret that the present moment is not yet
suitable . . .' ?   Or : ' Having read your letter with interest, we
should be glad if you would supply further details as to your
wishes concerning the restoration of the world to Baroque,
Gothic, and so forth ' ? "

Ulrich smiled.   Count Leinsdorf, however, thought him a little
too gay at the moment and twiddled his thumbs in concentrated
repudiation.   In the hardness that his face took on, with its
mustachios, it was reminiscent of the time of Wallenstein.   And
then he came out with a statement that was really most remarkable.

" My young friend," he said, " in the history of mankind there
is no turning back of one's own free will ! "

This statement surprised no one more than Count Leinsdorf
himself, for he had really meant to say something quite different.
Conservative as he was, he had been cross with Ulrich and had
wanted to say that the middle classes had spurned the universal
spirit of the Catholic Church and were now suffering the consequences.   It would also have been the most natural thing to laud
the times of absolute centralism, when the world was still directed
by persons conscious of their responsibilities, and according to
unified principles.   But while he was groping for words, it had

all at once occurred to him that he would in fact be disagreeably surprised if he were to wake up one morning to find no hot bath and no railways, and instead of getting the morning papers to have to make do with the Imperial town-crier riding through the streets. And so Count Leinsdorf thought : ' Things were like that once, but they will never be the same again,' and thinking that, he was amazed. For, assuming that there was no going back of one's own free will in history, then mankind resembled a man being urged forward by some uncanny *wanderlust*, a man for whom there is no returning home and no arriving anywhere ; and that seemed a very remarkable state to be in.

Now, although His Highness did possess an extraordinarily happy knack of keeping apart any two thoughts that were antagonistic to each other, so that they never really met in his conscious mind, this thought, which was contrary to all his principles, was one that he really ought to have rejected. Only he had taken rather a fancy to Ulrich, and in so far as his duties left him time he took great pleasure in explaining political subjects, in a strictly logical manner, to this intellectually alert young man, who had been so well recommended to him and whose only drawback was that, belonging to the middle class, he was a shade out of touch with the really great problems. But once one makes a beginning with logic, in which one thought arises inevitably out of the preceding one, the long and the short of it is that one can never know how it will all end. And so Count Leinsdorf did not take back his statement, but merely gazed at Ulrich searchingly and in silence.

Ulrich picked up a second file and took advantage of the pause to hand both of them to His Highness.

" I had to give the second one the heading ' Forward to ——', " he began to explain.

But His Highness started up and discovered that he had overrun his time. He begged to have the rest left for another occasion, when there would be leisure to think it all over. " By the way, your cousin is going to have a little gathering of our most distinguished men to discuss these very questions," he said, already on his feet. " Do go along. Do, please, be sure to go along. I don't know whether I myself will be permitted to be present."

Ulrich packed the files up again.

Count Leinsdorf, already in the darkness of the open door, turned back once more. "A great experiment naturally makes everyone downhearted. But never mind, we'll shake them up!" His sense of duty would not let him go away leaving Ulrich behind without comfort.

59   *Moosbrugger does some thinking.*

MEANWHILE Moosbrugger had settled down in his new prison as best he could. Scarcely had the gate shut when he was shouted at. When he resented this, they threatened to beat him—if he remembered rightly. He had been put into an isolation cell. When he was taken out for his walk in the yard his hands were thackled, and the warders' eyes were fastened on him all the time. They had cropped his hair, regardless of the fact that his sentence had not yet been confirmed, allegedly in order to take his measurements. They had lathered him with stinking soft soap, pretending it was for disinfection. He was an old hand and he knew that none of all this was according to regulations, but it was not so easy to hold one's own behind the iron gates. They did what they liked with him. He demanded an interview with the prison governor and made a complaint. The governor had to admit that some of it was not according to regulations, but it was not meant as punishment, he said, but as a precaution. Moosbrugger complained to the prison chaplain. But the chaplain was a kindly old man whose benevolent shepherding of souls had the old-fashioned fault that it could not cope with sexual crimes. He abhorred them with the incomprehension of one whose body had not even touched the fringe of such things, and was indeed dismayed to find that Moosbrugger, with his honest looks, moved him to the weakness of personal pity. He referred him to the prison doctor, while he himself, as in all such cases, merely sent up a great plea to the Creator, without entering into details and dealing with the errings of mortal man in such general terms that in the moment of prayer itself Moosbrugger was included as much as were free-thinkers and atheists. The prison doctor however gave it as his opinion to Moosbrugger that everything he was objecting to wasn't half as bad as all that, slapped him cheerfully on the back and absolutely refused to take any notice of his complaints, for—if Moosbrugger understood rightly—that was beside the point so long as the question whether he was insane or simulating had not been settled by the medical authorities. Moosbrugger was wrathfully aware that they all talked just as it suited them and that it was this talking that gave them the power to treat him any way they liked. He had the feeling, which simple people tend to have, that the educated ought to have their tongues cut out. He looked into the doctor's face with the duelling scars, into the priest's face that was withered away from within, into the austerely tidy office-face of the governor, and saw each gazing into his own in a different way ; and in these faces there was something beyond his reach but common to them all, something that all his life long had been his enemy.

The power of contraction by means of which every human being, with all his self-conceit, laboriously manages to squeeze in among all the other flesh in the outside world had somewhat lessened—in spite of all the discipline—under the roof of the jail, where life was made up of waiting, and the living relationship between human beings, coarse and violent though it was, was hollowed out by a shadowy unreality. The slackening of the tension after the struggles of the trial was something to which Moosbrugger reacted with the whole of his strong body. It was like being a loose tooth. His skin itched. He felt miserable, as though he had caught an infection. It was a plaintive, delicately nervous over-sensitivity, such as sometimes overcame him. The woman who now lay underground, who had got him into this mess, appeared to him, in comparison with himself, a coarse malignant wench confronting a child.

Nevertheless, Moosbrugger was on the whole not dissatisfied ; there were plenty of things by which he could tell that he was an important person here, and he relished that. Even the provisions made for all convicts alike were a source of satisfaction to him. The State had to feed, bath and clothe them and concern itself with their work, health, books, and singing, since the time when they had done wrong, whereas previously it had never done so. Moosbrugger enjoyed this attentiveness, in spite of its strictness, like a child that has succeeded in forcing its mother into paying it some angry attention.   But he did not want it to last long; the idea that he might be recommended to mercy and have his sentence commuted to imprisonment for life, or that he might be sent back again to a lunatic asylum, aroused in him the resistance that we feel when all our efforts to escape from our life lead us back, time and again, into the same hated conditions.   He knew that his counsel was trying to get the case re-opened and that he was to be examined yet once again.   But he made up his mind to take a stand against that in good time and to insist that they should kill him.

His departure must be worthy of him—so much was certain. For his whole life had been a battle for his rights.   In his solitary cell Moosbrugger did some thinking about what his rights were. He couldn't really tell.   But it was what had been withheld from him all his life long.   In the instant when he thought of that, his emotions began to swell.   His tongue arched and began to move like a stallion pacing in *haute école* style, so refinedly was it trying to put it. ' Rights,' he thought exceedingly slowly, in order to establish the meaning of it, and thought it just as though he were talking to someone, ' that's when you don't do anything that isn't right, or some such, isn't it ? '   And suddenly it struck him : ' Right is the law.'   That was it—his rights were his law ! He looked at his plank-bed, to sit down on it, turned round slowly and carefully, pulled in vain at the thing, which was screwed fast to the floor, and settled down hesitantly.

They had withheld his law from him !   He remembered his master's wife, when he was sixteen.   He had had a dream that something cold was blowing on his belly, then it disappeared inside him, he yelled and fell out of bed, and the next morning he felt as if he had been beaten black and blue.   Now, as it happened, other apprentices had once told him that if you showed a woman your fist with the thumb sticking out a little bit between the middle finger and the forefinger, she couldn't resist.   He didn't know what to make of it all.   They all said they had tried it out, but when he thought of it the ground seemed to slide away from under his feet, or his head suddenly seemed to be fixed on his neck differently from what he was used to. The long and the short of it was that something was going on in him that was a hair's-breadth out of the natural order of things and not quite safe. " Missus," he said, " I'd like to do something nice to you . . ." They were alone. And she looked into his eyes, must have read something there, and replied : " You just clear out of this kitchen ! " Thereupon he held up to her gaze the fist with the protruding thumb. But the magic only half worked. The missus turned dark red and hit him over the face with the wooden spoon she had in her hand, so swiftly that he couldn't dodge. He realised what had happened only when the blood began to trickle over his lips. But now he recalled that moment quite vividly, for there and then his blood turned the other way, flowed upwards and rose up over his eyes; he hurled himself upon the big strapping woman who had so outrageously insulted him, the master came running in, and what happened from then on, up to the moment when he found himself standing in the street, his legs giving way under him, and his things being thrown out after him, was as though a big red blanket were being torn to shreds. That was how they had mocked and beaten his law. He began to tramp the roads again. Could anyone find the law on the roads ? All women were already someone else's law, and so were all apples and all beds. And the gendarmes and the magistrates were worse than the dogs.

But what in fact it was by which people always got hold of him and why they threw him into prisons and asylums was something that Moosbrugger could never rightly make out. He stared long and hard at the floor and then into the corners of his cell, straining every nerve ; he felt like someone who had dropped a key on the ground. But he could not find it. The floor and the corners once more turned grey and ordinary in the daylight, after they had just been like the ground one walks on in dreams, where suddenly a thing or a person springs up where a word has dropped. Moosbrugger gathered up all his logic. What he could remember distinctly was only all the places where it began. He could have ticked them off on his fingers, describing them. Once it was in Linz, and another time in Braila. There were years between. And last of all now here in the city.

He saw every stone before him. Clear. The way stones don't usually stand out. He remembered too the bad temper that always went with it. Like having poison instead of blood in your veins, you might say, or something like that. For instance, he would be working in the open, and women would be going by. He would not look at them, because they bothered him, but again and again new ones would go by. Then in the end his eyes would follow them with loathing, and that again—that slow turning of the eyes to and fro—was like a stirring in tar or in stiffening cement. Then he would notice that his thoughts were beginning to get heavy.

He always thought slowly anyway, words cost him an effort, he never had enough words, and at times, when he was talking to someone, it would happen that the other person suddenly looked at him in astonishment, not realising how much there was in one single word when Moosbrugger brought it out so slowly. He envied all the people who had learnt when young how to talk easily. With him the words stuck like rubber to his gums, just to spite him, at the very times when he needed them most, and then sometimes an endless while passed before he could tear a syllable loose and get on again. There was no denying that a thing like that certainly had no natural cause. But when he told the court that it was the Freemasons or the Jesuits or the Socialists who were persecuting him in this way, nobody would understand him. Although the lawyers could talk better than he could and brought up all sorts of things against him, they had not the faintest idea of the way things really were.

And when that had gone on for some time, Moosbrugger got frightened. Just let anyone try standing in the street with his hands tied together and see how people behave ! Knowing that his tongue, or something else still deeper inside him, was stuck fast as though with glue gave him a feeling of miserable insecurity that it took him days of trouble to hide. But then there suddenly came a sharp and, one might almost say, soundless frontier. All at once there was a cold breath. Or in the air quite close to him a big ball loomed up and flew into his chest. And at the same moment he felt something about himself, in his eyes, on his lips or in the muscles of his face. All his surroundings went into a vanishing, a blackening, and while the houses lay down upon the trees, out of the bushes some cats might come darting and shooting away. It only lasted for a second, and then the whole thing was over.

And actually it was only then the time began that they all wanted to know about and all kept on talking about. They made the most senseless objections to what he said, and unfortunately he himself could remember his experiences only vaguely and by their meaning. For those times were all meaning! They sometimes lasted for minutes, but sometimes they went on for days on end, and sometimes they passed over into other similar ones, which might last for months. To begin with these, because they were the simpler ones, such as in Moosbrugger's opinion even a judge could grasp, then he would hear voices or music or a blowing and buzzing, also a whizzing and rattling, or shooting, thundering, laughing, shouting, talking and whispering. It came from everywhere at once; it was in the walls, in the air, in his clothes and in his body. It seemed to him that he carried it around with him in his body, so long as it kept silent; and as soon as it came out, it hid in the surroundings, but never very far away from him. When he was working, the voices would generally talk at him in scraps of words and short sentences, scolding and criticising him, and when he thought something, they said it out aloud before he himself had time to, or spitefully said the opposite of what he meant. Moosbrugger could only laugh at the idea that they wanted to declare him insane for that. He himself treated these voices and visions no differently from monkeys. It amused him to watch and listen to their goings-on. That was much, much better than the tough, heavy thoughts that he himself had. But when they annoyed him a lot, he got angry, and that after all was only natural. As he had always listened very carefully to all the words used in discussing him, Moosbrugger knew that it was called hallucinations, and it suited him very well that he should have this advantage of having hallucinations over other people, who couldn't do it. For he also saw many things that others did not see, beautiful scenery and hellish beasts; but he thought the importance attached to this was very much exaggerated, and when his stay in one or other of the asylums became too disagreeable he would without hesitation declare that he was only shamming. These people who thought

themselves so smart would ask him how loud it was. There
wasn't much sense in the question. Of course it was sometimes
as loud as a thunder-clap, the way he heard it, and sometimes it
was the faintest whisper. And the pains, too, that tormented
him at times could be unbearable or merely as slight as something
imaginary. That was not the important point. Often he could
not have exactly described what he saw, heard and felt; all the
same, he knew what it was. It was sometimes very blurred.
The visions came from outside, but at the same time a glimmer
of observation told him that they nevertheless came out of himself. The important point was that it was not in the least
important whether something was outside or inside: for him it
was like clear water on both sides of a transparent glass wall.

And in his great times Moosbrugger paid no attention at all
to the voices and visions. But he would think. That was what
he called it, because this word had always impressed him. He
thought better than other people, because he thought outside
and inside. Against his own will, thinking went on in him. He
said thoughts were put into him. And without losing his slow,
manly steadiness, he also got worked up about the merest trifles,
just as it is with a woman when her breasts are full of milk. His
thinking then flowed on as a brook swollen by hundreds of leaping
brooks flows through a lush meadow.

Now Moosbrugger had let his head sink and was looking down
at the wood between his fingers. 'In these parts they call a
squirrel an oak-pussy,' it occurred to him. 'But just let anyone try putting on a straight face and saying " oak-tree cat "!
They'd all prick their ears up, like when a real shot goes off in
the middle of the quick popping of the blanks on manoeuvres.
In Hessia, now, they say " tree-fox ". A much-travelled man
knows that sort of thing.'

And good heavens, how interested the psychiatrists made
believe they were when they showed Moosbrugger a painted
picture of a squirrel and he told them : " That'd be a fox, or
maybe a hare. Or it might be a cat, or some such." Every
time then they would ask him as fast as anything : " What does
fourteen and fourteen make ? " And he would answer slowly
and thoughtfully : " Well, about twenty-eight to forty." This
' about ' caused them difficulties that made Moosbrugger smirk.

For it was quite simple : he too knew that one gets to twenty-eight if one goes fourteen further on from fourteen—but who's to say that one has got to stop there ? Moosbrugger's gaze would always range a little further, like that of a man who has reached the top of a chain of hills outlined against the sky and now sees that beyond this again there are still more, similar chains of hills. And if an oak-pussy is not a cat and not a fox and not puss, the hare that the fox eats, one doesn't need to be so particular about the whole thing ; somehow or other it's patched together out of all of it and goes scampering over the trees. Moosbrugger's experience and conviction was that one could not pick any one thing out all by itself, because each one hangs together with the next one. And it had even happened before now in his life that he had said to a girl : " Your sweet rose-lips ", but suddenly the words gave way at the seams, and something came about that was very distressing : the face went grey, just like earth under the mist, and at the end of a long stem there was a rose. Then the temptation to take a knife and cut it off, or hit it to make it go back into the face, was enormous. True, Moosbrugger did not always at once get his knife out ; he only did that when he could not manage any other way. Generally he just used all his gigantic strength to hold the world together.

In a good mood he might look a man in the face and in it see his own face as it would gaze back at him from among the minnows and bright pebbles in a shallow stream. In a bad mood, however, he only had to cast a fleeting glance of scrutiny into a man's face and would recognise that it was the same man with whom he had always got mixed up in a row, everywhere, no matter how much the other one pretended to be a different person each time.

And who can blame him ? All of us quarrel with the same man almost every time. If one were to investigate who the people are with whom we get so senselessly entangled, it would surely turn out to be the man with the hook to which we are the eye. And what about love ? How many people look into the same loved face day in, day out, but when they shut their eyes could not say what it looks like ! Or even apart from love and hate : to what changes things are unceasingly exposed, according to habit, mood and point of view ! How often joy burns out, and what is left is an indestructible core of sadness !

How often one man calmly bangs away at another whom he could just as well leave in peace! Life forms a surface that pretends it has to be the way it is, but under its skin things are thrusting and jostling.

Moosbrugger always stood with his feet solidly on two feet of earth, keeping them together, sensibly striving to avoid everything that might confuse him. But sometimes a word burst open in his mouth—and what revolution and what dream of things welled up then out of a cold, burnt-out cinder of a double word like oak-pussy or rose-lips!

As he sat there in his cell, on the bench that was also his bed and his table, he mourned his upbringing, which had not taught him to express his experiences properly. The little person with the mouse-eyes, who was causing him so much trouble even now when she had been lying in the ground so long, annoyed him. They were all on her side. He stood up, heavily. He felt as brittle as charred wood. He was hungry again; the prison fare was not enough for a huge man like him, and he had no money to eke it out. In such a condition it was quite impossible for him to think of everything that they wanted him to tell them. It was just that one of those changes had come, for days, weeks even, as March comes, or April, and right on top of it then the whole thing had happened. Nor did he know any more about it than was in the police files, and he did not even know how it had got in there, either. The reasons, the considerations, that he remembered he had already stated in court anyway. But what had really happened seemed to him as though he had suddenly spoken fluently in a foreign language, saying something that had made him very happy, but which he could no longer repeat.

' I only hope to goodness it'll all be over and done with as soon as may be,' Moosbrugger thought.

60

Excursion into the realm of logic and morals.

WHAT there was to be said about Moosbrugger from the legal point of view could have been stated in one sentence. Moosbrugger was one of those borderline cases known to jurisprudence and forensic medicine, and indeed even to laymen, as cases of diminished responsibility.

It is characteristic of these unfortunate people that they have not only inferior health but also an inferior disease. Nature has a remarkable taste for producing a superabundance of such people. *Natura non fecit saltus*—she does nothing by leaps and bounds ; she prefers gradual transitions and on a large scale too keeps the world in a transitional state between imbecility and sanity. But jurisprudence takes no notice of this. It says : *non datur tertium sive medium inter duo contradictoria* ; in plain English : the individual is either capable of acting contrary to law or he is not, for between two contraries there is no third or middle term. As a result of this capacity he becomes liable to punishment ; as a result of his quality of being liable to punishment he becomes legally a ' person ', and as a ' person ' in the legal sense he has a share in the suprapersonal benefits of the law. Anyone who does not understand this at once should think of the cavalry. If a horse goes wild at every attempt to ride it, it will be groomed with especial care and be given the softest bandages, the best horsemen, the choicest fodder, and the most patient handling. If, however, a cavalryman commits some offence, he will be shut up in a flea-ridden cage, made to go without his food, and put into irons. The reason for this difference lies in the fact that the horse belongs merely to the empirically known animal kingdom, while the dragoon has a share in the realm of logic and morals. In this way man is distinguished from the animals— and, it may be added, also from the insane—by the fact that, having intellectual and moral faculties, he is capable of acting contrary to law and committing a crime ; and hence, as it is primarily the quality of being liable to punishment that elevates him to the status of a moral being, it is understandable that the lawyers must hold on to it like grim death.

Unfortunately there is also the fact that the psychiatrists, whose job it should be to counteract this, are usually much more timid in the execution of their professional duties than the lawyers are. They certify as really insane only such persons as they cannot cure—which is a mildly exaggerated way of putting it, since they cannot cure the others either. They distinguish between incurable mental diseases and such as by the help of God in time become better of their own accord and, finally, such as the doctor, admittedly, cannot cure either but which the patient could have avoided, assuming, of course, that by some disposition of providence the right influences and considerations had affected him in time. This second and third group supply those merely inferior sufferers whom the angel of medicine does of course treat as patients when they come to him in his private practice, but whom he shyly leaves to the angel of the law when he encounters them in his forensic practice.

Moosbrugger was such a case. In the course of his decent life, interrupted by the crimes of an uncanny intoxication with blood, he had been confined in mental institutions just as often as he had been released, and he had passed as a case of dementia praecox, as a paranoiac, an epileptic, and a manic depressive, until in the last proceedings two particularly conscientious medical experts had restored his sanity to him again. Naturally, in that large, crowded court there was no single person, the two of them included, who was not convinced that Moosbrugger was in some way or other insane; but it was not a way that complied with the conditions made by the law and could be acknowledged by conscientious minds. For if one is partly insane, according to the views of jurisprudence one is also partly sane; but if one is partly sane, then one is at least partly responsible for one's actions; and if one is partly responsible for one's actions, then one is wholly so; for responsibility for one's actions is, as they say, the state in which the individual possesses the power to devote himself to a definite purpose of his own free will, independently of any compelling necessity; and such self-determination is something one cannot simultaneously possess and lack.

Admittedly, this does not exclude the fact that there are persons whose conditions and predispositions make it difficult for them to resist ' immoral impulses ' and to ' tip the scale towards the good ', as the lawyers call it ; and Moosbrugger was such a person, in whom circumstances that simply would not affect anyone else at once produced the ' resolution ' to commit an offence.   But, first, his powers of reasoning and judgment were, in the view of the court, in so far unimpaired that if they had been exerted the act could just as well have remained unperformed ; hence there was no reason to exclude him from the moral estate of responsibility.   Secondly, a properly functioning judicial system demands that every culpable act shall be punished if it has been performed wittingly and willingly.   And, thirdly, judicial logic assumes that in all insane persons—with the exception of those utterly unfortunate ones who put their tongue out when asked how much seven times seven is, or say ' me ' when required to give the name of His Imperial and Royal Majesty— there is still present a minimum power of discrimination and self-determination, and that it would only have needed a special effort of intelligence and will-power to recognise the criminal character of the deed and resist the criminal impulses.   That is apparently the least that can be expected from such dangerous individuals !

Law-courts are like cellars where the wisdom of our forefathers lies bottled.   Opening these bottles, one could weep at how unpalatable the human striving for exactitude is at its highest degree of fermentation before reaching perfection.   Yet it does seem to intoxicate those who are not hardened.   It is a well-known phenomenon that the angel of medicine, when he has been listening to the expositions of the lawyers, very often forgets his own mission.   Then he folds his wings with a metallic clang and behaves before the court like a reservist-angel of jurisprudence.

61

The ideal of the three treatises, or the Utopian idea of exact living.

IN this way Moosbrugger had got to his death-sentence and owed it only to Count Leinsdorf's influence and friendly feelings towards Ulrich that there was a prospect of his mental condition being examined once again. Ulrich, however, was at that time far from having the intention of taking any further interest in Moosbrugger's fate. The discouraging mixture of cruelty and passive suffering that is in the nature of such people was just as disagreeable to him as the mixture of accuracy and negligence that is the characteristic mark of the verdicts usually pronounced upon them. He knew exactly what to think of him when he regarded the case soberly, and what methods might be tried with such people, whose place was neither in prison nor at liberty and for whom the asylums were not the right place either. But he was equally well aware that thousands of other people knew that too, that every such question was being continually discussed by them and regarded from the aspects in which they took a particular interest, and that the State would in the end kill Moosbrugger because, considering the imperfection of things, that was simply the cheapest, safest, and most clear-cut way of dealing with him. Putting up with this might indicate a callous attitude ; but, after all, our rapid means of transport exact more victims than all the tigers of India, and it is obvious that the ruthless, unscrupulous and utterly casual attitude with which we put up with this makes us capable, on the other hand, of the successes we have undeniably achieved.

This attitude of mind, which is so perspicacious in matters of detail and so blind to the whole, finds its most significant expression in an ideal that might be called the ideal of a life-opus consisting of not more than three treatises. There are intellectual activities in which it is not the big books but the little treatises that make up a man's pride. If for instance someone were to discover that in certain circumstances, never previously observed, stones were capable of speaking, he would need only a few pages for the presentation and exposition of such a revolutionary phenomenon. Right-mindedness on the other hand is something that one can always write another book about. And this is far from being a merely academic matter, for it indicates a method by which one never arrives at clarity in dealing with the most important questions in life. Human activities might be classified according to the number of words that they require; the more words there are, the worse case their character is in. All the knowledge by means of which our species has advanced from dressing in skins to flying through the air—with its proofs, all complete—would fill no more than the shelves of a small reference library, whereas a bookcase the size of the earth itself would be utterly insufficient to hold all the rest, quite apart from the very extensive discussion that has been conducted not with the pen but with chains and the sword. It seems fairly obvious that we carry on our human business in an extremely irrational manner whenever we do not go about it as the sciences do, which have forged ahead in such exemplary fashion along their own lines.

And this was indeed the mood and attitude of an era—a number of years, scarcely of decades—some of which Ulrich was just old enough to have known. At that time people were thinking—and 'people' is here a deliberately vague term, since no one could say who and how many were thinking it—well, anyway, it was in the air—that perhaps life could be lived with exactitude. Today it will be asked what was meant by that. The answer is doubtless this: a life-work can just as easily be thought of as consisting not of three treatises but of three poems, or actions, in which the individual's capacity for achievement is intensified to the highest degree. In other words, what this would come to would be remaining silent where one has nothing to say, doing only what is necessary where one has no particular business in mind, and—what is most important of all—remaining indifferent wherever one has not that ineffable sensation of spreading out one's arms and being borne upward on a wave of creativeness! It will be noticed that this would mean the greater part of our psychic life would inevitably have to cease; but that might, after all, be no such very grievous loss. The thesis that the great turn-over of soap is evidence of great cleanliness need not necessarily apply where morality is concerned ; there the more recent proposition is more correct, namely that a marked compulsion to wash is an indication of internal conditions that are not quite cleanly. It would be a useful experiment if one could for once confine to a minimum the consumption of morality (of whatever kind it may be) that accompanies all action, and content oneself with being moral only in the exceptional cases where it is worth while, in all other cases thinking of one's action not otherwise than one thinks of the necessary standardisation of pencils or screws. Admittedly, in this event not much would be done of what is called the good, but there would be some of the better. There would be no talent left, only genius. The dim transfer-pictures would disappear out of the picture of life—those images originating in the pale resemblance that actions have to virtues—and in their place there would arise intoxicating union of the virtues in holiness. In a word, from every hundredweight of morality there would be left one milligramme of an essence of which even a millionth part of a gramme can give magical happiness.

It will be objected that this is a Utopian idea. Certainly, it is. Utopian ideas amount to more or less the same as possibilities. The fact that a possibility is not reality means nothing else than that the circumstances with which it is at present interwoven are preventing it from being so ; for otherwise, of course, it would be merely an impossibility. If, however, the possibility is freed from its bonds and allowed to develop, the Utopian idea arises. There is a similar process when a scientist observes a change in one of the elements in a compound phenomenon and draws his conclusions from it. A Utopian idea is an experiment in which the possible changing of an element is observed, together with the effects that it would cause in that compound phenomenon we call life. If, now, the element under observation is exactitude itself, if one isolates it and allows it to develop, if one regards it as an intellectual habit and a way of living and lets it exert its exemplary influence on everything that comes into contact with it, the logical conclusion is a human being in whom there is a paradoxical combination of precision and indefiniteness. He possesses that incorruptible, deliberate cold-bloodedness, the temperament that goes with exactitude ; but apart from and beyond this quality all is indefinite. The solid internal conditions that are guaranteed by the possession of a morality have little value for a man whose imagination is geared to change ; and finally, when the demand for the greatest and most exact fulfilment is transferred from the intellectual realm into that of the passions, the remarkable result is, as has already been indicated, that the passions disappear and their place is taken by a kind of goodness that resembles primordial fire.

That is the Utopian idea of exactitude. It is hard to say how this human being is to spend his day, since he cannot remain continually poised in the act of creation and will have sacrificed the domestic fire of limited sensation to some imaginary conflagration. But this exact man is today in existence ! As a man within the man he lives not only in the scientist but in the business man, in the administrator, in the sportsman, in the technician— even if for the present only during those main parts of the day that they call not their life but their profession. For he who is so thorough and unprejudiced in everything abhors nothing so much as the idea of being thorough where he himself is concerned, and unfortunately it can scarcely be doubted that he would regard the Utopian idea of himself as an improper experiment carried out on persons occupied with serious business.

That was why Ulrich, in his concern with the question whether or not all other achievements should be adjusted to the most powerful group of inner achievements—in other words, whether a goal and a meaning could be found for something that happens to us and always has happened to us—had all his life long remained more or less alone.

62

The earth too, but Ulrich in particular, pays homage to the Utopian idea of Essayism.

PRECISION, as a human attitude, also requires precise action and precise living. It makes maximal demands on action and living. But here a distinction must be made.

For in reality, after all, there is not only the fantastical kind of precision (which does not yet exist in reality, of course) but also a pedantical one, and these two are distinct from each other in that the fantastical keeps to facts and the pedantical to the products of fantasy. The precision, for instance, with which the strange mind that was Moosbrugger's was fitted into a system of two-thousand-year-old legal concepts resembled a madman's pedantic efforts to spit a free-flying bird upon a pin; it was not in the least concerned with the facts, but only with the fantastic concept of the whole traditional code of laws. On the other hand, the precision that the psychiatrists displayed in their attitude to the great question whether or not it was permissible to condemn Moosbrugger to death was entirely and wholly exact, for it did not presume to say more than that the clinical picture he presented corresponded exactly to no clinical picture observed hitherto, and left the further decision to the lawyers.

It was a picture of life that the court-room presented on that occasion. For all those vigorous men of modern life, who would find it utterly impossible to use a car that was more than five years old or to have a disease treated by methods that were considered the best ten years ago, who furthermore devote all their time voluntarily-involuntarily to the promotion of such inventions, and are delighted with the idea of rationalising everything that comes into their domain, prefer to leave the questions of beauty, justice, love and faith, in short, all human questions, in so far as their business interests are not involved, to their wives, or, so long as the latter are not quite adequate to this task, to a sub-species of men who tell them in thousand-year-old phrases of the cup and sword of life and to whom they listen frivolously, peevishly and sceptically, without believing in any of it and without thinking of the possibility that everything might equally well be done quite differently.

So there are in reality two outlooks, which not only conflict with each other but—what is worse—usually exist side by side, without exchanging a word except to assure each other that they are both desirable, each in its place. The one contents itself with being precise, and sticks to facts ; the other does not content itself with that, but always looks at the Whole and draws its knowledge from what are called great and eternal verities. Thereby the one gains in success, and the other in scope and dignity. It is clear that a pessimist might also say the results of the one are worthless and those of the other not true. For where will it get one, on the Day of Judgment, when mankind's works are weighed in the balance, to come forward with three treatises on formic acid—or thirty, for that matter ? On the other hand, what can one know about the Day of Judgment if one does not even know what may have come of formic acid by then ?

It was between the two poles of this Neither-Nor that evolution was swinging to and fro when it was a bit more than eighteen and not yet twenty centuries since humanity was first informed that such a spiritual court would be held at the end of the world. Experience shows that in these things a swing in one direction is always followed by a swing in the opposite direction. And although it is conceivable and might be desirable for such turns in opposite directions to proceed on the same principle as the worm of a screw, which climbs higher at every change of direction, for some unknown reasons evolution seldom gains more in this process than it loses through detours and destruction. So Herr Dr. Paul Arnheim was quite right when he told Ulrich that history never permits anything negative. History is optimistic. It is always enthusiastically deciding for one thing, and only afterwards for the opposite.   So too the first fantasies of exactitude were by no means followed by any attempt to realise them, but were abandoned to uninspired use by engineers and scientists, and there was a return to the broader and more dignified outlook.

Ulrich could remember quite well how the element of uncertainty had come back into repute. More and more pronounc

ments began to pile up, in the complaints of such people as were carrying on a somewhat uncertain *métier*—poets, critics, women and those whose vocation was being a new generation—pronouncements to the effect that pure knowledge was like a fatal substance disrupting all mankind's sublime works, without ever being able to put them together again ; and the demand was for a new human faith, for a return to original values, for a spiritual revival and all sorts of similar things.   Ulrich had at first naïvely assumed that these were people who had ridden themselves sore and now, dismounted, limped about crying out for someone to come and rub them with essence of soul.   But he was gradually forced to recognise that this repeated cry, which had at first struck him as so comical, was being echoed far and wide.   Knowledge was beginning to be old-fashioned.   The inaccurate human type, which dominates the present, had begun to assert itself.

Ulrich had rebelled against taking this seriously, and went on developing his intellectual inclinations in his own way.

From the earliest times of the first self-confidence of youth, which it is often so touching, even moving, to look back upon later, all sorts of once-loved notions lingered in his memory even today, and among them was that of ' living hypothetically '. This phrase still expressed the courage and the involuntary ignorance involved in a life in which every step is an act of daring without experience behind it, and the desire for large terms of reference, and the breath of revocability that is felt by a young man hesitantly entering into life.   Ulrich thought that actually none of this need be taken back.   A thrilling sensation of being destined to something or other is the beautiful and only certain thing in him whose gaze surveys the world for the first time.   If he keeps a careful watch over his emotions he cannot say yes to anything without reservation ; he seeks the possible beloved, but does not know whether she is the right one ; he is capable of killing, without being sure that he must do it.   His own nature's will to develop forbids him to believe in anything perfect ; but everything that comes his way behaves as if it were perfect.   He has a vague intuitive feeling that this order of things is not as solid as it pretends to be ; nothing, no ego, no form, no principle, is safe, everything is in a process of invisible but never-ceasing transformation, there is more of the future in the unsolid than in the solid, and the present is nothing but a hypothesis that one has not yet finished with. What better can he do than hold aloof from the world, in that good sense exemplified by a scientist's attitude towards facts that are trying to tempt him into over-hastily believing in them ? This is why he hesitates to become anything. A character, a profession, a definite mode of existence —for him these are notions through which the skeleton is already peering, the skeleton that is all that will be left of him in the end. He tries to reach a different understanding of himself. With an inclination towards everything that inwardly enriches him— even though it may be morally or intellectually taboo—he feels himself to be like a stride that could be taken in any direction, but which leads from one instant of equilibrium to the next and always onward. And if one day it seems to him that what has just occurred to him is the very thing he wants, he then perceives that a drop of some indescribable incandescence has fallen into the world, and the earth looks different in the glow of it.

Later, as his intellectual capacity increased, this gave rise in Ulrich's mind to a notion that he no longer associated with the indeterminate word ' hypothesis ' but, for certain reasons, with the peculiar concept of the essay. It was approximately in the way that an essay, in the sequence of its paragraphs, takes a thing from many sides without comprehending it wholly—for a thing wholly comprehended instantly loses its bulk and melts down into a concept—that he believed he could best survey and handle the world and his own life. The value of an action or of a quality, indeed their essence and nature, seemed to him dependent on the circumstances surrounding them, on the ends that they served, in short, on the whole complex—constituted now thus, now otherwise—to which they belonged. Incidentally, this is only the simple description of the fact that a murder may appear to us as a crime or as an heroic deed, and the hour of love as a feather that has fallen from an angel's wing or one from the wing of a goose. But Ulrich generalised it. Then all moral events took place in a field of energy the constellation of which charged them with meaning, and they contained good and evil just as an atom contains the potentialities of chemical combination. They were, so to speak, what they became, and just as the one word ' hard ' describes four quite different entities according to whether the hardness relates to love, brutality, eagerness or severity, so the significance of all moral happenings appeared to him the dependent function of others. In this manner an endless system of relationships arose in which there was no longer any such thing as independent meanings, such as in ordinary life, at a crude first approach, are ascribed to actions and qualities. In this system the seemingly solid became a porous pretext for many other meanings ; what was happening became the symbol of something that was perhaps not happening but was felt through the medium of the first ; and man as the quintessence of human possibilities, potential man, the unwritten poem of his own existence, materialised as a record, a reality, and a character, confronting man in general. Fundamentally, and in keeping with this view, Ulrich felt himself capable of every virtue and every kind of badness ; and the fact that in a balanced social order virtues and vices are generally, though unconfessedly, felt to be equally tiresome, to him proved precisely what is always happening in Nature, namely that every play of forces tends in the course of time towards an average value and average condition, a compromise and a state of inertia. Morality in the usual sense was for Ulrich no more than the senile form of a system of forces that cannot be mistaken for morality without a loss of ethical force.

It may be that these views also indicated a certain unsureness about life ; however, unsureness is sometimes nothing but mistrust of the usual assurances and safeguards. For the rest, it may be recalled that even so experienced a person as mankind itself apparently acts according to quite similar principles. In the long run it revokes everything it has done and puts something else in the place of it ; and for it too crimes in the course of time change into virtues and vice versa ; it builds up great spiritual connections between all things and events and after some generations lets them collapse again. Only, this happens successively instead of in a single homogeneous awareness of life ; and the chain of mankind's experiments reveals no rising towards a climax, whereas a conscious human essayism would find itself confronted with something like the task of transforming the world's haphazard state of consciousness into a single will. And many individual lines of development indicate that this may happen soon. The bacteriologist's assistant in a hospital, who, clad in the whiteness of a lily, with the aid of acids thins out a patient's faeces in a white china bowl until they are a scarlet smear, the correct colour of which rewards her careful attention, is even now, and even although she may not know it, in a world more capable of under-going transformations than is the young lady who shudders at the sight of the same substance in the street. The criminal who has once entered the field of moral energy pertaining to his deed moves only like a swimmer being swept along by a strong current. Every mother whose child has once been caught up in this current knows this ; only up to now no one believed her, because there was no room for such belief. Psychiatry terms great elation a state of hypomanic disturbance, as though it were a hilarious dis-tress, and has made it clear that all high degrees of intensification, whether of chastity or of sensuality, of scruples or of negligence, of cruelty or of compassion, in the long run end up in something pathological. How meaningless healthy life would be if it had no other goal than a medial state between two extremes ! How paltry it would be if its ideal were in fact nothing but a refusal to exaggerate its ideals ! Recognising this brings us to the point where we no longer see the moral norm as the immobility of rigid commandments, but as a mobile equilibrium continually demand-ing exertions towards its renewal. One begins to feel increasingly how narrow-minded it is to ascribe to a person by way of a character a tendency to repetition that he has acquired involun-tarily, and then blame his character for the repetitions. One learns to recognise the inter-play between the internal and the external aspects of things, and it is precisely by way of under-standing the impersonal element in man that we have hit on new clues to the personality, on certain simple and fundamental patterns of behaviour, an ego-building instinct, like the nest-building instinct of birds, by which the ego is constructed of many materials according to a few methods. We are already so close to being able, by means of certain influences, to dam up degenerate conditions just like a mountain torrent that it no longer amounts to anything much more than social negligence or a residue of clumsiness if we do not promptly turn criminals into archangels. And much more of the same kind could be cited, random items such as have never come into contact with each other yet, the general effect of which is to make one tired of the crude approximations that came into existence and were applied under simpler conditions; and one gradually comes to feel a compulsion to change the fundamental forms of a morality that for two thousand years has been adjusted to changes of taste only in minor details, and to exchange it for another, one that will fit more closely and elastically to the mobility of facts.

According to Ulrich's conviction all that was actually still missing was only the formula, the particular terms in which the goal of a movement must express itself in some lucky moment, just before it is reached, so that the last lap of the journey can be done at all. And this expression is always a daring one that cannot be justified in the state of affairs as yet prevailing; it is always a combination of the exact and the non-exact, of precision and passion.

But precisely in the years that should have spurred him on, something queer happened to Ulrich. He was no philosopher. Philosophers are violent and aggressive persons who, having no army at their disposal, bring the world into subjection to themselves by means of locking it up in a system. Probably that is also the reason why there have been great philosophic minds in times of tyranny, whereas times of advanced civilisation and democracy do not succeed in producing a convincing philosophy, at least so far as one can judge from the lamentations one commonly hears on the subject. That is why nowadays there is a terrifying amount of philosophising done in small slices, so much so that shops are the only places where one can still get anything without a philosophic view being involved. There is, on the other hand, a definite mistrust of philosophy in large chunks, which is simply considered impossible. This was a prejudice from which Ulrich himself was by no means free; in the light of his scientific experience he was, indeed, inclined to think of philosophy rather scornfully. This helped to establish his attitude, and so he was constantly being forced to reflect on what he saw, and yet could not shake off a certain dread of too much thinking. But what finally determined his attitude was yet something else. There was something in Ulrich's nature that worked in a haphazard, paralysing, disarming manner against logical systematisation, against the one-track will, against the definitely directed urges of ambition; and it was also connected with his chosen expression, ' Essayism ', even although this something in him contained precisely those elements that he had, in the course of time and with unconscious care, eliminated from that concept. The translation of the word ' essay ' as ' attempt ', which is the generally accepted one, only approximately gives the most important allusion to the literary model. For an essay is not the provisional or incidental expression of a conviction that might on a more favourable occasion be elevated to the status of truth or that might just as easily be recognised as error (of that kind are only the articles and treatises, referred to as ' chips from their workshop ', with which learned persons favour us); an essay is the unique and unalterable form that a man's inner life assumes in a decisive thought. Nothing is more alien to it than that irresponsibility and semi-finishedness of mental images known as subjectivity ; but neither are ' true ' and ' false ', ' wise ' and ' unwise ', terms that can be applied to such thoughts, which are nevertheless subject to laws that are no less strict than they appear to be delicate and ineffable. There have been quite a number of such essayists and masters of the floating life within, but there would be no point in naming them. Their domain lies between religion and knowledge, between example and doctrine, between *amor intellectualis* and poetry, they are saints with and without religion, and sometimes too they are simply men who have gone out on an adventure and lost their way.

Nothing, incidentally, is more typical than one's involuntary experience of learned and rational attempts to provide a commentary on such great essayists, to transform the living wisdom, even as it is, into a theory of life, and so to extract some ' content ' from the motion of those who were moved : what is left over is about as much as remains of a jelly-fish's delicately opalescent body after it has been lifted out of the water and laid on the sand. The teachings of the inspired crumble into dust in the rationality of the uninspired, crumble into contradiction and nonsense ; and yet one cannot actually call them delicate and of unstable vitality, for in that case one would also have to call an elephant delicate because it cannot survive in a vacuum, an environment that does not answer its vital needs. It would be most deplorable if these descriptions were to suggest a mystery or, say, a kind of music in which the harp-notes and sighing *glissandi* predominate. The

contrary is true. And the question fundamental to them was
something that Ulrich experienced by no means merely in intuitive glimmerings, but also quite soberly in the following form :
a man who is after the truth sets out to be a man of learning ;
a man who wants to give free play to his subjectivity sets out,
perhaps, to be a writer. But what is a man to do who is after
something that lies between ? And yet such examples of lying
' between ' are provided by every moral maxim, for instance by
the well-known and simple one : thou shalt not kill. One can
see at the first glance that it is neither a verity nor a subjective
statement. We know that in many respects we keep to it strictly ;
in other respects certain very numerous but precisely defined
exceptions are admitted. But in a very large number of cases
of a third kind, as for instance in the imagination, in our desires,
in the drama, or in the enjoyment of newspaper reports, we roam
in a quite unregulated manner between abhorrence and allurement. Something that is neither a verity nor a subjective statement is sometimes called a requirement. This requirement has
been firmly attached to the dogmas of religion and those of the
law, and has thus been given the character of a truth arrived at
by a process of deduction. But the novelists tell us about the
exceptions, beginning with Abraham's sacrifice, down to the
latest pretty women who has shot her lover, and so dissolve it
again into a matter of subjectivity. So one can either hold on
to the stakes or let oneself be carried to and fro between them
on the swell of the tide. But with what feelings ! Man's feeling
towards this maxim is a mixture of blockheaded obedience (including the ' healthy nature ' that refuses even to think of such
a thing, but, if just slightly deranged by alcohol or passion, instantly does it) and thoughtless splashing in a wave of possibilities.
Is this maxim really only to be understood in such a way ? Ulrich
felt this meant that a man who wanted to do something with all
his heart and soul did not know whether he was supposed to do
it or to leave it undone. And yet he was intuitively aware that
one could put one's whole being into either doing it or leaving
it alone. Neither a fancy nor a taboo meant anything to him.
The linking of anything with a law above or within aroused
criticism from his intelligence ; more than that, indeed, one
merely devalued a moment that was sure of itself if one gave

way to one's craving to ennoble it by providing it with a pedigree. In all this his heart remained silent, and only his head spoke. But he felt that in some other way his decision might coincide with his happiness. He might be happy because he did not kill, or happy because he did kill, but he could never be the indifferent fulfiller of a demand made on him. What he felt at this moment was not a commandment : it was a realm into which he had entered. Here, he realised, everything was already decided, soothing to the mind as mother's milk. But what told him this was no longer thinking, neither was it feeling in the usual in-coherent way. It was a ' comprehending wholly ', and yet again only like what happens when a message from far away comes borne on the wind ; and it appeared to him neither true nor false, neither rational nor irrational, but took hold of him as though some faint blissful exaggeration had fallen into his heart.

And just as little as one can make a truth out of the genuine parts of an essay can one gain a conviction from such a state ; at least not without giving it up, just as a lover has to leave his love in order to describe it. The limitless emotion that at times stirred Ulrich, without activating him, was in contradiction to his urge towards activity, which insisted on limitation and form. Now, it is probably right and natural to want to *know* before one lets feeling speak ; and involuntarily he imagined that what he wanted to find some day would, even if it were not truth, never-theless yield nothing to truth in solidity. And this, in the special nature of his case, made him resemble a man who is getting his equipment together and whose intentions, even as he does so, are fading out. At any point during his work on mathematical and mathematico-logical problems or while he was concerned with natural science, if he had been asked what aim he had in mind, he would have answered that there was only one question really worth thinking about, and that was the question of right living. But when one has been making a demand for a long time without any result, the brain goes to sleep, just as the arm does when it has been holding something up for too long. Our thoughts can no more remain standing for an indefinite period than soldiers can on parade in summer ; if they have to wait too long, they simply fall down in a faint.

As Ulrich had completed the draft of his view of life when he was twenty-six, now, when he was thirty-two, it no longer seemed quite genuine. He had not elaborated his ideas any further, and apart from a vague, tense feeling, such as one has when waiting for something with one's eyes shut, there was not much sign of personal emotion in him, now that the days of the first tremulous revelations had passed. Yet it probably was a subterranean movement of such a kind that had gradually slowed him up in his scientific work and prevented him from applying all his will-power to it. This got him into a peculiar state of schism. It must not be forgotten that fundamentally the exact outlook is more religious than the aesthetic; for it would submit itself to 'Him' the moment He deigned to show Himself to it under the conditions it prescribes for the recognition of His reality, whereas our aesthetes, if He were to manifest Himself, would only find that His talent was not original and His view of the world not intelligible enough to put Him on one level with persons of really divinely inspired genius. So Ulrich could not abandon himself to vague glimpses and glimmers as easily as anyone of that species could; but neither could he conceal from himself that in all those years of pure exactitude he had merely been living against himself; and he wished something unforeseen might happen to him. For when he was doing what he somewhat mockingly called taking his 'holiday from life', he had nothing, in one direction or the other, that could give him peace.

It might be mentioned in his defence that at a certain age life runs away incredibly fast. But the day when one must begin to live out one's last will, before one leaves the residue of it behind, lies far ahead and cannot be shifted. That had become menacingly clear to him since almost six months had passed without anything's changing. While he let himself be moved to and fro in the minor and foolish activity that he had taken on, talking, liking to talk too much, living with the desperate persistence of a fisherman putting down his nets in an empty river, and yet doing nothing that was in accord with the person he nevertheless significantly was, and doing it deliberately, he waited. He waited hidden behind his person, in so far as this word refers to that part of a man formed by the world and the course of life; and his quiet desperation, dammed up behind it, rose higher every day. He was in the worst state of emergency in his life and despised himself for his omissions. Are great ordeals the privilege of great personalities? He would have liked to believe that. But it is not true, for even the simplest neurotic personalities have their crises. So all he was actually left with in this great perturbation was that residue of imperturbability possessed by all heroes and criminals—it is not courage, it is not will-power, it is not confidence, but simply a tough capacity to hold on—something that is as difficult to drive out as the life out of a cat even when it is utterly mangled by the dogs.

To anyone who wants to visualise how such a man lives when he is alone, the most that can be said is that by night the lighted window-panes gaze into his room, and the thoughts, after they have been used, sit about like the clients in the waiting-room of a lawyer with whom they are not satisfied. Or perhaps this—how once in such a night Ulrich opened the windows and looked out among the tree-trunks, smooth as snakes, their twistings strangely black and sleek between the blankets of snow on their tops and on the ground, and suddenly felt an urge to go down into the garden just as he was, in his pyjamas; he wanted to feel the cold in his hair. When he was downstairs, he turned the light off, in order not to be framed in the brilliance of the doorway, and only from his study a roof of light extended into the darkness. There was a path leading to the iron gate that opened into the street; a second path crossed it, darkly distinct. Ulrich walked slowly towards it. And then the darkness towering up between the tree-tops suddenly, fantastically, reminded him of Moosbrugger's gigantic form, and it seemed to him the naked trees were queerly physical—ugly and wet as worms and yet somehow making one want to embrace them and sink down beside them with tears on one's face. But he did not do it. The sentimentality of the impulse revolted him in the same instant that it touched him. Through the milky foam of the mist some late passers-by at this moment went along outside the iron railing, and he may well have looked like a lunatic to them, as his figure, in red pyjamas among black tree-trunks, detached itself from its background. But he stepped firmly on to the path and went back into his house comparatively contented: for whatever was in store for him, it must be something quite different.

63   *Bonadea has a vision.*

ON the morning after this night, when Ulrich got up, late, feeling very battered, he was told that Bonadea was there to see him. It was the first time they were to meet again since their quarrel.

Bonadea had wept much in the period of separation. She had often felt, during this time, that she had been ill-used. She had often resounded like the rolling of a muffled drum.

Bonadea had had many adventures and many disappointments. And although with each adventure the memory of Ulrich sank into a deep well, after every disappointment it rose out of it again, helpless and reproachful as the desolate grief in a child's face. In her thoughts she had a hundred times asked her lover's forgiveness for her jealousy—'punishing her wicked pride' was what she called it—and finally she resolved to propose terms of peace to him.

She was charming, melancholy, and beautiful as she sat before him, and she had a sick sensation in her stomach. He was standing there 'like a youth'. His skin had the marble polish that went with great happenings and diplomacy, such as she thought him capable of. She had never before noticed how energetic and determined his face looked. She would gladly have capitulated with her whole person, but she did not dare to go so far, and he made not the slightest attempt at inviting her to do so. This coldness was unspeakably sad for her, but over-lifesize, like a statue. Suddenly rising, she took his dangling hand and kissed it. Ulrich stroked her hair meditatively. Her legs became weak in the most womanly manner in the world, and she felt as though she must fall on her knees. At that moment Ulrich pushed her gently back into the chair, brought whisky and soda, and lit a cigarette.

"A lady doesn't drink whisky in the morning!" Bonadea protested. For an instant she regained the strength to be offended, and her heart rose up into her head, for it seemed to her that there was a heartless allusion implied in the matter-of-factness with which Ulrich offered such a crude and, as she thought, licentious drink.

But Ulrich said kindly : " It'll do you good. Anyway, all the women who have played a great part in politics have drunk whisky."

For in order to get into favour with Ulrich again, Bonadea had said that she admired the great patriotic Campaign and would very much like to help in it.

That was her plan. She always believed several things at once, and half-truths made it easier for her to tell lies.

The whisky had a thin golden radiance and was warming as May sunshine.

Bonadea felt as though she were seventy years old and sitting on a garden bench outside a house. She was getting on in years. Her children were growing up. The eldest was already twelve. It was undoubtedly disgraceful to follow a man, whom one did not even really know, into an apartment merely because he had eyes with which he looked at one like someone looking out through a window. One notices—she thought—little things about this man that one doesn't like, things one might take as a warning. Really, one might—if only something would pull one up at such moments !—break it all off, flooded with shame and perhaps even flaming with anger. But because that does not happen, the man grows more and more passionately into his role. And, oneself, one' feels quite clearly that one is like a piece of scenery in a glare of artificial light. These are stage-eyes, a stage-moustache, self-opening costume buttons, that one has before one ; and the moments from entering the room until the frightful first gesture of sobriety comes again are played out in a consciousness that has stepped right out of the head and covers the walls of the room with the wallpaper of illusion. Bonadea did not use quite these words, thinking it, indeed, only partly in words, but as she tried to visualise it she instantly felt herself once more at the mercy of that change of consciousness.

' Anyone who could describe this would be a great artist—no, he would be a pornographer ! ' she thought, gazing at Ulrich. For her good intentions and her firm will to decency were something that she did not for an instant lose even during such states ; only, then they stood outside, waiting, and simply had no say in this world so changed by desires. The moment when Bonadea's reason returned was that of her greatest anguish. The alteration of consciousness occasioned by sexual intoxication, which other people pass over as something natural, was so strong in her, as a result of the depth and suddenness not only of the ecstasy but also of the remorse, that as soon as she returned to the peaceful circle of the family she felt quite frightened. It seemed to her then that she must be mad. She could hardly bring herself to look at her children, for fear that her corrupted gaze might do them harm. And she jumped whenever her husband looked at her in a way that was especially fond, and was afraid of the unconstraint of solitude. This was why in the weeks of separation the plan had matured in her mind to stop having any lover except Ulrich ; he was to give her support and prevent her from committing excesses alien to her. ' How on earth could I presume to find fault with him ? ' she thought now, sitting opposite him for the first time after so long. ' He is so much more perfect than I am.' She gave him the credit for the fact that she had been a better woman during the time of his embraces, and was doubtless also thinking that at the next charity performance he would have to introduce her into his new social circle. Bonadea silently swore an oath of allegiance to this flag, and her eyes filled with pathetic tears as she turned it all over in her mind.

But Ulrich was finishing his whisky with the slowness of a man adding weight to a grave decision. At the moment, he explained to her, it was not possible to introduce her to Diotima.

Bonadea naturally wanted to be told exactly why it was not possible. And then she wanted to know exactly when it would be possible.

Ulrich had to explain to her at length that she was not prominent either in art or science or in the field of charitable endeavour, and that for this reason it would be a very long time before he would be able to make Diotima understand the necessity of her collaboration.

Now, as it happened, Bonadea had in the mean time come to have curious feelings towards Diotima. She had heard enough of Diotima's virtues not to be jealous ; on the contrary, she envied and admired this woman who grappled her, Bonadea's, lover to herself without making any improper concessions to him.

To this influence she ascribed the statuesque serenity that she thought she observed in Ulrich. Herself she thought of as 'passionate', whereby she meant both her depravity and a just about honourable excuse for it. But she admired cool women, with the same sensation with which the unfortunate possessors of everlastingly moist hands lay their hand in one that is particularly dry and beautiful. 'It is her doing!' she thought. 'She has changed Ulrich like this!' There was a hard drill boring into her heart, a sweet drill boring into her knees, and these two drills turning simultaneously and in opposite directions made Bonadea almost faint with helplessness when she came up against Ulrich's resistance. So she played her last trump-card: Moosbrugger!

By a process of painful reflection it had become clear to her that Ulrich had a strange liking for this frightful figure. She herself felt utterly sickened and revolted by the 'brutal sensuality' that was, in her opinion, expressed in Moosbrugger's deeds; the feelings she had in relation to this problem were, though naturally without her being aware of it, exactly like those of the prostitutes, whose reaction was quite straightforward and devoid of all bourgeois romanticism, in that they saw a murderous sexual maniac as nothing more or less than a threat to their profession. But even where her unavoidable lapses were concerned, she needed a true and tidy world, and Moosbrugger was to be of use to her in restoring it. As Ulrich had a weakness for him, and as she had a husband who was a judge and in a position to give useful information, in her desolation the thought had matured all on its own that she might combine her weakness with Ulrich's weakness through the medium of her husband; and this yearning fantasy had all the consoling strength of a sensuality blessed with a sense of justice.

But when she approached her worthy husband in this matter, he was amazed at her juristic ardour, although he knew how easily she became enthusiastic about all that was great and good in human nature; and as he happened to be not only a judge, but also a sportsman, fond of his day's shooting, he tried to put her off, good-humouredly enough, by saying that the only proper thing was to destroy beasts of prey wherever one came across them, without a lot of sentimental fuss, and he refused to enter into any further discussion. On a second attempt, which she made some time later, all that Bonadea could get out of him was the supplementary opinion that he regarded child-bearing as women's business and killing as a matter for men. And as she could not risk drawing suspicion on herself by taking too keen an interest in this dangerous problem, the path of the law was for the present barred to her. So she had entered upon the path of mercy, which was the only one left to her if, to please Ulrich, she was to do something for Moosbrugger; and this path led— not so much surprisingly, perhaps, as attractively—*via* Diotima.

In her mind's eye she saw herself as Diotima's friend and granted herself her wish in advance by believing she had to get to know her admired rival for the sake of the cause, which brooked no delay, even if she was certainly too proud to do it out of personal desire. She had resolved to win Diotima over to sympathy with Moosbrugger—which Ulrich, as she had at once guessed, was not succeeding in—and her imagination painted the whole picture in the fairest of colours. Tall and marble, Diotima would lay her arm round Bonadea's warm shoulders that were bowed under a load of sin. And Bonadea was looking forward to playing something like the part of anointing this divinely immaculate heart with a drop of mortal corruption. This was the plan she expounded to her ex-lover.

But today Ulrich was not at all susceptible to the idea of saving Moosbrugger. He was familiar with Bonadea's noble feelings and knew how easily the flaring up of a single beautiful impulse in her became the panic of wild-fire running through her whole body. He explained that he had not the slightest intention of meddling with the Moosbrugger case.

Bonadea gazed at him, deeply hurt, out of beautiful eyes in which the water floated over the ice as on the borderline between winter and spring.

Now, Ulrich had never quite lost a certain feeling of gratitude for their childishly beautiful first encounter in that night when he had lain senseless on the pavement, Bonadea crouching by his head, and the wavering romantic vagueness of the world, youth, and emotion had come trickling out of this young woman's eyes into his awakening consciousness. So he tried to make the hurtful refusal milder, dissolving it in a lengthy conversation.

" Supposing," he suggested, " you were walking through a

large park at night and were molested by a couple of ruffians—
would it occur to you that they were pitiable creatures and that
society was to blame for their brutality ? "

" But I never walk through a park at night," Bonadea instantly
retorted.

" But if a policeman came along, surely you would get him to
arrest the two of them ? "

" I would ask him to protect me ! "

" Well, then he would arrest them ! "

" I don't know what he does with them then. Anyway,
Moosbrugger isn't just a ruffian."

" All right then, assume he's working as a carpenter in your
house. You're alone in the place with him, and he begins
slithering his eyes to and fro that way."

Bonadea protested. " What an abominable thing you're asking
of me ! "

" Of course," Ulrich said. " But I'm just trying to show you
that people like that, who lose their balance so easily, are extremely
unpleasant. Impartiality is an attitude one can only really adopt
towards them when it's someone else who is taking the beating.
Then, I grant you, they bring out the very tenderest feelings in
us, then they're the victims of a social system, or of fate. You
must admit nobody can be blamed for his faults if one looks at
them through his own eyes. For him, at the worst they're mistakes or bad qualities that don't make the person as a whole any
the less good. And of course he's perfectly right."

Bonadea had to fix her suspender and felt compelled to look at
Ulrich while she did so, her head slightly tilted back, so that,
escaping the vigilance of her eye, in the region of the knee there
was revealed a pageant rich in contrasts between lacy frills, smooth
stocking, tensed fingers and the softly relaxed pearly gleam of
the skin.

Ulrich hastily lit a cigarette and went on : " It is not that man
is good, but that he is always good. That's a tremendous difference, do you see ? One is amused by the sophistry of self-love,
but one ought to draw from it the conclusion that man cannot
do anything evil at all. Evil is something he only brings about.
Recognising this would bring us to the proper starting-point for
a system of social morals."

With a sigh Bonadea let her skirt drop into its proper place again, straightened up and tried to calm herself with a sip of the pale golden-fiery drink.

"And now I will explain to you," Ulrich added smilingly, "why one can, of course, feel all sorts of things for Moosbrugger, but can't, all the same, do anything. In the last resort all these cases are like a loose end of thread hanging out, and if one pulls at it, the whole tightly-knit fabric of society begins to come undone. I shall demonstrate this to you first of all by means of purely rational examples."

In some inexplicable manner Bonadea lost a shoe. Ulrich bent down to pick it up, and the foot, with its warm toes, came like a little child to meet the shoe in his hand.

"Don't bother, don't bother, I'll do it myself," Bonadea said, while she held out her foot to him.

"First of all there are the psychiatric-juridical problems," Ulrich went on inexorably explaining, while the fragrance of a no longer complete responsibility for actions rose into his nostrils from her leg. "We know medicine has now practically reached the stage of being able to prevent most of such crimes, if only we were prepared to spend the necessary amount of money. So it's merely a social question now."

"Oh dear, can't you leave off?" Bonadea pleaded when he had said 'social' for the second time, "When such things are mentioned at home, I leave the room. It bores me to death."

"All right then," Ulrich conceded, "what I was getting at was that as there have long been technical means of making useful things out of corpses, sewage, scrap and toxins, it is just about time it became possible for psychological technique to do something similar. But the world is taking an unconscionable time to solve these problems. The State spends money on every kind of foolishness, but hasn't a copper to spare for solving the most important moral problems there are. That lies in its nature, for the State is collective man at his stupidest and most malign."

He spoke with conviction. But Bonadea tried to lead him back to the heart of the matter.

"Darling," she said languishingly, "but surely it's the very best thing for Moosbrugger that he's not responsible?"

"It would probably be more important," Ulrich said, sweeping that aside, " to exterminate a few responsible persons than to save one who cannot be held responsible from being exterminated."

He was now walking up and down quite close in front of her. Bonadea found him revolutionary and inflammatory. She succeeded in catching hold of his hand, and laid it on her bosom.

" All right," he said, " I shall now explain the emotional problems to you."

Bonadea opened his fingers and spread his hand out on her breast. The accompanying glance would have moved a heart of stone. In the next few moments it seemed to Ulrich that he felt two hearts in his breast, thumping a-rhythmically like the ticking of clocks in a watchmaker's shop. Exerting all his will-power, he restored order in his breast and said gently : " No, Bonadea."

Bonadea was now on the brink of tears, and Ulrich talked soothingly to her.

" Come to think of it, isn't it contradictory for you to get worked up about this particular affair, just because I happened to tell you about it, while you don't seem to be aware of the millions of equally great wrongs being done every day ? "

" But that hasn't anything at all to do with it ! " Bonadea protested. " The point is, I do know about this now. And it would be wicked of me to keep calm about it."

Ulrich remarked that one had to keep calm. Downright tempestuously calm, he added. He freed himself and sat down at some distance from Bonadea.

" Everything that goes on nowadays is ' meanwhile ' and ' for the time being ',," he observed. " It must be so. The scrupulousness of our mind forces us into a horrible unscrupulousness of the heart." He poured out some more whisky for himself too and put his feet up on the divan. He was beginning to feel tired. " Every human being begins by thinking about life as a whole," he explained, " but the more precisely he thinks about it, the more it all narrows down. By the time he has become mature, what you have is a man who knows his way about on one particular square millimetre so well that there are at the outside two dozen people in the world who know as much about it as he does, a man who is perfectly aware that all the rest, who don't know their way about his particular bit of the world so well, talk nonsense about it, and who mustn't stir from it himself, because if he shifts only a micromillimetre from his place, he will be talking nonsense too." His weariness was now transparently golden as the drink on the table. 'So what it comes to,' he thought, 'is that I myself have been talking nonsense for quite half an hour.' But this reduced condition was a pleasant one. There was only one thing he was afraid of, and that was that it might occur to Bonadea to come and sit down beside him. Well, the only one way to prevent it was to keep on talking. He had clasped his hands behind his head and lay stretched at full length like the effigies on the tombs in the Medici chapel. All at once he became conscious of this; and then indeed, as he lay in that attitude, magnificence flooded through his body, a kind of floating in the repose of those figures, and he felt himself mightier than he was. For the first time he felt, through the intervening distance, that he understood those works of art, which he had previously looked upon only as alien objects. And instead of talking, he remained silent. Bonadea felt something too. It was one of those ' moments ', as one calls what one cannot describe. Some theatrical exaltation united the two of them, who had suddenly fallen silent.

'What is there left of me?' Ulrich thought with bitterness. 'A man, perhaps, who is brave and incorruptible and imagines that for the sake of inner freedom he respects only a few external laws. But this inner freedom consists in being able to think everything, in knowing—in every human situation—why one need not bind oneself to it, and in never knowing what one would wish to be bound by!' In this far from happy moment when the queer little wave of emotion that had for an instant overwhelmed him ebbed out again, he would have been prepared to admit that he possessed nothing but a capacity for discovering two sides to everything—the moral ambivalence that characterised almost all his contemporaries and was the disposition of his generation, or, one might even say, its fate. His relation to the world had become pale, shadowy, and negative. What right had he to treat Bonadea badly? It was always the same frustrating talk that they had over and over again. It was caused by the acoustics of emptiness within, where a shot resounds twice as loudly and goes echoing on and on. It bothered him that he could no longer talk to her at all except in this manner; and for the peculiar torment that it caused them both there occurred to him now the half-witty, pretty name : the Baroque of the Void. And he sat up to say something pleasant to her.

" Something has just occurred to me," he said, turning to Bonadea, who was still sitting there in a dignified pose. " It's a funny thing. There's a remarkable difference—a person who is responsible for his actions can always do the other thing, too, but a person who is not *never* can ! "

Bonadea replied with significant emphasis : " Oh, Ulrich ! " That was the only interruption, and silence closed round them again.

She did not like it at all when Ulrich talked on general subjects in her presence. Quite rightly, in spite of all her lapses from virtue, she felt herself still one of a crowd of people like herself and she had a proper sense of what was unsociable, extravagant and solitary in his way of entertaining her with thoughts instead of feelings. All the same, the result was that crime, love and melancholy had fused in her to form one circuit of ideas, one that was highly dangerous. Ulrich now seemed to her far less intimidating and perfect than he had at the beginning of this reunion ; but to make up for that he had gained something boyish that excited her idealism, something of a child that does not dare to run past some obstacle in order to throw itself into its mother's arms. For quite a long time now she had been feeling a loosened-up, almost quite uncontrolled tenderness for him. But since Ulrich had rejected her first hint of it, she was exerting violent restraint on herself. She had not yet got over the memory of how, on her last visit here, she had lain undressed and helpless on his divan, and she had made up her mind if need be to sit on her chair in hat and veil to the very end, so that he might begin to realise that he had to deal with someone who could if necessary control herself every bit as much as her rival, Diotima. Bonadea could never find the great idea that should have gone with the great excitement she got into when in proximity to a lover. This is of course something that could, unfortunately, be said of the whole of life, which contains much excitement and little sense. But Bonadea did not know this, and she sought to utter some—any—idea. Ulrich's own ideas, she felt, lacked the dignity of which she was in need ; and it is probable that she was searching for one more beautiful and more emotional. But idealistic hesitation and low common attraction, attraction and a terrible fear of being too quickly attracted, mingled in all this with an urge to keep silence—silence in which the unaccomplished actions went on twitching—and with the memory of the great calm that had for a second united her with her lover. It was, in fact, like rain hovering in the air and no rain falling. It was a flickering numbness spreading out all over the skin, and it frightened Bonadea with the notion that she might lose control of herself without noticing it.

And suddenly a physical illusion came jumping out of it, a flea. Bonadea did not know whether it was reality or imagination. She felt a shudder in her brain, a scarcely credible sensation as though there an image had detached itself from the shadowy bondage of all the rest and yet was nothing more than imaginary ; and at the same time there was an undeniable, perfectly realistic shudder on her skin. She held her breath. When something starts coming up the stairs, pit-a-pat, and one knows there's no one there, and yet one quite distinctly hears it coming, pit-a-pat —that's it. As though in a flash, Bonadea realised that this was an involuntary continuation of the lost shoe. It was a desperate remedy for a lady to resort to. And yet, at this moment, when she wanted to conjure the spook away, she felt a sharp sting. She uttered a faint shriek, her cheeks flushed brightly, and she called upon Ulrich to assist her in the search. A flea favours the same areas as a lover. The stocking was examined down to the shoe, the blouse had to be unbuttoned in front. Bonadea declared she must have got it in the tram or from Ulrich. But it was not to be found and it had left no traces.

" I can't imagine what it can have been ! " Bonadea said.

Ulrich smiled in an unexpectedly kind manner.

And then Bonadea began to cry like a little girl who has just done something naughty.

64

*General Stumm von Bordwehr visits
Diotima.*

GENERAL Stumm von Bordwehr had paid his first call on
Diotima. He was that officer whom the War Ministry had sent
as a delegate to the great inaugural meeting, where he made a
speech that impressed everyone, without however being able to
prevent the Ministry of War from being passed over, for obvious
reasons, when committees for the great work of peace were being
set up on the pattern of the ministries.

He was a not very imposing general, with a little paunch and
a little toothbrush-moustache instead of real mustachios. His
face was round and had rather a look of the typical family man
with just enough money to put down the caution required of army
officers intending to marry, but no more than that. He told
Diotima that the role allotted to the soldier in the conference-
chamber was a modest one and that it went without saying that
for political reasons the War Ministry could not be considered in
the setting up of committees. Nevertheless, he would venture
to say that the proposed Campaign should have an influence
abroad, and what had an influence abroad was a nation's might.
He repeated what the celebrated philosopher Treitschke had
said : that the State was the power of maintaining one's existence
in the struggle of the nations. The power displayed in times of
peace, he said, averted war, or at least shortened its reign of terror.
He talked for another quarter of an hour, making use of several
classical quotations, which, as he added, he still remembered with
special enjoyment from his schooldays, and he asserted that those
years of classical studies had been the happiest of his life. He
sought to convey to Diotima a sense of his admiration for her and
his delight at the manner in which she had conducted the great
conference, and just wanted to say once again that, rightly understood, building up the armed forces, which were far behind those
of the other great powers, might well be the most effective
demonstration of a peace-loving attitude. He wound up by

declaring he confidently looked forward to a spontaneous rise of broad popular interest in army matters.

This amiable general gave Diotima the fright of her life. There were at that time in Kakania families whose houses were frequented by officers because their daughters married officers, and there were families whose daughters did not marry officers, either because there was no money to put down for the marriage-caution, or on principle, so that no officers frequented their houses. Diotima's family had belonged to the second group for both reasons, and the consequence was that this conscientiously beautiful woman entered into life with a conception of the military that was approximately that of Death decked out in a motley coat. She replied by saying that there was so much of the Great and the Good in the world that it was not easy to make a choice. It was a great privilege, she said, being allowed to give a great sign in the midst of the materialistic bustle of the world, but it was also a grave obligation. And, after all, the demonstration was to rise spontaneously out of the midst of the people, which was why she had to keep her own wishes somewhat in the background. She set her words carefully, as though stitching them together with black-and-yellow thread, and burned the mild incense of high bureaucratic phraseology upon her lips.

But when the General had taken his leave, this sublime woman's soul collapsed in a swoon. If she had been capable of such a low emotion as hatred, she would have hated that podgy little man with the waggling eyes and the gold buttons on his paunch. But as this was denied her, she had an obscure sense of being affronted, without being able to say why. In spite of the wintry coldness of the air, she opened the windows and walked, rustling, up and down the room several times. When she shut the windows again, there were tears in her eyes. She was quite astonished. This was now the second time she wept without cause. She recollected the night when she had shed tears at her husband's side without having an explanation for them. This time the purely nervous quality of the process, to which there was no adequate content, was even more marked: this fat officer had brought the tears to her eyes like an onion, without there being any rational feeling involved. She was justifiably disquieted. A premonitory anxiety told her that some invisible wolf was

prowling round her folds and it was high time for him to be exorcised by the power of the idea. This was why she resolved, after the General's visit, to bring about with all possible speed the intended gathering of great minds that was to aid her in assuring the great Campaign of a spiritual content.

65 *Extracts from the conversations between Arnheim and Diotima.*

IT took a load off Diotima's heart to know that Arnheim had just returned from a journey and was at her disposal.

" Only a few days ago I had a discussion with your cousin about generals," he at once replied, conveying this information with the mien of a man who alludes to an equivocal association of things without wanting to specify what it is. Diotima received the impression that her contradictory cousin, who had so little enthusiasm for the great idea of the Campaign, was in addition favourable to the vague dangers emanating from the General.

" I wouldn't like to expose this to scorn in your cousin's presence," Arnheim went on, giving the conversation a new turn, " but it means a lot to me to convey to you something that would otherwise scarcely occur to one so remote from these things—the connection between business and poetry. I mean of course business in the wider meaning of the word, global business such as I have been destined to carry on as a result of the position to which I was born. It is related to poetry, for it has irrational, indeed positively mystical aspects. I should even go so far as to say it is especially business that has them. I'm sure you realise that money is an extraordinarily intolerant power."

" There is probably a certain measure of intolerance in everything that people go in for with all the intensity of their being," Diotima answered, rather hesitantly, still musing over the unfinished first part of their talk.

"Particularly where money is concerned!" Arnheim said swiftly. "Foolish people imagine it is a pleasure to possess money. In fact it is an uncanny responsibility. I don't want to talk about the countless individual lives that are dependent on me, so that for them I almost occupy the place of destiny. Let me only speak of the fact that my grandfather started as a rag-and-bone dealer in a middle-sized town in the Rhineland."

At these words Diotima really did feel a sudden awe of something she took for economic imperialism. But here she was confusing two different things; for she was not quite free of the prejudices of her social class, and since the words 'rag-and-bone dealer' made her think of what she was accustomed to call 'the garbage-man', her friend's courageous confession made her blush.

"In this refuse-refining process," he went on with his confession, "my grandfather laid the foundations of the Arnheims' influence in the world. But even my father was still what one would call a self-made man, for one must bear in mind that inside forty years he expanded the firm to the dimensions of a world-wide concern. He had no more than two years at a commercial college, but he can see through the most involved world situation at a glance, and knows everything he needs to know sooner than anyone else does. I myself studied economics and every conceivable branch of science, but they are quite outside his ken and there is no way of explaining how he does it, yet nothing he touches ever goes wrong. That is the mystery of vigorous, simple, great and healthy life!"

When Arnheim spoke of his father, an unusual ring of reverence came into his voice, as though there were a little crack somewhere in its magisterial calm. It struck Diotima all the more since Ulrich had told her that old Arnheim was described as being just a broad-shouldered little chap, with a bony face and a nose like a button, who always wore a swallow-tail coat wide open and handled his stocks and shares as doggedly and carefully as a chess-player moving his pawns.

After only a brief pause, without giving her time to answer, Arnheim continued:

"When a business has reached a point of expansion like the very few of which I am here speaking, there is scarcely anything in life that it does not become involved with. It is a little cosmos

in itself. You would be amazed if you knew what seemingly quite uncommercial problems—artistic, moral and political—I sometimes have to bring up in conference with the senior chief of the firm. But the firm is no longer shooting up at the same speed as in its early days—what I should like to call its heroic days. No matter how prosperous a business firm may be, there is a mysterious limit to its growth, as there is with everything organic. Have you ever asked yourself why there is no animal nowadays that grows beyond the size of an elephant ? You find the same mystery in the history of art and in the strange relationships in the life of peoples, cultures and epochs."

Diotima now felt remorse for having shrunk from the refuse-refining process. She was bewildered.

" Life is full of such mysteries. There is something that the intellect is powerless against. My father is in league with it. But a person like your cousin," Arnheim said, " an activist whose head is always full of ideas about how to do things differently and better, is utterly insensitive to it."

When Ulrich was now mentioned once again, Diotima indicated by a smile that a man like her cousin was far from having any claim to exert an influence upon her. Arnheim's evenly coloured, somewhat sallow skin, which gave his face the smooth appearance of a pear, had flushed over the cheek-bones. He had yielded to a queer feeling of need, which Diotima had stirred in him for some time, to confide in her without reserve, down to the last unknown detail. Now he closed up again, took a book from the table, glanced at the title without really noticing what he read, put it back again impatiently, and said in his usual tone of voice, which at this moment affected Diotima as movingly as the gesture of a man who, by gathering up his clothes, makes one realise he has been naked : " I have wandered a long way from the point. What I have to say to you about the General is that you cannot do better than realise your plan as soon as possible and give our Campaign sublimity through the influence of the humanistic way of thinking and its recognised representatives. But you need not reject the General as a matter of principle. Personally he may be a man of good will, and after all you know my principle—one should never miss any opportunity of bringing what is spiritual into a sphere of mere power."

Diotima took his hand and summed up this conversation in the words of farewell : " I am so grateful to you for your frankness ! "

Arnheim let that mild hand lie in his own for one moment of indecision, gazing at it meditatively, as though there were something he had forgotten to say.

66   *All is not well between Ulrich and Arnheim.*

AT that time Diotima's cousin quite frequently amused himself by describing to her the official experience he was gathering at His Highness's side, and made a special point of time and again showing her the files with the suggestions that were pouring in at Count Leinsdorf's.

" O mighty cousin," he reported, a thick file in his hand, " I can't manage any more on my own. The whole world seems to be expecting us to undertake reforms, and one half begins with the words ' Free from——' and the other half with ' Onward to——'. I have here demands extending from ' Free from Rome ! ' to ' Onward to kitchen-garden-culture ! ' What will you settle on ? "

It was not easy to reduce to some form of order the wishes that the contemporary world was addressing to Count Leinsdorf, but there were two groups that definitely stood out because of the number of letters written in support of them. The one put the blame for the troubles of the age on one particular thing and demanded its abolition ; such particular items were nothing less than, for instance, the Jews, the Roman Church, socialism or capitalism, the mechanistic school of thought or the neglect of technical developments, miscegenation or the reverse of it, large-scale landowning or big cities, intellectualisation or the inadequacy of popular education. The second group, on the other hand, pointed to goals lying somewhere ahead, the reaching of which would be all that was needed ; and these highly desirable goals recommended by the second group usually differed from the particular things that the first group wanted to destroy in nothing more than their emotional key, obviously because the world is made up of both critical and positive temperaments. So it was that the communications from the second group would come forth with, say, the joyfully negative statement that it was high time to do away with this ridiculous cult of the arts, since life itself was a greater poet than all the scribblers rolled into one, and would demand collections of law-court reports and descriptions of travel for general use. Meanwhile the first group would be maintaining with happy assertiveness that the mountaineer's emotional experience of the peak was sublimer than all art, philosophy and religion, for which reason it would be better to drop these and support mountaineering associations. In such a dual manner demands were made as much for a slowing up of the tempo of the times as for a competition for the best *feuilleton*, on the grounds either that life is unendurably or that it is exquisitely short; and the liberation of mankind was clamoured for both from and by means of garden suburbs, the emancipation of women, dancing, sport or the cult of the home, and also by means of or by abolition of innumerable other things.

Ulrich shut his file and began a private conversation.

" O mighty cousin," he said, " it's an odd thing that one half of mankind is looking for salvation in the future and the other half in the past. I don't know what conclusion one should draw from this. His Highness would say the present time is past praying for."

" Has His Highness something religious in mind ? " Diotima asked.

" At the moment he has just arrived at the conviction that in the history of mankind there is no turning back of one's own free will. But what makes the situation so difficult is that there is no going forward that is much use either. I should like, if I may, to call it a remarkable situation in which one can't move either forwards or backwards and also feels the present moment quite unbearable."

As always when Ulrich talked like this, Diotima retreated behind the battlements of her tall figure as into a tower marked with three stars in Baedeker.

" Do you believe, dear lady," Ulrich asked, " that anyone today fighting for or against some cause or other, if by some miracle he were tomorrow made the all-powerful ruler of the world, would that same day do what he has been demanding all his life long ? I am convinced he would put it off for a few days."

As Ulrich then made a little pause, Diotima suddenly turned to him, and, without answering his question, asked sternly :

" Why did you hold out hopes to the General with regard to our Campaign ? "

" What general ? "

" General von Stumm ! "

" You mean the little round general who was at the first big meeting ? I ? I haven't even seen him again, far from holding out any hopes to him ! "

Ulrich's amazement was convincing and demanded an explanation. But since it was equally impossible that a man like Arnheim should speak anything but the truth, there must be some misunderstanding ; and Diotima explained what had led her to make this assumption.

" You mean to say I had a talk with Arnheim about General von Stumm ? But I hadn't—never ! " Ulrich assured her. " I've talked to Arnheim—just a minute, let me think for a moment——" he reflected, and suddenly laughed. " It would really be very flattering if Arnheim were to attach such importance to every word I say ! I have chatted with him several times recently—if you care to apply that term to our exchanges of antagonistic views—and as a matter of fact I did once say something about a general, but not a particular one and only incidentally, by way of example. I maintained that a general who for strategical reasons sends a battalion to its certain doom is a murderer if he is considered in relation to the fact that each of those men is some mother's son, but that he immediately turns out to be something else if one thinks of him in a different connection, for instance that of the necessity of sacrifice or the unimportance of this short life. I used a lot of other examples too. But here you must allow me to go off at a tangent. For very obvious reasons every generation treats the life it finds waiting for it as something definitely established, except for the few things it is interested in changing. This is useful, but mistaken. For the world could at any moment be changed in all directions or at any rate in any given one. It has it, so to speak, in its bones. And so it would be an original way of living if one were to try, for once, not to behave as a definite person in a definite world, in which, one might say, only a few buttons need shifting—the thing one calls evolution—but starting out as a man born to change and surrounded by a world created for change, in other words, pretty much like a little drop of water in a cloud. Are you despising me for being obscure again ? "

" I am not despising you, but I cannot understand you," Diotima said and commanded : " Please tell me the whole conversation."

" Well, Arnheim started it. He button-holed me and positively dragged me into a discussion," Ulrich began. " ' We business men,' he said to me with a rather puckish smile that was somewhat in contradiction to the reposeful attitude he usually preserves, and yet very majestic all the same, ' we business men don't make calculations, as you may perhaps believe. But we—I am speaking, of course, of the leading men—the little ones, admittedly, may spend all their time doing calculations—we learn to regard our really successful inspirations as something that defies all calculation, just as the personal success of the politician does, and of course the artist's as well.' Then he asked me to judge what he was going to say next with the indulgence due to something of an irrational nature. Since the first day he saw me—so he confided in me—he had had certain ideas about me, and although you, gracious cousin, had also told him various things about me, still, he assured me, he had not really needed to hear them in order to form a view, and he explained to me that it was odd that I had chosen a quite abstract, conceptual occupation, for whatever great gifts I might have for it, I was, nevertheless, on the wrong track in being a scientist, and my essential talent, however much it might surprise me to know it, lay in the realm of action and of personal effectiveness ! "

" Oh, indeed ? " Diotima said.

" I am entirely of your opinion," Ulrich hastened to say. " There is nothing I have less talent for than myself."

" You are always making a mock of things, instead of devoting yourself to life," Diotima commented, still annoyed with him on account of the files.

" Arnheim says the opposite. I have the urge to draw excessively profound conclusions about life from my own thoughts— so he says."

" You are sardonic and negative. You are always on the point of taking a leap into the impossible and you avoid every real decision," Diotima said, laying down the law.

" It is simply my conviction," Ulrich replied, " that thinking is an institution all on its own, and real life is another one. The difference between their respective levels of development is at present too great. . . . Our brain is several thousand years old, but if it had only half thought everything out and forgotten the other half, its accurate reflection would be reality. All one can do is refuse to take any intellectual share in it."

" Doesn't that mean making things too easy for oneself ? " Diotima asked without any offensive intention, simply gazing at him like a mountain gazing down at a little stream at its foot. " Arnheim likes theories too, but I think there is little he lets pass without examining it in all its aspects. Don't you really think that the meaning of all thinking is that it should be a concentrated capacity for application . . . ? "

" No," Ulrich said.

" I should like to hear what Arnheim said about it."

" He told me that the mind is today a helpless spectator of the real developments, because it dodges the great tasks life sets. He demanded that I should look around and consider what the arts are concerned with, what petty-mindedness preoccupies the churches, how narrow even scholarship's field of vision is ! And he wanted me to realise that the earth, meanwhile, is literally being shared out. And then he told me this was precisely what he had wanted to talk to me about."

" And what did you say ? " Diotima asked, agog, for she thought she could guess that Arnheim had been trying to reproach her cousin for his indifference to the Collateral Campaign's problems.

" I told him that realisation always attracts me less than nonrealisation, and by that I meant not only realisation of, say, the future, but also the past and its lost opportunities. It seems to me our history is made up of the fact that every time we fulfil just a little of an idea, in our delight we leave the greater part of it undone. Magnificent institutions are usually bungled drafts of ideas. Magnificent personalities too, for that matter. That's what I said to him. There was, in a manner of speaking, a difference in the direction of our gaze."

" That was quarrelsome of you ! " Diotima said in an injured tone.

" In exchange he informed me of the impression I make on him when I deny the active life for the sake of some unfulfilled intellectual settlement in general. Do you want to hear it ? That of a man lying down on the ground beside a bed that's been prepared for him. It's a squandering of energy, in fact something physically immoral, he added for my personal benefit. He worked on me to get me to understand that intellectual goals of great dimensions can only be reached by use of the present-day economic, political and, last but not least, intellectual balance of power. He, for his own part, considers it more ethical to make use of them than to neglect them. He worked very hard on me. He called me a man of action in a defensive attitude, in a cramped defensive attitude. I rather think he has some faintly sinister reason for wanting to win my respect."

" He means well by you ! " Diotima exclaimed severely.

" Oh no," Ulrich demurred. " I am, perhaps, only a little pebble, and he is like a magnificent bulgy glass ball. But I have the impression that he's frightened of me."

Diotima made no answer to this. What Ulrich had said might be presumptuous, but it had occurred to her that the conversation he had reproduced was by no means quite what it ought to have been like, judging by the impression of it she had received from Arnheim. It rather worried her. Although she thought Arnheim quite incapable of making any intriguing move, still, she was gaining confidence in Ulrich, and she turned to him with the question what then he would advise her to do about General Stumm.

" Keep him off ! " was Ulrich's answer.

And Diotima could not help feeling, though with some self-reproach, that this appealed to her.

67 *Diotima and Ulrich.*

DIOTIMA'S relationship to Ulrich had much improved recently through their being together as a matter of routine. They often had to drive out together to call on people, and he came to her house several times a week, not infrequently unannounced and at unusual times. In these circumstances it was convenient to both of them to take advantage of their family relationship and so relax the strict code prescribed by society. Diotima did not always receive him in the drawing-room and fully armoured from her bun down to the hem of her skirt, but occasionally in slight domestic disarray, even though it was only a very cautious disarray. A kind of fellow-feeling had grown up between them, which lay mainly in the form of their association ; but forms have an influence that works inward, and the emotions of which they are made up can also be aroused by them.

Ulrich sometimes felt with all possible intensity that Diotima was very beautiful. She then struck him as being like a tall, plump heifer of good stock, sure-footed and with deep gaze regarding the dry grasses on which she was grazing. In other words, even then he did not look at her without the malice and irony that took revenge on her spiritual nobility by using similes drawn from the animal kingdom and which originated in a profound annoyance directed less at this foolish model child than at the school in which its performances enjoyed success. ' How pleasant she would be,' he thought, ' if she were uneducated and easy-going and as good-natured as a big warm female body always is when it hasn't any particular idea in its head ! ' And then the celebrated wife of the much-whispered-of Permanent Secretary Tuzzi evaporated out of her body, and only the body itself remained behind, like a dream that was transformed, together with the pillows, the bed and the dreamer on it, into a white cloud all alone with its tenderness in the wide world.

But whenever Ulrich came back to earth from such a flight of fancy, he saw before him an eagerly industrious middle-class mind seeking to associate with aristocratic thoughts. And any-way, family relationship combined with intensely antagonistic temperaments is always disturbing ; in fact even the mere idea of kinship is enough, the consciousness of self. It often happens that brothers and sisters loathe each other in a manner far in excess of anything that could possibly be justified by the facts ; this is simply because they make each other questionable through their mere existence, having a faintly distorting-mirror effect on each other. Sometimes the mere fact that Diotima was about as tall as Ulrich was enough to waken the thought that she was related to him and to make him feel repugnance for her body. Here, even though with some alterations, he had passed on to her a function that otherwise was that of his boyhood friend Walter, namely that of humbling his pride and irritating it, rather as dis-agreeable old pictures, in which we see ourselves portrayed, humiliate us in our own eyes and at the same time are a challenge to our pride. The result was that even in the mistrust that Ulrich felt towards Diotima there was necessarily something binding and uniting, in short, a breath of genuine affection, just as the one-time cordial sense of fellowship with Walter still dragged on in the form of mistrust.

But since he did not like Diotima, for a long time this greatly disconcerted him, without his being able to get to the bottom of it. They sometimes made little expeditions together. With Tuzzi's encouragement the fine weather was made use of to show Arnheim, in spite of the unfavourable time of year, ' the beauties of Vienna's surroundings '—Diotima never used any other expression for it than this cliché—and Ulrich every time found himself taken along in the part, as it were, of an elderly female relative acting as chaperon, since Permanent Secretary Tuzzi could not spare the time ; and later on it came about that Ulrich also went driving alone with Diotima when Arnheim was out of town. Arnheim had made motor-cars available for such expedi-tions, as well as eventually for the immediate purposes of the Campaign—as many as were needed. For His Highness's vehicles, adorned with his coat of arms, were too well known about town, too conspicuous. As a matter of fact, the motors used were not Arnheim's own, since rich people always find other people who are delighted to be of service to them.

Such excursions were not only for pleasure ; they also had the object of canvassing for influential or wealthy persons' support for the patriotic enterprise, and took place within the bounds of the city more often than in the countryside.   The two relatives together saw many beautiful things : Maria-Theresa furniture, Baroque palaces, people who still had themselves wafted through the world by their servants, wrapped in cottonwool, modern houses with many rooms all opening out of each other, palatial banks, and the blend of Spanish austerity with the domestic habits of the middle class in the homes of high civil servants.   In general, so far as the aristocracy was concerned, what they saw was the remnants of a grand style of life without running water laid on, and this was repeated in the houses and conference-rooms of the wealthy bourgeoisie, in a hygienically improved version, which, though in better taste, was only a pale copy.   A caste of lords always remains somewhat barbaric.   Cinders and left-overs that the slow smouldering of time had not quite burnt away remained lying about in the aristocratic castles, just where they happened to lie, and close to the magnificent staircases one stepped on floorboards of soft wood, and abominable new furniture stood about unconcernedly among wonderful old pieces.   The *nouveau riche* class, on the other hand, in love with the imposing and grandiose eras of their predecessors, had involuntarily made a fastidious and refined selection.   Wherever a castle had passed into bourgeois possession, it was not merely that it was provided with modern conveniences, like an heirloom chandelier with electric wiring run through it ; in the furnishing of it, too, what was less good had been cleared out and things of value added, either according to personal choice or on the infallible advice of experts.   Incidentally, this process of refinement was demonstrated most impressively not in the castles but in the town houses, which had been furnished, in keeping with the times, with all the impersonal luxury of an ocean liner, but which—in this country of refined social ambition—still, in an ineffable breath, in a scarcely perceptible widening of the distance between the pieces of furniture, or in the dominating position of a picture on a wall, preserved the delicately clear reflected glint of a great glory that had passed away.

Diotima was in raptures over so much ' culture '.   She had

always known that her native country harboured such treasures, but their abundance surprised even her. The two of them would get joint invitations to pay visits in the country ; and on such occasions it struck Ulrich that he not infrequently saw fruit picked up in the fingers and eaten unpeeled, and similar things, whereas in the houses of the upper bourgeoisie the cere-monial of knife and fork was strictly observed. The same sort of observation could also be made with regard to conversation, which was of perfect distinction almost only in bourgeois houses, whereas in aristocratic circles the well-known informal idiom, reminiscent of cab-drivers, was predominant.

Diotima defended this with enthusiasm against her cousin. Bourgeois estates, she admitted, were equipped more hygienically and intelligently. The nobility's country seats were freezing cold in winter ; narrow, worn stairs were nothing rare ; and stuffy low-ceilinged bedrooms went together with the splendour of the drawing-rooms. And there were no service-lifts and no bath-rooms for the servants. But precisely that, after all, was in a sense the more heroic, the traditional and grandly nonchalant thing ! So she would conclude, quite enraptured.

Ulrich used these excursions for investigating the feeling that linked him to Diotima. But since there were so many digressions in all this, we must follow them up for a while before coming to the decisive point.

In those days women wore clothes that encased them from throat to ankles ; and although men wear pretty much the same clothes nowadays as then, it was more appropriate at that time, for their clothes were still an organic part of a way of life, an outward sign of the immaculate compactness and strict restraint that were regarded as the mark of a man of the world. The water-clear candour of exhibiting oneself naked would then have been regarded, even by a person who had few prejudices and was not hampered by any feelings of shame in his appreciation of the undraped body, as a relapse into the animal state, not because of the nakedness but because of the renunciation of the civilised erotic stimulus afforded by clothes. In fact at that time it would probably have been called : below the animal state. For a three-year-old horse of good stock and a playful greyhound are much more expressive in their nakedness than a human body can ever manage to be. On the other hand, they cannot wear clothes; they have only one skin, whereas human beings at that time still had many skins. In the enormous dress, with all its ruches, puffs, bell-skirts, cascading draperies, lace and pleatings, they had created a surface five times as large as the original one, forming a many-petalled, almost impenetrable chalice loaded with an erotic charge and concealing at its core the slim white animal that made itself fearfully desirable, letting itself be searched for. It was the standard process that Nature herself uses when she bids her creatures fluff out their plumage or ejaculate clouds of darkness in order to intensify the matter-of-fact operations that are what really counts into an unearthly state of madness.

For the first time in her life Diotima felt herself deeply affected by this play, even though in the most decorous manner. Coquetry was nothing strange to her, for it was one of the social accomplishments in which a lady had to be proficient. Nor had it ever escaped her when young men's glances expressed something other than respect for her; indeed, she even enjoyed this, because it made her feel the power of gentle feminine reproof when she compelled the eyes of a man intent on her, like the horns of a bull, to turn away, diverting them towards the idealistic sentiments she was uttering. But Ulrich, in the security of their kinship, which brought them near to each other, and of the unselfish help he was giving the Collateral Campaign, protected also by the codicil devised in his favour, permitted himself liberties that penetrated perpendicularly through the ramified wickerwork of her idealism.

For instance, it happened once when they were driving through the countryside, the car bowling past delightful valleys where hill-sides covered with dark pine-woods sloped down to the road, that Diotima pointed at them, quoting the lines:

" Who was it, lovely woods, did plant you there on high ? " (She quoted these lines as part of a poem, it goes without saying, and without even the faintest suggestion of the tune to which the song goes, for that she would have thought threadbare and trite.)

And Ulrich replied: " The Lower-Austrian Land Bank. Don't you know, cousin, that all the forests around here belong to the Land Bank ? And the creator you are intent on praising is a forester in its employ. Nature in these parts is a planned product of the forestry industry, a store-house—rank upon rank

—of cellulose manufacture, which is, indeed, what it looks like."

The answers he gave were very often of this kind. When she spoke of beauty, he spoke of the fat-tissues supporting the skin. When she spoke of love, he spoke of the annual curve showing the automatic rise and fall in the birth-rate. When she spoke of great men in art, he began talking about the chain of borrowings that links these great men to each other. What it really came to always was that Diotima began talking as though God had on the seventh day put man, like a pearl, into the shell of the world, and Ulrich then reminded her that mankind was a little heap of dots on the outermost crust of a midget globe.

It was by no means easy to see what Ulrich's object was in doing this. It was, however, obviously an attack on that sphere of greatness with which Diotima felt herself in communion, and to her it was, above all, offensive priggishness. She could not tolerate the idea that her cousin, whom she had made up her mind to regard as an *enfant terrible*, should know better about anything than she did herself; and his materialistic objections, which she did not in the least understand, because they were something he fetched up from the low regions of calculations and exactitude, thoroughly annoyed her.

" Thank goodness," she once retorted sharply, " there are still some people who are capable of believing in simple things, in spite of having great experience ! "

" Your husband, for instance," Ulrich answered. " I have been wanting to tell you for a long time how much I prefer him to Arnheim ! "

At that time they got into the habit of often exchanging ideas by way of talk about Arnheim. For like all people in love, Diotima enjoyed talking about the object of her love, without— or at least so she believed—betraying herself. And because Ulrich found this as insupportable as every man does who combines no ulterior motive with his own withdrawal, on such occasions it often happened that he lashed out against Arnheim. The way in which he began to be bound up with Arnheim produced a relationship of a peculiar kind. When Arnheim was not out of town, they met almost every day. Ulrich knew that Permanent Secretary Tuzzi regarded the stranger with suspicion, just like himself, who had been observing Arnheim's effect on Diotima from the first day onward. Admittedly there did not yet seem to be any impropriety between the two of them—so far as could be judged by a third person, he being confirmed in his conjecture by the fact that there was unendurably much propriety in the exchanges of this couple, who, it was obvious, were enthusiastically modelling themselves on the loftiest examples of a Platonic union of souls. At the same time Arnheim showed a striking inclination to draw the cousin of his friend (or *was* she, perhaps, his beloved ? Ulrich wondered and decided that the most probable thing was something like beloved plus friend divided by two) into this intimate relationship. Arnheim often addressed Ulrich in the tone of an older friend, a tone made permissible by the difference in age, but receiving a disagreeable touch of condescension from the difference in position. Ulrich almost always responded forbiddingly, indeed in a somewhat challenging manner, as though he did not in the least appreciate this acquaintance with a man who might well have discussed his ideas with kings and chancellors instead of with him, Ulrich. He contradicted him uncivilly often and with unseemly irony, and was himself annoyed by this lack of self-control, where he would have done better to enjoy himself by being the silent observer. But to his own amazement it kept on happening that he felt violently irritated by Arnheim. He saw in him, fattened by favourable circumstances, the exemplary special case of a line of intellectual development that he hated. For this celebrated writer was shrewd enough to understand the questionable situation into which man had got himself since he gave up looking for his image in the mirror of streams and looked for it, instead, in the sharp, broken surfaces of his intelligence ; but the book-writing iron-king put the blame for this not on the fact that intelligence was imperfect but that it had appeared on the scene at all. There was a confidence-trick involved in this union between the soul and the price of coal, a union that was at the same time a useful dividing-line between what Arnheim did with his eyes wide open and what he said and wrote when he was under the twilight spell of his intuitions. And there was something else, which caused an even greater sense of discomfort in Ulrich and which was new to him : things of the mind in combination with wealth. For when Arnheim talked more or less like a specialist on some particular subject and suddenly, with a negligent wave of the hand, caused the details to disappear in the light of a ' great thought ', his doing so might well originate in a not unjustifiable need, but the fact remained that this manner of disposing freely in two directions was strongly suggestive of the rich man who can afford to treat himself to the best of everything. He had at his disposal a wealth of ideas that was always a little reminiscent of the operations of real wealth. And perhaps even that was not what chiefly provoked Ulrich to make difficulties for the celebrated man ; it was perhaps rather the inclination Arnheim's mind showed towards a dignified mode of holding court and keeping house, which automatically led to an association with the best brands of whatever was traditional as of whatever was unusual. For in the mirror of this epicurean connoisseurship Ulrich saw the affectedly simpering grimace that was the face of the times minus the few really strong lines of passion and thought in it ; and all this left him hardly any opportunity to come to a better understanding of the man, who could probably be credited with all sorts of good points as well. It was of course an utterly senseless battle he was waging, in an environment that was all in Arnheim's favour, and for a cause that was of no importance at all ; the most one could have said was that the sense of this senseless behaviour was a complete expending of one's own resources. Apart from that, it was a quite hopeless struggle. For if Ulrich once really succeeded in wounding his enemy, he could not fail to recognise that he had hit the wrong side. When Arnheim the man of the mind seemed to be lying vanquished on the ground, then, like a winged being, Arnheim the man of reality rose up with an indulgent smile and hastened away from the idle toyings of such conversations towards action in Baghdad or Madrid.

This invulnerability enabled him to meet the younger man's bad manners with that man-to-man camaraderie the origin of which Ulrich could not satisfactorily explain to himself. Admittedly Ulrich himself was anxious not to depreciate his antagonist too much, for he had resolved to be chary of letting himself in again for the kind of half-baked and unworthy adventure in which his past was far too rich ; and the progress he observed in the relations between Arnheim and Diotima greatly strengthened him in this resolve. So he generally saw to it that the points of his attacks were like the point of a foil, elastically yielding and tipped with an amiable little rubber button to soften the blow.

It was actually Diotima who had originated this comparison. She fared strangely with this cousin of hers. His candid face with the clear brow, his calmly breathing chest, the free mobility of his limbs, all revealed to her that this was a body in which malicious, spiteful, perversely voluptuous urges could not be at home. Nor was she quite without pride in the good looks and easy bearing of this member of her family, and right at the beginning of their acquaintance she had made up her mind to take him under her wing. If he had happened to have black hair, a crooked shoulder, muddy skin and a low forehead she would have said that this harmonised with his views. But since he looked as he did, she was merely struck by a certain discrepancy between his looks and his ideas, which caused her an inexplicable uneasiness. The antennae of her famous intuition groped in vain for the cause ; but the groping in itself aroused pleasurable sensations at the other end of the antennae. In a sense, though not of course in an entirely serious one, she sometimes even preferred conversation with Ulrich to conversation with Arnheim. Her need to feel superior found more fulfilment in him ; she was surer of herself ; and what she considered his frivolity, eccentricity, or lack of maturity, gave her a certain satisfaction, which balanced the idealism, growing daily more dangerous, that she saw swelling to incalculable dimensions in her feelings for Arnheim. Soul is something frightfully ponderous, and hence materialism, by contrast, is cheerful. Managing her relations with Arnheim was sometimes as much of a strain on her as her *salon*, and her scorn for Ulrich made her life easier. She did not understand her own feelings, but she did notice this effect ; and this enabled her, whenever she was annoyed with her cousin on account of one of his remarks, to cast at him an oblique glance that was no more than a tiny smile in the corner of her eye, while the eye itself remained idealistically unmoved, indeed even gazed a little contemptuously straight ahead.

At any rate, whatever the reasons may have been, Diotima and Arnheim adopted towards Ulrich the attitude of two antagonists clutching at a third, whom they push to and from between themselves in constantly fluctuating waves of fear. Such a situation was not without its dangers for him, for through Diotima the question vividly arose : do people have to be in harmony with their bodies or not ?

68 *A digression : Do people have to be in harmony with their bodies ?*

INDEPENDENTLY of their talking faces and the subject of their conversation, the movement of the motor-car on these long trips rocked the two cousins to and fro so that their clothes touched, overlapped a little and shifted apart again. It could be observed only at their shoulders, because the rest of them was covered by the rug they shared, but the bodies felt this contact, muffled by the clothes, in as delicately blurred a way as things are seen on a moonlit night. Ulrich was not insensitive to this kind of subtle love-play, without taking it particularly seriously. The over-refined transference of the desire from the body to the clothes, from the embrace to the obstacles, or in short, from the goal to the approach, met his temperament half-way ; its sensuality drove it towards the woman, but its higher powers held it back from the alien, unsuitable person that it suddenly saw before it in inexorable clarity, so that it continually found itself tensely hovering between inclination and repulsion. But this meant that the sublime beauty of the body, the human beauty of it, the moment when the melody of the spirit soars up from Nature's instrument, or that other moment when the body is like a goblet being filled with a mystic potion, had remained unknown to Ulrich all his life long, apart from the dreams dreamt for the major's wife, which had set him free from such inclinations ever since.

All his relationships with women since then had been somehow wrong. With a certain amount of good will on both sides that unfortunately happens very easily. There is an underlying scheme of feelings, actions and complications that the man and the woman, as soon as they give it a thought at all, find ready waiting to take possession of them. It is a process the inner meaning of which is reversed, in which the last happenings push ahead first ; it is no longer a flowing from the source. In this psychic reversal two human beings' pure delight in each other, this simplest and deepest of all emotions in love, which is the natural origin of all the others, is not present at all.

So on his trips with Diotima Ulrich not infrequently remembered their leave-taking after his first call. He had held her mild hand in his, an artificially and nobly perfected hand without weight, while they had gazed into each other's eyes. They had certainly both felt repulsion, but had also been struck by the thought that they might yet intermingle to the point of dissolution. Something of this vision remained between them. So two heads, up in the air, turn a dreadful chill upon each other, while down below the unresistant bodies are melting into each other at white heat. There was something malignantly mythical about it, as about a two-headed god or the Devil's cloven hoof, something that had misled Ulrich much and often in his youth, when he had experienced it more frequently ; but with the passing of the years it had turned out to be nothing but an ordinary civilised erotic stimulus, exactly the same as the substitution of the unclothed state for that of nakedness. There is nothing that so inflames civilised love as the flattering discovery that one has the power to drive another human being into an ecstasy in which he or she behaves so crazily that one would positively have to become a murderer in order to produce such changes by any other means.

And indeed, that such changes in civilised people are possible, that such an influence can emanate from us—does this not account for the query, the bewilderment, in the daring and glassy eyes of all who put ashore on the lonely island of lust, where they are murderers, Destiny, and God, all rolled into one, and in the most comfortable way in the world experience the highest degree of irrationality and romance that is given to them ?

His gradually acquired repugnance for this kind of love finally extended to his own body as well, which had always encouraged these topsy-turvy relationships by presenting women with an illusion of staple masculinity—an ideal that Ulrich did not live up to, having too much of a mind and being made up, as he was, of too many inner contradictions. At times he was downright jealous of his appearance, as of a rival making use of cheap and rather unfair methods, which made apparent a contradiction that is also present in others who do not feel it. For it was he himself who kept this body in good trim by means of gymnastics, giving it the shape, expression and alertness whose inner influence may well be compared to the influence a permanently smiling or permanently grave face has on its owner's state of mind. And, oddly enough, the majority of people have either a neglected body, formed and deformed by accidental circumstances and seemingly in almost no relationship to their mind and character, or one hidden under the mask of sport, which gives it the look of those hours when it takes time off from being itself. For those are the hours when man continues the day-dream of wanting to look like something, which he has casually picked up from the illustrated papers of the smart, great world. All these bronzed and muscular tennis-players, horsemen and motorists, who all have a record-breaking look, although usually they are only moderately good at whatever it is they do, these ladies in full dress or undress, are day-dreamers, only distinguished from ordinary waking dreamers by the fact that their dreams do not remain inside the brain, but, issuing forth *en masse* into the open air, take shape as a formation of the mass-soul, physically, dramatically and (one feels inclined to say, thinking of certain more than dubious occult phenomena) ideoplastically. But they definitely have in common with the ordinary weavers of fantasies a certain shallowness of the dream, as regards both its nearness to the waking state and its content. Collective physiognomy, with all its problems, still seems to be evading definition in our days. Although from handwriting, voice, position in sleep, and heaven only knows what else besides, we have learnt to draw conclusions about people's character—conclusions that are indeed sometimes surprisingly correct—for the body as a whole we have only the examples of fashion, which it models itself on, or, at the outside, a kind of moral nature-cure philosophy.

But is this the body of our mind, of our ideas, institutions and plans, or—the pretty ones included—that of our follies? The fact that Ulrich had loved these follies and to some extent still possessed them did not prevent him from not feeling at home in the body they had created.

69   *Diotima and Ulrich (continued).*

AND it was above all Diotima who in a new way intensified this feeling of his that the surface and the depths of his living being were not one and the same. This manifested itself very clearly and suddenly on these trips with her, which were at times like drives in the moonlight, when this young woman's beauty became detached from her person as a whole and for instants laid itself upon his eyes like the gossamer of a dream. He knew of course that Diotima compared everything he said with what was said generally—even though at a certain height of generality—and he was pleased that she should think it ' immature ', so that he felt as though he were always sitting there with a reversed telescope trained on him. He became steadily smaller, and when talking to her believed, or at least was not far from believing, that in his own words, while he was playing the *advocatus diaboli* and sober-minded materialist, he could hear the discussions of his last terms at school, when he and his schoolmates had been enthusiastic about all the evil-doers and monstrous figures in history precisely because their teachers had referred to them as such in tones of idealistic abhorrence. And when Diotima looked at him in displeasure, he became smaller still and, moving further back from the morality of heroism and the urge towards expansion, arrived at the defiantly insincere, callously and uncertainly aberrant morality of his hobbledehoy years—only metaphorically speaking, of course, just as one can discover in a gesture or a word a remote resemblance to gestures or words that one has shed long ago, indeed even to gestures that one has only dreamt or seen and disliked in other people.

At any rate there was an echo of all this in his delight in affronting Diotima. The mind of this woman, who would have been so beautiful without her mind, aroused an inhuman feeling in him, perhaps a fear of the mind, a distaste for all great things, a feeling that was quite faint, scarcely detectable—and perhaps even the word ' feeling ' was far too pretentious an expression for something that was but a mere breath. But magnified into words it would have had to be put like this : at times he saw not only this woman's idealism but all the idealism in the world, in all its ramifications and extent, appear physically before him, floating a hand's-breadth above the crown of that Grecian head. It only just missed being the Devil's horns. Then he became even smaller still and—again metaphorically speaking—went back into the passionate first moral state of childhood, in whose gaze allurement and terror mingle as in the eye of a gazelle. The tender sensations of that age can in one single moment of abandonment set the whole as yet still tiny world in flames, for they have neither purpose nor means of bringing about anything whatsoever and are simply and solely an illimitable fire. It was not in keeping with what Ulrich was like, but these childhood feelings, which he could scarcely imagine now because they had so little in common with the condition under which an adult lived, were what he ultimately came to long for in Diotima's company.

And once he was on the verge of confessing this to her. On one of their trips they had got out of the motor and were walking down into a little valley like a river-mouth of meadows with steep wooded banks, forming a crooked triangle in the middle of which a meandering brook lay icy and brittle in the faint frost. The slopes had been partly cleared of timber, with a few trees left standing, looking like feather dusters stuck into the bare hill-sides and hill-tops. This scene had tempted them to get out and walk. It was one of those wistful snowless days in the middle of winter that are reminiscent of a faded, out-of-fashion cotton dress.

Diotima suddenly asked her cousin : " Tell me, why does Arnheim call you an activist ? He says you always have your head full of how to do things differently and better." She had all at once remembered that her conversation with Arnheim about Ulrich and the General had ended inconclusively. " I don't understand that," she went on, " for it seems to me that you rarely mean anything seriously. But I must ask you, since we

share such a responsible task.   Do you remember our last talk ?
There was something you said . . .   You maintained that nobody,
if he had complete power, would carry out what he really wanted.
I should like to know now what you meant by that.   Surely it
was a dreadful idea ? "

Ulrich was silent for a while.   And during this silence, after
she had said her say as pertly as she could, it became clear to her
how intensely she was preoccupied with the illicit question
whether Arnheim and she would carry out what each of them
secretly wanted.   Suddenly she believed she had betrayed herself
to Ulrich.   She blushed, tried not to, blushed even more, and
did her best to gaze out over the valley, and away from him, with
as *dégagé* an expression as possible.

Ulrich had observed this process.   " I am sadly afraid," he
answered, " that the only reason why Arnheim, as you say, calls
me an activist is that he overestimates my influence in the Tuzzi
family.   You know yourself how little importance you attach to
what I say.   But in this moment, now that you have asked me,
I realise what an influence I ought to have on you.   May I tell
you without your instantly finding fault with me again ? "

Diotima nodded mutely as a sign of agreement and tried to
compose herself behind an appearance of absent-mindedness.

" Well," Ulrich began, " so I maintained that nobody would
carry out what he wants even if he could.   You remember our
files full of suggestions ?   And now I ask you—is there anyone
who would not be at a loss if whatever he had been passionately
demanding all his life long were suddenly to happen ?   If for
instance the Kingdom of God were suddenly to burst on the
Catholics or the Utopian State on the Socialists ?   But perhaps
that doesn't prove anything.   One gets used to demanding and
isn't ready at a minute's notice for the realisation of it.   Many
people may think that only natural.   To pursue the enquiry,
therefore . . .   Undoubtedly a musician considers music the
most important thing there is, and a painter, painting.   Probably
even a concrete expert thinks the same about the building of
concrete houses.   Do you think that the one will therefore
imagine God Almighty as a super-specialist for reinforced concrete and the others will prefer a painted world, or a world blown
on the bugle, to the real one ?   You will think this question non-

sensical, but the deep seriousness of it lies in the fact that one ought to be demanding this nonsense.

"And please don't think now," he said, turning to her perfectly seriously, "that all I mean is that everyone is allured by what is difficult to put into practice and scorns what he can really have. What I do mean is that reality has in itself a nonsensical yearning for unreality."

He had quite inconsiderately taken Diotima a long way down into the little valley. The further they went, the wetter the ground became, perhaps from snow trickling down the slopes, and they had to jump from one of the little grassy hillocks to the next, which gave a special rhythm to the talk, making it possible for Ulrich to keep on continuing it in jumps. And that too was why there were so many obvious objections to what he said that Diotima could not decide on any one of them. She had got her feet wet and now stopped, led astray and a little frightened, standing on a grassy mound with her skirts slightly lifted.

Ulrich turned back and laughed. "You've started something extremely dangerous, O mighty cousin. People are unspeakably glad if they are left so that they can't put their ideas into practice!"

"And what then would you do," Diotima asked irritably, "if you were the ruler of the world for one day?"

"I suppose I would have no choice but to abolish reality!"

"I should be very much interested to know how you would do that!"

"I don't know myself. I don't even know exactly what I mean. We infinitely overvalue the present moment, the sense of the present, the Here and Now. I mean, the way you and I are here together now in this valley, as though we had been put into a basket and the lid of the moment had fallen shut. We overvalue that. We shall remember it. Perhaps even a year from now we shall be able to describe how we stood here. But what really moves us, speaking at least for myself, is always—to put it carefully, for I'm not looking for an explanation and a name for it!—to a certain extent in antagonism to this way of experiencing things. It is displaced by so much Here and Now, so much Present. So it can't force its way through to becoming present!"

What Ulrich had just said rang out, loud and confusing, in the narrow valley. Diotima all at once had an eerie feeling and set out to return to the car. But Ulrich detained her, showing her the scenery.

" A few thousand years ago that was a glacier," he explained. "The world itself isn't so very whole-heartedly what it's pretending to be at this moment, either. This roundish entity has an hysterical nature. Today it's playing the good middle-class mother nursing her children. In those days the world was frigid and icy as an ill-natured girl. And a few thousand years before that, again, it was carrying on voluptuously with hot fern-jungles, sultry swamps and demoniacal beasts. One can't say that it has been developing towards perfection, nor what its true condition is. And the same goes for its child, humanity. Just think of the clothes in which people have stood here in the course of the ages, here where we're standing now. Expressed in the language of the lunatic asylum, it all resembles chronic obsessions with sudden flights of ideas, after which a new picture of the world appears. So you see, reality is abolishing itself, isn't it ?

" There is something else I should like to say to you," Ulrich began all over again, after a while. " The feeling of having firm ground underfoot and a firm skin all round, which seems so natural to most people, is not very strongly developed in me. Just cast your mind back to when you were a child—how everything was a soft shapeless glow. And then as a young girl whose lips were scorched with yearning In me at any rate something rebels against the notion that what is called mature manhood is the peak of such a development. In a certain sense, yes. And in a certain sense, no. If I were a myrmeleonina, that delicate creature rather like a dragonfly, I would be utterly horrified to think that a year earlier I had been the squat grey myrmeleon, the ant-lion, running backwards and living at the edge of the forest, dug in at the bottom of a funnel-shaped hole in the sand, with invisible pincers catching ants by the waist, after previousyl reducing them to exhaustion by means of a mysterious bombardment with grains of sand. And at times, in fact, my youth does horrify me just like that, even though it may be that I was the dragonfly then and am the monster now." He himself did not quite know what he was getting at. He had produced the myrmeleon and myrmeleonina slightly in mimicry of Arnheim's cultured omniscience.   But he had it on the tip of his tongue to say : ' Bestow an embrace upon me, purely for kindness' sake. We are kindred—not quite separate, far from being quite one—anyway, the extreme contrast to an austere and dignified relationship.'

But Ulrich was at fault.   Diotima was one of those people who are contented with themselves and therefore regard the different stages of development through which they pass as a staircase leading upward from below.   So what he said was completely incomprehensible to her, all the more since she did not know, of course, what he had left unsaid.

But meanwhile they had reached the motor, and so she felt calm again, tolerating what he was saying as the accustomed sort of talk that hovered between the entertaining and the irritating, something to which she accorded no more than a glance from the corner of her eye.   At this moment he had in fact no influence whatsoever upon her, apart from that of bringing her down to earth.   A delicate cloud of embarrassment, which had arisen from some hidden recess of her heart, dissolved into dry emptiness.   Perhaps for the first time she got a hard, clear glimpse of the fact that her relations with Arnheim must sooner or later confront her with a decision that might change her whole life.   It could not have been said that this now made her happy ; but it had the weighty presence of a real mountain-range there before her.   A weakness had passed.   ' Not doing what one wants to do ' had for an instant had a quite absurd splendour that she no longer understood.

" Arnheim is the out-and-out opposite of me.   He is always overestimating the happiness it is for time and space to meet with him in forming the present moment," Ulrich said, smiling with a sigh, feeling a strong need to bring what he had been saying to a conclusion.   But still, he said no more about childhood, and so it did not come to the point where Diotima would have got to know him from the sentimental side.

70   *Clarisse visits Ulrich to tell him a story.*

RE-DESIGNING the interiors of old castles was the special forte of the well-known painter, van Helmond, whose most inspired work was his daughter Clarisse. And one day she walked in unexpectedly on Ulrich.

" Papa sent me," she informed him. " He wants me to see if you couldn't turn your marvellous aristocratic connections to some account on his behalf as well."

She looked round the room with curiosity, dropped into a chair and threw her hat on another. Then she held out her hand to Ulrich.

" Your papa has exaggerated ideas about me," he began. But she cut him short.

" Oh, nonsense ! You know quite well the old man's always hard up. Business isn't anything like what it used to be in the old days." She laughed. " Smart place you have here. Very nice ! " She scrutinised her surroundings again and then looked at Ulrich. Her whole attitude had something of the charming uncertainty of a little dog whose bad conscience is making its skin twitch. " Well then ! " she said. " So you'll do it if you can. And if not, not. I promised him you would, of course. But I've come for another reason. This request of his put an idea into my head. Fact is, it's something there is in our family. I should just like to hear what you have to say about it." Her mouth and eyes hesitated and flickered for a moment, then she took the first hurdle at a bound. " What does it mean to you if I say ' beauty-doctor ' ? A painter is a beauty-doctor."

Ulrich realised what she meant. He knew her parents' house.

" What I mean—dark, distinguished, splendid, luxurious, upholstered, frilled and tasselled ! " she went on. " Papa's a painter, a painter is a kind of beauty-doctor, and knowing us always counted in society as just as smart as going to a spa. You follow. And one of Papa's main sources of income has always been doing up palaces and big country houses. You know the Pachhofens ? "

They were a patrician family Ulrich knew of, but he had not met them. He had only once encountered a Fräulein Pachhofen years ago in Clarisse's company.

" She was a friend of mine," Clarisse explained. " She was seventeen then and I was fifteen. Papa was going to do up and renovate the castle. Well yes, the Pachhofens' castle, of course ! We were all asked. Walter was with us too, for the first time. And Meingast."

" Meingast ? " Ulrich did not know who Meingast was.

" Oh yes, but of course you know him too. Meingast. He went to Switzerland later on. He wasn't a philosopher then, he was cock of the walk in every family with daughters."

" I never met him," Ulrich pointed out. " But now I know whom you mean."

" All right then." Clarisse did some strenuous mental arithmetic. " Wait a minute. Walter was twenty-three then, and Meingast was a bit older. I think secretly Walter admired Papa terrifically. It was the first time he had been asked to stay at a castle. Papa often had something like an inward royal robe. I think at first Walter was more in love with Papa then with me. And Lucy——"

" For heaven's sake, Clarisse, go a bit slower ! " Ulrich implored. " I seem to have lost the thread."

" Lucy," Clarisse said, " is Fräulein Pachhofen, of course, the daughter of the Pachhofens with whom we were all staying. Do you understand now ? Very well then, so you understand. When Papa wrapped Lucy in velvet or brocade, with a long train, and put her on one of their horses, she imagined he was Titian or Tintoretto. They were absolutely mad about each other."

" That's to say, Papa about Lucy, and Walter about Papa ? "

" Wait, I haven't got to that yet. At that time they had Impressionism. Papa's painting was all old-fashioned-musical, the same as what he is still doing today, brown gravy and peacocks' tails. But Walter went in for light and air, clean-lined English functional forms, everything that was new and sincere. Privately Papa could endure him about as much as a Protestant sermon. He couldn't stand Meingast either, for that matter. But he had two daughters to marry off, and he'd always spent more money than he earned, so he was indulgent towards the souls of these two young men. Walter, on the other hand, was secretly in love with Papa, I've told you that already. But publicly he had to despise him because of the new movement in art, and Lucy had never known anything about art, but she was afraid of making a fool of herself in front of Walter and frightened that if Walter turned out to be right, Papa would look like nothing but a funny old man. Now do you see how things stood?"

There was just one thing more Ulrich wanted to know, and that was where Mama had been.

"Mama was there too, of course. They quarrelled every day, the same as usual, no more and no less. You can see that under such conditions Walter was in a favourable position. He made a sort of point of intersection for all of us. Papa was afraid of him, Mama egged him on, and I began to fall in love with him. But Lucy played up to him. So Walter had a certain amount of power over Papa, and he began savouring it in a cautiously voluptuous way. I mean, at that time he was coming to realise his own importance. Without Papa and me he would never have become anything at all. Do you see how it all hangs together?"

Ulrich thought he could answer this question in the affirmative.

"But it was something else I wanted to tell you about," Clarisse assured him. She reflected for a while and then said: "Wait! To start with, just think of me and Lucy. That was an excitingly complicated relationship! Of course I was worried about Father, who was so far gone in love 'that he looked like wrecking the whole family. And at the same time of course I did want to know how a thing like that actually works. They were both quite crazy. In Lucy, naturally, friendship for me got mixed up with the feeling that the man she had for a lover was the same man whom I still had to say 'Papa' to like a good little girl. She was pretty conceited about it, but she was also frightfully ashamed towards me. I think the old castle can never have had such complications going on under its roof since the day it was built! Lucy used to hang around with Papa wherever she could, all day long. And at night she came up to the tower to confess to me. I used to sleep in the tower, you see, and we kept the light on almost all night."

"How far did Lucy actually go with your father?"

"That was the only thing I could never find out. But just

think of summer nights like those ! The owls whimpering, the night groaning—and when it got too uncanny for us, we both got into my bed and went on talking there. We couldn't imagine the whole thing any other way than that a man who had been seized with such a fatal passion would have to shoot himself. In fact we were waiting for it from day to day. . : ."

" I rather have the impression," Ulrich interrupted, " that not very much happened between them."

" That's what I think too—not everything. But quite a lot, all the same. You'll see what I mean in a minute The thing was, Lucy suddenly had to go away from the castle, because her father arrived unexpectedly and took her off on a journey to Spain. You just ought to have seen Papa when he was left on his own ! I think sometimes it was only touch and go whether he throttled Mama. He used to go riding around from morning till evening with a folding easel strapped on behind the saddle, without ever painting a stroke, and he didn't touch a brush when he stayed at home either. The point is he usually paints like a machine, but at that time I often used to come across him sitting in one of those big empty rooms with a book in front of him, which he hadn't even opened. Sometimes he used to brood like that for hours, then he would get up, and then the same thing happened all over again in another room or in the garden. Sometimes all day long. After all, he was an old man, and youth had left him in the lurch. Well, it's understandable, isn't it ? And I should think the picture he must often have had of Lucy and me, two girl friends with their arms round each other's waist, chatting to each other intimately, must have shot up in him then—like a wild seed. Perhaps he even knew, too, that Lucy always used to come up to me in the tower. To cut a long story short, once, about eleven o'clock at night, when all the lights in the castle were out, there he was ! I say, that was quite something ! " Clarisse was swept away with enthusiasm about the significance of her own story. " There was this fumbling and scraping on the stairs, and not knowing what it was. And then the clumsy fiddling with the door-handle and the door opening, like something in an adventure story . . ."

" Why didn't you call for help ? "

" That's the queer thing. From the very first sound I knew

who it was. He must have stayed standing motionless in the doorway, because for quite a time there wasn't a sound. Probably it was a shock for him too. Then he shut the door carefully and called me in a low voice. I was simply thunderstruck. I didn't at all mean to answer, but that's the queer thing—it came out of the depths of me as though I were a deep well, a sound like a little whimper. You know what I mean?"

"No. Go on!"

"Well, just like that. And the next moment he was clutching at me in endless despair. He almost fell on my bed, and his head was on the pillow beside my own."

"Tears?"

"Dry paroxysms! An old, deserted body! I understood that instantly. Oh, I tell you, if one could say later on what one thought at such moments, it would be something simply great! I think he was in a mad rage with all morality because of what he had missed. Well then, I noticed all at once that he had waked up again, and although it was pitch dark I knew immediately he was all convulsed with ruthless hunger for me. I knew now there was no mercy or consideration. Since I had groaned there hadn't been a sound. My body was burning hot and dry, and his was like a piece of paper put close to the edge of the fire. He positively grew quite light. I felt his arm letting go of my shoulder and snaking down along my body. And by the way, there's something I wanted to ask you. That's what I've come about——" Clarisse broke off.

"What? You haven't asked me anything!" Ulrich prompted her after a short pause.

"No. There's something else I must say first. The thought that he must be taking my keeping quite still for a sign of consent made me loathe myself. But I lay there quite bewildered, with fear like a stone on top of me. What do you think about that?"

"I can't say anything at all about it."

"With one hand he kept stroking my face all the time, and the other one wandered about. Trembling, pretending it wasn't really doing anything at all, you know, away over my breast like a kiss, then as though it were waiting and listening for an answer. And finally it was going—well, I dare say you understand, and at the same time his face came close to mine. But at that point

I did summon up all my strength and slipped away from him, turning on my side. And again there was this sound I've never heard from myself at any other time, sort of half-way between pleading and moaning, that came out of my chest. You see, I have a birthmark, a black medallion——"

" And how did your father react ? " Ulrich interrupted her coolly.

But Clarisse did not let herself be interrupted. " Here ! " She smiled tensely and pointed through her dress to a spot on the inner side of her hip. " That's how far he got, this is where the medallion is. This medallion has a miraculous power—or else there's something queer about it."

The blood suddenly flooded into her face. Ulrich's silence sobered her up and dissolved the thought that had been holding her captive. She smiled awkwardly and concluded, speaking rapidly : " My father ? He straightened up at once. I couldn't see what went on in his face. I think it was probably embarrassment. Perhaps gratitude. After all, I had saved him at the last moment. Imagine it—an old man, and a young girl has the strength to do that ! I must have seemed remarkable to him, for he pressed my hand quite gently and stroked my head twice, and then he went away without saying anything. Well, you'll do what you can for him, won't you ? But after all I had to explain to you about that too."

Trim and correct, in a tailor-made that she wore only when coming into town, she stood there on the point of departure and held out her hand to say good-bye.

71   *The Committee for the Drafting of a Guiding Resolution with reference to the Jubilee Celebrations of the Seventieth Anniversary of His Majesty's Accession to the Throne opens its sessions.*

CLARISSE had not uttered a word about her letter to Count Leinsdorf and her demand that Ulrich should save Moosbrugger; she seemed to have forgotten all that. But Ulrich did not have a chance to remember it for some time either. For Diotima's preparations had at last reached such a stage that within the framework of the ' Enquiry as to the Drafting of a Guiding Resolution and the Ascertaining of the Wishes of all Participant Circles of the Population with reference to the Jubilee Celebrations of the Seventieth Anniversary of His Majesty's Accession to the Throne ' there could now be summoned a meeting of the special ' Committee for the Drafting of a Guiding Resolution with reference to the Jubilee Celebrations of the Seventieth Anniversary of His Majesty's Accession to the Throne ', chairmanship of which Diotima had reserved for herself personally. His Highness had himself composed the invitation, Tuzzi had gone over it, and Arnheim had been shown his emendations by Diotima before they were allowed to pass. For all that, it contained everything that occupied His Highness's mind.

" What brings us together in this gathering," so the text went, " is our agreement on the question that a mighty demonstration rising out of the midst of the people must not be left to chance, but calls for far-sighted influence from a quarter with a broad general view, in other words, an influence from above." Then followed the " almost unique celebration of the seventieth anniversary of an accession to a throne so rich in blessing ", the " gratefully thronging nations ", the Emperor of Peace, the lack of political maturity, the Universal-Austrian Year ; and finally there was the appeal to " culture and capital " to transform all this into a glorious demonstration of the " true " Austrian spirit but never-theless to give it their most cautious consideration.

From Diotima's lists of names the groups Art, Literature and Science had been formed and, after painstaking and exhaustive research, carefully enlarged ; then, however, of all those persons who had come under consideration as possibly suitable to be present at the event, although without being expected to take any active part in it, after the most thorough sifting only a very small number remained. Nevertheless, the number of those who received invitations was still so high that there could be no question of sitting round the green baize table in the orthodox manner, and the informal evening at-home with a cold buffet was the only alternative left. People sat or stood as arrangements permitted, and Diotima's rooms resembled the encampment of a spiritual army, which had to be supplied with sandwiches, cake, wine, liqueurs, and tea in quantities such as were only made possible by special subsidies that Tuzzi had granted his wife—without a word of protest, it must be added, from which it can be concluded that he had resolved to make use of new, intellectual methods of diplomacy.

The handling of these throngs, from the hostess's point of view, made great demands on Diotima, and she would perhaps have taken exception to a number of things had her head not resembled a superb fruit-bowl, a superabundance with the words continually brimming over the edge—words with which the lady of the house welcomed each arriving guest, delighting him with her detailed knowledge of his latest work. The preparations for this had been extraordinary, and it could not have been accomplished without the help of Arnheim, who had placed his private secretary at her disposal in order to arrange the material and make extracts of what was most important. The wonderful cinders of this fiery zeal were a large collection of books, acquired with the funds that Count Leinsdorf had provided for the starting of the Collateral Campaign, and these, together with Diotima's own books, were set up as the only decoration in the last one of the rooms that had been cleared of their usual furniture, its flowered wallpaper, in so far as it could still be seen at all, betraying the boudoir—a juxtaposition of unusual elements stimulating the beholder to flattering reflections about the fair owner. In another way as well, however, this assemblage of books turned out to be a profitable investment. For every one of the guests, after having received Diotima's gracious welcome, drifted irresolutely through the rooms and was unfailingly drawn to the wall of books at the far end as soon as he caught sight of it. There was always a throng of backs rising and sinking in scrutiny before it, like bees along a flowering hedge ; and even if the cause was only the noble curiosity that every creative person cherishes for collections of books, yet a sweet contentment entered into the very marrow when the beholder at last discovered his own works. This was good for the patriotic enterprise.

In the intellectual direction of this assembly Diotima at first let things go at their own sweet will, even though at the same time she made a point of assuring everyone, and the poets in particular, that fundamentally all life rested upon an inward poetry —even, indeed, the life of commerce, if one ' took the larger view ' of it. Nobody was startled by this, only it turned out that most of those distinguished by being addressed in such a manner had come in the conviction that they had been invited in order that they themselves might briefly—that is to say, in anything between five and forty-five minutes—give the Collateral Campaign some advice, following which it could not miss its way in future, even though subsequent speakers might waste time with pointless and mistaken suggestions. For a while this got Diotima into a positively tearful state of mind, and it was only with an effort that she could preserve her ease and calm of manner, for it seemed to her that everyone was saying something different, without her being able to find a common denominator for all of it. She had no experience as yet where such degrees of concentration of the Mind Beautiful were concerned, and since so universal a gathering of great men is not the sort of thing that happens every day, understanding of it could only be arrived at in a very laborious and methodical way, step by step.

There are, incidentally, many things in the world that singly mean something quite different to people from what they mean in the mass. For instance, water in excessive quantities is a pleasure less pleasing, by precisely the difference between drinking and drowning, than it is in small quantities. It is similar with poisons, amusements, leisure, piano music, and ideals, probably indeed with everything ; in other words, what a thing is depends entirely on the degree of its density and other conditions. So it must only be added that genius is no exception to this rule, lest anyone should see in the following impressions anything like depreciation of the distinguished personalities who had so selflessly put themselves at Diotima's disposal

For even at this first gathering one could not fail to have the impression that every great mind feels itself in an extremely unsafe position as soon as it leaves the shelter of its cliff-top eyrie and has to be comprehensible on common ground. The extraordinary eloquence that passed away over Diotima's head like a celestial event, as it were, so long as she was alone in conversation with one of the mighty, gave way to a painful inability to keep to the point as soon as a second or third of the mighty joined them and several speeches went on at cross-purposes with each other. (Anyone who does not shrink from such similes may think of a swan descending after its proud flight and moving along the ground.) However, on longer acquaintance even that becomes quite easy to understand. Nowadays the life of great minds rests on the principle of ' no one knows what for '. They enjoy great veneration, which manifests itself on their fiftieth to their hundredth birthday or on the occasion of celebrating the tenth anniversary of the founding of an agricultural college, which bedizens itself by conferring honorary degrees, but also on various other occasions when one is bound to hold forth about the treasures of the German mind. In the course of our history we have had great men, and we regard it as an institution that goes with us, just the same as prisons or the army : once it is there, someone has to be put into it. And so, with a certain automatism that is inherent in such social needs, one always takes whoever happens to be next and pays him whatever honours are ripe for bestowal. But this veneration is not quite genuine ; at the bottom of it lurks the familiar conviction that actually not a single one of them deserves it, and it is hard to be sure whether the mouths that open do so in enthusiasm or in a yawn. There is something of the cult of the dead about it these days when a man is referred to as a genius, with the unuttered supplementary remark that there really isn't such a thing any more ; and it is something like the hysterical love that makes a tremendous fuss for no other reason than that it lacks real feeling.

Such a state of things is, quite understandably, not agreeable to sensitive minds, and they try various ways of getting out of it. Some get rich in sheer despair, by learning to exploit the demand that there is, as it happens, not only for great minds, but also for wild men, sophisticated novelists, bulging children of Nature, and leaders of the new generation. Others wear on their heads an invisible royal crown, which they do not remove in any circumstances at all, and assure one, with embittered modesty, that they do not want any judgments passed on the value of their work for another three to ten centuries. All, however, feel it is a terrible tragedy for the German people that the really great men never become part of its living culture, since they are too far ahead.

It must be emphasised, all the same, that up to this point it is what is called the artistic creative mind that has been under discussion, for there is a very remarkable difference in the relations of different types of mind to the world. The artistic mind claims admiration of the same kind as that accorded to Goethe and Michelangelo, Napoleon and Luther. But scarcely anyone remembers even the name of the man who gave mankind the untold blessing of anaesthetics ; nobody probes into the lives of Gauss, Euler or Maxwell in the hope of finding a Frau von Stein ; and hardly a soul cares where Lavoisier and Cardanus were born and died. Instead, one learns about how their ideas and inventions were further developed by the ideas and inventions of other, equally uninteresting people, and one concentrates exclusively on their achievements, which live on in others long after the short-lived fire of the personality has burnt out. One is amazed in the first instant of perceiving how sharply this difference separates two kinds of human attitude ; but almost at once the counter-examples come into one's mind, and it begins to look like the most natural of all borderlines. Familiar habit assures us it is the borderline between the personality and the work, between the greatness of a man and that of a cause, between culture and knowledge, Humanity and Nature. Work and industrious genius do not increase moral greatness, or how *a man's a man for a' that* under the gaze of heaven, that indivisible and indefinable doctrine of life handed down only in examples, by statesmen, heroes, saints,

singers, and admittedly also by film-actors—that great irrational
power in which the poet feels he has his share too, so long as he
believes in his own words and holds fast to the thought that what
speaks out of him is, according to the circumstances of his life,
the inner voice, the voice of the blood, of the heart, of the nation,
of Europe, or of all mankind. He feels himself to be the instrument of the mysterious Whole, whereas the others are merely
grubbing about in what is tangible. And this mission of the
artistic mind is one that must be believed in before one can learn
to see it ! What assures us of all this is undoubtedly a voice of
truth. But is there not something strange adhering to this truth ?
For wherever less attention is paid to the personality than to the
cause there is, oddly enough, time and again a new personality
to carry the cause on ; on the other hand, wherever the personality
is what counts, after a certain height is reached the feeling occurs
that there is no longer any adequate personality there, and that
all that is truly great belongs to the past.

These were all integral men that had gathered at Diotima's,
each of them a Whole, and that was a great deal all at once.
Writing and thinking, something as natural to everyone else as
swimming is to a duckling, they practised as a profession, and,
what was more, they really were better at it than other people.
But what for ? What they did was beautiful and great and
unique, but the atmosphere of so much uniqueness was like that
of a graveyard, like the concentrated breath of transience, without
straightforward meaning and purpose, origin and continuation.
Innumerable reminiscences of experiences, myriads of criss-
crossing spiritual vibrations, were assembled inside these heads,
which were like a carpet-weaver's needles sticking in a web spread
out all around them, in front of them, and behind them, without
seam or border, and there, in some place or other, they were
working a pattern, which was repeated somewhere else very like
and yet just a little different. But is putting such a little patch
on the fabric of eternity making the proper use of oneself ?

It would probably be going much too far to say that Diotima
had understood this. But she felt the graveyard wind blowing
over the fields of the spirit, and the further this first day moved
on towards its end, the deeper she sank into despair. Luckily
she remembered a certain hopelessness to which Arnheim had

given utterance on another occasion, when such problems had been under discussion, and which she had not quite understood at the time. Her friend Arnheim was now away, but she thought of how he had warned her against setting too great hopes on·this gathering. And so it was actually this Arnheimian melancholy into which she was sinking, which did after all, in the long run, afford her a noble, almost sensually mournful and flattering sense of enjoyment. ' Isn't this fundamentally,' she wondered, musing over his prophecy, ' the pessimism that men and women of action always feel when they come into contact with those whose medium is words ? '

72 Science smiling into its beard, or first full-dress encounter with Evil.

A few words must now be said about a smile, a masculine smile at that, with a beard attached to it, whereby the general activity of smiling in one's sleeve was transposed into the masculine one of smiling into one's beard. It was the smiling of the men of science and learning who had accepted Diotima's invitation and were listening to the celebrated men of the arts. Although they smiled, it must on no account whatever be believed that they did so ironically. On the contrary, it was their way of expressing homage and incompetence, a matter that has already been mentioned. But one must not let oneself be deceived by that either. It was true enough where their conscious mind was concerned ; yet in their subconscious—to make use of this customary word—or, to put it more exactly, in the sum total of their being, they were people in whom a propensity to Evil crackled like the fire under a cauldron.

Now that, of course, looks like a paradoxical remark, and any professor at a university, if it were made in his presence, would presumably retort that he simply serves the cause of truth and progress and has no other concerns : for that is his professional ideology. But all professional ideologies are high-minded. Hunters, for instance, would not dream of calling themselves the butchers of the woods ; they prefer to call themselves the real friends of animals and Nature, just as business men uphold the principle of fair profit, and the god that thieves also take for their own is the business men's god, that distinguished promotor of international concord, Mercury. So not much importance need be attached to the way an activity is mirrored in the consciousness of those who practise it.

If one asks oneself in an unprejudiced way how science came to have its present-day aspect (which is in itself important, since after all it dominates us, not even an illiterate being safe from it, because he learns to live together with countless things that are born of science) one gets a quite different picture. According to credible traditions it was in the sixteenth century, an age of very intense spiritual emotions, that people gradually ceased trying, as they had been trying all through two thousand years of religious and philosophic speculation, to penetrate into the secrets of Nature, and instead contented themselves, in a way that can only be called superficial, with investigations of its surface. The great Galileo, who is always the first to be mentioned in this connection, did away with the problem, for instance, of the intrinsic reasons why Nature abhors a vacuum, so that it will cause a falling body to enter into and occupy space after space until it finally comes to rest on solid ground, and contented himself with a much more general observation : he simply established the speed at which such a body falls, what course it takes, what time it takes, and what its rate of acceleration is. The Catholic Church made a grave mistake in threatening this man with death and forcing him to recant, instead of exterminating him without more ado. For from his way of looking at things, and that of those whose outlook was similar, there sprang—in almost no time at all, if one applies historical measurements—railway time-tables, factory machines, physiological psychology, and the moral ruin of the present age, against which the Church no longer stands a chance. It probably made this mistake from an excess of shrewdness, for Galileo was, after all, not only the discoverer of the law of gravitation and of the earth's motion, but also an inventor in whom, as one would put it today, high finance took an interest; and he was, besides, not the only one at that time seized by the new spirit. On the contrary, the historical reports show that the matter-of-factness that inspired him spread and raged like an infection. And however disconcerting it may sound today to speak of anyone's being inspired with matter-of-factness, when we think we have too much of it already, at that time the awakening out of metaphysics to clear-cut scrutiny of things must, to judge by all the evidence, have been an out-and-out intoxication, a very fire of matter-of-factness!

But if one asks oneself why humanity took it into its head to change in this manner, the answer is that all it was doing was what every sensible child does when it has tried to walk too soon: it sat down on the ground, making the contact with a dependable and not really dignified part of the body, in other words, precisely the part on which one does sit. And the remarkable thing is that the earth has shown itself uncommonly susceptible, and since that contact took place has let inventions, conveniences and discoveries be wormed out of it in downright miraculous quantities.

After such a history one might think, and not quite without justification, it was the miracle of the Anti-Christ that we find ourselves in the midst of now. For the 'contact' simile that has just been used is to be interpreted with reference not only to the dependability of the part of the body that is involved, but also to its aspect of the unseemly and taboo. The point is, before intellectual man discovered his delight in facts, the only people who had such a delight were warriors, hunters and merchants, that is to say, the people whose nature it was to be cunning and violent. In the struggle for existence there are no philosophical sentimentalities, but only the wish to kill off one's opponent by the shortest and most practical method. There everyone is a positivist. Nor would it be a virtue, in commerce, to let oneself be taken in instead of putting one's trust in solid facts, profit being in the last resort a psychological vanquishing of one's opponent, arising out of the particular circumstances. However, if one investigates what qualities it is that lead to discoveries, what one finds is freedom from traditional scruples and inhibitions, courage, as much initiative as destructive spirit, the exclusion of moral considerations, patient bargaining for the smallest advantage, dogged endurance on the way to the goal, if necessary, and a veneration for measure and number amounting to the most acute mistrust of all uncertainty ; in other words, one sees nothing but the old hunter's, soldier's and merchant's vices, simply transposed into intellectual terms and re-interpreted as virtues. And though by this means they are raised above the urge for personal and comparatively vulgar advantage, yet the element of primal Evil, as it might be called, is something they do not lose even in undergoing this transformation. It is apparently indestructible and eternal, or at least as eternal as everything humanly sublime, since it consists in nothing less, nothing other, than the pleasure of tripping that sublimity up and watching it fall flat on its face. Who does not know the malicious temptation—when contemplating a beautifully glazed vase, all voluptuous curves—that lies in the thought that one could smash it to smithereens with a single blow of one's stick ? Intensified into the heroically bitter realisation that one cannot rely on anything in life except what is clinched and riveted, it is a basic emotion enclosed within the soberness of science, and even if, for reasons of respect, one does not want to call it the Devil, the fact remains that it brings with it a faint whiff of brimstone.

One can begin at once with scientific thinking's curious preference for mechanical, statistical, material explanations that have, as it were, the heart cut out of them. Regarding goodness as only a particular form of egoism ; relating emotions to internal secretions ; asserting that man is eight or nine tenths water ; explaining the character's celebrated moral freedom as an automatically evolved philosophical appendix of free trade ; reducing beauty to a matter of good digestion and well-developed fat-tissue ; reducing procreation and suicide to annual curves, showing what seems to be the result of absolute free will as a matter of compulsion ; feeling that ecstasy and mental derangement are akin ; putting anus and mouth on one level, as the rectal and oral ends of one and the same thing—such ideas, which, in a manner of speaking, lay bare the sleight of hand in the conjuring-trick of human illusion, always meet with something like a prejudice in their favour, which allows them to pass as particularly scientific.

Admittedly, it is truth that one so loves here. But all round this shining love is a partiality for disillusion, compulsion, inexorability, cold intimidation and dry reproof, a malicious partiality or at least an involuntary emotional radiation of this kind.

In short, the voice of truth has a suspicious undertone of 'interference', but those most closely concerned pretend they don't hear it. Now, modern psychology is acquainted with many such suppressed undertones, or 'interferences', and is ready with the advice that one should haul them out and make them as clear to oneself as possible, in order to prevent their having harmful effects. How would it be, then, if one were to put it to the test and give way to the temptation to bring that ambiguous taste for truth, and its malign undertones of misanthropy and hell-houndishness, out into public view, as it were trustfully bringing it forth into the world? Well, what would come out is pretty much the same lack of idealism that has already been described under the heading of the Utopian idea of exact living, an outlook based on experiment and revocation, but subject to the iron laws of warfare involved in all intellectual conquests. Of course, this attitude to the conduct of life by no means tends towards preserving and appeasing. Instead of regarding all that is endowed with the dignity of life merely with respect, it would look on it as a line of demarcation constantly getting shifted about in the battle for inner truth. It would question the sanctity of the state the world is in at any particular moment, not from scepticism, but because of being in the attitude of climbing, where the foot that has the firm hold is always the lower one. And in the fire of such a Church Militant, hating the teaching for the sake of a revelation that has not yet taken place, and thrusting aside law and tradition in the name of an exacting love for the next form they are to assume, the Devil would find his way back to God, or, to put it more simply, then Truth would once again be Virtue's sister and no longer have to commit against it the covert acts of malice that a young niece plots against an elderly maiden aunt.

Now, all this is more or less consciously absorbed by a young man in the lecture-halls of knowledge, where he also picks up the elements of a great constructive outlook, which with the greatest of ease can associate things as remote from each other as a falling stone and a revolving star and dissect something that is seemingly one and indivisible, like a simple action's origin in the centres of consciousness, into currents whose inner sources are thousands of years apart from each other. But if someone took it into his head, after so acquiring such an outlook, to make use of it outside the limits of specialised professional tasks, it would instantly be made plain to him that life's requirements are different from those of thought. What happens in life is, roughly speaking, the opposite of what the trained mind is accustomed to. In life the natural differences and likenesses are very highly esteemed. Whatever exists—be it what it may—is to a certain extent felt to be natural, and there is a disinclination to tamper with it. The changes that become necessary only come about slowly and as though trundling first this way and then that. And if someone were, from a pure vegetarian conviction, to say ' ma'am ' to a cow (bearing in mind that one is much more likely to behave inconsiderately to a being that one addresses as ' hi, you ! ') he would be regarded as a prig, if not a madman—but not on account of his animal-loving or vegetarian convictions, which are considered highly humane, but on account of their being directly applied to reality. In short, there is an elaborate compromise between the mind and life, one in which the mind gets at the most one half per thousand of its claims paid up, and to make up for that is awarded the title of creditor *honoris causa*.

But if the mind, in its most recent mighty form, is, as was assumed a short way back, a very masculine saint with the secondary vices of the warrior and the hunter, one might be justified in concluding from the circumstances described that its inherent tendency towards depravity can nowhere come out in all its magnificent completeness and has no chance to purify itself through contact with reality, so that it is likely to be found on all sorts of thoroughly queer, unsupervised roads along which it escapes from its barren captivity. It may be left open whether everything hitherto has been a game with illusions. But undeniably this last surmise is in its own peculiar way confirmed. There is a nameless attitude to life that quite a number of people have in their blood these days, an awareness of the greater evil, a readiness to riot, a mistrust of everything one respects. There are people who complain about youth's lack of ideals, but who, in the moment when they must act, automatically come to the same decision as anyone who, from a very healthy mistrust of ideas, reinforces their gentle power with a blackjack. Is there, in other words, any one pious aim that would not have to provide itself with just a shade of corruption and a reckoning with the lower human qualities in order to pass, in this world, as serious and seriously intended ? Expressions like ' tie down ', ' force ', ' put the screws on ', ' not shrink from stepping on a few toes ', and ' take strong measures ' have a pleasant ring of reliability. Such notions as that the greatest of minds, put on the barrack-square, will inside a week have learnt to move at the double at the sound of the sergeant-major's voice, or that a lieutenant and eight men suffice to arrest any parliament of orators in the world, did, admittedly, only later find their classical expression in the discovery that a few spoonfuls of castor oil, poured down an idealist's throat, can make the staunchest of convictions ridiculous ; but although they were indignantly banished from sight, they had already long had the wild buoyancy of sinister dreams.

The fact of the matter nowadays is that the second thought, at least, of every one confronted with an overwhelming phenomenon —and even if it is the beauty of it that overwhelms him—is : ' You needn't think you can take me in ! I'll soon put you in your place ! ' This frenzied determination to get things down into their places and make them smaller—typical of this epoch, which is not only cunning as a fox but runs with the hounds as well—is hardly as yet life's natural division into the crude and the sublime ; it is, rather, a self-tormenting feature of the mind, an unspeakable enjoyment of the spectacle of how the good can be humiliated and how wonderfully easily it can be destroyed. It looks not unlike a frantic way of trying to give oneself the lie. Perhaps, indeed, it is not so dismal after all to have faith in an epoch that has come into the world buttocks first and only needs the Creator's hand to turn it up the other way.

Well, then, a masculine smile will express many things of such a kind, even if it escapes self-observation or even never passes through the consciousness at all ; and this was the nature of the smile with which most of the celebrated specialists who had been invited to Diotima's adjusted themselves to her laudable exertions.

It was a tickling sensation climbing up the legs, which did not rightly know in what direction they ought to turn here, and it ended its journey in the face as a benevolent expression of wonderment. Everyone was glad when he caught sight of an acquaintance or a fairly close colleague and could go up and speak to him. There was a general feeling that on leaving, passing through the door, one would take a few experimental steps, bringing one's foot down smartly to see if one kept one's balance. Still, it was all very nice, of course. Such enterprises of a general nature are naturally something that never gets a real content, just like all very general and very lofty concepts. Even ' dog ' is something no one can imagine ; it is only a token of particular dogs and doggy qualities. And patriotism or the most splendid patriotic idea is still more impossible to imagine. But even if it has no content, it has a meaning all right, and it is certainly a good thing to quicken that meaning into life from time to time. This was the drift of most of the talk here, although the actual words remained unuttered, in the silence of the unconscious.

But Diotima, who was still standing in the chief receptionroom and bestowing little speeches on late-comers, hearing lively conversations starting up all around her, was astounded to catch now and then, even though indistinctly, scraps of what, if she was not utterly mistaken, were discussions about the difference between Bohemian and Bavarian beer or on the subject of publishers and royalties.

It was a pity that she could not also watch her reception from the street. From out there it looked wonderful. The light gleamed brightly through the curtains of the high windows along the front of the house, the glory of it all intensified by the nimbus of authority and distinction that the waiting carriages and motorcars lent to the scene, and by the gaping of idle passers-by who stopped and looked up for a while, without quite knowing why. It would have pleased Diotima if she could have seen it. There were always people standing in the half-light that this festivity cast out upon the street; and behind their backs the great darkness began and only a short distance further on rapidly became impenetrable.

END OF VOLUME ONE

Robert Musil
The Man Without Qualities
Vol. II: £3.95; **Vol. III:** £4.95

'The only writer in any language as exciting as Proust' ELIAS CANETTI

A vast and complex novel of ideas – funny and disturbing by turns.

Vienna at the eve of World War I: the Austro-Hungarian Empire totters
disastrously. How can Ulrich, the Man Without Qualities, or any individual,
find a link between himself and a society which has less and less place for
everything the individual represents? Ulrich has, in fact, qualities in
abundance; but faced with the unrealities and idiocies of life around him, he
decides to stand aside and drift with the tide. Meanwhile Moosbrugger, the
amiable psychopath, sits in jail awaiting trial for the murder of a prostitute –
he is the ominous savage, never far from the surface of civilized behaviour,
the harbinger of catastrophe . . .

'Glorious fun' JOHN LEHMANN

'One of the very few great comic writers of this century' PHILIP TOYNBEE

'A wonderful and prolonged firework display' V. S. PRITCHETT

and intimidated by the general prejudice. Indeed, it was even bound to happen that, contending with the increasingly marked incompatibility of herself and her husband—and when, for reasons that he would never properly account for, he did not climb higher than the rank of manager and lost all prospect of ever becoming a real director—she came to explain many things that wounded her by assuming, with a shrug of the shoulders, that Leo's character was after all alien to her own, even if, where outsiders were concerned, she would never yield an inch of the principles of her youth.

This incompatibility consisted fundamentally, of course, in nothing but a lack of harmony, as in many marriages, where an as it were natural unhappiness comes to the surface as soon as the bedazzlement of happiness wears off. Since Leo's career had slowed up and he had got stuck at the position of head of the stock office, Klementine was no longer able to excuse certain of his peculiarities by telling herself that after all he did not sit in the mirror-stillness of an old ministerial office, but at the ' whirring loom of time '—and who knows whether she had not married him precisely on the strength of that quotation from Goethe ? His side-whiskers, which, combined with the pince-nez perched on the middle of his nose, had in those days seemed reminiscent of a Dundreary-whiskered English lord, now suggested a stockbroker, and certain habits of his, certain gestures and turns of phrase, began to be positively unendurable to her. Klementine at first tried to reform her husband. But she came up against extra-ordinary difficulties ; for it turned out there was nowhere in the world any criterion of whether Dundreary whiskers were reminiscent of a lord or of a broker and at what precise place on a nose a pince-nez combined with a wave of the hand to be expressive of enthusiasm or cynicism. Apart from that, however, Leo Fischel was not at all the man to let himself be reformed. He declared that this fault-finding, which was aimed at turning him into a civil servant's Germanico-Christian beau-ideal, was mere social faddiness, and he refused to listen to her disquisitions, as unworthy of a rational man. And the more his wife objected to certain details, the more he emphasised the great guiding-lines of reason. So the Fischel household was gradually transformed into a field of battle between two different attitudes to life.

discomfort that had been inflicted on him must be connected
with Arnheim. He slept through till morning in anger, as it
were, and woke up with the firm resolve to get himself a clear
picture of this intruder.

51   *Fischel and his family.*

DIRECTOR Fischel of Lloyd's Bank was that bank-director, or,
more accurately, manager with the title of director, who had
forgotten, for reasons at first incomprehensible, to answer Count
Leinsdorf's invitation and afterwards had not received another.
Even that first invitation he owed only to the connections of his
wife, Klementine. Klementine Fischel came from an old civil-
service family ; her father had been Auditor General, her grandfather had been a *Kameralrat*, and three of her brothers held
high positions in their respective ministries. Twenty-four years
earlier she had married Leo for two reasons : first of all because
the families of high civil servants sometimes have more children
than means, but secondly, too, out of romanticism, because in
contrast with the meticulously thrifty narrowness of her parental
home banking appeared to her a latitudinarian, essentially modern
vocation, and in the nineteenth century a cultivated person did
not judge another person's value according to whether he was
a Jew or a Catholic—indeed, as things were then she practically
felt there was something particularly cultivated in disregarding
the crude anti-semitic prejudice of the common people.

Later the poor woman found a spirit of nationalism welling up
all over Europe, and with it a surge of hostility to Jews, which
transformed her husband, so to speak in her arms, from a respected
liberalist into a member of a destructively analytical-minded alien
race. At first she had rebelled against this with all the wrath of
' a great heart ' ; but with the passing of the years she was worn
down by the naïvely cruel and continually extending hostility

armed force or by using the military against strikers. But it is along this road that business leads to philosophy (for it is only criminals who presume to damage other people nowadays without the aid of philosophy). And so they became accustomed to regarding Arnheim junior as a kind of papal legate in their affairs. For all the irony with which they regarded his tastes, it was agreeable to them to possess, in him, a man who was capable of presenting their case just as well to a conclave of bishops as to a sociologists' congress ; indeed he finally gained an influence over them similar to that exercised by a beautiful and intellectual wife, who looks down on the everlasting office work but is useful to the business because she is admired by one and all. Now, one only needs to imagine the effect of Maeterlinckian or Bergsonian philosophy when applied to the problems of the price of coal or cartelisation policy in order to estimate how depressingly the younger Arnheim's presence could affect industrialists' conferences and directorial meetings in Paris, say, or in Petersburg, or in Cape Town, the moment he appeared there as his father's ambassador and had to be heard out, from the beginning to the end. The results, where business was concerned, were as great as they were mysterious ; and out of it all there arose the well-known legend of the surpassing greatness of the man and his lucky hand.

Much else of the same kind could be told of Arnheim's successes ; for instance with diplomats, who approached the important, though to them alien, realm of commerce with the caution of men who have been given the care of a not entirely reliable elephant, while he treated it with the careless unconcern of a native keeper ; and with artists, to whom he was seldom of any use, in spite of which they contrived to feel that they were dealing with a Maecenas ; and with journalists, who should really have the first claim to be mentioned, because it was they with their admiration who first made a great man of Arnheim, without noticing that this was putting things back to front, for once having got this bee in their bonnet, they were deceived by the buzzing of it into believing they could hear the grass of time growing . . .

The fundamental pattern of his success was everywhere the same. Surrounded by the magical halo of his wealth and the legend of his importance, he always had to associate with people who towered over him in their own field, but who took a fancy to him as an outsider with a surprising knowledge of their special subject and were intimidated by the fact that in his person he represented connections between their world and other worlds of which they had no idea at all. So it had become second nature with him, in a gathering of very specialised men, to appear as one who was complete, both as a man and as an entity. At times he had imaginative glimmerings of a kind of Weimarian or Florentine epoch of industry and commerce, an epoch under the leadership of strong personalities who would increase prosperity, who would have to be capable of combining in themselves the individual achievements of the technical, scientific and artistic realms and of guiding developments from an exalted standpoint. He felt in himself the capacity to do this. He possessed the gift of never being superior in any detail, in anything that could be put to the test, but of always coming to the top in every situation, by means of a fluid, perpetually self-restoring equilibrium. This may perhaps really be the fundamental makings of a politician, but Arnheim was convinced, besides, that it was a profound mystery. He called it 'the Mystery of the Whole'. For even a person's beauty consists of almost nothing that is detail and can be put to the test, but is that magical something that even turns little defects to good account; and in exactly the same way the profound goodness and love, the dignity and greatness of a human being are almost independent of what he does, indeed they are capable of ennobling everything he does. In some mysterious way the whole counts for more in life than the details do. So although small people may be made up of their virtues and faults, the great man is he who himself endows his qualities with their rank. And if it is the secret of his success that it cannot quite be explained by any of his merits or any of his qualities, the fact is that the presence of a force greater than any single one of its manifestations is the mystery on which all the greatness in life finally rests. This was the way in which Arnheim described it in one of his books; and when he wrote this down, he almost believed he had caught the supernatural by the hem of its cloak, and let as much become apparent in the text.

will feel obliged to utter a reminder of the connection between the kidneys and the nation as a whole. That is why Goethe is so much quoted in Germany. But if an academic personage wishes to make it particularly evident that he possesses not only learning but also a mind that is alive and joyfully aware of the possibilities the future holds, he will best prove his claim by referring to writings acquaintance with which not only reflects honour at the moment but also promises more honour, like bonds that are going up in value ; and in such cases quotations from Paul Arnheim enjoyed increasing popularity. The expeditions that he undertook into the territory of the sciences in order to support his general ideas did not, frankly, always satisfy the strictest demands. They did doubtless show an easy command of great reading ; but the specialist unfailingly found in them those little errors and misunderstandings that enable one to recognise a dilettante's work, as surely as a dress made by the sewing-woman who comes to the house by the day can be distinguished from one made by a real *couturier*. However, it must by no means be thought that this prevented the specialists from admiring Arnheim. They smiled complacently. He impressed them as something utterly modern, as a man of whom there was talk in all the newspapers, a king of commerce, one whose achievements, compared with the intellectual achievements of more ancient kings, were certainly outstanding ; and if they had occasion to observe that they themselves did, after all, represent something rather different in their own field from what he did, they proved themselves grateful for that by calling him a man of great brilliance, of genius, or quite simply a man with an all-round mind, which among specialists amounts to much the same as when men among themselves say of a woman that women think her good-looking.

The third source of Arnheim's fame lay in commerce. He did not do too badly with those old salts, the seasoned captains of industry ; when he had a big deal to bring off, he did down even the most wide-awake of them. As a matter of fact, they did not think much of him as a business man and called him ' the Crown Prince ', to distinguish him from his father, whose short thick tongue was not mobile enough to talk with ease but made up for that by picking up the subtlest taste of anything like business for miles around.   Him they feared and revered.   But when they heard of the philosophic demands that the Crown Prince made on business men as such, and even wove into the most matter-of-fact discussions, they could not help smiling.   He was notorious for quoting the poets at board-meetings and insisting that commerce was something that could not be kept apart from all other human activities, that ought, indeed, to be considered only in the larger context of all the problems of national life, including the life of the mind and indeed even of the spirit itself.   And yet, even though they smiled at these things, they could not entirely fail to see that it was precisely the fact that Arnheim junior adorned business with these trimmings that made him of steadily increasing interest to public opinion.   News of him appeared now in the financial, now in the political, now in the literary and artistic columns of the leading newspapers of all nations : a review of a book that he had written, a report of a noteworthy speech that he had made somewhere, news of his having been received by some ruler or some art association.   And in the circle of great industrial magnates, who for the most part operate in silence behind double-locked doors, there was soon no man of whom there was so much talk outside as there was of him.   And it must not be thought that the presidents, chairmen of boards of directors, governors, directors, or managers of banks, concerns, mines, and shipping companies were at heart the bad men that they are often represented as being.   Apart from their very highly developed family sense, the inner reason of their life is money ; and it is a kind of reason with very strong teeth and a hearty digestion.   They were all convinced that the world would be much better if it were simply left to the free play of supply and demand, instead of being run with the help of men-o'-war, bayonets, potentates and financial ignoramuses of diplomats. But the world being what it is, and there being an old prejudice to the effect that a life that primarily promotes one's own and only secondarily and indirectly the public advantage is less estimable than chivalry and loyalty to the State, and public commissions ranking, as they do, morally higher than private ones, they were the last people not to reckon with all this ; and it is well known that they made thoroughly sound use of the advantages to the public welfare offered by customs negotiations backed up by

helpless in the face of the external authority of the police-sergeant. At last, however, he glimpsed a possibility of saving the situation. Although, when he was asked his occupation and made the statement " independent " (he could not have brought himself to say he was ' engaged in independent research ') the gaze he felt fixed on him was still of exactly the sort that might have been expected if he had said ' of no settled abode ', when his father's status was enquired into and it appeared that he was a member of the Upper House, the gaze underwent a transformation. It was still mistrustful, but something about it at once gave Ulrich a feeling such as a man tossed to and fro by the ocean waves might have when his big toe scrapes on solid ground.

With rapidly awakening presence of mind he turned this to account. He instantly modified everything he had so far admitted ; he confronted this authority, these ears that had heard it all in their capacity as ears under official oath, with the insistent request that he should be interrogated by the superintendent himself ; and, when this merely caused a smile, he lied—with an utterly natural air, quite casually, and prepared to go back on the assertion immediately in the event of its being knotted into the noose of a demand for precise details—saying that he was a friend of Count Leinsdorf's and secretary to the great patriotic Campaign of which everyone had doubtless read in the newspapers. He at once observed that this produced the graver state of thoughtfulness as to his person that had up to now been denied him, and he held on to his advantage.

The result was that the sergeant eyed him wrathfully, for he did not want to take the responsibility either of detaining this catch any longer or of letting it go ; and because at this hour there was no higher official in the building, he resorted to a way out that was a handsome testimonial to the fact that he, a simple sergeant, had learnt something of the way in which his superiors handled awkward cases. He put on an important air and expressed grave surmises as to how Ulrich seemed to be not only guilty of having insulted an officer of the law and of having interfered with the execution of his duty, but, worse still, considering the position he claimed to hold, also came under suspicion of being involved in obscure and perhaps political machinations, for which reason he must take the consequences of being handed over to the political department at police head-quarters.

So a few minutes later Ulrich was driving through the night in a cab that he had been permitted to take, at his side a plain-clothes man who was little disposed to conversation. As they approached headquarters, Ulrich saw the windows on the first floor festively illumined, for there was an important conference still going on at this late hour in the office of the President of Police himself. The building was far from being a dim and gloomy hole; it quite resembled a ministry. He began to breathe more familiar air. He soon noticed, too, that the officer on night-duty, to whom he was brought, was quick to see the foolishness committed by the exasperated peripheral arm in arresting him. Nevertheless, it seemed utterly inadvisable to release from the clutches of the law anyone who had been so reckless as to run into them of his own accord. The officer here at headquarters also wore an iron machine in his face and assured the prisoner that his rashness made it appear extremely difficult to warrant his release. Ulrich had already twice gone over every-thing that had such a favourable effect on the sergeant, but where this higher-ranking officer was concerned it was all in vain. He was beginning to give himself up for lost, when all at once a remarkable, almost happy change occurred in the expression of the man in whose hands his fate lay. He read the charge again carefully, asked Ulrich for his name once more, made sure of his address and then very civilly asked him to wait a moment, where-upon he left the room.

It was ten minutes before he returned, looking like a man who had recollected something pleasant, and with marked courtesy invited the prisoner to follow him. At the door of a room where light was burning, a storey higher, he said no more than: " The President of Police wishes to speak to you personally ", and the next moment Ulrich stood before a gentleman with the mutton-chop whiskers that had lately become familiar to him, who had just come in from the conference-room next door.

He was determined to explain his presence as a mistake on the part of the district station, and in a tone of gentle reproach. But the President anticipated him, greeting him with the words: " A misunderstanding, my dear Herr von ——, the Inspector

has already told me all about it.   All the same, we must impose
a little penalty, for——" and with these words he looked at him
roguishly (in so far as the word ' roguish ' can at all be applied
to the most exalted of police officials), as though he wanted him
to solve the riddle himself.

But Ulrich entirely failed to guess.

" His Highness ! " the President helped him on.   " His Highness Count Leinsdorf," he added, " just a few hours ago came
to me, enquiring for you most anxiously."

Ulrich only half understood this.

" You are not in the directory, my dear Herr von ——," the
President explained in a tone of jesting reproach, as though that
were Ulrich's only offence.

Ulrich bowed, smiling formally.

" I gather that you must call upon His Highness tomorrow on
a matter of great public importance, and I cannot take it upon
myself to prevent you from doing so by incarcerating you."   In
this manner the master of the iron machine concluded his little
joke.

It may be assumed that the President would also in any other
case have considered the arrest wrongful and that the Inspector,
who happened to recollect the connection in which Ulrich's
name had come up for the first time in this building a few hours
earlier, had represented the incident to the President in such a
way that the President was bound to come to this conclusion : in
other words, no one had arbitrarily interfered with the course of
events.   His Highness, by the way, never learnt how it all came
about.   Ulrich felt obliged to call on him on the day after this
evening of *lèse-majesté*, and on this occasion was at once appointed
honorary secretary to the great patriotic Campaign.   Count
Leinsdorf, had he known how it all came about, would not have
been able to say anything but that it was like a miracle.

41   *Rachel and Diotima.*

SHORTLY afterwards the patriotic Campaign's first great committee meeting was held at Diotima's.

The dining-room next to the drawing-room had been transformed into a conference-room. The dining-table, extended to its full length and covered with green baize, occupied the middle of the room. Sheets of ivory-white hand-made paper and pencils of various degrees of hardness were laid in each place. The sideboard had been removed. The corners of the room were empty and austere. The walls were awe-inspiringly bare except for a portrait of His Majesty, which Diotima had hung up, and that of a lady with a wasp waist, which was only something that Herr Tuzzi had once brought home from somewhere when he was a consul, but which could just as well be taken for the portrait of an ancestress. Diotima really would have liked to put a crucifix at the head of the table, as a finishing touch, but Permanent Secretary Tuzzi had laughed her out of it before discreetly absenting himself from his house for the day.

For the Collateral Campaign was to be inaugurated quite privately. No ministers or official bigwigs were asked. There were no politicians either. This was intentional ; for the beginning only a small, select circle was to meet, composed of selfless servants of the Idea : the Governor of the National Bank, Herr von Holtzkopf and Baron Wisnieczky, several ladies belonging to the high nobility, well-known figures associated with the city's charitable and welfare organisations, and, faithful to the Leinsdorfian principle of ' Capital and Culture ', representatives of the universities, of the academies of arts, of industry, of the old hereditary landowners, and of the Church. The government departments were represented by inconspicuous young officials who fitted into this circle socially and who enjoyed the confidence of their chiefs. The constitution of the meeting was in keeping with the wishes of Count Leinsdorf, whose idea, it will be remembered, was a demonstration rising spontaneously from the midst of the people, but who, after his experience of reformist enthusiasm, felt it was after all a great relief to know whom one was dealing with.

The little maid Rachel (whose name her mistress somewhat fancifully translated into the French Rachelle) had been up since six o'clock that morning. She had extended the big dining-table, pushed two card-tables up to it, spread green baize, and dusted with special care, performing each of these tedious operations in a state of rapture. The evening before Diotima had said to her : " History may be made in this house tomorrow," and Rachel's whole body glowed with happiness at being an inmate of a house where such an event could take place—and this said a great deal for the event, for Rachel's body, under its little black dress, was as exquisite as Meissen porcelain.

Rachel was nineteen years old and believed in miracles. She had been born in a squalid cabin in Galicia, where the *mesusa* was nailed to the door-post and the earth came up through cracks in the floorboards. She had been cursed and turned out of doors. Her mother had looked on with a helpless expression, and her brothers and sisters had grinned timidly. She had knelt there, pleading, and shame had nearly choked her ; but it had all been of no avail. A young fellow without any conscience had seduced her, she no longer knew how. She had had to give birth to the child in the house of strangers, and then she had left the country. She had travelled far, and under the dirty cart in which she travelled despair bowled along with her. Empty of tears, she saw the capital, to which some instinct had driven her on her flight, only as a vast brick wall, red as flames, that she wanted to fling herself at and so die. But—oh, true miracle !— this wall divided and let her in. Since then Rachel had always felt as though she were living at the heart of a red-gold flame. Chance had brought her to Diotima's house ; and Diotima found running away from under one's parents' roof in Galicia very natural if it brought one to her. After they had got to know each other well she sometimes talked to the little thing about the famous and highly placed people who came to the house where ' Rachelle ' enjoyed the privilege of waiting on them ; and she had even told her something about the Collateral Campaign, for the joy of seeing how Rachel's starry eyes flashed as she listened, like golden mirrors radiantly reflecting her mistress's image.

Although little Rachel had been cursed by her father because of a young fellow without any conscience, she was a respectable girl, and she loved simply everything about Diotima : the soft, dark hair that she was allowed to brush morning and evening, the dresses that she helped her into, the Chinese lacquer-work and the little carved Indian tables, the books in foreign languages that lay about and of which she did not understand a word. . . . She loved Herr Tuzzi too, and of late the nabob who had visited her mistress on the second (she made it into the first) day after his arrival.   Rachel had stared at him in the hall in such rapturous excitement as at the Christians' Saviour stepping down from His golden shrine ; and the only thing that marred her delight was that he had not brought his Soliman with him to do homage to her mistress.

But today, so close to an event of world importance, she was convinced that something must happen for her too, and she assumed that this time Soliman would probably accompany his master, as the solemnity of the occasion demanded.   This expectation was however by no means the main point, but only the proper entanglement, the complication of the plot, the amorous intrigue never missing from any of the novels on which she was educating herself.   For Rachel was allowed to read the novels that Diotima had finished with, just as she was also allowed to cut down and alter for herself the underclothes that Diotima no longer wore.   Rachel sewed and read fluently—that was her Jewish heritage—but when she had a novel in her hand that Diotima had pointed out to her as a great work of art—and it was these that she was fondest of reading—then she naturally understood the events only as one watches lively happenings from a great distance or in a strange country : she was absorbed in and deeply moved by performances unintelligible to her, without being able to intervene in any way, and this was something she loved especially.   In the same way, when she was sent out on an errand or when distinguished visitors came to the house, she enjoyed the grand and exciting demeanour of an imperial city, an abundance of brilliant details surpassing all understanding, of which she partook simply through being in a privileged place in the midst of it all.   She did not in the least want to understand it any better.   Her elementary Jewish education, the wise maxims heard at home, she had angrily forgotten; and she had as little need of them as a flower has need of spoon and fork in order to nourish itself with the juices of the earth and the air.

So now she collected all the pencils once again and carefully put their gleaming points into the little machine fixed to the corner of the table, which, when one turned the handle, peeled the wood off so perfectly that on a repetition of the process not even the tiniest chip fell. Then she put the pencils back beside the velvet-soft sheets of paper, three different ones in each place, and thought about how this perfect machine, which she was allowed to work, had come from the Ministry of Foreign Affairs and of the Imperial House, brought by a messenger from there the previous evening, and the pencils and the paper too.

It was now seven o'clock. Rachel cast a swift strategic glance over all the details of the arrangement and hurried out of the room to wake Diotima, for the meeting was to begin at a quarter past ten and Diotima had stayed in bed a little longer after the master had left the house.

These mornings with Diotima were Rachel's particular joy. The word 'love' does not describe it; the words 'selfless veneration' meet the case better, implying as they do that a person can be so filled with profound respect and devotion to the depths of his innermost being that there is no more room left for himself. Since her adventure at home Rachel had a baby girl, who was now eighteen months old, and regularly, on every first Sunday of the month, she took a large part of her wages to the foster-mother, on which occasion she also saw her daughter; but although she did not neglect her duty as a mother, she saw it only as a punishment incurred in the past, and her feelings had again become those of a girl whose chaste body has not yet been opened by love.

She went up to Diotima's bed, and, adoring as that of a mountaineer who catches sight of the snowy peak rising out of the darkness of dawn into the early blue, her gaze glided over Diotima's shoulder before she touched the mother-of-pearly, delicate, warm skin with her fingers. Then she savoured the subtly mingled aroma of the hand that crept out sleepily from under the bedclothes to be kissed, smelling of the previous day's scent, but also of the vapours of the night's sleep.   She held out the morning slipper for the groping, naked foot and met the awakening gaze. But the sensual contact with that magnificent female body would not have been so wonderful for her, by far, had it not been irradiated though and through by Diotima's moral significance.

" Have you put the chair with the arms in His Highness's place ? And the little silver bell in mine ? Have you put out twelve sheets of paper for the secretary ? And six pencils, Rachelle, six, not merely three, in his place ? "   That was what Diotima said this morning.

At each of these questions Rachel inwardly ticked off on her fingers all that she had done, a shock of excitement and ambition going through her as though a life were at stake.   Her mistress had thrown on a dressing-gown and now went into the committee-room.   Her way of training ' Rachelle ' consisted in reminding her, in connection with everything she did or left undone, that one must never merely consider it one's personal affair, but always think of its general significance.   If Rachel broke a glass, then ' Rachelle ' was told that the damage in itself was quite insignificant, but that transparent glass was a symbol of the little everyday duties that the eye scarcely perceived because it liked to gaze at higher things, and so for that very reason it was to these little everyday duties that one must pay particular attention.   And under such ministerially courteous treatment the tears would come into Rachel's eyes while she was sweeping up the fragments, tears of remorse and happiness.   Cooks, from whom Diotima expected correct thinking and recognition of past errors, had changed often enough since Rachel had been in service here ; but Rachel herself loved this wonderful phraseology from the bottom of her heart, just as she loved the Emperor, funerals, and the twinkling candles in the gloom of Catholic churches.   Now and then she told a lie in order to get herself out of a scrape, but afterwards she always felt very wicked.   Perhaps indeed she was fond of small lies, because in telling them she felt all her own badness in comparison with Diotima ; but in general she only told them when she hoped to be able secretly and swiftly to transform a falsehood into truth.

It sometimes happens when one human being looks up to another like this in all things, in all ways, that his body is, as it were, drawn out of its own orbit and plunges like a little meteorite into the sun of the other body.

Diotima had found nothing to criticise and had amiably patted her little maid on the shoulder. Then they both went into the bath-room and began the toilet for the great day. When Rachel tested the water for the right heat, lathered soap and was permitted to rub Diotima's body down with the bath-towel as hardily as though it had been her own body, it gave her much more pleasure than if it had really been merely her own body. For her own, it seemed to her, was base and untrustworthy, and she was far from thinking of it even by way of comparison. When she touched Diotima's statuesque fullness, her feelings were like those of a yokel who is a raw recruit in a brilliantly dashing regiment.

Thus was Diotima girded for the great day.

42   *The great conference.*

WHEN the last minute swung over to the appointed hour, Count Leinsdorf appeared, accompanied by Ulrich. Rachel, already glowing because visitors had been arriving ceaselessly and she had all the time been opening the door to them and helping them out of their coats, recognised Ulrich at once and with some satisfaction recorded the fact that he too had been no casual visitor but a man who had been brought to her mistress's house by a significant chain of events, as became apparent now on his returning in the company of His Highness. She fluttered to the door of the room, which she opened ceremonially, and then crouched down at the key-hole to see what would happen now. It was a large key-hole, and she could see the clean-shaven chin of the Governor, the purple neck-band of the prelate Niedomansky, and also the golden sword-knot of General Stumm von Bordwehr. This general had been sent along by the War Ministry, which, although it had actually not been invited, had nevertheless declared, in a letter to Count Leinsdorf, that it did not wish to be absent from such a ' highly patriotic occasion ', even though it had no direct concern either with the origin or with the expected development of the matter. This, however, Diotima had forgotten to tell Rachel, and as a result the latter was very excited by the presence of an officer at the conference. But for the present she could not discover anything further about what was going on in the room.

Meanwhile Diotima had welcomed His Highness, not paying Ulrich much attention, for she was introducing the other people present. The first person she introduced to His Highness was Herr Dr. Paul Arnheim, declaring that a fortunate chance had brought this very distinguished friend of her family here, and even though as a foreigner he could not claim to take a formal part in their conferences, yet she hoped he might be permitted to attend as her personal adviser. For—and here she lost no time in slipping in a gentle menace—his great experience and great connections in the realm of international culture and in the relations between these problems and those of economics were of invaluable help to her, these being subjects that she had previously had to deal with single-handed and in which, in all probability, no substitute for her would be found in the near future, although she herself was only too conscious of her inadequacy.

Count Leinsdorf saw that he had been ambushed, and for the first time since the beginning of their relationship he was taken aback by a *faux pas* on the part of this middle-class lady whom he had made his friend. Arnheim too felt slightly ruffled, like a sovereign whose entry has not been properly prepared for ; he had been firmly convinced that Count Leinsdorf knew of his invitation and approved of it. But Diotima, whose face at that moment was flushed and obstinate-looking, would not let go ; and like all women who have too clear a conscience in matters of matrimonial morality, she was capable of producing an insufferable feminine importunity whenever she was dealing with an affair of entire respectability.

She was then already in love with Arnheim, who had called on her several times meanwhile ; but inexperienced as she was, she had no notion of the nature of her feeling. They had discussions about what moves a soul that ennobles the flesh between the sole of the foot and the crown of the head and transforms the confused impressions of civilised life into harmonious spiritual vibrations. But even that was a great deal, and because Diotima was habitually cautious and all her life long had taken care never to compromise herself, this intimacy seemed to her too sudden, and she had to mobilise very great feelings, feelings that were positively downright great. And where is one most likely to find them ? Precisely where everyone expects them to be : in the drama of history. The Collateral Campaign was for Diotima and Arnheim a little island, so to speak the street-refuge in the rising flood of their spiritual inter-traffic. They regarded what had brought them together at so important a moment as a special destiny, and there was not the slightest difference of opinion between them as to the fact that the great patriotic enterprise was an immense opportunity and responsibility for people with minds. Not only she said so. Arnheim said the same, although he never forgot to add that what was primarily important was strong personalities with experience equally great in both realms, that of economics and that of ideas, the scope of the organisation being of secondary importance. So for Diotima the Collateral Campaign had become inextricably tied up with Arnheim, and the intellectual void that had originally been associated with this enterprise had been replaced by intellectual superabundance. The expectation that the treasure of emotions stored up in everything Austrian could be strengthened by Prussian intellectual discipline turned out to be most happily justified ; and so strong were these impressions that this very correct woman lost all sense of what a *coup de main* she was about to effect when she invited Arnheim to be present at the inaugural meeting.

Now it was too late to think better of it. But Arnheim, who intuitively understood what was behind all this, could not help feeling that there was something essentially conciliatory in it, however irritated he was by the situation into which he had been put. And His Highness was actually far too fond of his friend Diotima to express his astonishment otherwise than in his first involuntary reaction. He met Diotima's explanation with silence, and after an awkward little pause he amiably held out his hand to Herr Dr. Arnheim, in the most civil and complimentary way making him as welcome as in fact he was. Most of the other people present had probably noticed the little incident, and those who knew who Arnheim was were certainly surprised at his presence. But among well-bred people it is generally assumed that there is a good reason for everything, and it is considered poor form to enquire inquisitively as to what that reason is.

Meanwhile Diotima had recovered her statuesque repose. After a few moments she declared the meeting open and asked His Highness to honour her house by taking the chair.

His Highness made a speech. He had prepared it days before-hand, and his mind was of much too solid a nature for him to be able to change anything at the last minute; he could only just manage to modify the most outspoken allusions to the Prussian needle-gun, which had cunningly got the better of the Austrian muzzle-loaders in '66.

"What has brought us together," Count Leinsdorf said, " is the shared conviction that a mighty demonstration rising out of the midst of the people must not be left to chance, but calls for far-sighted direction from a quarter with a broad general view, in other words, from above. In the year 1918 His Majesty, our beloved Emperor and Sovereign, will celebrate the almost unique jubilee of the seventieth year of his richly blessed reign—please God still enjoying the same strength and vigour that we are accustomed to admire in him. We are sure that this festival will be celebrated by Austria's grateful peoples in a manner that will not only show the world our deep love, but also show that the Austro-Hungarian Monarchy stands gathered round its Sovereign, as firm as a rock."

Here Count Leinsdorf wavered, wondering whether he should make any mention of the symptoms of decay to which this rock was exposed, even on the occasion of a joint celebration in honour of its Emperor and King; for in all this resistance must be reckoned with on the part of Hungary, which only acknowledged a King. Hence His Highness had originally intended speaking of two rocks standing firmly gathered. But even that did not quite express his sense of Austro-Hungarian nationhood.

This sense of Austro-Hungarian nationhood was an entity so strangely formed that it seems almost futile to try to explain it to anyone who has not experienced it himself. It did not consist of an Austrian and a Hungarian part that, as one might imagine, combined to form a unity, but of a whole and a part, namely of a Hungarian and an Austro-Hungarian sense of nationhood ; and the latter was at home in Austria, whereby the Austrian sense of nationhood actually became homeless. The Austrian himself was only to be found in Hungary, and there as an object of dislike ; at home he called himself a citizen of the kingdoms and realms of the Austro-Hungarian Monarchy as represented in the Imperial Council, which means the same as an Austrian plus a Hungarian minus this Hungarian, and he did this not, as one might imagine, with enthusiasm, but for the sake of an idea that he detested, for he could not endure the Hungarians any more than they could endure him, which made the whole connection more involved than ever. As a result, many people simply called themselves Czechs, Poles, Slovenes or Germans, and this was where that further decay began, together with those well-known ' disagreeable phenomena of a domestic-political nature ', as Count Leinsdorf called them, which according to him were ' the work of irresponsible, callow and sensation-seeking riff-raff ' that did not meet with the necessary check from the mass of the population, which was all too ill-informed in political matters. After these allusions, the subject of which has since been dealt with in many well-informed and intelligent books, the reader will gladly accept the assurance that neither at this point nor subsequently will any serious attempt be made to paint an historical picture and enter into competition with reality. It entirely suffices if it is noticed that the mysteries of this dualism (such is the technical expression) are at least as difficult to understand as those of the Trinity ; for the historical process more or less everywhere resembles a juridical one, with hundreds of clauses, appendices, compromises and protests, and it is only to this that attention should be drawn. All unsuspectingly the common man lives and dies in the midst of it all, and lucky for him that it is so ; for if he were to realise in what a process, what an action, he is involved, with how many lawyers, what costs and motives, he might be driven into persecution mania, whatever country he lived in. Understanding reality is exclusively a matter for the historico-political thinker. For him the present time follows the battle of Mohács or of Lietzen as the entrée follows the soup. He has all the records at his fingertips, and at every moment feels the necessity arising out of the nature of the process. And if, what is more, he is, like Count Leinsdorf, an aristocratic politico-historically trained thinker, whose forefathers, agnates and kindred on the distaff side themselves played their part in the preliminary operations, he can survey the result as a line smoothly ascending.

So His Highness Count Leinsdorf had said to himself before the conference : 'We must not forget that His Majesty's noble and generous resolve to give the people a certain degree of enfranchisement in the conduct of its affairs is after all not so old that there could yet have resulted a political maturity in every respect worthy of the confidence graciously shown by our Sovereign. Hence such phenomena as those we unfortunately endure, damnable as they are in themselves, will not be seen by us as they are seen by the jealous world beyond our frontiers, as symptoms of senile decay, but, on the contrary, as a sign of not yet mature, and therefore inexhaustible, youthful strength in the Austrian people.' And this was something that he had wished to call to mind at the meeting ; but because Arnheim was present, he did not say everything that he had thought out, contenting himself with a hint about foreign ignorance of true Austrian conditions and the over-estimation of certain disagreeable phenomena. " For," His Highness concluded, " if we wish for an unmistakable indication of our strength and unity, we do so very much also in the international interest, since a happy relationship within the European family of nations is based on mutual regard and respect for the other's power." He then only repeated once more that such a sturdy native display of strength must really come out of the people's midst and hence must be directed from above, the purpose of this meeting being to find ways of doing so. When one recalls that all that had occurred to Count Leinsdorf a short time ago was a list of names, in addition to which he had received the idea of an Austrian Year from external sources, this must be accounted great progress, particularly if one bears in mind that His Highness did not even say all that he had thought.

After this speech Diotima said a few words, expounding the Chairman's intentions. The great patriotic Campaign, she explained, must seek to find a great aim, rising, as His Highness had said, out of the midst of the people. " We who are gathered here today for the first time do not feel ourselves called upon to define this aim as yet. We have met together this time only so that we may create an organisation to prepare the way for the framing of suggestions leading towards this aim." With these words she opened the discussion.

The first thing was that silence fell. If one shuts birds of different species and song, which do not know what is going to happen to them, into one common cage, for the first moment they will be silent in exactly this way.

At last a professor asked for permission to speak. Ulrich did not know him. Presumably His Highness had got his private secretary to send this gentleman an invitation at the last moment. He spoke about the road of history. If we look ahead—he said—we see an impenetrable wall. If we look left and right, we see an overwhelming mass of important events, without any recognisable direction. He would mention only a few instances : the presens conflict with Montenegro, the heavy fighting that the Spaniardt had to face in Morocco, the Ukrainian obstructionism in the Austrian Imperial Council . . . But if one looks back, as though by a miraculous dispensation everything has turned into order and purpose . . . Therefore, if he might put it so : in every instant we experience the mystery of a miraculous guidance. And he welcomed it as a great thought that a nation's eyes should in a manner of speaking be opened to this, that it should be allowed to cast a conscious glance into the ways of Providence as a result of being called upon, on a definite occasion of particular sub-limity . . . That was all he had wanted to say. It was the same as in modern methods of teaching, according to which the pupil worked together with the teacher instead of being confronted with ready-made results.

The assembled company stared stonily at the green table-cloth, all wearing pleasant expressions. Even the prelate, who was representing the Archbishop, during this spiritual performance on the part of a layman merely maintained the same polite attitude of reserve as the gentlemen from the ministries, without letting any slightest indication of cordial agreement slip into his face. There seemed to be a general feeling such as when someone in the street unexpectedly begins talking loudly to all and sundry ;

everyone, even those who had not been thinking of anything at all, then suddenly feel that they are out on serious, businesslike errands or that the street is being put to an improper use. While he was speaking the professor had had to struggle with a feeling of embarrassment, against which he had squeezed his words out, jerkily and constrainedly, as though a strong wind were making breathing difficult for him. He waited to see whether anyone would reply, and then withdrew the expectant look from his face, not without dignity.

Everyone had the same sense of being rescued when, after this incident, the representative of the Imperial Privy Purse quickly asked for permission to speak and gave the meeting a survey of the foundations and endowments that were to be expected from His Majesty's private purse in the year of jubilee. It began with the bestowal of a sum for the building of a pilgrims' church and a foundation for the support of penurious deacons, then came The Archduke Karl and The Field-Marshal Radetzky Veterans' Associations, and the soldiers' widows and orphans from the campaigns of '66 and '78; then came funds for the support of pensioned non-commissioned officers and for the Academy of Science and Learning; and so it went on. These lists were not in any way exciting, but they had their definite course and accustomed place in connection with all public expressions of Imperial benevolence. When they had all been read out, a Frau Weghuber immediately rose, a manufacturer's wife, who was a lady of great merit in all charitable affairs and utterly unsusceptible to the notion that there could be anything more important than the objects of her concern. She put to the meeting a proposal for a Greater-Austrian Francis-Joseph Soup-Kitchen, which was received with sympathy. The representative of the Ministry of Public Worship and Education remarked, however, that his own department had actually received a somewhat similar suggestion, namely for the publication of a jubilee folio gift-book, ' The Emperor Francis Joseph the First and His Time '. But after this fortunate start silence settled down again, and most of those present felt themselves in an awkward situation.

If they had been asked, on their way to the meeting, whether they knew what historical, great, and such-like events were, they would certainly have answered in the affirmative. Yet, confronted with the tense expectation that they should produce such an event, they gradually began to feel quite faint, and something like the rumblings of a very natural nature stirred within them.

At this dangerous moment the ever-tactful Diotima, who had prepared refreshments, adjourned the meeting.

43

Ulrich's first encounter with the great man. In the history of the world nothing irrational happens, but Diotima asserts that True Austria is the whole world.

IN the interval Arnheim observed that the more all-embracing the organisation was, the further the suggestions would diverge from each other. This, he said, was a characteristic symptom of the present state of development, which was based on intellect alone. But precisely for this reason it was a tremendous undertaking to force a whole people into the awareness of will and inspiration and those essentials that lay deeper than the intellect.

Ulrich answered with the question whether this meant that he believed anything would come of this Campaign.

" Undoubtedly," Arnheim replied. " Great events are always the expression of a general situation." This situation, he went on, existed nowadays. And the mere fact that a meeting like today's was possible anywhere proved its profound necessity.

All the same, discrimination in such things seemed difficult, Ulrich said. Supposing, for instance, the composer of the latest operetta with world-wide success were a conspirator and suddenly set himself up as president of the world, which, considering his enormous popularity, was quite within the bounds of possibility— would this be a great leap in history or an expression of the general state of mind ?

" That is quite impossible ! " Herr Dr. Arnheim said earnestly. " Such a composer cannot be either a conspirator or a politician.

If he were, his genius for light music would be unthinkable. And nothing irrational happens in the history of the world."

" But so much does in the world, surely ? "

" In the history of the world *never*."

Arnheim was visibly on edge. Nearby, Diotima and Count Leinsdorf stood in lively, low-voiced conversation. His Highness had after all expressed his amazement to his friend at meeting a Prussian on this exceptionally Austrian occasion. For reasons of discretion, if nothing else, he considered it entirely out of the question that a foreigner should play a leading part in the Collateral Campaign, although Diotima pointed out the excellent and confidence-inspiring impression that such freedom from political egotism must make abroad. At this point, however, she changed her tactics, enlarging her plan surprisingly. She spoke of a woman's tact, which was a sureness of feeling utterly indifferent to the prejudices of society. If His Highness would listen to this voice, just this once . . . Arnheim was a European, one the power of whose mind was known throughout Europe. And precisely because he was not an Austrian, his participation would prove that the mind as such was at home in Austria. And suddenly she made the assertion that True Austria was the whole world. The world, she explained, would not find peace and rest until the nations in it lived in higher unity like the Austrian peoples in their fatherland. A Greater Austria, a Universal Austria, that was what had occurred to her, thanks to His Highness, in this happy moment. That was the crowning idea that the Collateral Campaign had hitherto lacked.

Sweepingly, pacifistically commanding, the beautiful Diotima stood before her exalted friend. Count Leinsdorf could not yet make up his mind to abandon his objections, but once again he admired this woman's fiery idealism and breadth of vision, and he pondered on whether it might not be more advantageous to draw Arnheim into the conversation than to give an immediate answer to suggestions so pregnant with significance.

Arnheim was restless, for he sensed this discussion, without being able to have any influence on it. He and Ulrich were surrounded by the curious, who had been attracted by the presence of the Croesus. Ulrich was just saying : " There are several thousands of occupations that people give themselves up to entirely. It is there that their intelligence lies. But if one tries to get the general human element out of them—that which is common to them all—there are actually only three things that can be left over : stupidity, money, or, at the most, a trace of religious memory."

"Religion ! That's precisely it ! " Arnheim interpolated emphatically and asked Ulrich whether he believed, then, that it had disappeared completely, down to the very roots. He had uttered the world ' religion ' so loudly and distinctly that Count Leinsdorf could not fail to hear it.

His Highness seemed in the mean time to have arrived at a compromise with Diotima, for, with her leading the way, he now approached the group, which tactfully dissolved, and addressed Herr Dr. Arnheim.

Ulrich all at once found himself alone and left to gnaw his lips.

Heaven knows why—perhaps to while the time away or not to stand there so forlorn—he began thinking of the drive to this meeting. Count Leinsdorf, who had brought him along, possessed motor-cars, for he was a man who moved with the times ; but since he also clung to tradition, he occasionally used a pair of superb chestnuts that he kept, together with a coachman and a calash, and when the major-domo had come for his instructions, His Highness had decided it would be appropriate to drive to the inaugural meeting of the Collateral Campaign with those two beautiful creatures that now almost belonged to the past.

" This is Pepi, and that is Hans," Count Leinsdorf explained on the way. One saw the dancing brown hillocks of the cruppers and now and then one of the nodding heads, moving rhythmically sideways so that the foam flew from the mouth. It was hard to imagine what was going on in the animals. It was a beautiful morning, and they went at a fast trot. Perhaps fodder and speed were the only great horse-passions left in such a case as that of Pepi and Hans, for they were geldings and did not know love as tangible desire, but only as a filmy haze that at times veiled their vision of the world with thin, lucent clouds. The passion for fodder was housed in a marble manger full of delicious oats, in a hay-rack full of fresh hay, the sound of the stable halter rubbing on the ring, and concentrated in the warm stable-smell of bread, a spicy, smooth smell through which the ammonia-laden sense of self penetrated like needles : Here Are Horses ! Where speed was concerned, it was probably rather different. There the poor soul is still linked together with the herd, and into the great stallion there ahead, the leader, or into all of them at once, movement suddenly comes from somewhere, and the whole host of them goes galloping into wind and sun. And when the animal is solitary and all the four quarters of space are open to it, a sudden mad shudder will often run through its skull and it will go storming aimlessly away, plunging into a terrible freedom that is as empty in one direction as in any other, until in bewilderment it stands still and can be lured back with a basinful of oats.

Pepi and Hans were quiet horses, well used to running in harness. They pulled eagerly, their hooves beating on the sun-shiny street with its tall hedges of houses. The people for them were a grey swarming, a cause neither of joy nor of fear. The variegated displays in the shop-windows, the women gay in brilliant colours, were no more than patches of meadow no good for grazing ; the hats, ties, books, diamonds along the street—a desert. Only the two dream-islands of stable and trotting loomed out of it all, and at times, as though in dream or play, Hans and Pepi shied at a shadow, thrust against the shafts, were freshened again by a flat flick of the whip, and leaned thankfully into the curb.

And suddenly Count Leinsdorf had sat up straight on the upholstered seat and said queryingly to Ulrich : " Stallburg tells me that you are applying yourself to a man's case ? " In his surprise, Ulrich did not at once grasp the connection. However, Count Leinsdorf continued : " Very good of you. I've heard all about it. I'm afraid there isn't much that can be done—terrible fellow he is. But it often happens that the intangible personal thing, the thing that's in need of grace, which is there in every Christian being, shows itself precisely in such an individual. And if one sets out, oneself, to do something great, one should think most humbly of those who can't help themselves. Per-haps one could have him medically examined again." After Count Leinsdorf had delivered this long speech sitting upright in the jolting carriage, he dropped back into the soft upholstery and added : " But we must not forget that at the moment we owe all our strength to an historic event."

49

The beginnings of antagonism between the old and the new schools of diplomacy.

HIS association with persons whose speciality was being the hereditary aristocracy constituted no exception. Arnheim so muted his own distinguished urbanity, modestly confining himself to nobility of the mind, which knows its own merits and limits, that after a while those who bore ancient aristocratic names seemed, beside him, to have the bent backs of labourers, bowed under the weight of that burden. It was Diotima who observed this most acutely. She recognised the Mystery of the Whole with the mind of an artist who sees his life's dream realised in a way that excludes any possiblity of improvement.

She was now again completely reconciled to her *salon*. Arnheim uttered a warning against the over-estimation of external organisation. Crude material interests would overwhelm the pure intention. He attached more value to the *salon*.

Permanent Secretary Tuzzi, on the other hand, expressed a misgiving lest in this way there should be no bridging an abyss of talk.

He had crossed one leg over the other and clasped his lean, dark hands with the protruding veins over his knees. With his little beard and his southern eyes, as he sat beside Arnheim, who was sitting upright in his faultless suit of very soft material, he looked like a Levantine pickpocket beside a patrician Hanseatic merchant. Here two kinds of urbanity came into collision, and the Austrian one, which, going as it did with a highly cultivated and complex taste, was inclined to have a touch of negligence about it, considered itself by no means the lesser. Permanent Secretary Tuzzi had a pleasant way of enquiring after the progress of the Collateral Campaign as though it were not permissible for him to know at first hand what was going on in his house. " It would be a help to us if we could be informed as soon as possible what is being planned," he said, gazing at his wife and Arnheim with an amiable smile that was meant to convey : ' In this case of course

I'm a mere stranger here.' Afterwards he told them that his wife's and Count Leinsdorf's joint work was already causing profound concern in official quarters. While making his last report to His Majesty, the Minister had taken soundings as to what external demonstrations, on the occasion of the jubilee, might eventually count on receiving gracious approval, in particular, in how far gracious favour would be conferred on the plan of anticipating the trend of the time by taking the lead in an international pacifist campaign. For that would be the only possibility, Tuzzi explained, if the idea of Universal Austria, with which His Highness had been inspired, were to be translated into political terms. But, he went on, His Gracious Majesty, with his world-famed sense of responsibility and reserve, had at once waved it all aside with the vigorous remark : " Oh, I don't like being pushed into the limelight, don't you know." And now one did not know whether or not this indicated definite opposition so far as His Gracious Majesty's wishes were concerned.

In such a gentle manner did Tuzzi treat the little secrets of his profession ungently, as does a man who is at the same time well able to keep greater secrets. He concluded by saying that it was now for the embassies to enquire as to the feeling at their respective foreign Courts, since one was not sure of the feelings at one's own and yet must somehow get something to hold on to. For even from the technical point of view there were, after all, many possibilities, from a general peace conference to a meeting of twenty sovereigns, down to adorning the walls of the Hague Palace with frescoes by Austrian artists, or a foundation for the benefit of the children and orphans of those employed in the Hague Palace.

He went on to raise the question of what the Prussian Court thought about the jubilee year.

Arnheim declared he had no information on this point.

This Austrian cynicism was repugnant to him. He, who himself so well understood the art of conversation, in Tuzzi's vicinity felt as buttoned-up as a man who wishes to emphasise that everything must become cold and grave the moment affairs of State come under discussion. In this manner two opposing kinds of *savoir vivre*, two styles of official and of private life, displayed themselves before Diotima, not quite without rival intentions.

But put a greyhound beside a pug-dog, a willow beside a poplar, a wine-glass on a freshly ploughed field, or a portrait into a sailing-boat instead of an art exhibition, in short, put side by side two highly bred and distinct forms of life, and what happens is that between them a void comes into existence, a mutual cancelling out, an utterly malicious absurdity with no bottom to it. Diotima felt this in her eyes and ears, without understanding it, and, somewhat frightened, gave the conversation a different turn by telling her husband with great decisiveness that primarily she intended to achieve something spiritually great with the Collateral Campaign and would let no demands other than those of really modern people enter into the conduct of it.

Arnheim was thankfully conscious that the idea had had its dignity restored to it ; for precisely because he was having at certain moments to resist the danger of going under, he no more wished to trifle with the events that grandly justified his being in Diotima's company than a drowning man does with his life-belt. But to his own surprise he asked Diotima, not without doubt in his voice, whom then she would choose for the intellectual spearhead of the Collateral Campaign.

This was of course not yet at all clear to Diotima. The days of being in Arnheim's company had given her such an abundance of ideas and stimulation that she had had no time as yet to make a definite choice. Although indeed Arnheim had several times declared to her that what was important was not the democracy of the committees but strong personalities with breadth of grasp, in all this she had simply had the feeling ' you and I ', though she was still far from any resolve or, indeed, insight. Now probably it was precisely this of which she was reminded by the tone of pessimism in Arnheim's voice, for she answered : " Is there anything at all today that one can call so important and great that one would wish to devote all one's strength to making it come true ? "

" It is the mark of a time that has lost the inner certainty of healthy times," Arnheim commented, " that it is difficult for anything to crystallise in it as what is greatest and most important."

Permanent Secretary Tuzzi lowered his gaze to a speck of dust on his trousers, so that his smile could be interpreted as one of agreement.

" And indeed, what should it be ? " Arnheim continued search-ingly. " Religion ? "

Permanent Secretary Tuzzi now directed his smile upwards. Arnheim, it is true, pronounced the word, not as emphatically and unsceptically as on a previous occasion in His Highness's presence, but nevertheless with sonorous gravity.

In protest against her husband's smile, Diotima interpolated : " Why not ?   Religion too ! "

" Certainly.   But since we must come to a practical decision —have you ever thought of appointing a bishop to the com-mittee, with the task of finding a contemporary aim for the Campaign ?   God is in the profoundest sense old-fashioned.   We are incapable of imagining Him in tails, clean-shaven, with a parting in His hair, but still think of Him in patriarchal terms. And what have we apart from religion ?   The nation ?   The State ? "

Diotima was pleased at this, because Tuzzi generally treated the State as a masculine affair that one did not discuss with women.   But now he remained silent, only his eyes betraying that there might be something more to be said on this score.

" Science ? " Arnheim went on.   " Culture ?   There remains art.   Truly, it is art that primarily ought to reflect the unity of life and life's inner order.   But how well we know the picture it presents today !   General disintegration, extremes without any connection . . .   The epic of the new mechanised social and emotional life was created right at the beginning by Stendhal, Balzac and Flaubert.   It is Dostoievsky, Strindberg and Freud who have laid bare the demonic sub-strata.   We who live today have the profound feeling that in all this there is nothing left for us to do."

Here Permanent Secretary Tuzzi interjected that when he wanted to read something solid he took down Homer or good old Peter Rosegger.

Arnheim instantly picked up the thread.   " You should add the Bible too.   With the Bible, Homer, and Rosegger or Reuter one can get along very well.   And there we are, right at the heart of the problem !   Supposing we had a new Homer . . .   Let us ask ourselves with complete candour whether we would be capable of listening to him at all.   I think we must answer in the negative.

We have not got him because we do not need him ! " Arnheim was now in the saddle and in full gallop. " If we did need him, we should have him ! For in the last resort nothing negative happens in history. What therefore can be the meaning of the fact that we transpose all that is truly great and essential into the past ? Homer and Christ have not found their equal since, to say nothing of having been surpassed. There is nothing more beautiful than the Song of Songs. The Gothic and the Renaissance stand before our modern times like mountainous country before the entry into a plain. Where today are the great rulers of the world ? How inadequate even Napoleon's deeds appear compared with those of the Pharaohs, Kant's doctrines compared with those of the Buddha, or Goethe's work compared with that of Homer ! But after all we live, and must live, for something. And so what conclusion are we to draw ? None other than that——" here, however, Arnheim broke off and assured them that he hesitated to put it into words, for the only conclusion left was that everything one took seriously and considered great had nothing to do with what was the innermost force in one's life.

" And what is this force ? " Permanent Secretary Tuzzi asked. He had no objection to the statement that most things were taken far too seriously.

" No man of our time can say," Arnheim answered. " The problem of civilisation can be solved only by the heart. By the appearance of a new personality. By inner vision and a pure will. The intellect has achieved nothing but a watering down of the great past into merest liberalism. But perhaps we do not see far enough, perhaps we are reckoning on too small a scale. Any moment may be a turning-point in the world's history ! "

Diotima had been about to object that then there would be nothing at all left for the Collateral Campaign. But, strangely enough, she was entranced by Arnheim's sombre visions. Perhaps there was still a residual awareness in her of tedious school-tasks, which weighed her down when time and again she had to read the latest books and talk about the latest pictures. Pessimism as an attitude to art liberated her from much beauty that fundamentally she had not liked at all ; as an attitude to science it diminished her fear of civilisation, of the excessive quantity of all that was worth knowing and far-reaching in its importance.

Hence Arnheim's judgment on the age, devoid of hope as it was, was balm to her, she felt all at once. And agreeably the thought darted through her heart that Arnheim's melancholy was somehow connected with her.

50

Further developments. Permanent Secretary Tuzzi resolves to get himself a clear picture of Arnheim.

DIOTIMA had guessed right. Since the moment when Arnheim had become aware that the bosom of this wonderful woman who had read his books on the soul was being expanded and moved by a power that could not be misunderstood, he had fallen a prey to a despondency not usual with him. To put it briefly and in the terms of his own experience, it was the despondency of the moralist who all at once and unexpectedly encounters heaven upon earth. If one wishes to feel what he felt, one only needs to imagine what it would be like if all around us there lay nothing but the quiet blue pool of the heavens, full of floating, soft, white bales of feathers.

Regarded *per se* moral man is ridiculous and unsavoury, as we know from the odour of those resigned poor people who have nothing to call their own but their morality. Morality needs great tasks to lend it significance. And that is why Arnheim had always sought the complement of his moralising nature in world events, in history, in the ideological interpenetration of his activities. It was his favourite notion to bring ideas into spheres of power and always to regard business in connection with intellectual problems. He liked to provide himself with comparisons from history, in order to fill them with new life. The role of finance at the present day seemed to him similar to that of the Catholic Church, a power exerting influence from behind the scenes, unyieldingly yielding in its intercourse with the ruling powers, and at times he looked upon himself, in his activities, as something like a cardinal. But this time he had set out on his journey more or less as a result of a whim ; and although he did not undertake even a journey that was more or less a whim without having some intentions, yet he could not recall how the plan that had brought it about, which had incidentally been a plan of some importance, had originally arisen in his mind. Something like unpremeditated inspiration and sudden resolve presided over his journey. It was probably this little circumstance of liberty that brought it about that a holiday voyage to Bombay could scarcely have made a more exotic impression on him than did this out-of-the-way German-speaking metropolis where he now found himself. The thought, completely impossible in Prussia, of being invited to play a part in the Collateral Campaign, had done the rest, making his mood as imaginatively illogical as a dream, and though the nonsensical character of it did not escape his practical intelligence, this did not enable him to break through the spell of the fairy-tale situation. He could probably have achieved the purpose of his coming much more easily by direct means ; but he regarded it as a holiday and a rest from reason to return here time and again, and for these excursions into fairy-land he was punished by his business sense, which smudged the black conduct-mark that he should have given himself into a grey blur all over everything.

Admittedly, there was no repetition of such extensive reflections in a sombre key as those that time in Tuzzi's presence, if for no other reason than that Permanent Secretary Tuzzi generally only put in a fleeting appearance and Arnheim had to distribute his words among the most various persons—and he found people amazingly receptive in this beautiful country. In His Highness's presence he called criticism unfruitful and the modern age void of the divine, whereby he once more let it be understood that man could only be redeemed from such a negative existence through the heart, adding, for Diotima's sake, the statement that only the South of Germany, rich in culture as it was, was still capable of liberating the German spirit, and so perhaps the world too, from the excesses of rationalism and the mania for petty arithmetic. Surrounded by ladies, he talked of the necessary organisation of inward tenderness, if mankind was to be saved from an armaments race and utter soullessness. To a circle of active professional men he expounded Hölderlin's saying that there were no longer any human beings in Germany, only occupations. " And no one can achieve anything in his occupation without a feeling for some higher unity—least of all the financier ! " he concluded his exposition.

People liked listening to him because it was so nice that a man who had so many ideas also had money. And the circumstance that everyone who spoke to him went away with the impression that an enterprise like the Collateral Campaign was a highly suspect affair, full of the most dangerous intellectual contradictions, reinforced the general impression that no one would be as suitable as he to take over the leadership in this adventure.

However, Permanent Secretary Tuzzi would not have been, in his quiet way, one of his country's leading diplomats if he had not noticed anything of Arnheim's fundamental presence in his house. It was only that he could make nothing of it. But he did not show this, because a diplomat never shows what he is thinking. This stranger was in the highest degree disagreeable to him personally, but also, so to speak, in principle ; and the fact that he had manifestly selected Tuzzi's wife's *salon* for the scene of his operations in pursuit of some hidden intention or other was something that Tuzzi felt to be a challenge. He did not for an instant believe Diotima's assurances that the Nabob visited the imperial city on the Danube so often only because his spirit felt most at home in the midst of its ancient culture. But he was confronted first of all by a task for the solution of which he lacked any point of reference, for in his official relations he had never yet come across such a person as Arnheim.

And since Diotima had expounded to him her plan of giving Arnheim a leading position in the Collateral Campaign, and had complained about His Highness's resistance, Tuzzi was considerably perturbed. He did not think much either of the Collateral Campaign or of Count Leinsdorf, but he regarded his wife's notion as politically so surprisingly indiscreet that in that moment he felt as though long years of masculine work in educating her, such as he flattered himself he had accomplished, had collapsed like a house of cards. Permanent Secretary Tuzzi had in his own mind even used this very simile, although at other times he never

Director Fischel of Lloyd's Bank enjoyed philosophising, but only for ten minutes daily. He liked to contemplate the rational foundations of human life and believed in its intellectual lucrative ness, which he imagined as something like the well-constructed order of a large banking concern ; and he daily noted with approval whatever he read in the newspaper about new progress. This belief in the unswerving guiding-lines of reason and progress had for a long time made it possible for him to dispose of his wife's carpings with a shrug of the shoulders or a cutting retort. But as misfortune would have it, in the course of this marriage the mood of the times had turned away from the old principles of liberalism, so favourable to Leo Fischel—from the great guiding ideals of tolerance, the dignity of man, and free trade—and reason and progress in the western world had been displaced by racial theories and street-slogans ; and he too was not unscathed by it. He had at first denied outright the existence of these develop-ments, precisely as Count Leinsdorf was accustomed to deny the existence of certain ' displeasing phenomena of a public nature ' ; and he waited for them to disappear of their own accord. This waiting is the first, as yet scarcely perceptible degree of the torture of exasperation that life imposes on men of upright principles. The second degree they generally call—and hence Fischel also called—' poison '. This poison is the appearance, by drip and by drop, of new views in morality, art, politics, the family, news-papers, books and social intercourse, which is from the very beginning accompanied by a helpless feeling of irrevocability and by indignant denials, which cannot avoid to a certain extent acknowledging the existence of what is denied. Yet Director Fischel was not spared the third and final degree, in which the isolated showers and sprinklings of the new attitudes condensed into a steady rain. This in time becomes one of the most dreadful torments that can be experienced by a man who has only ten minutes a day to give to philosophy.

Leo came to know in how many things people can be of different opinions. The urge to be right—a need that is almost equivalent to the dignity of man—began to commit excesses in the Fischel household. In thousands of years this urge has produced thou-sands of admirable philosophies, works of art, books, deeds and allegiances ; and if this admirable, but also fanatical and monstrous congenital human urge has to be content with ten minutes for the philosophy of life or discussion of the fundamental household problems, then it is inevitable that it will burst, like a drop of red-hot lead, into innumerable points and sharp edges, which can cause extremely painful injuries. It burst on the question whether a maid was to be given notice or not, and whether or not it was right to have toothpicks on the table. But whatever was the cause of its bursting, it had the capacity to re-form itself immediately into two views of the world, each inexhaustibly rich in detail.

That was all very well by day, for then Director Fischel was in his office. But by night he was human, and this did a very great deal to worsen relations between himself and Klementine. What it comes to is that with the complexity of everything these days a man can really know everything only in one field, which with him was stocks and shares; and this was why at night he had a slight tendency towards indulgence. But Klementine even then remained sharp and unyielding, for she had grown up in the steady atmosphere of a civil-service household, with its strong sense of duty. In addition to this her consciousness of social position did not permit their having separate bedrooms, for this would only have meant making the already inadequate apartment even smaller. A shared bedroom, however, particularly when the light is out, puts a man in the situation of an actor who has to play, before an invisible audience, the rewarding but by now thoroughly worn-out part of a hero snarling like a lion. For years Leo's dark auditorium had not let slip the faintest hint of applause or the slightest sign of disapproval, and this was surely enough to shatter the strongest nerves. In the morning, when, in keeping with respectable tradition, they met at breakfast, Klementine was as stiff as a frozen corpse and Leo twitching with touchiness. Even their daughter Gerda always noticed something of it and was filled with horror and bitter disgust, imagining married life as a cat-fight in the darkness of the night.

Gerda was twenty-three years old and constituted the favourite bone of contention between her two progenitors. Leo Fischel thought it was about time to let him think out a good marriage for her. Gerda however said : " You're old-fashioned, my dear

permitted himself the use of similes because they were too literary and had an odour of poor social tone. But on this occasion he was really upset.

Later on Diotima did actually improve her position again by her stubbornness. She became gently aggressive and talked about a new kind of man who could no longer passively leave the spiritual responsibility for the course of world events to the professional helmsmen. Then she spoke of a woman's tact, which at times could be a visionary gift and might even direct the gaze to further vistas than everyday professional work could. Finally she said Arnheim was a European, a man whose mind was recognised throughout Europe, and that the conduct of affairs of State in Europe was not sufficiently European, and much too unspiritual, and that the world would not know peace until it was permeated by a universally Austrian spirit, just as the old Austrian culture wound its tendrils round the many peoples of many tongues within the frontiers of the Monarchy.

She had never before dared to stand up so resolutely against her husband's superiority. But Permanent Secretary Tuzzi was temporarily reassured by this. He had never considered his wife's aspirations any more important than questions of dress-making; he was pleased when others admired her; and now he regarded this matter more mildly and in much the same way as if a woman with a vivid sense of colour had for once chosen too gaudy a ribbon. He confined himself to repeating to her, with grave courtesy, the reasons why in the world of men it was impossible publicly to entrust the decision of Austrian affairs to a Prussian, at the same time, however, admitting the possibility that there might be advantages in being on friendly terms with a man in so unique a position, and he assured Diotima that she would be misinterpreting his scruples if she were to conclude from what he had said that he did not care to see Arnheim in her company as often as possible. Privately he hoped that in this way sooner or later the opportunity would arise to lay a trap for the outsider.

Only when Tuzzi had to stand by and see Arnheim being a success everywhere, he returned to the point that Diotima was showing herself somewhat too *engagée* with this man. But once more he found that she did not show her usual respect for his wishes. She argued with him and declared he was worrying about a mere figment of his imagination. He resolved that as a man he would not enter into combat with a woman's dialectics, but wait for the hour when his foresight would be proved right by circumstances. Then, however, it happened that he received a tremendous impetus.

For one night he was made uneasy by something that seemed to him like an infinitely distant weeping. At first it hardly disturbed him ; he simply did not understand what it was. But from time to time the spiritual distance was reduced at a leap, and all at once the menacing uneasiness was close to his ears and he started out of his sleep so abruptly that he sat straight up in bed. Diotima was lying on her side and gave no sign, but something made him feel that she was awake. He called her by her name, in a low voice, and then again, and with gentle fingers tried to turn her white shoulder to him. But as he turned her and her face rose over her shoulder in the darkness, he saw it looking at him angrily, expressing defiance, and bearing traces of tears. Unfortunately his sound sleep in the mean time had half overwhelmed him again, insistently drawing him back on to the pillows, and Diotima's face was then no more than a mere hovering, painfully bright distortion before him, something that he could no longer understand at all.

" What's matter ? " he muttered in the quiet bass of dropping off to sleep, and received a clear, irritated, disagreeable answer, imprinted on his hearing, falling into his drowsiness and there lying like a twinkling coin in the water.

" You toss about so much in your sleep, no one can sleep next to you ! " Diotima had said harshly and distinctly.

His ear had taken it in, but by that time he had already slipped out of the waking state, without being able to go into the reproach any further.

He merely felt that grave wrong had been done him. To sleep quietly was in his view one of the chief virtues of a diplomat, for it was a condition of all success. It was a point on which he was sensitive, and he felt Diotima's remark as a serious challenge to his whole existence. He realised that she had changed. It did not occur to him, even in his sleep, to suspect his wife of tangible infidelity, but he did not for an instant doubt that the personal

of the world. It must not be merely practical, it must be sheer poetry. It must be a landmark. It must be a mirror for the world to gaze into and blush. And not only blush, but, as in the fairy-tale, see its true face and never be able to forget it again. For this His Highness had made the inspiring suggestion : ' Emperor of Peace '. So much having been said, it could not fail to be recognised—she went on—that the suggestions so far discussed did not meet the requirement. If in the first part of the meeting she had mentioned symbols, of course she did not mean soup-kitchens. What was to be achieved was nothing less than the rediscovery of that human unity which had been lost as a result of the great discrepancies that had developed in human interests. Here, admittedly, the question arose whether the present time and the nations of today were still at all capable of such great ideas in common. All the suggestions that had been made were of course excellent, but they diverged widely, which in itself showed that none of them possessed the unifying force that was so much needed.

While Diotima was speaking, Ulrich was observing Arnheim. It was not any details of his physiognomy to which his distaste attached itself, but simply the whole of it. Although these details—the Phoenician hardness of the master-merchant's skull, the sharp face that was yet flat, as though formed out of too little material, the English-tailored repose of the figure, and, at that second place where man peers out of his clothes, the somewhat too short-fingered hands—were sufficiently remarkable, it was the good proportions between all these elements that irritated Ulrich. It was this sureness that Arnheim's books also had : the world was all right as soon as Arnheim had regarded it. Ulrich suddenly felt a guttersnipe desire to throw stones or mud at this man who had grown up in wealth and perfection, now while he was watching him display so much attention in following the silly procedure at which they had to be present. Arnheim was positively sipping it like a connoisseur, on his face an expression that signified : Without wishing to exaggerate, I must say this is a really noble vintage !

Diotima had meanwhile come to the end of her speech. Immediately after the interval, when they had taken their seats again, all those present clearly showed they were convinced that now a result would be arrived at. Nobody had been thinking about it in the mean time, but all adopted the attitude of people expecting something important. And now Diotima concluded: And so if the question arose whether the present time and the nations of today were still at all capable of great ideas in common, one might, indeed one must add—were they capable of bringing forth the redeeming power? For it was all a matter of redemption, of a redeeming upsurge. This was putting it briefly. Though, admittedly, one could not yet quite picture it. It must come out of the totality, or it would not come at all. Therefore she took it upon herself, after consultation with His Highness, to put forward the following proposal concluding this day's meeting: His Highness had rightly observed that the illustrious ministerial departments did in fact represent a division of the world according to its main aspects, such as religion and education, commerce, industry, law and so on. If therefore the meeting would resolve to set up committees, with an envoy of these government departments at the head of each, and elect representatives of the respective institutions and strata of the population to be at his side, it would mean the creation of an organisation already embodying the main moral forces of the world in their proper order, an instrument through which these forces could pour in and in which they could be sifted. The final summing up would then take place in the executive committee, and all that this organisation still needed was to be supplemented by some special committees and sub-committees, such as a propaganda committee, a committee of ways and means, and the like, whereby she personally would like to reserve to herself the foundation of a committee dealing with the spiritual approach, for the further elaboration of the fundamental ideas, of course in constant co-operation with all the other committees.

Again everyone was silent, but this time in relief. Count Leinsdorf nodded several times. Someone asked, for the sake of more complete clarity, how the peculiarly Austrian element would enter into the campaign as thus conceived.

General Stumm von Bordwehr rose to reply. (All the previous speakers had remained seated.) He was well aware—he said— that in the council-chamber the role allotted to the soldier was a modest one. If nevertheless he did speak, it was not in order